D0743969

Sign up for our newsletter to hear
about new releases, read interviews with
authors, enter giveaways,
and more.

www.ylva-publishing.com

a collection of erotic lesbian stories

DON'T
BE SHY

edited by:
Astrid Ohletz and Jae

Ylva

INTRODUCTION

In this book you will find volumes 1 and 2 of the *Don't Be Shy* erotic short story series as one compendium. These twenty-five stories had previously only been available as two separate e-books.

What you'll encounter inside are stories about women getting what they want, about women loving women in all their diverse beauty—all shapes, sizes, and ages. We had a lot of fun selecting these stories; there's hardly anything more entertaining for us than getting to read stories about women finding their bliss. And there's plenty of that here. Within these pages, you'll find red-hot scenarios as well as quietly titillating situations, with established couples exploring new pleasures together as well as strangers in chance encounters enjoying the heady rush of sexual pursuit.

Of course, you'll have to judge for yourself how well we've done in our selections. (Oh, the burden of hands-on research!)

So don't be shy: go find someplace to yourself where you won't be disturbed for a while, curl up with these stories, and go find your bliss.

We won't wait up for you.

Astrid Ohletz & Jae

TABLE OF CONTENTS

CUSTOMER SERVICE

BY LILA BRUCE

As weekends go, this one had started off pretty crappy.

Erin had thought things couldn't get any worse when her boyfriend suddenly up and moved out, taking all his belongings and a few of hers along with him. But then the dishwasher blew up.

God, she was going to miss that dishwasher.

Sure, she was going to miss Corey too, but men came and went—a dishwasher, though? It had been her first big purchase after moving out on her own four years ago. Fresh out of college, she had found a cozy two-bedroom starter house, made an offer, closed the deal, and finally had a place that she could call her own. It had been that first weekend at the house, just after hosting all her friends and their plates and bowls and cups, that she came to the adult decision that a dishwasher was more important than the new flat-screen television she had been saving for.

And now here it was, gurgling pitifully as it drew its last breath in the corner of the kitchen.

Erin felt like crying.

Almost as a side thought, it occurred to her that with Corey gone there would be no one to take the soap-stained carcass out to the curb. That morning he had packed his beat-up burgundy sedan and announced that he was leaving. Not just leaving, but leaving for another woman. He'd met the woman, Toffee, at a work function, he told her. They'd been e-mailing and texting each other for a couple of months, and he had finally realized that Erin didn't get him the way that Toffee did. Toffee understood his feelings, and she would support his dreams of becoming a Hollywood actor. She too was leaving her boyfriend, and together, she and Corey were moving to California. Having made that proclamation, Corey walked out the kitchen door and then squealed off.

Deep down inside, Erin was not sad to see him go.

Not really.

As Corey would have said, they both had "checked out" of the relationship months ago. Little things that he had done during the early days of their relationship, things she had once thought were cute, now made her want to strangle him. After dating for just over a year and living together almost seven months, Corey had gotten too settled in and comfortable around her. Passing gas as he walked by—crop dusting as he called it—and leaving his dirty clothes on the floor for her to wash had begun to be a daily thing. And they argued all the time. The simplest discussion would turn into a shouting match: what to have for dinner, whose turn it was to take the trash out, whether it was appropriate for Corey to watch one of his disgusting porn movies while Erin was on the phone to her mother, anything really. So no, she was not surprised or even overly upset that he had left her for the woman with the ridiculous name.

Erin shook her head and looked at the dishwasher in disgust. Corey's leaving was what she had expected. The dishwasher breaking down, now that felt like a betrayal.

It was more than she could take in one day. Erin grabbed her purse and her keys and headed out the door.

———◦◦◦◦———

"Anything I can help you with, little lady?"

Erin stood in the appliance section of the big box store located a few miles from her house. There were refrigerators and stoves by the dozen, but not a dishwasher to be found.

"Yes, please. I'm looking for the dishwashers," she answered back to the fifty-something man in a blue shirt and red vest. A nametag that was pinned on at an angle pronounced that his name was Dan and that he thought customer service was his number one priority.

Who the hell says little lady? She followed Dan past a row of microwaves to finally arrive at the dishwasher section.

"Looking for any model in particular?" he asked.

Erin shook her head. "No, just something dependable," she said with a tinge of bitterness. "Something that will live up to my expectations. Something that won't up and leave me with no warning one day."

Dan gave her an odd look and then pointed to a stainless steel model. "Well…um…this one here has five wash cycles, fourteen place settings, an auto soil sensor, plus a silverware basket that you can move to any position within the washer."

"That sounds interesting. How much?"

"Seven hundred and sixty five dollars."

For just a moment, Erin forgot how to breathe. "What? For a dishwasher? When I bought my last one three or four years ago, it was around three hundred dollars!"

"Well…" Dan drawled out, "that was four years ago and prices have gone up as the technology has improved. We do have this one." He pointed to a plain white dishwasher with a bright red sticker labeling it as energy efficient. "It's three ninety-nine but only has two cycles and doesn't come with the auto soil sensor—"

"Does it wash dishes?" Erin asked.

"Well, yes, of course it does, but—"

"Then I'll take it."

Dan opened his mouth as if to say something, then thought better of it. "All righty, then. Let's get you ready to go."

As Erin stood there, thinking of all the shoes she could buy with three hundred and ninety-nine dollars, Dan pulled a notepad out of his back pocket and began to write numbers on it.

"Will you need it delivered?" he asked.

Erin nodded.

"Okay, and what about your old one? Will you need that one taken away as well?"

Erin thought about her dishwasher, sitting cold and lifeless in the corner of her kitchen. "Yes, please," she said softly, a touch of sadness in her voice.

"Okay, then. Carter!" Dan screamed, making Erin jump back a step. "Carter!" Erin looked at the salesman as if he was crazy. Noticing her stare, Dan smiled and explained, "Carter here is our runner."

What the hell is a runner? Erin thought. *And why you are screaming at the top of your lungs in the middle of a store?*

"Yes, Dan?" a deep, sultry voice called back.

She twirled around to see the tall, tanned specimen that was Carter smiling behind her. To Erin's surprise, Carter was a girl. Well, a woman really. Her close-cropped hair was the most startling shade of red, almost a burgundy.

She wore a shirt similar to Dan's, but, unlike Dan, she *wore* the shirt. The navy-blue button-up hugged her lithe form, accentuating the fullness of her breasts. The short sleeves cut tight around the woman's toned arms, while the faintest trace of a tattoo peeked out from edge of the fabric. She flashed white teeth at Erin and then winked at her.

Erin realized then that she had been staring.

"Carter, this lady just purchased a dishwasher. We are going to need the old one picked up and the new model delivered." Dan pointed at the white dishwasher as he spoke. Then he turned back to Erin and said, "Ma'am, if you will just give her your address, she'll take care of everything you need. After all, customer service is our number one priority."

For a brief instant Erin thought of several things that Carter could take care of but then shook her head as she realized both employees were staring at her, waiting for a response. Slightly embarrassed and not sure what had gotten into her, Erin rattled off her address.

Surely it was just the stress of losing the dishwasher, Erin thought as she thanked them and made her departure.

* * *

Erin sat on the couch, eating a bowl of cereal and watching the evening news. She hadn't planned to have cereal for dinner, but the bulk of her dishware lay entombed in the broken dishwasher and she didn't feel like eating a frozen dinner. As she listened to the newscaster talk about the latest out of Washington, she thought back over the day's events.

She thought about the loss of the dishwasher and what bills she would be unable to pay to make up for the cost of the three-hundred-and-ninety-nine-dollar-plus-tax purchase.

She thought about Corey.

She thought again what an epically stupid name Toffee was.

And she thought of Carter.

Erin wasn't sure what made her think of the store employee in *that* way. She had only ever strayed from the straight and narrow one time, during her junior year of college. While the sex with Leanne had been amazing, that was where the connection ended. After a few wild weeks, Erin parted ways with the big-busted blonde from Nebraska who lived in the dorm room down the hall to fall back into her nice and quiet heterosexual rut.

Flipping off the television with the remote, Erin rose from the couch and walked the cereal bowl to the kitchen sink. She shook her head in response to the memory of the attractive woman from the store, not sure what it was that had brought on this line of thinking. *Maybe it was the baby blue eyes that smiled when she spoke.* Whatever it was, Erin was sure that it had been way too long since she had last had sex. She briefly turned on the spigot and swirled water around the bowl before setting it down in the sink. She turned off the lights in the living room and then headed back to the bedroom, where she stumbled face-first onto the king-sized mattress, relieved that the day was over.

Lying on the secluded beach, Erin gave a contented sigh. It was not quite noon, but already the hot tropical sun was beating down on her back. She thought about rolling over on the towel but was too comfortable to move right now. Wearing only a string bikini, she was sure to pay the price for it later.

"Need some help?" a husky voice asked.

Erin opened one eye to see Carter standing beside her. Her bronzed skin and wine-red hair glistened in the sunlight. A black bathing suit hugged the curve of her hips and the swell of her ample breasts. Baby blue eyes smiled at her as the woman held up a bottle of sunblock.

"I'd hate to see skin as soft as yours get burned out here."

Erin smiled at her and nodded, closing her eyes as Carter fell to her knees in the sand. She popped open the lid of the lotion bottle and poured a generous amount on her hand. Erin gave a slight squeal and a shiver as the cold lotion touched her hot back.

"Sorry," Carter breathed into her ear. "Didn't mean to startle you."

She began to massage the lotion onto Erin's shoulders, running long, slender fingers down Erin's back in a slow, caressing motion.

Moaning as Carter swirled the lotion erotically around the small of her back and onto her hips, Erin felt herself become liquid under the other woman's hands.

"Tell me if this okay," Carter said softly.

"Yes," Erin whispered. "It's more than okay."

Carter continued her caress of Erin's shoulders and back, then lowered her head to kiss and nip the back of her neck and ears. Shivers ran down her spine as Carter flicked her tongue along the lobe of one ear. Erin's hips moved in time with Carter's tongue, grinding back and forth against her taut, athletic body.

She moved from Erin's neck and slowly began to make her way down Erin's back and then to her side. Erin moaned as electric waves of pleasure rippled through her. When Carter reached the bikini bottoms, tongue gave way to teeth. Erin shuddered as the other woman pulled down the flimsy material with her mouth and used her hands to knead and caress Erin's hips and thighs.

It was almost more than Erin could handle, and she struggled to turn over.

Carter gently but firmly held her in place, gripping each hip with a lotion-covered hand. She kneeled on either side of Erin's body and nipped again at Erin's neck.

Erin was unable to do anything but whimper. "Please. I need you…"

"Soon," came the sultry promise. "Let me worship you a little while longer." With that, Carter rolled Erin over onto her back. The unlatched bikini top fell away to the sand, freeing Erin's breasts. Carter took one breast into her palm, caressing it as she had done Erin's shoulders. The other breast found its way to Carter's lips, and she licked around its edge as Erin writhed beneath her. When Carter took one hard nipple into her mouth and suckled, Erin whimpered in pure pleasure and begged for release.

"Soon," Carter breathed, continuing her fondling of Erin's other breast. As Carter drew the hardened nipple between her lips, Erin breathed in sharply. Carter dove into the valley of Erin's breasts, then showered her stomach with kisses before continuing south.

Erin bucked up beneath Carter, but she had nowhere to go since Carter held the underside of her knees in place. She arched and nearly screamed as Carter's flattened tongue licked the length of her channel in one long, slow motion.

Erin reached down and twisted her fingers into Carter's short, spiky hair. She tumbled closer and closer to the edge.

Undaunted, Carter continued her onslaught, alternately licking and sucking Erin's clit.

When Erin felt two slender fingers slide into her, it was too much. She screamed in sheer pleasure and writhed uncontrollably in the sand.

Erin suddenly sat up in bed.

What. The. Fuck?

She lay back down and rolled to her side, breathless. Sure, it had been two months or maybe more since she'd had anything that would even remotely resemble satisfying sex with Corey, but to have an erotic dream about some random *female* salesperson she had just met at the appliance store was unlike anything that had ever happened before.

Erin closed her eyes. Tomorrow was Saturday, and she had a lot to do around the house before the delivery people came with the new dishwasher. She closed her eyes and drifted back off to sleep.

———————— ⟞⟝ ————————

It was half past twelve and there still wasn't the first sign of any delivery person.

Erin was beginning to get frustrated. She'd gotten up early that morning, cleaned up the kitchen, swept the floor, and did what she could around the house to make it look as if Harriet Homemaker lived there. Erin had completed the daunting task of cleaning out the dozen or so dirty dishes that were inside the old dishwasher. She had even lit candles around the kitchen and living room to conceal the odors of foul milk and garbage.

And then she spent the next four hours waiting.

On a usual Saturday she would have slept in, drunk a cup of coffee while reading the morning paper on the back porch, argued with Corey over dirty laundry left on the bathroom floor, and then maybe gone to the mall with her friend Leigh to do a little shopping. Now that Corey had left her for the girl with the ridiculous name, the Saturday morning arguments were certainly at an end. And any shopping trips she had thought about making were going to have to be put on hold after the major purchase of the new dishwasher.

Just when she was about to give up on the dishwasher being delivered at all, a white paneled van with bright green letters backed into her driveway. She peeked out the front window and watched with disappointment as two burly men in their late forties stepped out and unloaded the large, brown box from the back of the van. A little part of her had hoped that Carter would be the one doing the delivery.

Well, a big part of her, to be honest.

She opened the door and led the deliverymen to the kitchen. They smelled vaguely of pepperoni and garlic. The shorter of the two bore a red stain on the front of his gray shirt that looked suspiciously like marinara sauce; the mystery of what had taken them so long to get there was solved.

7

In a surprisingly short time, the deliverymen had removed her old dishwasher and rolled it out to the van. The short one drew a box cutter from his back pocket and slashed to pieces the cardboard box they had brought in the house, revealing the shiny new dishwasher, all covered in clear plastic. They deftly eased it into place and hooked up the assorted wires and hoses. When they were done, Erin and the two men stood in the kitchen, silently admiring the new machine.

"Thank you so much," Erin said with a smile.

"Nothing to it, ma'am," the tall one answered. "Just doing our job. Customer service is our number one priority."

They asked her to have a good rest of the weekend and headed out to their van.

She watched them back out of the driveway and then disappear down the street from the kitchen window. When they were gone, she walked back into the kitchen to stare again at the new dishwasher.

She opened the door and breathed in the smell of new plastic. Rolling the top basket out and then back in again, she again thought of all the things she could have done with three hundred and ninety-nine dollars.

So much for the day's excitement. She retreated back to the TV to channel surf.

A knock at the door interrupted her thoughts.

Erin frowned and turned down the volume on a blonde TV woman in leopard skin pants who was explaining the benefits of owning a stand-mixer. Erin peeked out the window. The white delivery van was back in the driveway. Wondering what the men had forgotten, she opened the back door.

It was Carter.

They stood there in silence, staring at one another.

"Hi, Miss Greene?" she said, her husky tones sending shivers down Erin's spine.

For a second she forgot how to speak. Finally, Erin was able to get out, "Um, yes."

"We really hate to bother you again, but the deliverymen forgot to have you sign some paperwork earlier today." She held up a clipboard.

"Oh, I see. Please, come in." Erin motioned to her and then took a step back into the kitchen.

Carter walked to the table and set the clipboard down. After reaching for a pen from her front pocket, she presented it to Erin. "Again," she said,

"I'm sorry they didn't get this earlier. If you will just sign on this front page and then initial the last two pages stating that you received delivery of the dishwasher and we removed the old one for you."

As she spoke, all Erin could do was think how well the tight green polo shirt fit around Carter's body. She couldn't help looking Carter up and down, taking time to linger at the round breasts pressing against the cotton-polyester blend.

"Miss Greene?"

Erin realized, flushing, that she had been staring maybe a little too long. "I'm sorry. Let me take care of that for you." She took the pen from Carter's hand and flipped through the paperwork. "All right, here you go."

"Thanks." Carter took the clipboard back from her, hugged it to her chest, and glanced over at the dishwasher. "Looks good," she said. "Is there anything I can explain about it for you or any questions you may have?"

"Would you like something to drink?" Erin asked. *Where did that come from? Now I sound like some little old woman.*

"No, thank you. I'm fine."

"Okay."

"Well, if you don't have anything, I'll be going. Thanks again for your understanding." Carter smiled and began to walk toward the door.

Want to have sex?

"I'm sorry, what?" Carter stopped just short of the door.

The blood ran out of Erin's face as she wondered if she had said that aloud. "Um, I was wondering if you could maybe show me how the cycles work on the machine?" she said quickly and then thought how stupid that sounded.

"Uh, sure, no problem." Carter walked over to the dishwasher. She opened the door and pulled out the racks, explaining how the machine worked as she did. She went through the various controls on the front of the dishwasher and described what each one did.

All Erin could think about during the demonstration was how good Carter looked in those jeans. For a moment she flashed to a scene from one of those disgusting pornos that Corey watched all the time, the one where the blonde with the absurdly large breasts didn't have the money to pay the pizza delivery guy and an alternative method of payment was worked out between them. God, how embarrassing! After months of chiding Corey for watching films that were so blatantly demeaning to women, here she was now in her own fantasy with Carter in the starring role.

"…and this button will delay the cycle either two or four hours, depending on what your need may be," Carter was saying. She turned to Erin. "And that's pretty much it. Do you have any more questions?"

Erin shook her head. "No, I think that covers everything, thank you."

"Okay, great." Carter smiled, her blue eyes dancing.

Finding herself lost in those eyes, Erin stood there, transfixed.

As a result, Carter had to sidestep around her, brushing against Erin as she turned to collect her clipboard from the counter top.

Erin sucked in a breath as the touch sent a shiver through her. She had a sudden flash of memory, recalling the feel of Dream-Carter's skin against her own. Looking at the woman standing before her now, Erin found the impulse to touch her was getting harder and harder to deny. *What the hell…* Erin stepped up behind Carter as she adjusted the papers on the clipboard and wrapped her arms around the woman's waist.

For a moment, the kitchen fell silent.

"Um, Miss Greene?" Carter's voice went an octave higher than it had been.

Erin said nothing, instead lightly running her hands across the front of Carter's polo shirt, just brushing over her breasts.

Carter gave a soft moan, making no attempt to pull away.

Emboldened by the sound, Erin brought her hands lower, feeling up and around Carter's thighs.

"Miss Greene…um…" Her husky voice trailed off as Erin began to untuck the green polo shirt from Carter's jeans. When Carter turned to face Erin, she was smiling and flushed.

"Tell me you don't want me," Erin murmured.

Carter seemed to swallow first before saying, "Excuse me?"

"I said, tell me you don't want me and I'll stop. I want you. I've wanted you from the moment I saw you in the store yesterday." She flashed Carter what she hoped was a seductive look as she finished untucking the polo from the other woman's jeans. "Tell me that you don't want me…say that I'm making an incredible fool of myself…that I've embarrassed and humiliated both of us and I'll step back." Erin ran her hands up Carter's stomach, this time touching flesh as she put her hands under the shirt. "I've never done anything like this before in my life, so I need you to say something. What do you want?" She leveled her eyes at Carter. "I know what I want."

Carter drew in a heavy breath and licked her lips. "I really don't know if this…um…appropriate," she said quietly.

Heat rose to Erin's cheeks, and she stepped back from Carter, wiping her palms on her pants. She cleared her throat and then turned away. "Of course. I don't know what I was thinking. Please, I'm so sorry if I've embarrassed you. I…I just don't know what got into me." She silently wished that the ground would open up and swallow her whole.

"Um, no, not at all. Don't worry about it," Carter said, tucking her shirt back into her jeans. "I'll, uh, just see myself out."

Nodding, Erin watched quietly as Carter collected her clipboard from the countertop and quickly exited the kitchen. The door closed, and Erin blew out a breath. She wiped her hands over her face and groaned. *What the hell was I thinking?* She turned to make her way back into the living room. She'd only taken a step when there was a knock at the kitchen door. Erin walked back and tentatively swung it open.

It was Carter.

They stood there in silence, staring at one another.

"It just occurred to me," Carter said finally, "that they told me to make sure that all your needs were taken care of." Taking a step forward, she wrapped an arm around Erin's waist and drew her in close. Carter dipped her head and took Erin's mouth in a hungry urgency.

Erin surrendered to the softness of Carter's lips, then moaned softly as Carter's teeth lightly grazed her bottom lip.

Carter ran her hands slowly down Erin's back, reaching lower while their kissing deepened. She lifted her off the ground with surprising strength and placed her on the kitchen table.

Continuing to hold the kiss, Erin jerked the shirt out of Carter's jeans so that she could softly caress the skin along her ribs and back.

Carter made short work of Erin's own blouse, deftly working the buttons and then sliding it off Erin's shoulders in what seemed to be a single motion.

Erin shivered under the dual sensations of her bra being pushed away and the cool wooden surface of the table making contact with her naked back.

Holding her around the hips, Carter bent down and began to kiss and lick Erin's breasts. She nipped softly with her teeth and then kissed and lightly licked her exposed stomach.

Flutters ran across Erin's body, making her shudder.

Carter stopped and took a step back, pulling the polo over her head.

Erin rose up from the table to admire Carter's creamy, pink-tipped breasts. She licked her lips, fighting the urge to taste them.

Carter reached down to unzip her pants, but Erin reached out a hand.

"Let me help you with that." She pulled her closer and breathed in a faint scent of vanilla. With one hand on either side of the jeans, she slid them down Carter's lithe frame while bending forward and kissing the top of one breast.

Carter inhaled sharply as she captured one nipple between her lips.

Unable to get enough of the taste of Carter's honey soft skin, Erin moaned softly as she suckled the beautifully formed breast. Continuing to feast, Erin moved her hand to its twin, cupping it in her palm while circling the nipple with her thumb.

Strong arms enveloped Erin's waist, and she felt herself being lifted up once again.

"Bedroom." Carter panted.

Erin grinned up at her and then motioned with one hand while licking around the edge of Carter's breast.

"Jesus," Carter muttered and carried Erin effortlessly from the kitchen.

They made it as far as the living room, where Carter lowered Erin down onto the soft cushion of the sofa. With one quick motion, she removed the remainder of Erin's clothes, covered her body with her own, and captured Erin's lips again in an intoxicatingly slow kiss.

The feel of Carter's naked skin inflamed Erin. Her senses felt on overload, but not enough to make her stop wanting more of Carter's body. She ran her hands along the soft skin of Carter's back, tightly gripping her naked hips and sinking in her nails as Carter's tongue slipped between her lips, making sweeping, swirling motions inside her mouth.

Erin slid her hand under Carter to find her throbbing wet heat. With a satisfied moan, she pushed a finger inside and then quickly added a second. As Carter began to nip and lap along the side of Erin's neck, Erin thrust her fingers into Carter's liquid warmth. She knew by Carter's moans that she'd found the right spot and began making long, deliberate strokes, relishing the feel. She glided her fingers upward, sliding deep inside Carter's pulsating core.

Carter began to gasp for air and arched her back. She trembled and shuddered against Erin, wrapping her thighs tightly around Erin's hand as she cried out in pleasure. Finally, she stilled and then collapsed on top of her.

Erin smiled and lightly ran her fingers along the back of Carter's neck.

After a moment, Carter propped her head up and grinned. To Erin's delight, she began to delicately flick her tongue along the edge of Erin's collarbone and then nipped and kissed along her chest and down her stomach. She stopped at her navel and then licked upward to the underside of Erin's breasts.

Oh God! Erin moaned and arched, fisting the couch cushion as streaks of electricity shot through her.

Carter gave the smallest of nips to one breast and then reached down and spread Erin's legs apart with one knee. She licked slow circles around Erin's navel as she cupped and teased at Erin's breasts. Moving lower still, she bent between Erin's thighs and ran her tongue up and down the edge of her clit.

Erin cried out and caught her lower lip between her teeth as Carter continued licking and suckling, then parted the sensitive folds with one finger and thrust her tongue between them. Carter darted her tongue in and out, relentlessly bringing Erin to the edge of climax as she writhed on the soft cushions.

"Please…" Erin didn't know exactly what she was begging for, whether it was for her to stop or keep going.

Carter flicked her tongue and then grazed Erin's clit with her teeth.

It was all she could take.

Erin screamed and bucked uncontrollably as the orgasm washed over her in endless waves. With a ragged gasp she fell back against the couch.

"Oh my God."

Carter smiled and leisurely kissed her way back up Erin's body. They drew close, Carter turning Erin in her strong arms so that they lay face to face.

Erin gazed up into Carter's baby blue eyes and smiled. "That was…wow, that was just wow," she murmured.

Carter kissed along her neck and face as she lightly traced the edge of Erin's ribs with her fingers, sending little shivers down her body. "Customer service is my number one priority."

BEST IDEA EVER

BY JOVE BELLE

THE BLACK PLASTIC BAG CRINKLED loudly when Van tightened her grip. The common area of the dorms was especially full, and she felt her face flush hot with embarrassment when a sophomore from her comparative lit class glanced at her. The thought that maybe the other girl knew what was in the bag made her look away sharply and increase her pace.

This proved just how much she was willing to do for Sophie. Last night, when they'd been tangled beneath the blankets, sweaty and naked and on the verge of coming, all she had managed was a hurried *yes* when Sophie asked her to get it. This morning, when Sophie reminded her, Van had choked on her cereal. She'd been certain that she'd imagined the promise, high on lust and unable to hear properly with the rush of blood in her ears.

"I want to try it," Sophie had smiled and twisted her fingers into Van's hair in the way that made Van helpless to do anything but nod in agreement.

"Are you sure?" Van had just managed to squeak out her response as she tried to fit Sophie's request into her mind... Her body flushed with desire, and she came with a hot, wet rush as Sophie had whispered into Van's ear the dirty details of things she wanted her to do. Sophie knew what Van wanted even if Van herself couldn't admit it.

Van's hesitation hadn't stopped Sophie from assigning her the job of shopping. She'd cited her own busy class load compared to Van's light Wednesday schedule. And so Van had gone downtown and stammered out her request as the shop girl laughed and checked her out at the same time.

"If you need help figuring it out..." she'd said, her fingers loose against Van's wrist. Her touch burned into Van's hammering pulse as she imagined exactly what the clerk was offering. She'd snatched up her bag and ran, her Chucks pounding loud and fast against the pavement in time with her heart.

She entered Sophie's dorm room without knocking and almost lost her mind when she found Sophie sitting on her bed, naked and anxiously watching the door.

"You're back." Sophie stood, hands clasped together.

"You're naked," Van blurted.

Sophie's cheeks turned pink. "Yes, well, I thought it would be easier this way."

"Oh. Right." Van pushed the door closed with her foot.

"You got it?"

She thrust the bag into Sophie's hands. "Here."

She felt instantly better having successfully completed her mission.

"Should we, you know, open it?" Sophie asked without looking at the bag.

"Okay. Sure. Go ahead."

Sophie dumped the contents onto the bed. The black leather harness landed flatly, but the clamshell package holding the dildo bounced before coming to a rest. The bottle that the sales clerk swore she needed rolled off the bed and onto the floor. Van picked it up, hoping Sophie wouldn't ask about it. Of course, she did.

"What's that?"

Van laid the bottle on the bed next to the other items. "Lube."

"Why?"

"The girl at the store said...She thought..." Van scratched the back of her neck and waited for Sophie to figure it out on her own.

"Oh!" Sophie picked it up and read the label. "I don't think that will be necessary."

"Yeah?" Van asked, one side of her mouth curving up into a lopsided smile.

"Yeah. Pretty sure."

"Awesome." Van kissed Sophie, because she was naked and she wanted to touch her boobs, but it seemed crass to do that without at least warming her up first. But first they needed to sort out their new purchase, so she pulled away before she could get too caught up. "How should we...um?"

Sophie draped her arms around Van's neck and played with the short hair at the back of her neck. "I thought you would, you know, put it on and..."

Van jerked away, Sophie's fingers tugging sharply with the unexpected movement. "You what? You want me to what?"

As ridiculous as it seemed now, Van hadn't really thought about *how* they would use it, only that Sophie said she wanted to. As shocked as she was to realize Sophie wanted her to wear it, she couldn't even imagine it the other way around.

"I just…" Sophie stepped close again and rested her hand against Van's chest, her fingertips grazing along the top of her shoulder and base of her palm just touching the swell of Van's breast. Sophie shrugged and looked away. "I think it would be hot, that's all."

Van's mind flashed to the image of Sophie naked beneath her, panting as Van pushed the dildo into her with her hips. A loud buzzing grew in her ears and the edges of her vision blurred as a bolt of arousal shot through her, so fierce it made her sway on her feet.

"Okay." She struggled to remove her T-shirt and pants at the same time, tripping when her jeans got caught on her shoes.

Sophie laughed. "Calm down. Let me help."

She pushed Van onto the bed next to the harness and dildo, and Van blushed even harder as the cock bounced obscenely, the clear plastic package glinting as it caught the light. Someday, she'd be suave with all this sex stuff. For now, though, she couldn't believe that Sophie wanted her, that she'd let Van touch her *there*. And now she wanted Van to…

Van took a deep breath and tried to calm herself as she watched Sophie kneel between her legs. She kissed Van softly on the mouth, then bent to remove Van's shoes. Before Van realized, Sophie stripped away her clothing from the waist down, with her T-shirt still hanging awkwardly around her neck. She tugged the shirt off, along with her sports bra. Van didn't feel very sexy, but the look Sophie gave her, as if she was burning up from the inside out, fixed that. Her muscles clenched way down low in her belly, and she shifted slightly to ease the pressure. The movement sent a sharp zap of arousal through her, starting at her clit and radiating outward. She froze in place and sat stiffly as she waited for Sophie to speak.

"So far so good," Sophie said with a slow, wicked smile.

Van nodded stupidly. They were both naked, but she still had no idea what to do next. "Now what?"

Sophie picked up the harness. "Now you put this on. I'm just going to…" She handed off the harness and took up the dildo, "…figure this out."

By the time Van decided which leg went where and how to get the O-ring part in the front—that's where the dildo went, said the shop girl—Sophie had the package open. She hefted the cock in her hand as if testing the weight of it.

"It's kinda big, isn't it?"

Van had worried about the opposite in the store. Compared to some of the others, it was positively tiny. It seemed such a simple idea when Sophie had sent her off on her errand. She had no idea that dildos came in so many sizes and colors. Ultimately, she'd opted for one that didn't remind her of some sort of dirty circus accessory and hoped that Sophie would like it, too. Van had never seen an actual penis before, so she had no idea how this fake one compared. But she really, *really* wanted to get it on and inside of Sophie.

"Is it?"

Sophie nodded, eyes wide. "It'll work, I think."

"Good." Van was past being embarrassed by how much this turned her on. She just needed to figure out how to get the cock into the ring. There were snaps and leather straps and she'd barely managed to get the harness on right.

"So, where does it, you know…go?" Sophie pointed at the harness with the tip of the dildo and Van took it from her. The situation was awkward enough without Sophie tugging on the harness trying to figure out how to get the cock through the ring properly.

"Like this, I think." Van unsnapped one side and freed the ring the way the shop girl had shown her, then slipped the dildo inside. When she finished, the dildo jutted out from her crotch, listing to one side. She felt even more ridiculous than she had walking down the hall with the black bag.

Sophie stared at her with dark pupils blown wide. She licked her lips. "That's fucking hot."

"Yeah?" Van didn't feel ridiculous anymore.

"Definitely," Sophie said breathlessly. She ran one finger from the tip to the base, then back up.

The motion made Van shudder with want.

"Wait. We should clean it first, shouldn't we?" God, Van hated to stop Sophie from doing whatever she wanted to do next, but they needed to be smart about this. Judging from how her body was reacting, she would want to do this again. If they did it wrong this time and made Sophie hate it, Van would probably cry.

"How?"

"Fuck. I don't know." Cleaning seemed like a really good idea, but how they were going to do that with it already strapped in was beyond Van. She'd probably have to take it off and that seemed really wrong.

"I know." Sophie smiled brightly and went to her desk. "This!"

She held a half-empty bottle of Absolute. They'd drunk a good portion of it the night before, so it seemed oddly fitting that it would make an appearance today. Sophie grabbed a box of tissue from the desk, too.

"Gimme."

"I'll do it." Sophie twisted the cap off and knelt between Van's knees. She braced the dildo in one hand, her fingers wrapped loosely around it, and drizzled vodka over the surface. She wiped it down, the tugging and pushing moved the cock against Van's clit. She tried to stay still, but when Sophie swiveled the dildo in the ring to clean the other side, she couldn't hold back her moan.

Sophie watched Van's face closely as she finished cleaning the dildo. She tossed the tissue in the general direction of the trash can, then pumped her fist up and down the length of the cock.

Van groaned and pushed her hips against Sophie's hand to draw out the pressure.

"You like it." Sophie smiled.

Van nodded, her hands clenched tight around the edge of the mattress. "Very much."

"Mmmm… I want to try…" Sophie's voice drifted away as she lowered her mouth to the cock and ran her tongue over the tip.

Van couldn't feel the fleeting pressure, but a burst of arousal jolted through her at the sight. She struggled to keep her hips still, whimpering with the effort. Sophie smiled and wrapped her lips around the head. She dipped her head down, taking the cock into her mouth and increasing the pressure on Van's clit. Van moved her hands from the bed to the back of Sophie's head, tightening them in Sophie's hair as her head bobbed up and down.

"God, Sophie…please." Van tugged on Sophie's shoulders and pulled her up into a sloppy, open-mouthed kiss. She could taste the hint of vodka and silicone in Sophie's mouth and it made her hips jerk.

Sophie gripped at her waist, her hands just above the straps of the harness and her fingers scratching restlessly at her skin.

"I want…" Van gasped, her tongue still partially inside Sophie's open mouth. She clutched Sophie to her, holding tight to her shoulders and unsure what to do next.

Sophie ended the kiss, her chest heaving as she tried to catch her breath. "What? What do you want?"

18

"I want…" Van kissed her again, thrusting with her tongue the way she wanted to thrust with her hips. She licked the inside of Sophie's mouth, pushing deeper and harder than she ever had before. Sophie straddled her, the cock pressed up between their bellies. Van rocked her hips and broke away. "I want inside."

"Yes," Sophie hissed as her mouth descended onto Van's. Her hand inched upward until she cupped Van's breast in her hand. When she rolled the nipple between her thumb and forefinger, Van pushed her down onto the bed.

"How do we…" Van gestured toward their pelvic area. "…you know?"

"Just kiss me." Sophie pulled Van into another kiss and as Sophie pushed her tongue into Van's mouth, Van felt the growing pressure deep inside compelling her to do *more*. Sophie spread her legs and Van fell into the open space, the cock hard between them. Sophie moaned and thrust, rubbing herself against the dildo, and the sensation was almost enough to make Van come.

"I just…" Van pushed herself up until she was kneeling between Sophie's legs. Having Sophie beneath her—her legs splayed open, her hips thrusting against nothing—made her breath catch in her throat. "I can…"

She positioned the head of the cock at Sophie's opening and Sophie froze. God, she was so wet, Van could feel it everywhere, brushing the back of her knuckles and coating her thighs. The bottle of lube, wherever it was, *really* wasn't necessary. She pushed forwarded the tiniest bit and Sophie's face contorted as Van entered her.

"Are you okay?" She held herself above Sophie, watching her face, mesmerized by the sight of the cock, *her* cock, partially inside her girlfriend. In that moment Van knew she'd selected the right one, flesh colored to match her own complexion. She braced one hand near Sophie's head, her hair soft as silk against Van's fingers, and braced the other against Sophie's chest for leverage, her thumb stretched out to swipe over her nipple.

"God, yes," Sophie gasped, her voice high and tight, her words stilted. She gripped Van tight at the hips, her fingers scratching and digging into the sweat-slicked skin of Van's ass. "Just…wait."

Van trembled against her body's desire to thrust, to claim Sophie and make her feel how much Van needed her. She wasn't sure if she loved Sophie, but in that moment, as she saw Sophie's face etched with desire as Van's cock slid slowly into her, she couldn't imagine anything more perfect. She was willing to declare her love before everyone if Sophie would just let her *move*.

"Sophie, please." She smoothed Sophie's hair away from her face and kissed her as gently as she could.

Sophie nodded as she pulled Van's hips down against her. "Slow. Go slow."

"Yes." Van eased her hips forward, watching as her cock disappeared little by little inside of Sophie. "God, you're so beautiful."

Sophie arched against her, urging her to pull out and thrust in again. Van moved carefully, her body thrumming with desire and the knowledge that this is the way it should have always been. Nothing would ever top this. Visions of her fucking Sophie consumed her—of her bending Sophie over her desk and taking her from behind, of Sophie riding her cock, of Sophie with her cock in her mouth—and she had to stop moving to keep from coming. Every fantasy that crossed her mind involved two constants: Sophie and her new cock.

"Baby, don't stop," Sophie begged. Her legs circled around Van's hips as she thrust upward.

"No, never." She stopped holding back and let herself thrust into Sophie the way her body had wanted to since Sophie first whispered the idea into her ear. She arched up, her hands on Sophie's breasts, because they were perfect and she loved the way Sophie whimpered when she teased her nipples.

"Deeper, God, Van, fuck me harder, please."

Sophie stared up at her with her mouth slightly open and her eyes dark with desire and Van felt something break loose inside her. She adjusted her position, reaching behind herself to grab Sophie's ankles. She pushed Sophie's legs up until her feet were next to her head and her body lay split open for Van. She held Sophie down and fucked her with her whole body. The coiling heat built inside her and she wouldn't be able to hold out for much longer.

"Touch yourself. God, Sophie, baby, let me see you touch yourself while I fuck you."

Sophie slipped her hand between them to find her clit. Her knuckles bumped into Van as she jerked her fingers against herself. Van moved faster. Seconds later, Sophie's eyes closed, her head snapped back and her whole body tensed. Van thrust harder, letting herself feel the way her cock bottomed out and the way Sophie sucked her back in every time she withdrew. She came with her cock buried deep inside Sophie.

They lay together, panting with exertion, sweat covering their bodies.

"Please tell me we can do that again," Van asked as her body drifted close to sleep, her cock still inside Sophie. She would leave it there forever if it was up to her. She wanted to wake up inside her girlfriend and fuck her again.

"Yes, best idea ever," Sophie agreed. She dropped her feet back to the bed, and Van slid out a bit with the motion. She looped her legs around Van's waist and pulled her in tight again. "Not yet. I'm not ready yet."

"Again?" Van thrust lightly against Sophie. She was exhausted, and her muscles were loose, but Sophie's bare breasts and thought of doing what they just did woke her up. She'd be ready again soon.

"Maybe." Sophie swatted her bottom easily. "In a little bit."

"Okay." Van bent low enough to take one of Sophie's nipples between her lips. She sucked on it gently, then scraped her teeth over the tip. Sophie moaned and moved beneath her. Van smiled and sucked a little harder.

Sophie pushed her away, even as her hips rocked against Van. "Baby, stop."

"You sure?"

"No." Sophie laughed. Van modified her position so that her full weight was no longer on Sophie. Her cock slipped a little until Sophie rolled with her. When they stopped adjusting, Van was on bottom and Sophie was on top. "Now stop fussing."

Sophie laid her head on Van's shoulder, her smaller body fitting perfectly over Van. She nuzzled her face into Van's neck and pressed her hips down until Van was seated inside her again. Van's body twitched to life with the feel of Sophie's body against hers, pushing tight onto Van's cock.

"Sophie..." Van's voice sounded as strained as her body felt. Just moments ago, she was ready to sleep; now she felt primed, as if she would come apart completely if she didn't fuck Sophie soon.

"Seriously?" The heat of Sophie's question washed over Van's neck, her lips brushing the skin and making it tingle. She adjusted her hips slightly and Van gasped. Sophie laughed and said, "Okay, maybe now."

Sophie sat up, her body rising above Van as she flexed and eased her hips in soft, exploratory circles. Van held tightly to Sophie's hips and simply let her move. She lifted herself, slipping up the length of the cock and tugging on it. She circled her hips with just the bare tip inside her. Van let her head fall back and closed her eyes. Sophie felt so fucking good moving above her and she wanted to enjoy it for as long as possible. It was different without the sharp, urgent edge driving her.

Sophie dropped down, then rose up again immediately with a long, deep moan.

"Fuck, baby, that's so hot. Ride me just like that." Van tightened her grip on Sophie's hips, pulling her down hard, then pushing her back up. She wanted to thrust, but more than that, she wanted Sophie to feel the power of being in control. Sophie arched her back and threw her head back.

"This won't take long." She moaned, moving up and down fast enough to make her boobs bounce.

"Don't hold back." Van wasn't there yet, but, God, if Sophie could come so easily like this, she wanted to watch it happen. She moved her hands from Sophie's hips to her breasts, taking her nipples lightly between her thumbs and forefingers. When Sophie gasped and moved faster, Van increased the pressure. She squeezed hard as her own orgasm grew.

Van thrust her hips upward, unable to hold herself back any longer. The sight of Sophie—the line of her throat as she threw her head back and screamed, her body covered with sweat and her breasts heavy in Van's hands as she bounced on Van's cock—was too much. Van's orgasm gathered quickly and swept over her like a storm. She came at the same time that Sophie cried out her name.

Sophie collapsed on top of her, her breath hot and loud in Van's ear. She stayed there for several moments, and Van luxuriated in the feel of Sophie's body pressing her into the bed. Eventually, Sophie shifted, making Van's cock slip out of her. Van didn't want to let it happen, but she understood. Sophie needed rest, and so did Van herself. If she left the cock inside Sophie, she'd be ready to go again in minutes.

"So what do you think?" Sophie teased without raising her head. Her body lay limp against Van.

"Best idea ever."

"Yeah? I was thinking maybe next we could try…"

ENCORE

BY JESS LEA

NETTY ADJUSTED THE GAS LAMP in the hall, nudged open the dressing room door, and dodged the powder puff that was flung in her direction.

"Five minutes, please."

"Wretched girl!" The rich, dark voice that had made Marianna the toast of Venice, Berlin, and St. Petersburg still managed to sound divine even when shouting insults. "How many times have I told you to knock?"

In fact, Marianna was fully clothed, encased in red wine satin to play *Carmen*, the bodice stiff with whalebone and flaring out into extravagant hooped skirts, so wide they hid the carpet at her feet. So really, there was no need to make such a fuss about her privacy. But Netty's mistress, the one they called *prima donna assoluta e sola*, absolute and only, was as famed for her temper as for her voice, a voice which made audience members leap to their feet like pilgrims in some revivalist tent, and drew a cascade of rose petals every night.

"Forgive me, Madam."

"I'll do no such thing! I've tolerated your insolence for far too long." Marianna leaned forward to adjust the coils of her black wig, and to colour in a beauty spot on one powdered cheekbone. Her bodice, cut low and fringed with ticklish black lace, held her breasts firmly in position, their alabaster tops straining above the fabric. A costume more suited to the court of Versailles than to the Gypsy camps of *Carmen*, in Netty's opinion. But as Marianna had made clear several times—punctuated by cushions hurled with impressive accuracy—Netty's opinions were not welcome.

"If I weren't afraid of dirtying my hands, I would thrash you," the diva snarled, still glaring at her own reflection as if this were preferable to looking at her maid. "Now get out, before I pick you up and throw you down the grand staircase!"

In a costume so unwieldy, Netty doubted her mistress could walk all the way to the staircase, much less engage in gymnastic feats there. Still, she felt herself flush at the insult. Netty could hand in her notice; Marianna had plenty of rivals who would take on the prima donna's attendant, if only out of spite. But some of them were said to behave even more outrageously towards those in their service. In Netty's experience, there was nothing that brought out a performer's nasty side more than a small amount of success. That mezzo-soprano Antoinette, for instance, was rumoured to dole out bare-bottom spankings to maidservants who displeased her, and Netty wasn't sure she could tolerate that. Certainly not from such a second-rate talent.

And besides, there were things Netty would miss about being in Marianna's service—sneaking looks at her scandal sheets and risqué novels from Paris, picking through the offerings of Turkish delight and champagne from the diva's admirers, and finishing off their cigars. After bobbing into a curtsy, she retreated, shutting the door behind herself with exaggerated care.

⟡

Still grumbling, Marianna craned closer to the mirror to touch up the kohl around her wide, dark eyes. Even the back stalls must get the full impact of her stare. Regarding herself critically, she gave a little nod. She might be well past thirty, might lack the crystal purity of a true coloratura soprano— but who cared? In Marianna's experience, it did not take long for fresh young soubrettes to lose their appeal. She'd finished both eyes and was refreshing the dark red paint that glistened across her lips, when her hooped skirts began to stir.

"That," said Lady S., emerging from Marianna's froth of petticoats and smoothing back her own glossy, cropped hair, "was not kind."

Marianna gazed down at her and arched one eyebrow. "Kind?"

Lady S. had been kneeling there without complaint while Marianna applied her cosmetics. The warm shape of her head had kept Marianna's thighs apart, while Lady S. teased the diva at length with her mouth. As a vocalist, Marianna could not help marvelling at the agility of the other woman's tongue; Marianna could have sworn she felt the shape of a treble clef at one point. Her nether regions were hot and tingling, rippling with enjoyment, but she saw no reason to say so. It would not do to seem too impressed by one's followers.

Still, of Marianna's many suitors, Lady S. was undoubtedly the most exotic. With her sharply tailored suits, bright cravats, and gold-tipped walking stick, she cut a swath through every crowd. Even the most worldly opera-goers would turn to stare at this creature, from her top hats to her leather shoes, which flashed with the sort of sheen that young ladies were warned to stand well away from, lest it reflect back their own shapely ankles and other attractions further north. If not for her wealth, lineage, and unshakeable pride, such a woman would never have been permitted inside this theatre. As it was, she'd been waiting at the stage door since opening night.

Against her will, Marianna smiled, recalling that first carriage ride. How warm Lady S.'s fingers had felt, as they toyed with the silk button that held Marianna's glove at the wrist. How she had traced it around and around, brushing the sensitive flesh beneath it, working the button loose with such tantalising slowness that by the time the fabric had peeled away and Marianna's hand was free, she scarcely knew whether to plunge it inside Lady S.'s clothing, or just slap her with it.

Tonight Lady S. had kept her own gloves on. The dressing rooms were unseasonably chilly, despite Marianna's many vocal and bloodcurdling complaints to the management. Lady S.'s hands, sheathed in fine chocolate leather, slid up and down Marianna's thighs. In spite of her cool demeanour, Marianna could not help wriggling in her seat; the sleek sensations above her stocking tops were hard to resist.

She cleared her throat and said "I will tell you what is unkind—distracting me like this when I should be in the wings already!"

"You take people for granted. It isn't right." Lady S. was still making a show of enjoying Marianna's plump, creamy flesh, stroking and tweaking it until Marianna gasped and would have smacked the roving hands, had she been able to reach them. Unfortunately the costume had been designed for aesthetic, not practical, purposes. Her boned bodice held her upright, and the wide cage of fabric and cane made things damnably complicated below the waist. Her womanly parts could only be reached by someone positioned— well, where Lady S. was now.

"Since when do you care so much about servants?" Marianna demanded. "Don't waste your concern on... What's her name? Nelly? She's a saucy little pest, hoping to discomfit me by charging in like that. For all I know, she's a spy for the newspapers. Perhaps she even suspects about us—"

Marianna's voice, so disciplined and powerful, broke off then in a sigh of delight. Lady S.'s hand had ventured higher, opening the thin muslin drawers with their lace edging. A ribbon held them up at the waist, but there was no need to fumble with that, thanks to the open seam that ran the full length of a woman's crotch. Such a sensible design, as Lady S. had often observed.

Marianna heard the creak of the leather. She felt its coolness against her most sensitive flesh, sensed the friction between the slightly stiff material and the nimble fingers that curved and flexed inside it.

"I think I love that thrilling voice of yours best of all when it does that," Lady S. mused as Marianna gave a faint moan.

Her lips were swollen and tender from Lady S.'s earlier attentions. This new contact made her twitch and jerk in surprise, wondering that a barrier between them could make her lover's touch feel more intimate than ever.

Lady S. scolded, "But don't try to distract me with a private performance, my darling. I was saying that you should be more generous to those who serve you. You could never have achieved greatness if not for the likes of her."

"Absurd." Marianna's hips were rocking, her breath coming hard as the pressure between her thighs grew firmer, more purposeful. She could hear the bell in the foyer, the dense hush of the auditorium, the opening blasts of the orchestra. "Oh, my love, please hurry…"

Lady S. smiled, craning forward to kiss the swell of Marianna's breasts above the satin. "See, you can speak quite sweetly when you want something."

The diva could feel her nipples tightening inside the gown, achingly conscious of her lover's mouth so close, but loosening that wretched bodice was out of the question now. It would take half an hour to get back into it again.

"That's my girl," said Lady S. "A firm hand, and you become quite civilised."

So saying, she eased Marianna's thighs further apart, and Marianna felt those fingers in their supple leather stroking open her lips and entering her one by one.

"I…I'm due out there—" Marianna gasped at the new incursion, a fiery pressure inside her.

"Won't take a moment."

That same devilish wink that had dared her into Lady S.'s carriage on their first night together was followed by a twisting, slithering sensation. Lady S.'s other hand seemed to be wrestling with something unseen, then her lover's fingers retreated but something was still...there.

Lady S. withdrew her hand to brush back her hair once again, and Marianna saw that her lover's smooth olive skin was bare. She had left the leather glove in place.

"What are you—"

"Shh, hold still." That smile again, as Lady S. straightened Marianna's drawers and shook down her skirts. "You never agreed to wear my flowers onstage, did you? But I think I like this arrangement better."

"That is..." Marianna squirmed and glowered in outrage. Bad enough that Lady S. should stop touching her, just when Marianna was almost—and now this ridiculous game? This was worse than the night when Lady S. had tied Marianna's wrists to the bedpost, then retreated to her armchair to sip brandy and smoke a leisurely cigarette while Marianna, quite naked, had panted and cursed and been obliged to rub herself against the linens for some measure of relief while her lover looked on. She'd known it was a mistake, letting Lady S. get away with that one. A sound thrashing would have put things right.

She struggled to her feet and discovered, to her dismay, that Lady S.'s calling card stayed where it was. Marianna was intending to retreat behind the Japanese screen and retrieve it—somehow—when a knock sounded again.

Netty's voice was breathless. "Oh, Madam, you're terribly late! The factory girls have had to do their dance twice, and Don José looks ready to explode!"

What was there for Marianna to do but hurry to the door, which Lady S. held open for her with impeccable courtesy and a neat little bow? Marianna would certainly have slapped her for that if the maid hadn't been watching. Not that Netty's presence was a problem in itself; the diva had smacked quite a few importunate callers in her time, and rather appreciated an audience. But she couldn't risk a witness seeing what would doubtless be the look of shameless enjoyment on Lady S.'s face.

Those who witnessed Marianna's performance of *Carmen* that night would go on to argue passionately over it for years. Her dancing was uncharacteristically stiff and hesitant, and she missed several cues. Although as some people pointed out, that might have been the diva's vanity, forcing her co-star and the orchestra to slow to a pace that suited her. It wouldn't be the first time she'd pulled a stunt like that. But her lyrics of free living and loving were delivered with a seductive force that surpassed all previous performances; her enslavement of the gullible Don José seemed all too believable. And her sensual trill on the line "If I love you, beware!" made many in the crowd whoop and rise to their feet in rapture.

Marianna had seldom been so furious. Bad enough that she should be distracted during a show, but that her distraction should take a form so very pleasurable... Every pose and dance step, every wriggle in the arms of her gaolers caused the leather to rub against her and inside her in the most indescribable ways. She feared her voice would crack, feared some quiver of her body or trembling of her lips would show that her voluptuous portrayal was more than just a performance. She even feared her growing slickness would make it impossible to keep the glove in place. What if it fell onto the stage? And when she gazed out across the theatre at the acres of plush red velvet, the flashes of gold, the rearing statues of nymphs, leering satyrs, and naked gods, her eyes fell on Lady S., seated in a private box. She was watching with her usual keen attention; she was a scrupulous and attentive viewer, Marianna had always appreciated that. But when she caught Marianna's gaze, she drew something—the remaining glove—from her pocket and rubbed it, between her fingers, very slowly.

Seated in the box beside Lady S., Claudine twisted her auburn hair around one finger and murmured, "Do you suppose I'll ever be a legend like her?"

"Without question." Lady S. lifted her companion's palm and kissed it, inhaling the scent of lilies. That was the only trouble with girls from the ballet, Lady S. reflected. They needed such constant reassurance. Still, Claudine was a darling when she wasn't sulking, and delectable to look at too, with her bright green eyes and sprinkling of freckles. Not to mention being quite startlingly flexible.

Pouting, the young women said, "Why should I believe you? Don't think I don't know where you were before the curtain went up."

"Beloved, you were so busy flirting in the foyer, I'm amazed you noticed I was gone." After another kiss, Lady S. coaxed, "Don't be cross, I'll make it up to you." She slid her arm around Claudine, stroking the bare white flesh of the young woman's throat, shoulders, and décolletage. There was quite a bit to caress, for Claudine—sensibly, in Lady S.'s view—saw no sense in possessing such beauty and hiding it.

The young woman scowled and slapped at Lady S.'s fingers, but permitted her admirer to lean in and kiss the line of her neck, the delicate shell ridge of her ear.

Lady S. glanced around to see if they were being observed. Here in the box, they had a certain privacy, although a spectator with opera glasses might be able to catch a more interesting view. From the vantage point of someone on the stage, however, the two of them were quite exposed. Lady S. knew Marianna would be able to follow every move. And Claudine's evening wear was a good deal more accessible than Marianna's.

Claudine gave a little yelp as Lady S. slipped her hand right inside the young woman's bodice. "That's quite enough of that!" The ballerina wriggled free. She didn't mind a little scandal, but there were limits.

"Oh, you are so proper." Lady S. sighed in disappointment, but retreated willingly enough. In the glare of the stage lights, she had caught a look from Marianna that confirmed that the diva had seen it all. A risky game to play, but prima donnas, in Lady S.'s experience, thrived on conflict.

"Why do you think I brought this for you?" Lady S. asked Claudine, flicking open the lace-edged fan in Japanese silk she had presented to her young companion earlier that evening. A handsome token, and quite wide enough for a modest woman to take cover behind. Pressing this screen into Claudine's trembling fingers, Lady S. got to work behind it, fondling Claudine's breasts and murmuring appreciatively in her ear. No chance of greater intimacy, alas. Public lovemaking would be a little too outré, even for them. But Lady S. always took care to get her companions comfortably settled before a show. Tonight she had been especially solicitous, positioning one silken cushion behind Claudine's back, another beneath her dainty feet and, while she'd been kneeling there, another underneath Claudine's skirts, wedged between her thighs.

The young woman began to stir and sigh, moving to and fro in her seat, the fan fluttering in her hand. Down on the stage, Marianna was beginning her final chorus for Act One. Lady S. smiled and prepared to enjoy the show.

———— ✦⊰✦⊱✦ ————

The curtain fell, and Marianna nearly ran for her dressing room. That wicked, heartless, trifling bitch! Marianna could not have cared less about pretty little Claudine, but for Lady S. to undermine her performance like that—it was unforgivable, and so was her own body's reaction. She was thoroughly and quite unbearably aroused.

Once inside her dressing room, Marianna grappled with her skirts in vain, but the costume was built for effect, not ease. And admirers, patrons, or murderous co-stars might invade the room at any moment! Her chest clenched in panic when she heard a knock and the door inched open, but it was only Netty, bearing an armload of flowers.

"You're in sweet voice tonight, Madam." Then, laying the flowers down, "Madam? Are you well?"

"Netty." Marianna grimaced, but what choice was there? She tiptoed around her maid to shut the door. "I find myself in some difficulty here." She closed her eyes. "Could you assist me? Please?"

<hr>

"Easy when you know how."

Netty's voice was calm as she dealt with the layers of satin and linen, bending and collapsing the cane scaffolding in ways Marianna had never learned. Despite her mortification, the singer felt some relief at her employee's skill.

"If you could lean further forward, Madam?"

Marianna grasped the edge of the dressing table and felt the rustle of fabric, then the cool air of the dressing room brushing the backs of her ankles, her naked thighs. Then, to her surprise, she felt the ribbon loosening at her waist, felt a tickle as her drawers fell around her ankles.

"There's no need for that—"

"Shh. I trained as a dresser at the Paris Opera." Netty's tone was quieter, more respectful than Marianna had heard it before, and firmer, too. "I know what I'm doing."

And to Marianna's amazement, it seemed that she did. Netty's hands felt small but unexpectedly strong as they moulded to the curves of Marianna's splendid white buttocks, fondling, kneading and squeezing.

"Luckily, Madam, I'm not in the least afraid of dirtying *my* hands," she whispered, drawing away to give the exposed bottom a good smack. When this was greeted with a cry of delight—the jolt had reverberated right into Marianna's sweet spot—Netty gave her another.

"Oh, my dear…" Marianna caught her breath, astonished by this turn of events and by the ease with which her body gave in to Netty's touch. She had felt those hands on her so many times before, fastening buttons and tugging corset laces. Was that why it seemed so natural to trust Netty now? Or was the singer just too aroused to refuse? "My dear, lock the door. Someone might—"

"Since when are you afraid of an audience, Madam?" Netty teased, caressing Marianna's soft rump again before taking pity on her. "Very well, I'll see to it." Stepping back, she added, "But don't you move, you promise? If you do, I will tire of your insults once and for all, and walk out of here."

"I…promise." Breathing hard, her hips thrusting back and forth, Marianna gripped the edge of the dressing table. She could hear a shivering sound as the little bottles of cosmetics clinked together. Netty crossed the room to jam a chair beneath the door handle, then paused. Not daring to look back, Marianna could nonetheless sense her enjoying the view.

"Now then, Madam," she said, "let's deal with this difficulty of yours."

Marianna had thought Netty would draw the glove straight out, and braced herself for the likelihood that she would climax, as she had always found withdrawal a more powerful sensation than entry. She promised herself she would be discreet about it. Well, silent, at least. But instead Netty took her time, working the object loose little by little, and pausing, it seemed, to make frequent adjustments.

"What on earth—" Marianna caught her breath, feeling a swelling, a filling out of those smooth leather fingers. The glove seemed to be coming to life; with great care, Netty had slipped her hand where Lady S.'s had been. "Oh…"

One finger was free, poised teasingly above her clit as Marianna began to churn her hips without modesty or restraint, conscious of nothing now but her body's own need. Netty's other fingers were curved inside her. She caught Marianna's rhythm and, like a skilled conductor, coaxed her to move slower, harder.

"That's it, Madam. Just let me…"

Marianna's ankles were still hobbled by her drawers. She struggled to part them wider. Lifting her head, she saw in the glass her own face flushed and open with pleasure, but could glimpse nothing but the mountain range of bright skirts behind her. She dropped her brow back to the table, breathed in the ticklish aroma of perfumes and powders…and came with a rush so drawn out and so sweet that she could hear, outside in the hallway, a passing contralto wondering aloud what sort of vocal warm-ups La Marianna could possibly be using.

Netty hadn't been exaggerating about her training. She had the prima donna fully dressed again, turned her around, and was powdering her blushing face almost before Marianna had gotten her breath back. Although she never admitted to such things, Marianna was impressed.

"By the way," said Netty, touching up Marianna's lip paint. "I meant it before. You are in exquisite voice tonight. Never better."

"You expected otherwise?" Marianna raised one eyebrow, her imperious manner returning. She allowed herself a tiny smile as Netty hesitated, then leaned forward to kiss her lips at last, swiftly and lightly, so as not to disturb the gloss.

"I wouldn't have walked out," Netty said, her tone almost shy now. "Not really."

"Of course not." Marianna turned away to skewer her wig in place. "Who else would keep you in sweets and cigarettes? Don't think I haven't noticed your pilfering."

"I'm sorry, Madam."

"You will be! If I catch you at it again, I'll—"

"Throw me into the orchestra pit?" Netty smiled.

"Head first into a tuba." Marianna's lips flickered as she fought not to smile back. "Now shoo. I have proper vocal exercises to do, and for these I do not require your assistance."

As Netty made her way down the narrow stairs that led from the dressing rooms, someone caught her elbow.

"Netty?" Lady S.'s voice sounded behind her, crisp and cultured. Her top hat was in place, Netty noticed. Her silk scarf and pearl cufflinks were impeccable. "Please permit me to apologise for what happened before the show. Your mistress should not have spoken to you so harshly."

"How do you know she spoke harshly, my lady?" Netty's eyes were wide, her expression all innocence. "Surely you were not there?"

"Well, I..."

Noting the stammer, most unusual for Lady S., and a faint flush of embarrassment, Netty said, "But it's all better now, thank you." Her smile softened, and the two women shared a confidential look. "Thank you," Netty repeated in a whisper.

Both fell silent and backed against the wall as the stairs creaked above them and the prima donna approached.

Marianna favoured Netty with a small, indulgent nod as she passed. To Lady S., she gave the sort of icy sneer she usually reserved for journalists, and for chorus girls who held their notes too long.

As she vanished from view, Lady S. sighed. "Do you think she'll ever forgive me?"

"You could have ruined her performance. *That* was inexcusable." Netty's voice was stern. "I'd give her till tomorrow night, at least."

"Fair enough." Lady S. watched Marianna's retreating back for a moment, then turned to her companion. "May I have my glove back? It's wretchedly cold in here."

Netty reached inside the folds of her dress and passed it across. As Lady S. pulled both gloves back on, straightening them with fussy care, it was Netty's turn to sigh. "They're beautifully made. You always have the prettiest things."

"Well..." Lady S.'s sharp brown eyes caught Netty's. She reached out to stroke Netty's face, to trace the bend of her lips with those gloved fingers, still scented with Marianna's pleasure. Netty's eyes fluttered closed, and she breathed in deeply. "I wouldn't say that, my dear," Lady S. winked. "I haven't had all of them yet."

Feeling the colour rising in her face, Netty glanced away, back up the stairs towards the prima donna's dressing room. It would be empty now, and heaped with flowers.

"Do you know what I thought the first time I stole into the theatre to watch a real opera?" For a moment, Netty's expression grew wistful. "I wondered how something so wonderful could possibly last so very, very long." She slipped her small, bare fingers through Lady S.'s leather-clad ones, and gave them a little squeeze. "So there's always Act Two."

TREATMENT NURSE

BY CHERI CRYSTAL

It was eight in the morning on Friday the thirteenth, the day before Valentine's Day, and it had been a particularly trying week in the Oncology ward at the hospital. We celebrated the remissions, cancer-free x-rays, an extra pain-free week, of course, but we had also had to send a beloved patient who had spent close to a year in our care to hospice, and that was a dreadful reminder of how short and precarious life was. These numbered days are too few to stand on ceremony, wait for rainy days, or cry over spilled milk, along with all the other cliché procrastination schemes we've all been guilty of from time to time. Not appreciating life was a luxury for those not surrounded by human frailty on a daily basis.

I'd worked a double shift and was looking forward to having the next three days off. When I was too tired to think, eat, or sleep, and at my most vulnerable, that was when I most needed a powerful orgasm, nature's best sedative, to regain a sense of invincibility. It helped me to feel as far far away from the inevitability of death as I possibly could. I was anticipating the release that happened when I totally abandoned all reservations, lost my mind to lust, forgot my inner self even existed, and let primal urges satisfy my most basic needs.

I wanted sex—it had to be hot, kinky wouldn't hurt—and I wanted it tonight. I wasn't going to beat around the bush. I didn't care who, what, where, or how. I just wanted to fuck the pants off some fetching woman who'd reciprocate by making me come until I was comatose. But before that could happen, I had to finish my shift.

When I signed up for this job ten years ago, I knew what I was getting myself into, but my compassion for the stricken seemed boundless. I would make a difference, do all I could to offer an extra kind word, administer meds in just the right dosage, and hold someone's hand while truly listening. It sucked that there weren't enough hours in a nurse's day to do all that, but I tried my hardest. I really did.

Sex was a great distractor, and there were sexcapades between staff members both on and off hospital grounds. It worked. It's what made us know we were alive. Some survived by having frequent sex, others by joking around to ease the tension, and still others by eating or drinking to excess, otherwise, we'd all be weeping. It's not to say there were never any tears, quite the opposite. Tonight I needed to come not just twice, but maybe a dozen times.

There was a smart, sweet, really cute nurse I'd been eyeing for months. She was coming to the end of her contract in Oncology, where she had been temping as coverage for a full-timer out on maternity leave. If things went well between us, I would miss her when she was gone, but if she turned me down or our tryst turned to shit, at least I wouldn't have to see her again. I figured I had nothing to lose by trying.

I initialled the treatment plan and placed the patient's chart on the rack by the nurses' station. As I walked off the unit, I noticed Betsy Turner, the very nurse I had just been thinking about, was in the supply room…alone. I mustered up all the calm, cool, collected tough dyke bravado I could. As I raised my arms to slick back my hair, I got a whiff of my armpits and quickly realized I needed a shower and shampoo as soon as possible. But given this opportunity, I decided to ask her point blank whether she would even entertain the notion of having sex with me, and she just had to say yes.

"Hey, Betts," I said casually. I was unable to call this total babe Betsy; it was way too cutesy. Her smile widened when she looked up and saw that it was me. At least I liked to think she was responding to me. "Busy day?"

I knew damn well the day had been especially horrendous. The evening would bring with it a full moon. Something about changes in barometric pressure made the patients particularly irritable and demanding, and some of them seemed to experience significantly greater pain as well. There was nothing worse than seeing an already vulnerable person suffering needlessly.

"Hi. I'm so glad you're still here. You're just in time to witness this oxycodone removal. Could you please sign for the morphine too?"

She showed me the requisition sheet, and I scribbled my name, the date and time.

Betts shoved the paperwork into her uniform pocket, and I couldn't help noticing, not for the first time, that she had nice hips. She was wearing the dress version of my pants and tunic. I appreciated what I could see of her toned calf muscles, despite the opaque pantyhose that covered them. Too bad the hem of her dress fell just above the knees and not mid-thigh like some of the younger interns wore. I would have loved to see more of Betts' thighs.

She was around my age, early thirties. We were young enough to withstand the gruelling pressures and work conditions, like being on our feet for hours without end, but old enough to appreciate the gravity of our roles. I sure had lightened up from the hot-blooded woman I was in my twenties, but I still had lots of steam left.

"You should be about done with your shift," Betts said.

"Yeah. Leaving in a few. You?"

"I want to check the stock one last time to make sure the weekend staff won't run short. I'm so happy that I'm off, I don't want to do anything to make them jealous that it's me and not them."

"You're too nice."

"You're too kind." She closed the cabinet and locked it, then turned and looked directly into my eyes. Hers were the most erotic shade of blue, and contrasted sharply with the pale of her skin. At that moment, she was a bit dishevelled, with subtly smudged eyeliner and strands of tousled brown escaping the confines of her hair band. If she was as exhausted as I was, she didn't show it. A tiny hint of pink lip gloss and those piercing blue eyes alone gave color to her face. I was taken in at once by her natural beauty. I imagined putting the red back into her cheeks. I wanted to kiss her right then, but I kept my cool.

"Do you have any plans this weekend?" she asked coyly.

It was exactly the opportunity I'd been waiting for. I couldn't blow it. I hesitated. The seconds ticked loudly in my ears; or was it my heartbeat? I crossed my arms over my chest and shoved my wet palms under my armpits to dry them surreptitiously. She waited. I knew I would kick myself if I didn't dive right in. I dropped my hands in a kind of surrender.

"I'm spending it with you!" I'd said it. I breathed a sigh of relief, becoming aware only then that I had been holding my breath.

She smiled. "Good answer. Do you want to meet up tonight?" She glanced at the watch pinned above her left breast, where it hung upside down for easy reading. Watches couldn't be worn on the wrist, as all staff had to be bare from the elbows down for proper hand-washing and infection control. "It's nearly eight-thirty now. If we get together at eight tonight, will that give you enough time to take care of whatever else you need to do today?"

"Well, yes. Yeah." I was about to bolt out of there, when I realized I didn't have her contact information and we hadn't made any specific plans about where to meet.

She handed me a Post-it note with her number and address. I left the ward dumfounded but in high spirits, thanking my good fortune. I reminded myself it was Friday the thirteenth, not April Fool's Day.

Already contemplating the evening, I headed to the staff locker room. I punched the door code into the numerical lock and went inside. The room was empty. I couldn't wait to clean up and get into street clothes. Most of us left our scrubs and uniforms at the hospital or bagged them to avoid carrying contamination to the world outside the hospital. My unit typically didn't encounter as much risk of infection, but it wasn't out of the question. Patients on chemo and radiation often were riddled with opportunistic infections due to their weakened immune systems. Cancer wasn't contagious, and I wasn't the only one on the Oncology staff who was guilty of deciding that gowning up safely was enough protection against spreading disease, so that we could skip the hospital shower and changing into clean clothes in order to get home sooner.

I preferred my own soap and shampoo, but the hospital soap dispensers, patient wash-up kits, and clean towels were fine in a pinch. I stripped quickly, shivering in the locker room that was several degrees cooler than the temperatures in the ward. Patients were easily chilled, so we kept the heat at seventy-two degrees. At least the shower room would warm up once the hot water was running. I quickly turned on the taps to let the water heat.

Despite the chilly air, my body thrummed as I thought about Betts. I couldn't believe my fantasies were about to come true, and I hadn't even had to seek a willing mate. I was sure I could have dug someone up at Lucille's Brasserie, a number one lesbian hangout, but I hadn't even had to go to that trouble. I planned to run my fingers through Betts' long brown waves as I kissed her perfect skin.

Completely lost in fantasy—the way she smiled after she caught me watching her when I didn't think she was looking—had me forgetting my own strength. I yanked open the shower curtain, and it ripped even further than it had been. It was missing rings, hanging off the bar to one side, letting the water out of the stall. Housekeeping kept promising a replacement. And now it had been made worse by yours truly. I was so tired, all I wanted was to wash away the last twenty-four hours. I quickly soaped up from my hair to my toes. It wasn't great that I now smelled the same as my patients after they'd been washed up bedside, but I was squeaky clean, refreshed, and, best of all, I had a date!

The shower's powerful jet spray was soothing my sore muscles and promoting deep relaxation, and I didn't dare risk shutting my eyes, or I just might have dozed off. I was planning to catch up on a little sleep before that evening, when I heard a firm knock at the door. I was naked, dripping, but there was a fellow nurse in need of a shower, so I opened up.

It was Betts. She had the foresight to lock the door and secure it with a chair under the handle. I gulped, but didn't bother to grab a clean towel off the cart. The towels were small and didn't cover much anyway. Besides, I had her right where I wanted her.

Her eyes were wide. The brilliant blue darkening as she made no secret of sizing me up. I allowed her the luxury and even turned around slowly so she could see all of me, including my best side. I'd so often been told I had a great ass, that I had started to believe it. Might as well flaunt it.

She took the bait. "Nice ass, Andrea." She cupped my butt cheeks, and my inner stirrings flared into a slow burn. "Mind if I call you Andi, like I've heard some of the others do?"

I turned to face her, and my voice was thick as I said, "Wouldn't want it any other way."

Stepping closer, I pulled her in by her notched collar, the top two buttons of her uniform opening under the pressure. Our lips were soon intimately pressed together. I parted hers with my tongue, and when she accepted it, I deepened our contact with my tongue probing further. Her hands were busy exploring each inch of my naked flesh, my skin prickling with delight in response to her touch.

I unbuttoned the remaining six buttons on the front of her dress and slid my hands inside. My cool palms skimmed her heated silken flesh until my fingertips reached the back of her bodice. I slipped the brushed cotton/poly twill off her shoulders, exposing her supple neck. Her white uniform landed in a heap on the damp tile floor. She kicked off her Crocs. There were still a bra, panties, slip, and tights to tackle, but I didn't see how she could be any sexier than she was at that moment. What a total turn on. The uniform didn't do justice to this fine woman and her admirable curves. If I was hot for her before, I was sizzling for her now.

I stepped back to take a long, appreciative look. She had a sultry smile that I committed to memory. My gaze moved down her body. I was instantly jealous of the underwire bra that squeezed her ample breasts into a fine cleavage. Reaching behind, I tried to unhook it with one hand. That was usually a snap for my practiced fingers, but my hands shook, either from fatigue or from something more—like struggling to withstand the temptation to rip it off. We laughed at my ineptitude. This faltering could have undermined my confidence, but with Betts, my heart rate soared and my worry vanished. Apparently she had the knack of making people feel safe, even at their most susceptible moments.

I took a deep breath and exhaled slowly, and with my hands steadied, the tiny hooks yielded as if by magic. I slowly removed both bra straps at the same time, releasing her perky tits from their confines. Betts rewarded me with moans of pleasure. Or perhaps the guttural sounds were emanating from me as I pressed her breasts together, which elicited a louder response from us both. Her nipples were soon the desired pert points. I hated to abandon them just then, but there was still the urgent matter of getting the rest of her naked. I thought back to all the times she had put an extra wiggle in her walk when I was close behind her, and it hit me that perhaps this romp was the result she'd planned all along. My hunger for her became even greater from knowing that was a distinct possibility.

Her half-slip was a virginal lacy fineness beneath otherwise extremely practical material, and I pushed it down around her ankles and whisked it off. The white support hose wasn't as easy to remove, but she helped. With that out of the way, I got the biggest kick out of seeing that she wore a white thong with a pink bow to match a pin she had on her ID card holder. Betts had a charity pin for every cause imaginable, including breast cancer. I banished the C-word from my mind; Betts had to consume my every thought.

She had the most amazing breasts. I loved them already, and showed her how much by kissing the nipples, licking and sucking them. I hadn't even noticed where her hands were until she tugged at my hair.

"Andi, you're driving me wild."

"Not as much as you are me. Please, let me relieve you of your panties."

"With pleasure."

In an instant, I was down on my knees. I pulled the thong off her hips and down her lean thighs, inhaling the incredible scent of her sex. I traced my finger along the landing strip of hair, but didn't venture any closer to the spot we both knew we were eventually going to go. She groaned softly, but spread her legs, lifting one foot at a time so I could remove the thong and cast it aside. She was warm and fragrant.

"Wash me good, Andi, and do hurry."

I turned on the shower, got the temperature just right, and led her under the spray.

"Don't miss anything. Especially the important parts."

"I'll pay extra attention to the important parts."

I stood behind her, my tits pressed just above her shoulder blades, my pubes against her butt. She was short-waisted; I had a long torso. She leaned her head back against my shoulder, lengthening her neck. I removed the ponytail holder and ran my fingers through her hair, utterly enjoying myself as I shampooed her silken mane.

"I love what you're doing to my scalp."

I massaged more vigorously for a bit, but she had places that were more urgently in need of tending. I quickly rinsed the soap from her hair, then lathered up her breasts, where I lingered a bit before I washed her armpits, and down along her waist and hips. After thoroughly lathering up my fingers, I was delighted to wash her pussy. Just touching hers made mine clench uncontrollably, threatening orgasm number one. I rinsed her off well. She was putty in my hands, whimpering and protesting if I stopped for even a second, so I tried my best to touch her at all times. I soaped up again and washed between her butt cheeks. She had a finer ass than I did, and I told her so. She protested, but I didn't concede.

"Your derriere is better, and that's final. One more word, and I'll—"

"Shhhh, okay," she said. "You win."

After washing her entire body, including between her toes while she giggled, she delivered a fiery kiss that paid me in full for services rendered.

"I'm not done yet," I said against her lips, returning her kiss.

"Neither am I." She kissed her index finger and lightly tapped my lips.

"Hold that thought," she said, leaving the shower to quickly towel off.

I shut the tap and followed her out.

She reached inside her gym bag. I had sometimes wondered what all she carried in there, and I was about to find out. Out came a yoga mat, which

41

she placed on the floor outside the shower area. Next came a box of rubber gloves—from CVS, not the ones we used on the wards, followed by a bottle of fancy lube, a foot or so of rope… that shocked me and made me hornier… and a fully loaded strap on.

"I thought I was the suit and you were the skirt."

"Suit yourself." Betts handed me the belt.

I didn't waste a minute getting it on. She assisted in readying us for anything. I had a good idea what "anything" I was hoping for, but she did me one better. After she put a condom on the dildo, she greased it up. She snapped on gloves, then lubed them up, too.

"Are you ready for the treatment of your life?" She arched an eyebrow.

I didn't have to think about it, just blurted, "You bet your beautiful ass I am."

Her wink said it all. "This is a multifaceted program. More than one treatment is necessary to achieve the desired results."

"I'm already on the brink of coming, if that's the plan."

"That may be, but the goal is to take our time and make it last."

"Of course it is." I already liked this game.

"And doctor's orders clearly dictate that if the current interventions are too rigorous, then subtler alternatives are to be adopted STAT. Are you ready?"

"I was born ready."

"Please sit down on the treatment table. I must examine you first to make sure you're fit enough to participate in this challenging protocol."

I laughed out loud when she handed me a privacy gown from the hospital out-patient supply closet, not that I would blow the whistle on her. She then put on an apron that was painted as a nurse's uniform. She used alcohol wipes to clean off her stethoscope, placed the sphygmomanometer, not one of ours but her own personal blood pressure cuff, by my feet, and even positioned a thermometer under my tongue. It didn't stay put long because I couldn't stop laughing. I hadn't played doctor in so long, I had forgotten how sexy it was. The gown smelled of fabric softener, a stimulating scent that was a far cry from the disinfectant detergents the hospital used in the laundry department. I had to wonder if she had washed it at home. It sure smelled like it. I smiled at her foresight.

"Try and keep your mouth closed."

"Yes, nurse." I doubted she had had a more compliant patient in her whole career.

She read my temperature. "Just as suspected, you're febrile. In fact, you're burning up."

She got that right. I was going to combust if she didn't let me fuck her soon.

"Do I really need my pressure taken? I can tell you right now, I'm a heart attack waiting to happen if I don't come soon."

"Okay, lie down. I must do a quick pelvic exam."

"That's more like it." I had my back on the yoga mat and my knees bent and spread before she could say lickety split.

She gasped. "Oh my!"

I leaned up on my elbows and took a peek at my pussy in case something was amiss. It looked okay to me.

"Just as I suspected, I'd better get started."

"You'd better," I urged. "And hurry."

She spread my lips and began a torturously light brushing of the tip of my clit using a gloved finger. My hips rose to meet her hand, but she clucked her tongue. "I see I'm going to have to restrain you. I'm sorry, but it's the only way to get a truly thorough examination." Without another word, she literally tied my hands to the padlocks on a couple of lockers behind my head. "Try not to move your feet, or I'll find a way to restrain them, too," she warned.

I couldn't believe this sweet nurse could be so cruel, but it sure stimulated my libido. I was already hornier than hell, but this was taking me to heights I'd never reached.

"I'll be good. I promise."

"Good patient." She spread my outer lips again, gently pulling at slick inner lips to separate the folds before she palpated my clit, which grew harder until I thought I'd pop. "I'll just pull back its hood and expose it for a second. Nothing to worry about. You might feel a slight tug."

My back arched. "Oh...my...God, that's...ah...may...zing," I said, willing her not to stop.

"We'll come back to that."

She released me, and I swore under my breath. She was a terrible tease. She had pulled the rug out from under my needy clit. I could have cried. I bit my lower lip to keep it from trembling.

She used her other hand to enter my pussy. "Relax your vaginal muscles. You're so tight. It's a good tight, but let's test those Kegels now, shall we?"

"Kegels? Please, Betts, fuck me. I'm dying here."

"This is going to hurt me much more than it hurts you."

"I doubt that. I need to come, and I need it now."

She inserted two fingers into my deepest recesses and pumped me with determined movements. My clit pulsated. It needed attention. If I hadn't been tied up, I'd have taken care of it myself. She must have read my thoughts, because she pumped my pussy with two, then three fingers while rubbing my aching clit with her thumb. I was nearly delirious, each movement bringing me closer to coming.

Someone knocked on the door.

"Go away!" we shouted in unison.

We waited a beat, and the knocking stopped. We had deterred whoever it was that wanted access to our temporary love nest.

I wasn't distracted by the intrusion for long, because Betts managed to fuck me despite the strap-on I was wearing and despite the uncontrollable thrusting of my hips, and finally, despite the orgasm that had my legs thrashing about.

"Slow down. Easy," she crooned. "Draw it out." Still in the throes, I nearly knocked her over. "Kicking is unacceptable." Her stern glance slipped into a smile. "Looks to me like your condition is completely cured, but one last test will satisfy me that the cure is permanent."

She bent down and licked my clit, swirling her tongue around it, sucking it in, and before I knew it, I came again. Following another amazing climax, a warm gush escaped me.

"Excellent. How do you feel now?" She placed a stethoscope to my heart. "Oh my. I'd say this treatment has achieved desirable results."

When I could catch my breath, I said. "Untie me."

She did and I quickly sat up, grabbed her by the shoulders, flipped her onto her back, and pinned her to the mat. Her body was extremely pliable.

"This is not a wrestling match," she chided.

"Says who? It's my turn to choose the scenario."

I removed every trace of healthcare equipment by thrusting it roughly into her bag. I had all the arsenal I would need, courtesy of one very well stocked woman with premeditated sex romps on her mind, especially the strap-on. I never wanted to take it off. She was my kind of woman, no doubt about that. We were evenly matched. I liked my women versatile, and Betts was proving to be that and more.

"For this part, I'm going to have you perform detailed tasks. If done to specifications, then you'll be richly rewarded."

"What if I can't manage it?"

"Then there'll be repercussions, but I doubt we'll have to resort to those."

"Good, 'cause my pussy is on fire for a strapping woman to save my poor battered soul."

"Then you're in good hands."

"I thought so."

"Lie down on your belly. All you need to do in this exercise is lie still, stay quiet, and follow directions. I may ask you to move. Do it swiftly, with no extra movements. Can you handle that?"

"Yes, ma'am."

My index finger traced an imaginary line from the top of her scalp, down past the indent of her neck, past her shoulder blades. When I got down to just above the middle of her back, she flinched.

I smacked her buttocks, just hard enough to get her attention. "I said not to move. Consequence number one. I'm keeping track. Don't let it happen again."

"What if I like being spanked?"

I slapped her again. "Don't get naughty. You only get three warnings, and then you won't be allowed to come."

"That's not fair. You can't wait until we're into the game before you explain the rules. I want a do-over."

I thought about it. Her request sounded reasonable enough. "Okay, you have three chances to prove you can lie still and not make a sound, no matter what I may do to you."

"I'm ticklish."

"Not my problem." I inwardly enjoyed this information. Very much. "I'll give you five chances."

"Thank you."

"Starting now." I again traced my finger along the entire length of her head, down her spine, to her back. She held her breath but didn't flinch as I glided over the small of her back and ended between her butt cheeks. She exhaled and inhaled deeply at that point, but did not move. Her control was formidable. I had to up the ante.

I reached into her bag and donned one of the gloves from the box. I put copious amounts of lube on it and again reached between her legs. "You have a fine ass, very fine. I wonder if you'll move if I just pass it by and head right into your even finer pussy."

The moment my fingers reached her entrance, she yelped. I smacked her bottom and said, "One."

She yelped again. "Just testing."

I swatted her again. She enjoyed it much too much, so I did it again. "That's very naughty. That's two and three. You're trying my patience, and there's only two left before you miss out on the fuck of your life."

She became like stone after that. I tickled and tortured her to no avail. "Turn over."

She complied, still stone. I kissed her everywhere—the sides of her waist, the soles of her feet, the inner recesses of her thighs. I even pressed the sides of her knees until I suspected she was sound asleep. The soft rise and fall of her chest would have had me convinced she was napping, but her eyes gave her away. They followed my every movement. Had she been in Dreamland, she wouldn't have maintained as sharp a focus.

"How do you do it?"

Her body was wet between her trembling thighs, and her expression was pleading, but she didn't utter a single sound. I couldn't take it; this game was going nowhere fast. "You may speak. How can you stay this still?"

"I teach mediation and yoga in my free time."

She smiled, and I had to kiss that smile. I grasped my phallus, checked the status of the lubey-doobie, and lowered my pelvis closer to hers. She immediately spread her legs wider and parted her lips with alacrity. I assisted the dildo as I inserted it into her pussy, gently at first, but then at her insistent urging, with increasing vigour. She bucked and grunted and rode me as I rode her. I kept up the rhythm. So did she. We became a duet of carnal vocalizations. The end of the dick dug into my clit and with each thrust, I came closer to letting go again.

"May I come now, please?" Betts cried.

"Yes. Come with me."

I rode her and she responded. Her internal muscles gripped the strap-on and made me work harder and faster, until our skin glistened from the exertion. Just as my arms were about to give out, she cried out my name. It sounded lovely coming from her lips. I came seconds after she had started writhing, and we finished together with a bang. I shuddered, and promptly collapsed beside her.

"That was wicked," I groaned. "But I don't think I can move ever again."

"Me neither. You're a pro at using that thing."

"Just doing what comes naturally when in the company of an amazing woman I want so very much to please. If I wasn't so exhausted, I'd fuck you again, but I'm seriously immobile. What if it's permanent paralysis?"

"I'm on the same page, but I highly doubt it."

We lay quietly recuperating, but it soon grew too cold. The heat of our lust-fest was fading, but our desire seemed to be just as strong as before we'd started. Physically, we couldn't go on, but mentally, I knew there was lots more lust to sate.

Betts sighed. "I guess we need to vacate this room."

"You reckon?"

"Yep."

We helped each other up, and then got dressed. I trashed the condom, cleaned up the dildo and handed it back to her with the belt. I hated to part with it. She gelled my hair, and I ran a comb through hers.

"I can French braid if for you," I offered with a shrug.

"A tough dyke like you? No way!"

"I have many talents."

"I've seen some truly unique ones today. I hope I get the opportunity to experience them all."

She located her ponytail holder and turned around so I could show her I knew how to plait hair. I had four sisters and was the designated braider, since I was the only one with short hair. I finished the braid and tied it up at the end, then turned her to face me.

"Thank you for today." I gave her a kiss.

"No, thank you. I'll miss you, Andi. The girl I'm covering for is coming back soon, too soon. I'm not ready to leave. I feel I'm really meant to be a part of the team."

"You are. They...we all love you. You're an amazing nurse, and I don't only mean the kinky kind, although that was totally incredible nursing. I feel quite fit, but I'm sure ongoing treatments will be needed to ensure I stay in shape."

She managed a smile, but a frown threatened to replace it. I knew it must be hard to lose a job she really loved, even if she had accepted the position knowing it was only temporary.

"I'm sure you'll find something permanent soon. I'll put in a good word, if that would help."

This cheered her somewhat, and she beamed as she asked, "Are we still on for tonight?"

"You bet!"

We left the locker room together, and then went our separate ways.

I was about to climb onto my bike when my cell phone pinged. I read her text: *Until tonight, Love, Betts XXX*

Later XXX I texted back. Triple X—how appropriate.

MELTDOWN

BY SACCHI GREEN

"SOME PIECE OF WORK YOU got there." Sigri jerked her head toward the door. Or maybe she was just flicking a trickle of sweat out of one eye, since her hands were occupied with hammering a rod of red-hot iron into submission. She'd been wearing goggles but shed them when we came in. "Ought to keep a shorter tether on your toys, Roby."

It was just as well Maura had already flounced out in a snit when she realized that we weren't going to focus on her—except that Maura's every movement was far too elegant to be termed "flouncing." Even when she'd knocked over a short trollish creature built using trowel hands and garden-rake teeth, tried to right it, got those long auburn waves that had sold ten million crates of shampoo tangled in another contraption, and knocked that one over too, her taut ass was as elegant as it was enticing. She could have been modeling those stretch ski pants for a fashion spread in *Vogue*. Probably had been, in fact, when she'd been here in New Hampshire in October for an autumn leaves photo shoot. Now, in January, the outfit suited the snow coming down outside.

Sigri's boi, Rif, edged deftly among the metal sculptures, righting the ones Maura had knocked over, touching some of the others as though they were friends. Or lovers. In their shadows, her slight body and pale short hair were nearly invisible. She hadn't spoken a word since I'd been here. Now, at a gesture from Sigri, she followed Maura out of the barn.

Maura needed to be the center of attention. Someplace deep inside being in the spotlight terrified her, but she still craved it. She didn't know how lucky she was that Sig and I had been ignoring her, catching up on old times and our lives over the past twenty years. She'd brought us together for her own convoluted purpose and pushed me over the edge of anger into rage once I knew what she was up to. Could have been part of her plan; Maura's plans were never straightforward. I didn't care whether she was listening outside the door or not.

"I'm not her goddamned keeper!"

"No? Somebody sure ought to be, and I get the impression she thinks it's you."

I perched gingerly on the seat of an antique hay baler stripped of its wheels, waiting its turn to be cannibalized into parts for the metal scrap beasts and demons Sig sold to tourists and the occasional high-end craft gallery. "Not a chance. Don't tell me she hasn't been trying you on for size."

Sig concentrated more intently than necessary on the metal she was bending across the edge of her anvil. "'Trying' is the word, all right." Her hammer came down hard. "The magazine crew was doing a photo shoot down the road with my neighbor's big black Percheron mare close by and sugar maples in the background. Rif hung around watching, kind of dazzled by the glitz, I guess, so when Maura asked about the weird iron critters out front here, Rif dragged her to the barn to see more. I knew you'd worked with her—Rif keeps some of those fashion mags around for some strange reason, and I don't deny taking a look now and then. Just to see whether your name's in the small print as photographer, of course. Not for those skinny-ass models." That brazenly lecherous grin was just the way I remembered it.

"Yeah, Maura has a thing for sharp scary things, the weirder the better. So I guess one thing led to another?"

"One thing led to—zip! Nothing but some crazy maze of 'yes…no…wait, maybe…' Does she have any fucking idea what she wants? Won't negotiate, won't submit, won't bend, likes to be hurt but mustn't be marked anyplace it would show when she models bikinis. I tell you, Roby, I don't have the energy anymore for games like that. No topping from the bottom." One more hammer blow and a curse, and then the warped metal was cast into a tank of water where it hissed as it cooled. From what little I'd glimpsed, I didn't think it had turned out as Sig intended.

"She doesn't know what she wants until she gets it," I said. "Looks like just now she thinks she wants it from you." *And she has the gall to want me to show you how to give it to her.* I'd given in to Maura's pleas to come back with her to the Mount Washington Valley in New Hampshire for a long weekend visit with my old friend Sigri, which did sound tempting, and then just as we arrived at the farmhouse, Maura had told me casually that she wished I'd teach Sigri the right way to hurt her. I had never come closer to hurting her in all the wrong ways.

"Screw it. I wouldn't have bothered at all if Rif hadn't been all for it." Sig pulled off her heavy leather apron and straddled a wooden bench. "Why'd she drag you here, then? Not that I'm not glad to see you. Every time I see your name on one of those photo spreads in a nature magazine I think about getting in touch, but somehow I never get around to it." She considered me for a moment, the fire from the forge casting a red glow over her square, sweaty face and muscular arms. "Good thing you moved on from the fashion ads racket. Your stuff is too good for that."

"The fashion biz pays better." I didn't quite meet Sig's gaze. "I still do it once in a while."

"You didn't come when Miss Fancypants threw a fit last October and insisted they had to get you because she wouldn't work with anybody else. So why now?"

"I was in Labrador on assignment from the Sierra Club magazine! And next month I head for Patagonia. In any case, I do have my limits. The guy they had here was good and needed the work." I looked her full in the face—a face I've seen in my dreams through the years more often than I'd like to admit. "This location is a big draw, though. So many memories..."

"Ohhh yeah!" Her smile this time was slow, reflective, and genuine. I wondered what she was remembering. My second most vivid image from those days was Sigri's fine broad, muscular butt in tight jeans twenty feet above me on the face of Cathedral Ledge.

We'd been casual friends, members of a fluctuating group of dykes renting this very same farmhouse for a few weeks in the summer while we hiked and climbed, and again in the winter as a ski lodge. Both of us usually had a girlfriend in tow, but when it came to rock climbing, we trusted each other and no one else. Even on easy climbs with iron bolts not more than twenty-five feet apart, when you take the lead with a belaying rope and call "Watch me," you damned sure need to know that when your partner on the other end answers "Go for it, I've got you," she has absolutely got you, her end of the rope firmly anchored, and will hold on if your grip fails or a rock edge breaks away and you start to plummet down the unforgiving cliff face.

We'd only admitted to figuring in each other's fantasies back then as mead companions, playing at being Viking warriors ravaging villages side by side as we bore off not-unwilling maidens. She still wore her yellow hair in that thick

51

Viking braid down her back; I couldn't tell in this unreliable light whether there were silver strands mixed in with the gold. My own dark cropped hair was still more pepper than salt, but not by much.

"Well, you're here now, and I'm glad. No need to let that glitzy bitch spoil things." She put away her tools and adjusted the damper on the furnace to let the fire die down. "Think we could make her sleep out here in the barn?"

"Not unless we made it seem like her own idea. Which isn't impossible."

"Never mind for now. Rif'll show you your room, and once you're settled in, we'll eat dinner. She'll have it the oven by now."

"Rif sounds like a real treasure."

"More than I deserve, that's for sure," Sig muttered, almost too low for me to hear. She made for the door. I followed, admiring that rear view the way I used to when no one was looking. Just a bit broader now, but even more muscular since she'd turned to blacksmithing. The front view had been admirable, too, but harder to enjoy covertly. Back then butch buddies did not openly ogle each other's chests, and things hadn't changed in that department. I could tell now that it was still remarkable, even hidden behind the leather apron shielding her from any runaway sparks or splinters of metal.

Snow was building up fast along the short path from the barn to the house, piling the existing banks along the sides even higher. Good thing we didn't have to drive anywhere tonight. Maura had damned well better not make me wish we could get away.

Dinner was maple bourbon-glazed salmon with hot cornbread, mushroom risotto, and tossed salad with pecans and dried cranberries. Perfection. Rif was perfection, too. Maybe too perfect. Her cooking was excellent, and her serving of it—well, let's just say she epitomized service in more ways than one while managing to sit for long enough to eat her own food. Quiet, efficient, never speaking without being spoken to, anticipating our needs, all with downcast eyes, at least whenever I glanced at her. Just the same, I could feel her gaze on me from time to time, and I was pretty sure she was sizing up Maura, too.

Maura was sizing up Rif right back, maybe taking notes on how to appeal to Sigri. At least she was putting on a pretty good demure act. Sig and I were wallowing in nostalgia, swapping recollections of cliffs we'd climbed, mountains we'd summited, ice walls we'd conquered, and après-ski orgies we'd enjoyed the hell out of.

Finally, when we were about done eating our desserts of individual pumpkin custards and sipping Rif's excellent coffee, Sig turned to Maura like a good host. "How about you, Maura? Done any climbing?"

"Oh yes, I've been on some jaunts with Roby out in the Sierras." She gave that trademark toss of her head that made strands of chestnut mane drift across one or another of her perfect breasts. Her navy silk shirt was conservative but clingy in all the right places. "You know how it is, though, hiking with somebody so much older, having to take things slower than you'd like."

Sig shot me a "what the fuck!" look.

Okay, Maura was asking for it. I smiled, genuinely amused, but also irritated as hell. "Got a mouth on her, hasn't she. Don't worry. It's just that insults are the best Maura can manage as foreplay."

"So how does that work out for her?"

Maura's glare in my direction was weakened by her belated realization that Sigri was just as old as I was.

"Depends on the circumstances. The last time she called me too old, she was already spread-eagled, tied to the four corners of a tent frame, and demanding to be gagged."

Rif's eyes flashed wide open for just a second. Sig nodded judiciously. "I can see getting a little something out of that."

"What I got was a bent tent frame. What Maura got was my mark in a place even a bikini won't reveal."

Maura apparently decided to go with the flow. "Isn't it cute," she said with a sultry smile, "the way old folks' memories get so fuzzy?"

Sigrid leaned forward and looked from Maura to me. "More foreplay?"

"Well, *she* seems to think so. It'd be cute if it weren't so juvenile."

Sig almost asked another question, thought better of it, pushed back her chair, and stood up. "Rif, how about you kids go take a walk while Roby and I have a nice chat about grown-up matters."

"Is it still snowing?" But I knew perfectly well that it was. "They could just stroll around inside the barn, and Maura could decide which sharp-edged, long-toothed demon there she'd most like to fuck her in her dreams."

Maura managed to stifle a smartass retort. Rif stifled a smile, then went to stand beside Sig with head meekly bent, speaking softly, before leading Maura away. Sigri and I moved into the cozy living room to sit by the fire and savor our after-dinner port, like any Old Country lords of the manor. Except that, instead of port, we savored excellent home-brewed mead a friend had given Sig and Rif at Christmas.

While Sig bent to pour a little of the golden elixir into my genuine bull-horn cup set in its own wrought iron stand, I felt her closeness with a jolt that startled me. In the old days, no matter what girl I was with, if Sig was in the room, I was more aware of her than of anyone else. Comradeship, sure, but I couldn't deny that there'd been an intensely sensual element as well. Now she was so close I could have reached out and touched her breast, guarded now only by flannel instead of the leather apron.

"Your work?" I switched my gaze quickly to the elaborate Celtic swirls of the cup stand. "And this?" I ran a finger over the spiraling dragon shape carved into the horn cup in exquisite detail.

"The metalwork, sure. The carving is all Rif's, though. She's an incredible artist, hands steady, fingers strong and flexible, every stroke precise…"

Sig might or might not have seen the slight quirk of my eyebrow. The reddening of her face might or might not have been due to a sudden flare-up of the fire. She went on in hurry, "She did these in the tenth-century Norwegian Ringerike style, but she can do just about anything."

"She's really amazing, isn't she? I hope Maura isn't giving her a rough time." If Rif had been dazzled by the October photo shoot and "all for" some D/s play between Sig and Maura, it would be a shame if Maura's rudeness shattered her fantasies.

"Don't worry. Rif can take care of herself, and then some. She—" Sig shook her head. "Well, enough about that. Tell me more about Maura. Did she really let you make a mark on her precious skin?"

"You might put it that way. It's not just vanity. Her agency takes out insurance on every inch of her, and at the slightest marking, the agency collects and she gets fired. It's a clause from the days before everything and anything could be photoshopped, but they still demand it. Sometimes she really, really wants to be marked and hurt, to feel like a real person instead of a very expensive commodity. Even dreams of a scar on the face that the world sees so it will be all her own again. But she doesn't want any of that enough to give up the life she has, and she trusts me to take her almost as far as she wants to go without going over the edge."

Sigri was shaking her head by the end of my revelations. I picked up my drinking horn and took a sip of mead. "As you said, that's enough about that. Too much, in fact." Another sip. "Hey, this is really fine stuff! Smooth and intense. Wish we'd had something this good back in the day."

"Nah, we'd've been too dumb to appreciate it." She sank down on the couch by my side, took a longer sip than I had, licked her lips, and looked slantwise at me. "We were too dumb to appreciate a hell of a lot."

"No kidding." I raised my horn. Hers met it halfway. "Here's to our wasted youth."

A few more sips of mead later, I was on the verge of blurting out a maudlin confession, but Sig beat me to it.

"That pool." She looked into the fireplace, not at me. "That day..."

I finished for her. "We bushwhacked off the Slippery Brook trail, discovered that huge gorgeous pool, and went skinny-dipping. The goddess place, I called it, and you told me not to go all woo-woo."

"But you did. And you scrambled naked back up that rock to where we'd left our stuff before we jumped off, got your camera, and yammered on about how the rocks on each side of the little waterfall looked like spread thighs, and the knobby stone in between with moss on it was the pussy, and the—the water of life, I think you said, was pouring into the sacred pool."

"Yeah, I guess that's what I said. And you dived into the deepest part and came up with handfuls of pebbles that you kept throwing at me while I tried to get pictures from just the right angle."

"Well, maybe I was as bad as your Maura at foreplay when it came to somebody like you. Girly types, no problem, but you? I figured you'd either laugh in my face or punch it if I made a move."

I shook my head in self-disgust. "And I just kept on yammering to keep from jumping you and getting slammed for it. Talk about dumb kids! When you got fed up and left, I was desperate for the chance to jerk off, fantasizing about what it would feel like to be in a clinch with you."

"Hah! I only made it to that other stream coming out of the beaver pond before my hand was in my pants. If you'd caught up with me then..."

I reached for the decanter of mead, poured us each a little more, and raised my horn again. "Well, here's to the years of steamy dreams inspired by the sight of you naked in that pool." Just as well not to reveal that I'd snapped a picture of her from behind that day, right when her muscular body arched, butt high, into the dive that got her those pebbles to throw at me. I'd carried a print of the photo around with me until I literally wore it out.

We were half facing each other by that time, up close. Somehow my left hand had reached over to her nearest thigh, and her right hand had done the same to me.

"You know that time when we arm wrestled a couple of nights later?" Sig's grip on my thigh tightened. "The only time you ever beat me? Shouldn't count as a win. I only lost because I was so distracted remembering how you'd looked naked, like a tougher, stronger version of those nymphs in old paintings. But I paid for that round of drinks anyway."

"No kidding? I thought I only won because I was so mad at myself for thinking of you in pretty much the same way, and the adrenaline gave me extra strength."

"How about—"

"A rematch? Not a chance. I've been hiking and toting my camera gear over some pretty rough terrain, but you've been hammering iron. No contest." I set my cup back on its stand on an end table to free up a hand so I could grip her bicep for emphasis—and for something more. But Rif's dragon carved into the horn seemed to be looking right at me. I paused. "Rif..." I said uncertainly, and as though the name worked a magic spell, the outside door opened and Rif herself came in. A brief gust of cold air blew right through the entrance hall, past the dining room, and into our cozy fireside haven.

She came right to Sigri, looked for a moment as though she were going to kneel before her, then thought better of it and just bent her head. "Excuse me, but Maura thinks it's getting too cold in the barn with the forge turned so low, and anyway, I started up the fire in the sauna hut a while ago, like you said I could, and it should be getting nearly hot enough."

"You still use the sauna? Great!" I hadn't moved my hand from Sig's thigh, so I gave her a squeeze, which she returned with interest. "All those rocks we dragged up from the river and the logs we cut!"

"We've upgraded it a bit since then, but yeah, the same old place. We use it quite a bit, and this time I'm pretty sure Rif thinks it'll be the easiest way to get Maura's clothes off."

Maura herself came in just in time to hear that last part. "The fastest way, at least," she said companionably, and from the look she exchanged with Rif, I figured they were up to something. If it got us all naked in the sauna, it was definitely a step in the right direction. And if they were in it together, I didn't need to worry. Right?

"Upgraded" was an understatement. Besides the structural improvements, there were birchwood benches with armrests carved like voluptuous mermaids, leering gargoyle heads at the ends of the towel bars, and the coatracks where we hung our clothes looked like giant sets of antlers with minidragons twining through them. Not that I noticed all these details right away in the shock of coming into intense heat out of the cold and snow outside and then the delirious distraction of such a variety of naked bodies.

Maura's delectable form was, of course, familiar to me, far more than it was to viewers of her photos even in bikini ads. Rif's slim body seemed more graceful in the freedom of nakedness than it had clothed; she could easily have been a sprite or nymph out of mythology, and her open smile and gleaming eyes gave her face a kind of elfin beauty.

Sigri… I'd seen her naked often enough in this same sauna years ago, but now I hardly dared look at her, and when I did, a flush of heat beyond anything the fire pit could produce swept through me. We'd both changed over the years, Sig with somewhat more flesh and a lot more muscle, me with some shifting of what flesh and muscle I had in spite of gym workouts when I'd lived in the city and strenuous trekking once I'd switched my focus to wilderness themes; but I'd never needed so intensely to get my hands on her. And in her. I could already feel her eyes on me, sharing that hunger.

But we both glanced toward Rif, who stood between Maura's spread legs gazing down at the shaved, smooth pussy on display. "That's the mark?" Rif said. "What does it mean?"

Sig went to look, too, with a lingering stroke across my flank as she passed me. I knew what they saw on that triangle of smooth skin just low enough to be covered by the skimpiest bikini bottom; four tiny curving arcs, not quite meeting, formed a delicate circle like a secret mandala. Maura just smiled mysteriously and leaned far back, her long hair flowing downward, her face clean of makeup, beads of sweat beginning to show between her breasts, looking more beautifully alive than any fashion ad could ever show.

We were all sweating by then. Rif took down two of the birch switch bundles hanging on the wall, laid one across Maura's lap, then approached Sigri with bowed head. "May I be of service?" she asked in a low, formal tone. Sigri looked toward me, shrugged, and took a position facing the wall with her hands braced against it. Maura was suddenly there beside me with her own bundle of switches, gesturing at me to do the same. I went along with it. We'd done this same sort of thing in the old days, ratcheting it up well beyond the traditional therapeutic usage. The idea of letting Maura use the switches on me was a bit disturbing, but at least it might distract me from the urge to shove Sigri hard against the wall and rub myself against her.

Apparently Rif knew all about the ratcheting-up part, and so did Maura. The sting of the pliant birch twigs went up and down my back, lingered on my ass, then traveled down my legs and up again, over and over, more stimulating the harder they struck. All I could think of beyond my own throbbing backside was how red Sigri's must be, and how hot to the touch.

Sweat ran down my face, between my breasts, along my spine, between my ass cheeks, and down my inner thighs, although I couldn't be sure how much of that last substantial trickle was sweat and how much wild arousal. Any second I would pull back, turn around, get to Sig—but just before I tensed to move, another movement distracted me—Rif darting between our arched bodies and the wall. Suddenly a rope was pulling me toward Sig and winding around her as well while Maura shoved me from behind so that I faced Sig and Rif tugged at the crossed rope ends so that Sig faced me.

We had to clutch at each other to keep from stumbling, and then the clutching seemed like such a good idea that I dug my fingers into the clenched muscles of her butt while she yanked me by my shoulder blades hard up against her big breasts. Resistance was so futile, it ceased to exist.

The girls wrapped more of the rope around us, but we scarcely noticed. Sigri's mouth tasted of fine mead, and mine must have, too, but however intoxicating that contact was, there were other places that needed tasting. I licked sweat from the hollow of her throat and then down between and around her breasts while she kneaded my back and as far along my birch-switched ass as she could reach until she pushed my torso back enough to work her tongue and teeth down my chest to my belly.

Standing ceased being an option. The rope loosened, and a burst of steam swept over us. Someone, probably Rif, had poured water on the white-hot stones of the fire pit. As the steam cloud rose upward, Sig and I rolled on the floor, where there was slightly more air, first one on top, then the other, one knee thrusting and sliding between the other's sweaty thighs until the positions reversed. Finally Sig growled "Dammit, Roby!" and held me down with her greater weight. What the heck, she was the host here. I let her big hand work into where I needed it most, arching my hips to meet her thrusts with equal force. A wave that had been building for over twenty years swelled, crested, and crashed down over me, through me.

In its ebb, still quivering and scarcely able to breathe, I swung above her, grabbed onto her wide hips, and went at her with tongue and mouth and teeth and, for all I know, nose and chin until she was as spent and breathless as I was. With all the meager strength we had left, we pulled each other upright, hands sliding along our sweaty bodies, and made for the door.

The snow was powdery, deep, and searingly cold on our superheated flesh. Just what we needed. We rolled together, still hot where our bodies pressed together, melting mystical runes into the white surface touched by our backs. When we finally chased each other back into the lingering heat of the sauna hut, Maura and Rif passed us, laughing, on their way out. Whatever they'd been up to, which wasn't hard to guess, they'd clearly had a fine time.

Later, dressed again and heading back toward the house, Maura tugged me aside along the path to the barn. "Don't you want to know which demon I picked for my dream lover?"

The others followed us into the dim space, now only slightly warmed by the embers in the forge and lit only by a single naked light bulb by the door. Maura proceeded along rows of strange figures made even eerier by the shadows. She paused once in front of a creature with a horned helmet, long braid made of straw-colored rope and sled-runner arms holding a shield made from a woodstove door embossed with a dragon silhouette, considered for a moment, then shrugged and moved on.

She stopped at last before a figure in the corner, limbs constructed from tent poles, one hand a saw-toothed adze blade used in ice climbing, and the other with a single digit, seven thick inches of spiral-machined, nickel-plated steel rod. She touched the tip of her own delicate finger to the tip of that rod where four tiny curving arcs of metal, not quite meeting, formed a delicate circle like a secret mandala.

"I might as well stick with this one," she said casually.

"An ice screw! I knew it!" Sigri muttered behind us. Rif tugged at her gently and led her away, maybe thinking Maura and I would have some kind of tender interlude.

What actually happened was that Maura said, almost as casually, "I got a call yesterday from my agent, right before you picked me up at the airport. She said I got that movie role I was after. Not a lead, just the "bad girl" character, but terrific exposure. We'll be shooting mostly on location in France and Switzerland."

"Good going, kid," I said, and put a comradely arm across her shoulders. We didn't have anything close to what Sigri and Rif had, and that was fine with me. Maura three or four times a year was about all I could handle, and if she really needed me in between, she knew that I'd come. Even from Patagonia.

INSOMNIA
BY R.G. EMANUELLE

JANA SHUT DOWN HER COMPUTER and closed her folder with a weary slap. What a long day. Her eyes felt like cotton balls and her butt was numb. As she got up and stretched, she vowed, as she did every day at five o'clock, that she was not going to spend one more day writing grants for the Behavioral Science Institute. But she knew that she'd be back Monday morning at nine a.m. sharp. But today was Friday and she was going to get some pizza, go home, and watch old movies.

She pulled on her jacket, grabbed her backpack, and opened the door of her office. She was surprised to find the research suite empty. Where was everyone? She looked up at the wall. Six o'clock. Damn. She'd forgotten to change her watch to Daylight Savings Time. Oh, well. An extra hour of comp time wouldn't hurt. *Thanks for letting me know, everyone.*

As Jana walked down the hall toward the elevators, a figure in a white lab coat approached her from the other direction. "Hey, Jana!" the person called out.

"Oh, hey, Mike. Have a good night."

Mike was a wiry, kooky-haired guy, who looked the way you'd expect a science geek to look, and he was always hyper and twitchy, the way you'd expect a wiry guy to be. Unlike his usual bouncy self, though, he seemed a little haggard tonight.

"Wait. Don't leave." Mike picked up his pace and trotted up to her. "Listen, I need a favor. Would you help us out in the lab?"

"What? Uh, no. I'm really tired and I just want to go home. I'll see you Monday, okay?" She started toward the elevator again. Mike followed.

"Please, we're really stuck."

She sighed. Mike was a nice guy and he'd helped her out numerous times when her computer had acted stupid. It's always good to have someone like that on your side. With another quiet sigh, she relented. "Okay, fine. What do you need?"

"Awesome. You're the best." He smiled and kissed her on the cheek. He had a thing for Jana but he was respectful, even after she'd made it clear that nothing would ever happen between them. It only seemed to make him like her more, and this endeared him to her.

Taking her arm, he guided her to the sleep lab at the other end of the corridor. Jana was familiar with this room. She had allowed them to study her once. After her ex had broken her heart, she'd battled insomnia for months. It got so bad that she couldn't function anymore. She tried everything from herbs to yoga to visualization techniques. The lab finally confirmed that racing thoughts were the source of her problem, and they helped her work through it. It still fascinated her that they could figure out what was happening in her brain while she slept, or was trying to sleep. The experience had bored her, though. Just lying there staring at the ceiling in a little room with electrodes dotting your head.

"What exactly do you need me to do?" she asked him as they walked down the hall.

"Babysit."

"What?"

"Perry and Steve both got food poisoning from the shrimp they had last night."

"Oh, God. That's awful. You didn't get sick?"

"No. By the time our food came, I was three sheets to the wind and couldn't eat anything." He cracked a rueful smile. "Although, I did wake up with a splitting headache and my nasal passages completely shut. Alcohol does that to me sometimes." He attempted a deep, congested breath through his nose for effect.

Jana rolled her eyes. "That explains how you look."

He gave her a pained expression, but then went back to his usual upbeat self. "Anyway, I'm the only one left who can monitor the patient, but I have to pick up my car from the mechanic's and I have to do it tonight."

"Why?"

"The guy's closing for a week to go on vacation. He's staying open late just for me." His eyes pleaded with her. "All you have to do is stay in here and keep an eye on things until I get back."

"But I don't know anything about this equipment."

"You don't have to. She's all set up. Someone just needs to be here to watch and to make sure she doesn't get up and start doing weird things. You know, like sleepwalking and possibly hurting herself."

"And what am I supposed to do if she does?"

"Just let her be. If she hurts herself, call six-three-seven-two, and let them know what's happening. They'll page Dr. Wagner."

Jana looked at him. "Great," she said sarcastically. "Won't you get in trouble for leaving me in here?"

"I won't tell if you don't," he said with a boyish grin.

Against her better judgment, she agreed. "Okay, okay."

"You're the best! I'll be back as soon as I can."

Jana sat down in the chair in the console room and peered into the chamber beyond the glass. The two-way observation window allowed researchers to communicate with patients with body language and not just through the intercom, which sometimes disrupted patients' sleep rhythms. The sleep chamber was softly lit by a table lamp and decorated in peaceful peachy tones, accessorized by Turkish-looking throw pillows and green plants. *Looks nicer than my living room in there.* But where was the patient? Electrodes were bunched up on the nightstand.

Then she heard a flush and saw a woman walk out of the bathroom, which was accessible only from the sleep room. Was she supposed to help the patient put the electrodes back on? She didn't remember having to remove the electrodes to go to the bathroom when she was a patient.

She debated this for a moment until the woman moved into the light, and Jana's thoughts went somewhere else.

The woman sat down on the bed and stretched her back. The ends of her black, wavy hair rested softly in the crook of her elbows, and although Jana couldn't see their color, her eyes were dark, deep, and outlined by thick black pencil. Her sleepwear consisted of a button-down shirt over a pair of boy-shorts underwear. Her nipples poked at the shirt's fabric, and Jana's breath caught in her throat. It had been a long time since she'd been with anyone. And just as long since she'd reacted like this to anyone. It was then that it occurred to her that the woman looked just like Catherine Zeta-Jones.

"Catherine" casually ran her hand through her hair, then stopped and looked up at the window with her fingers buried in the strands. Her eyes met

62

Jana's and both women were still for several moments, staring at each other. Jana shifted nervously. Catherine was evaluating her.

Jana scanned the woman's legs from toe to thigh, entranced by their smoothness and perfect tan, and at that moment, she wondered why Catherine had so much trouble sleeping that she'd participate in a sleep study. *If I were with her, I'd find a way to help her sleep every night.*

The console room was situated at a slightly higher level than the sleep chamber, so observers could have a better view of the room from above. At that angle, Jana could see down Catherine's shirt, buttoned to the middle of her cleavage, and she wished that one more button were open. Then she caught herself. She felt like a pervert peeping in some woman's bedroom window.

What the hell was she doing fantasizing about this complete stranger? A patient, no less. Not very professional. But Catherine's stare made her loins tighten.

Catherine broke the moment by sliding up to the center of the bed. She drew her knees up and rested her hands behind her, a strange look crossing her face. Was that mischief in her eyes?

Then she slowly, languorously, got up and turned around, displaying the most perfect ass Jana had ever seen. The boy shorts rose up slightly, revealing round, tanned flesh.

Damn, I have to get back to the gym, Jana thought. She sighed and closed her eyes for a moment. When she opened them again, Catherine was back on the bed, facing her and kneeling.

What the hell was she doing?

The woman's eyes moved down Jana's face to her breasts, and Jana's skin grew hot all over.

Catherine undid one more button of her shirt and stopped again, her eyes never leaving Jana's. She tugged at the shirt once, twice, again and again, as if trying to say something.

Jana tried to figure out what Catherine wanted. A different shirt? A robe? Was it too hot for her? It took a minute, but Jana finally understood. She lightly pinched the placket of her shirt and rubbed it between her fingers. *No way. No way this is what she means. Am I fucking nuts?* But Catherine nodded and smiled.

So Jana began unbuttoning her shirt, hesitantly, praying that she wasn't wrong and wouldn't humiliate herself. Catherine resumed unbuttoning her own shirt.

What the hell was with this woman, anyway? Was she doing a strip show? Jana's throat constricted. *Dear Penthouse Forum...*

Good thing she was wearing a button-down shirt, too. She'd almost worn a pullover. That wouldn't have been as sexy. Her hair would've gotten messed up, her make-up would've smudged...

Each button Catherine undid, Jana followed suit, pausing between each one, waiting for Jana to catch up. Jana mimicked each move until she was moving in tandem with Catherine. Catherine slipped the shirt off and left it in a heap on the bed.

Her breasts were deliciously round, and her gaze seemed to pierce Jana's. She sat there, as if she were allowing Jana adequate time to take in the view. As if in a slow-motion film, Catherine then brought her hand up, lightly touched the middle of her chest with her fingertips, and then ran them down the length of her stomach.

Jana's heart thudded in her chest and sweat trickled down the back of her neck. As fast as her heart was beating, it almost stopped completely when Catherine's hand slipped into her boy shorts.

Up until then, Jana had mimicked all of her moves, but this was getting a little too crazy. Catherine's gaze was dark and intense. Her breathing got harder, but she kept her hand inside the elastic. Jana finally got the hint and unzipped her fly. When Jana's pants were undone and pooled around her hips on the seat, she stopped, terrified. Her clit throbbed with a dull ache, but she couldn't do this. She just couldn't go any further.

Catherine moved her fingers beneath the cotton fabric. Tentatively, Jana slid her hand down into her underwear.

Both women, with their hands in their pants, stared at each other. Blood pounded in Jana's temples as she tried to resist. Finally, she couldn't take the need any longer. She slipped her hand further down and her finger glided easily in a slick of smooth wetness. Her clit was hard under her fingertips.

With her cheeks flushed and her forehead glistening, Catherine's stroked herself faster and faster and her breathing was hard and labored. Jana silently gasped when Catherine pulled her hand out of her underpants. *Is that it? She gets me all worked up and that's it? Is she sick?*

But Catherine did not stop the show. Instead, with quick, desperate moves, she pulled off her underwear and tossed it aside before scooching to the edge of the bed, giving Jana a direct view of her wet, swollen pussy. She wished like hell that the Plexiglas between them would just disappear.

She watched as Catherine stroked herself slowly, her fingers luxuriating in the silky wetness, a strip of finely trimmed hair glistening. With her free hand, Jana clicked on the intercom and her ears filled with Catherine's moaning and heavy breathing. Then Catherine closed her eyes and threw her head back. With her lips slightly parted, she slowed her hand down to a barely perceptible caress, then shuddered for a good long while, her breaths ragged and clipped. Jana paused her own hand, transfixed by this hot, gorgeous woman bringing herself to exquisite orgasm.

When Catherine was finished, she opened her eyes, withdrew her hand from between her legs, and slid it up her belly, leaving a wet streak along her still-trembling flesh. She leaned back on her elbows but kept her knees up and far apart. She was enticing Jana to come, too, giving her something way better than *Playboy* as incentive.

Jana sat frozen for a moment. She couldn't continue masturbating while someone was watching, let alone come. Not if she was the only one doing it. It would be too embarrassing. The grunting, the moaning, and worst of all, the sex face. Jana didn't know what kind of sex face she made. What if it was freaky, or funny-looking with squinched eyes or snarly teeth?

Catherine didn't move. Her legs remained wide apart and her pussy remained on view as an offering. God, how Jana wanted to just jump through that window and dive into the glory of Catherine's Brazilian muff.

Jana swallowed hard. She couldn't stand it anymore. She began moving her hand again. She worked her fingers faster and harder, her own eyes closed in pleasure, her breath turning into pants, until she, too, began trembling and an orgasm ripped its way through her body.

Jana withdrew her hand and looked around for something, anything, to wipe her fingers. She found a napkin on the desk beneath Mike's coffee cup, used it, and tossed it in the trash can. She stared at it for a moment, wondering if she should go flush it. A can of room freshener would've been good right about now, too. With any luck, Mike's sinuses were still as closed as a dead clam. She turned back to the Plexiglas. Catherine was dressing, her face placid as she nonchalantly put herself back together. Jana pulled her pants back up around her hips.

The lights on the console reminded her that she was there for a purpose. She was supposed to be making sure that Catherine—the patient, she reminded herself—didn't do anything freaky. Too late for that.

Catherine was lying in bed on her stomach, her breathing regular, her eyes closed, her face peaceful. Her cheeks were still pink from her activities, and her lips had the hint of a satisfied smile.

I guess all you need is a little sex. That sounded like a good plan.

She watched Catherine a little longer and glanced at the nightstand. The electrodes. They had to go back onto her head. Oh, well. Jana would not wake her up for that. She was sleeping so peacefully.

Was it unethical to ask a subject of a scientific study out on a date? There was no confidentiality thing, was there? She wasn't a doctor. In fact, she had nothing at all to do with this study. There would be nothing wrong in asking Catherine out. Jana leaned back in her chair. *As if.*

Jana watched her for about twenty minutes, then Mike walked in. "Hey, Jana. How's it going? That wasn't too bad, was it?"

Jana suppressed a smile. "No, not too bad."

"So did she do anything?" Mike looked through the observation window. "Hey, what happened to her electrodes?"

"Oh, uh, she went to the bathroom and took them off," she said, her voice cracking.

"Well, how are we supposed to get a reading?" Mike moved toward the door that separated the rooms.

"No, wait." Jana put her hand on his arm to stop him, but quickly pulled it back. "Leave her alone. She's sleeping peacefully now. Who knows, maybe this is the best sleep she's had in a while."

Mike stood facing the window, looking thoughtful for a moment. He attempted to inhale, but it turned into a congested snuffle. Jana didn't realize that she had been holding in her own breath, and she exhaled.

"Yeah, I suppose," Mike said. "But the research won't be accurate. Or useful. This patient hasn't slept well in six months." He pursed his lips. "I wonder why she was able to fall asleep now? And so early."

Jana declined to inform him of her theory. "Maybe she can stay an extra day. That'll give you a chance to make up for tonight."

"That goes into Monday. No one's on shift that night." Mike ran his hand through his short, scruffy hair. "I guess I could get someone."

"I'll do it."

"You'd stay over Monday? Why would you want to do that?"

Although Jana glanced at Catherine for only a second or two, she felt the heat in her cheeks.

"I've taken an interest in the study. Because of my own experience. Ya know?"

"Okay, that would be great. I'll have to get it okay'd, but I can be persuasive," Mike said with a grin. He walked out, leaving Jana in the sex-scented room.

Catherine continued to sleep. If sex put her to sleep like this and she was experiencing insomnia, did that mean she didn't have sex very often? Jana couldn't imagine that. Catherine probably had women lined up at the door, eager to fuck her, and she could probably have a different woman every night. Jana wished she could be one of them. Just once.

As Jana explored Catherine's body in her thoughts again, her clit began to throb. She squeezed her thighs together to stop it. Mike would be back any minute.

Maybe she would ask Catherine out and offer her the most natural sleep aid available.

Whatever Catherine was dreaming about, it made her smile and moan happily.

"Goodnight, Catherine," Jana whispered. "I'll see you on Monday."

FIT FOR FORTY
BY HARPER BLISS

"FOR CRYING OUT LOUD." I can't hold my frustration any longer. "Are you trying to kill me?" But Kate has already hopped halfway up the steep path, as though it's easy for her, which is probably what's pissing me off the most. It *is* easy for her. For me, it's pure hell. And what's the point of going on a hike 'together' if she walks a few yards in front of me most of the time? I have half a mind to turn back, and let her reach the top—and the glorious view she's promised—on her own. For the life of me, however, I can't remember how to get back. We've already hiked up one mountain and retracing my steps would only lead to the same agony as following Kate. But no vista, no matter how spectacular, is worth the cramps in my calves, and the blisters forming on my big toe that will take days to heal.

She turns around, hands at her sides, smirking down at me. How can she be so sweaty, yet still look so hot? As if she's part of a commercial for hiking gear with the cameras hiding in the bushes beside her.

"Come on, babe." She beckons with one arm. "You can catch a glimpse of the ocean from here."

I don't give a toss about glimpsing the ocean. I've seen plenty stunning views in my life, and I have absolutely no desire to break my back climbing two mountains to see another. The ups don't really outweigh the downs, which is exactly what I wanted to tell Kate this morning before we set off, but it's not really something to say to your wife on her birthday.

"I want to be fit for forty," she told me eight months ago, and suddenly started using her overpriced gym membership again.

"You look fine, babe," I said to her.

"No." She shook her head. "It's not about how I look. It's about how I feel inside."

"Oh, it's like that," I had wanted to say, remembering my own approach to my fortieth five years earlier, but instead murmured some vague words of support.

"Birgit, come on," she insists. "It's really not that bad."

But I hadn't returned with her to the gym. I was glad to point out the new study that had proven a glass of red wine in the evening is just as good for your cardiac health as an hour on the treadmill. And a whole lot more fun. Not that I restrict myself to one serving per night. Hence my current state on this wretched mountainside. I gasp for air while glancing at my wife, who seems so far away. But I have no choice. I took the day off from work for her birthday, and she wants to climb a few mountains and take in a magnificent view together. It's what she wanted. What was I going to say? No thanks, dear, the view from our window is plenty for me? I would have if it wasn't her fortieth. In my defense, when I turned forty, I asked for an evening cruise across the harbor, not a torturously long trek through the wild. And I'm supposed to be the high maintenance one.

"We're almost there," she shouts.

So, I straighten my posture and start by putting one foot in front of the other. I'd developed this coping mechanism when we reached the hiking trail more than two hours ago. It feels more like days than hours.

One step at a time, that's how all great accomplishments are achieved. Up I go. I try to ignore the sting in my thigh every time my weight shifts to my left foot and focus solely on the triumphant smile Kate's sure to give me when we reach the top.

"That was worth it, wasn't it?" she'll say. "Don't you think, babe?" And at first I'll be annoyed, but then she'll lean into me with those strong hips of hers and I'll melt a little because she hasn't looked better in years.

I focus on that as my breath transitions to short stutters. On the sight of her dark-skinned arms against the white of her tank top, and the delicious curve of her ass in these shorts she's wearing. I'm here for her. I repeat it in my head like a mantra. I'm here for my wife because I love her and it's her blooming birthday.

Mid-slope, I look down at my feet instead of the top of the mountain. On days off, I prefer not to face reality, especially if that reality promises another hour of unfortunate muscle spasms and further proof of my very pathetic lung capacity.

Kate moves to the side of the path and drinks water from a bottle, exposing the line of her throat as she tilts her head back. Oh, that neck of hers. If I wasn't suffering so much, I'd surely have some raunchy thoughts running through my mind, but alas. I'm too preoccupied with feeling sorry for myself because my wife went on a health-kick to stave off feelings of midlife worthlessness, instead of binging on champagne and a trip to a tropical island.

I pause again, bending at the waist. I'm almost to her, but not quite. A few short, but very steep yards stretch between us like hot coals I'm intended to walk over barefoot. I can't say these things to Kate, because she takes too much pleasure in making fun of my theatrics.

I take the twenty—I count them to stop my mind from going elsewhere—steps needed to reach her side, and can't help but say something dramatic anyway. "Jesus fucking Christ, babe," is all that comes out between my ragged breaths.

Kate slings an arm around my shoulders, and I can feel her biceps press against the skin of my neck. She's been doing pushups, or CrossFit, or something like that. We only have five years between us but sometimes I feel at least twenty years older when she talks about compound movements and dead lifts and whatnot.

"Why does it have to be so hardcore, babe?" I asked her once. "Why can't our after-work life consist of gentle yoga and wine and dinner parties?" But Kate wouldn't have any of it.

"I want to be strong," was all she said, and how could I argue with that?

"Look," she says, while pulling me up, her arm still around my neck. "Look at the color of that ocean."

And it's true, it's very blue, and the waves crash photogenically against the rocks, but I'm too busy tallying up all the places where I'm in pain to fully absorb the beauty around us.

"Once we get to the top, we'll have an overview of the entire bay."

"Argh," I moan—dramatically. "I'm not sure I can do it, babe."

"Of course you can. The body is always capable of much more than you think." Another Fit-for-Forty Kate-ism. Statements like that drive me crazy. They don't lessen my pain in any way, only promise more.

I grumble under my breath. It's her birthday and I'm trying to keep up my good spirits, but I lost my sunny disposition a few blisters ago.

"It's fucking gorgeous," she says in a way that bears no contesting. "Nature at its very finest." She slips her arm from my shoulder and just stands there

71

gazing into the blue in front of her. The sky is a few shades lighter than the ocean, surrounded by the vivid green of the bushes and the darker green of the mountain looming ahead, and it is, objectively speaking, staggering. But fuck me. I'm still panting after having stood still for several minutes, and the prospect of finding the will power to tackle the rest of the mountain is killing me.

"You're right, babe," I mumble, still trying to be the bigger person.

"Shall we continue?" She looks at me with those dark eyes of hers, but Kate comes across more like a drill sergeant—a really hot one—than my wife right now.

"I need a few more minutes. You've been resting for ages."

"Fair enough." She sends me one of those loopy, crooked smiles I fell so hard for years ago. Hairstyles change, and the way jeans are worn switches from pulled high over the waist to slung low on the hips, but the shape of a smile always remains. And it's that very smile that got me here in the first place, the one I can never resist.

"Let's take the day off on the fifth," she'd said, "and finally go on that hike." I'd barely woken up and she was grinning down at me, her lips all asymmetrical and seductive. I'd pulled her back down under the covers with me and I guess that meant yes to her. My bad.

Kate hands me the water and I gulp it down. I'd rather splash it all over my face and neck, but I refused to carry my own backpack and I don't want to run out later. There are only so many sacrifices my out-of-shape body can make.

A few minutes later, we start climbing again. I'm too out of breath to complain but my inner monologue is going bonkers. This feels more like bloody rock climbing than a hike. The path we're on is thin and ridged with tree roots, and some stretches are covered with bits of rock and stones. I'm hardly a princess who fancies high heels, but this is fucking dangerous. Not life-threatening, but I bet bones have been broken on this surface. I focus my attention on maintaining my balance, which is a blessing because it keeps my mind off the steepness of the slope.

The torment continues for an eternity, only interspersed with brief breaks to admire the view, which, according to Kate, grows more impressive with every step. But my eyes are exhausted, and twisting my head to look would burn too much energy.

When we've almost reached the top, the bushes around us growing denser, it looks as if we're entering previously unchartered territory. Then, I feel something akin to pleasure. The maddest, craziest, most masochistic pleasure you could imagine, but pleasure nonetheless. Because, fuck, I'm about to reach the top of this damned mountain. No one else operated my feet. No machinery was involved to hoist me up. I did it all myself.

And then there's the absolute quiet around us, except for the forest sounds and the distant slap of the waves against the majestic shoreline beneath. And the fresh air in my tortured lungs, and the subsiding ache in my glutes, and the sweat on my brow dripping down my cheeks into my mouth. And I must admit, I'm feeling it. I get why she wanted to come here. It feels as though, because it's just us on this mountaintop, we're alone on the planet. A foolish notion, and perhaps I'm suffering from a lack of oxygen to the brain, but I'm enraptured nonetheless. God knows which permanent injuries this hike will cause, but right now, when I'm at the top with my girl on her birthday, I don't care about anything but this moment.

Below, the ocean is ink-blue in bits, while other patches are indigo and the caps of the waves are the purest of white. The sky stretches endlessly in front of us and for a minute, I feel like I might cry.

"Happy birthday," I say, and press a kiss to Kate's sweaty cheek.

She turns towards me, folding her arms around my waist. "Thank you for coming with me, babe. I know it was hard."

"No sweat," I lie, fooling no one.

"I feel so, so good. Like I can do anything." She tilts her head a bit. "It's hard to describe, but let's just say I feel exactly how I wanted to feel on this day."

"And it's only midday." I pull her a little closer towards me.

"Well." There's that smile again. "As outstanding as this view is, it *could* be enhanced."

"Oh, really?" I play dumb, but I know what she's getting at. You can't spend two decades with someone and not be aware of her love for alfresco hanky-panky. We've done it in more parks and alleyways and deserted parking lots than I can count.

"I see a tree with your name on it, babe." Kate doesn't look at a tree though; she looks straight into my eyes, sporting that look she gets when her mind goes there. This hike was foreplay for her. I guess when you're fit at forty it can be more than torture. Not for me, though. I'm happy I made it to the top, exhilarated, in fact, to share this moment with her, but I'm nowhere near horny. This, however, doesn't worry me in the slightest. I know Kate. I know what she can do to me.

"Do you now?" I play along. "And, say you get to push me up against said tree, what would you do?"

"Oh, I will push you against it, babe. There are really no two ways about it."

This is how it starts. This is how she gets my blood to heat up in my veins, and the hairs to stand up on the back of my neck.

"Once I do, I will make you come so hard, make you scream so loud, the birds won't know what hit them. They'll all fly off in submission, convinced there's a new top bird on the mountain. Which will be true. At least for a little while."

Kate doesn't touch me while she says this, doesn't try to sneak a hand underneath my top and brush a finger against my sweat-drenched flesh. And I realize that I knew this would happen—how could I not?—and it's most likely what kept me going in the end.

"Now, tell me," she continues, narrowing her eyes. "Do you want a sea view with your climax or do you prefer a mountain view?" She cocks her head to the right a bit.

I try to hold back a snicker, but fail. I burst out laughing, which might not be conducive to the atmosphere she's creating. My brain is flooded with endorphins from the climb, my limbs loose, and my psyche not quite where she wants it yet.

"It's your birthday babe. You choose." I trace the back of my fingers over her glistening upper arm. Her skin is soft, but underneath her biceps is flexed and hard.

"I say sea." Her hand approaches my belly, catches the waistband of my shorts. She pulls me close. She doesn't smile. I know what that means. "Why don't you have a look in my backpack. I brought us something." She ducks down quickly to pick it up and offers it to me.

Shaking my head at her audacity—because I can easily guess what I'll find—I zip the backpack open. Sure enough, wrapped in a towel, but poking ostentatiously upwards nonetheless, is my favorite purple dildo. The one she got me for *my* fortieth.

"You are unbelievable." The sight of my preferred toy makes my pussy twitch. I look up and stare into her dark, dark eyes. I'd better not burst out laughing again. I don't think her backpack is big enough to hold a paddle as well, but I know what her hands can do.

"It was a rough climb, babe. I intend for us to stay here a while." A soft smile breaks through the serious expression on her face, then she goes all stern on me again. "For my birthday, I want you to come four times on this mountain. I just turned forty, after all."

"But, what if someone comes along?" I object, although I don't feel much like complaining.

"That's why we came on a weekday." That grin again. "And if someone were to pass by, well, good for them then."

"But—" She moves in closer, taking the backpack from my hands.

"No buts. Time for Number One." She curls her fingers around my wrists and coaxes me towards the tree. Adding another year to her life hasn't made her less bossy.

The trunk of the tree is rough and I can easily feel it scratch my skin through the fabric of my lycra top. But fuck, the view she has me facing is breathtaking, and then she kisses me. A soft peck at first, followed by another, after which her tongue demands access and I happily surrender my mouth. Our lip-lock seems to last forever, and I feel it tingle in every extremity of my body. I haven't tasted another pair of lips in decades, and I know I haven't missed much. Ever since meeting Kate I've wondered if there's such a thing as meeting your perfect kissing companion, sort of like a soul mate, but for lips. From the very first time her mouth touched mine, I knew. I knew I would never need to be kissed by anyone else again because our lips met in such a definite and determined way that all other lips suddenly seemed obsolete. I'd found my matching pair.

Kate's mouth is soft on mine, and sometimes hard, like now, when she sinks her teeth into my bottom lip. Soon, she has me gasping for air—and I prefer the reason for this particular bout of breathlessness infinitely over the previous one.

When we finally break, and she looks into my eyes, I know that Number One won't be far off. My only worry is how the hell I'll ever get down this mountain after four orgasms. She'll have to carry me on her back. Maybe this is what all the CrossFit was about. "It's functional," Kate said, and up until now I had no idea what that was supposed to mean.

"I'm going to take your top off," she says. It's not a question, and I know there's no use in contesting it.

"As long as you take yours off as well." I can't help myself. The mountain air must make me mouthier than usual. Plus, I really want to see her take her top off. The mere thought of drops of sweat shimmering on her taut skin is enough for another round of clenches between my legs. I do hope she packed spare underwear in that bag of hers, because the pair I'm wearing now is as good as ruined.

"You know I like to bare it all when I'm outside." It's true. If it were up to her, we'd go on holiday to a nudist enclave every year. She doesn't waste any time and starts hoisting up her top. It's tight and clings to her flesh, but her strong arms have no problem with that. The sports bra, with extra support she wears for activities like this, comes off quickly and I have to catch my breath again. I'm floored by the sight of her naked breasts. I have no eyes for the wild beauty of the ocean behind her. It's all Kate for me.

She cocks her head again, as though saying, "Like what you see?" But she doesn't ask because she knows the answer all too well.

"Come on." She reaches for my top next and peels it off my skin slowly, gently exposing my flesh to the air. When my bra comes off, the faint breeze catches my nipples and the sensation is overwhelmingly pleasant. In no time, they grow hard, and I already know what will come next. Although, I wouldn't be entirely surprised if she produced a pair of nipple clamps from the backpack, but I'm guessing she didn't want to carry our entire drawer of sex toys on her back.

Kate presses her body against mine, our stiff nipples meeting, her breath husky in my ears. "I want you naked," she whispers, and her voice is low and gravelly, as though she's losing control a little.

It's a bit of a kerfuffle to hitch my shorts over my sturdy hiking shoes, but she gets the job done. And there I stand. Naked from the ankles up. I have to draw the line somewhere. I'm not taking off my footwear in this place.

"Look at you, babe," she says as she overlooks the situation. "Bloody gorgeous."

"How about you?" I ask, and motion with my hand towards her shorts, but she swats it away.

"No need." Her lips curl into a grin. "You know that."

I've been with Kate for such a long time, I can't even remember if I was such a pillow princess before we met. I am now. Well, at the moment more of a tree princess, but still. It's where she wants me, so that's how it is.

"Now." She inches closer, her nipples denting my skin, her lips hovering over mine. Her hand is sliding down my belly. "Spread your legs, babe," she asks, but does it for me anyway. She slants her body away from me and cups my breast with her other hand.

Her fingers are on my pussy lips, ever so gently sliding through the wetness there. Suddenly, the wind in the trees intensifies to a roar, and the sound of the sea is loud in my ears—despite our altitude and the distance separating us from the ocean. I have to hand it to her, there is something to be said for sex surrounded by nothing but the elements. She catches my nipple between two fingers and squeezes hard and quick. Her hand between my legs remains gentle, soft even, just gliding back and forth, staying too far away from my clit. She gazes into my eyes while she continues to pinch my nipple. Every tweak sends a fresh jolt of lust straight to my pussy, as if what her two hands are doing separately, connects there. If she weren't such a tease and lavished some attention on my clit, Number One would soon be a fact.

"I'm going to fuck you against this tree," she says. And then she does. A finger slides all the way in, and everything I have clamps around it. She brings her other hand to my face now, fingers rubbing my lips, negotiating entrance. She has one finger in my cunt and one in my mouth. That's new. And incredibly arousing. I suck on her finger for dear life. My knees give a little when she pushes deeper inside of me. Soon, a second one follows, spreading me wide—everywhere. I twirl my tongue around her fingers in my mouth and shove my pelvis towards her other hand. I can't say it out loud, but we've been together long enough for her to know. I want more.

"Come for me like this," she says, slipping a third finger in both orifices. Earlier, while suffering on that steep incline, I never imagined this was the view she was talking about. Her view of me, like this, totally at her mercy. Her fingers in my mouth are a huge turn-on and, yes, I think I might be able to do what she asks. I close my eyes and focus only on what my body is experiencing, on the tight grasp of her fingers deep inside of me, inhabiting me—that's what she calls it and the word seems to fit—and taking me there.

My breasts bounce slightly, and the breeze and sun on my skin awaken other senses, stir up an unusual sensation, seizing my entire body through the expanse of my skin. It all comes together in a point somewhere deep in my body. That's where it starts, somewhere below my stomach, or perhaps in my brain, who knows? All I know is that Number One is coming. My birthday present to my wife, because to her, it is a gift when I come for her the way she demands it. She knows what it takes. It's not mere rubbing of fingers and manipulation of body parts. It's trust, and the years between us, and all this love that has blossomed, and now she's forty and more gorgeous than ever.

Oh, fuck. I can't say it out loud because my mouth is full of her fingers, full of her, and so is my cunt. It starts the way the waves crash into the rocks below us, with a steady, sturdy slap, but then it transforms into an explosion of heat in my flesh and lightning in my blood. Her fingers in my cunt touch that spot over and over, and my knees give a little more, and that's how she knows.

She removes her fingers from my mouth and presses a kiss on my lips instead. Kate's usual M.O. after she's fucked me like this is to have me lick my own juices from her fingers. Today, she surprises me again and brings them to her own lips and stares deep into my eyes as she licks my wetness from her hand. Already, I can't wait for Number Two.

"Isn't it amazing?" she asks when she's done sucking her fingers.

"Oh yes," I say, not referring to our surroundings at all.

"Are you cold?" It's true that my skin has broken out in goose bumps, but that's hardly because of a drop in body temperature. I notice the gooseflesh on Kate's skin as well, and although there's some sweat on her brow, I realize it's due to the exhilaration of fucking on this mountaintop. I can't keep my eyes off her breasts. Off her small, rock-hard, earth-colored nipples, and how they point upwards, like an invitation to take them in my mouth. And fuck, I want to, but long ago, it was decided that Kate is calling the shots. It wasn't a decision as such, more of an organic unfolding of events over and over again that established patterns along the way. We both have very few reasons to complain.

If she hadn't said anything about four orgasms, I'd be content right now, sated, ready for one of those protein bars she packed in that seemingly bottomless backpack of hers, but now that I know there will be encores, a stirring remains in my blood—a sense of unfinished business.

I pull her towards me and kiss her, smelling and tasting myself on her lips. Her body is warm against mine, comforting, and restoring.

"Let me know when you're ready," she breathes into my ear after we break from the kiss. "I'm nowhere near done with you yet." She nuzzles my neck, before finding my eyes and painting that wicked grin on her face again. "On second thought, you'd best be ready now." She throws in a quick wink before grabbing me by the shoulders and spinning me around. Her knee is between my thighs, spreading them again. Her hand curves around my hip and pushes against my belly, indicating that I should stick my bottom out. My tummy tingles at the prospect of what that could mean—as if I don't know.

She bends her body over mine. I feel her nipples poke into the flesh of my back as she finds my ear.

"Permission to touch yourself," she says, "while I do this." With that, her hand glides down my spine, until it reaches my crack, and it still doesn't stop. She just spreads my cheeks. She wouldn't venture further without some preparation. My clit tightens with the confirmation of her plans for Number Two. And, yay me, I get to touch myself. What does she have in mind for the dildo, though? Then my thoughts freeze because Kate starts kissing her way down my back. She kisses with lots of teeth and tongue, and soon enough her teeth bite down on the curve of my ass. She must be on her knees behind me, but the view beyond the tree I'm facing is too overwhelming to look back, and I know she didn't put me in this position so I could check up on her.

The first drizzle of saliva slides down my cleft, and it's as though the entire expanse of my skin is hyper-sensitized and I feel everything tenfold. The birds in the trees chipper away in high-pitched tones, and the smell in my nose is decidedly green. Fresh. Alive.

There comes her tongue, and I immediately know she doesn't want to draw this one out. She's insistent, firm, entering me with the tip from the first go. So I rebalance and steady myself against the tree trunk with one hand while my other goes to my clit. It's still a little delicate, but also throbbing wildly. I circle my finger without hesitation. The same way Kate is feasting on my ass.

I rest my forehead against the tree for extra support, because I know what comes next. Kate's finger, the same one that fucked me earlier, will soon seek entrance, and once it does, the fireworks will come. And I'll be lost.

She doesn't push it deep, barely skirting the rim, but it's enough—it always is. That glorious, tight, all-in sensation engulfs me from the first little probe, like a promise of much bigger things to come. But there they come already. I can never help myself when she touches me there, especially not now, out in the open on this mountain with the sun warming our skin. The exposure adds an extra, illicit, earthy awareness, and I rub my clit frantically while Kate fucks me very carefully, very controlled from behind. I open my eyes when I come, but everything blurs into a big smudge when my brain gives up its power to pure sensation, to the utmost pleasure of my wife possessing my ass.

"Oh god." My forehead presses against my arm as I try to regroup and I hear Kate shuffle behind me. I can just imagine the smug grin on her face. I can't wait to kiss it off her.

She spins me around with those strong, dark arms of her, and I swoon a little. This particular type of climax is still rather new to me, and was only discovered because Kate kept gently coaxing me onto my belly, venturing a little bit farther every time over the course of months. It has only made me fall in love with her all over again.

"Let's sit for a minute." Her dark-brown eyes sparkle as she points towards a flat, wide rock skirting the spot where we've stopped. She grabs her tank top from where she let it drop on her backpack earlier and fashions a tiny blanket out of it. The rock is cold and hard, but I'm glad to be sitting for a bit, even though I'm completely naked for all the mountain creatures to see.

Kate reaches for her backpack and, instantly, the thought of what's inside ignites something in my belly again. But, damn, I need a break. I'm not an orgasm machine. Also, this spot doesn't seem ideal for a bout of dildo-fucking. I eye her as she rummages inside her bag and wonder how she's going to swing this one.

She produces a towel and bunches it up before handing it to me. "For your head," she simply says.

"What?" My brain is still a bit fuzzy from Number One and Two and I don't know what she means.

"The rock is big enough for you to lie down on. You can use the towel as a pillow."

"Lie down? What, erm, I don't know." I can't really seem to find my words either. They stall even more when the dildo materializes from the gaping mouth of her bag.

"For my birthday," she says as she crouches beside me, "I would like you to fuck yourself with this." She brings the dildo towards her mouth and slips it between her lips, coating it in saliva. "You should be wet enough, but just in case." She gives me the dildo and takes the towel from my hands, bunches it up some more and puts it behind me. "Take all the time you need, babe." She pushes herself up, ducks down one more time, and shows me her phone. "I'm going to take some snaps."

She doesn't mean of the view.

I open my mouth to speak, but no words come out.

"As a souvenir."

I scrunch my eyebrows together and realize she must have planned this entire day to a tee. She must have come here and scouted this spot, this rock, and the trees.

"Ready when you are." She just stands there grinning, mightily pleased with herself.

Heat rises from my belly to fill the tiniest cells in my body. Of course she knew exhibitionism times two would turn me on exponentially.

I stretch out on the rock as instructed, putting my head on the makeshift towel-pillow, spreading my legs wide for her, and her camera. The rock cools my overheated body, and a subtle breeze skims along my pulsing pussy lips. I take the dildo into my own mouth to warm it up some more, because Kate was right, I should be plenty wet to provide it easy access to my cunt. I slip and slide it between my lips and Kate takes pictures, or a video. I have no idea, but I'm sure she'll show me later. After we watch it, we'll fuck again.

"Fuck yourself, babe," she spurs me on, and she must be so aroused from all the things she has done to me. Doesn't she need some relief?

I bring the toy between my legs, easily finding my opening with the tip, and it slides in swiftly. It's big, and a little bit curved towards the top, and I'm spread so wide—even wider than when she fucked me with three fingers—that it feels like surrender all over again. I imagine what Kate is seeing, what the pictures will show, and it speeds up my heartbeat, which seems to be in direct connection to my pulsing clit.

I fuck myself for her with slow, luxurious strokes of our purple dildo that she carried with her up this mountain. I have to admit it's freeing, exhilarating in its boldness. More than the thrusts I deliver myself, it's the entire picture that excites me most. Kate with her camera and intense gaze—and her top off. The green and blue above me, the crisp air, the heat of the sun, that inexplicable delight of engaging in these acts outside, and me buck naked on a rock in the mountains. It's a feast for all my senses, so I have no trouble going there again. As though my previous orgasm still lingers and I can easily tune back in and pick up where we left off. As though it's not a string of climaxes but an interwoven pattern of highs with some breathing room thrown in.

Then again, I know this toy well. I know exactly how to position it for maximum effect, the slightly upward curve touching me precisely where I need to be touched. When extreme arousal and excellent knowledge of mechanics meet, in a steady rhythm, there's only one outcome: me, panting on a rock, crying out loudly as I come at my own hands, for her.

She takes the dildo from me after it slips out of my pussy. All the smugness has left her face. Is that a tear glittering in the corner of her eye? She's touched by my complete abandon for her, I can tell. In return, it moves me deeply, too. Usually, I'm the one doing all the crying in the bedroom. But we're not in the bedroom. We're in the wilderness, giving in completely to our animalistic, base urges, and it's sensational.

"Make me come," she says, completely out of character. "I need to. Now."

I'm more than happy to oblige. I push myself up from the rock and kneel next to her, not caring about what I'm shoving my knees into. "Take my spot."

As soon as she's on her back, I tug off Kate's shorts and underwear, exposing her to me, and the elements. Number Four will be for her, then.

She lets her legs fall open, and the sight of her like that sends my heart aflutter. I find a semi-comfortable position between her legs so I can lick her until she howls. I hunker down, bringing my face towards her glistening cunt. I want to lap at it as though it's the first drop of water I see after climbing another mountain like this, but first I take a moment to admire my view. So much better than any I've seen today.

"Please, Birgit." Kate is not the pleading kind—more the commanding one—so I know her need is urgent. I let my tongue wander over her slick lips for a few seconds. She grabs me by the hair. She can't wait. I don't have the heart to try her patience. Not after Number One, Two, and Three. I suck my lips around her clit and let my tongue go wild. Her nails dig into my skull; her pelvis pushes towards me. She's trapping me with her body, welding my mouth to her pussy, and it feels just as freeing as being naked on the rock.

I revel in the little sounds she makes; tiny, throaty guttural groans fill the air around us, and it makes a nice difference from the bird chatter. I taste her, drink her in, lick her clit until she's writhing underneath me. Until she loses control.

"Oh fuck," she screams, and presses her palms against either side of my head, before slowly pulling me away from her.

"Happy birthday," I say when she opens her eyes, her mouth slightly agape.

"Come here." She motions for me to join her on the rock, which seems rather unrealistic to me, but I try anyway. I sit on the ledge, my hips glued to her side, and stroke her face with my fingers.

"Definitely the best hike I've ever been on." I shoot her a schmaltzy grin.

"Shall we make it a weekly thing then?"

"Maybe, but either way, let's keep these particular antics for special occasions." Although I'm not sure I can ever go hiking without this sort of incentive again.

"Our wedding anniversary is coming up." She smiles up at me from her spot on the rock, her head still pressed into the heap of towel.

"And the anniversary of when we first met, and the one of our first kiss a few weeks after." I'm starting to come back to my full senses though, and it hits me that we're both sitting on this rock stark naked. "It's going to be a fun walk down." I bend over and kiss her on the lips.

As it turns out, on the way back, we walk hand in hand, the pair of us smelling like sex, that strong, heady scent that even nature can't erase. We're giddy, and loved-up, and I brush my hand against Kate's biceps now and then, just to cop a feel of exactly how fit she is for forty. My legs are light, my spirit soaring high, like the birds above us, and a new benchmark has been set for celebrating birthdays.

SLAMMIN' SUNDAY

BY ANNIE ANTHONY

IN COLLEGE, I HAD A poetry instructor who fronted a band in the eighties that opened for hard-core metal acts. She was from North Dakota. Had run away at fourteen. Married at fifteen. Divorced at seventeen. At nineteen, after years of living in vans and singing in dives, she landed a deal with a small label. But road life never really paid the bills, and while she'd never intended to settle down, by forty, she had a *job*.

Trading in shredded jeans and midriff tees for pencil skirts and cashmere wraps, she accepted an assistant professorship at a land-grant state college. She paced the classroom as though it were her private greenroom, and she couldn't wait for the show to start. I watched her closely, hoping to catch the moment when she stutter-stepped between the present and the past. I imagined her tossing down the syllabus, kicking off her shoes, and striding barefoot to the back of the class. In my mind, she turned the desks upside down and screeched metal instead of spoken word poetry.

She taught us very little about poetry, believing that "writing is a gift of the soul which cannot be taught in workshops." So instead of an academic analysis of verse and themes, Dennie—she preferred we call her by her first name—told us stories. She would sit on top of the desk, her eyes half closed as if the memories she fought were more real than the bodies and faces of the students in front of her. Her outstretched hands met loosely in front of her chest, as if reaching for a mic that was no longer there. Maybe not all of the undergrads in upper-division poetry spent the ninety-minute seminar fantasizing about her legs and her ass. But for an entire semester, while her words kaleidoscoped across our landlocked, windowless classroom, I focused as much on the shape of her lips as her stories.

She didn't just preach at us, though. She put us on the spot, believing in what she called "incidental genius." A lot of students grumbled, but I never minded taking my turn. Tingling after Dennie's voice called my name, I felt as though she absolutely believed I could combine colors and textures and objects in a way that revealed my vulnerability, my fear, my hope. All in two minutes or less. I loved poetry, but my undeniable reactions to Dennie allowed me to embrace the growing awareness that I loved women. Until her class, I had tolerated sex with guys—random dates and mediocre couplings that left me wondering if something was wrong with me. I loved sex, was horny all the time. But somehow the way Tyler Hansen's chest felt above mine left me feeling more alone than when I actually was alone.

By the time I reached thirty, I still loved poetry, still loved women but wasn't much different than the student I'd been. Unfulfilled longing was my loveless partner. Bland people, tedious work, and uninspired meetings hadn't been objectives on my resume, but poetry doesn't pay back student loans. This creative writing student ended up in another nearly windowless building, working a corporate insurance job.

One afternoon, my boss asked if we could chat. He leaned his ass against my desk and moved so close I could smell the stink from his lunch on his breath. We discussed a problem with a bulk reserve for far longer than the issue deserved, and by the time he moved on to another victim, I literally needed some fresh air. I grabbed my key card and headed out for some coffee.

I wandered up to Café Q, an artsy little cafe that specialized in drip coffee, loose teas, and artisan pastries. Every table was taken, mostly by people in suits chatting on phones or tapping at laptops. Students sat on oversized floor pillows while a homeless guy pilfered napkins and honey packets from the self-serve bar.

I ordered a small decaf and checked the community board. A neon green flyer caught my attention. Slammin' Sundays. Café Q was pleased to host an inaugural Sunday morning poetry slam. All participating poets were given a free small beverage and would be entered into a drawing for a $50 Q's gift card. *Sunday mornings don't have to suck… now they can slam!*

Corny flyer, yes. But it had been a long time since I'd had a moment of "incidental genius," or even just listened to a poet live. I folded the flyer in thirds and then in half again and slipped it into my wallet.

Apparently, most of the city thinks Sunday mornings suck, because by 8:30am almost every seat in Q's was taken. I'd tucked a copy of one of Dennie's old volumes of poetry into my messenger bag for inspiration along with a notebook filled with my own old poems…just in case. I waited in line for coffee at the counter and scanned the café for a space to sit.

A single stool opened up at a long varnished table lining the back wall of the café. I stepped over a pair of long legs that stretched past a floor cushion and took the seat next to a bearded, flannel-wearing hipster. I sipped my coffee and took in the crowd. A baby cried and a stroller edged awkwardly around the tangles of people sitting on the floor, all drawn in by the promise of words sweet enough to taste, yet sharp enough to feel.

At precisely nine o'clock, a barista with purple hair walked through the crowd, holding half-sheets of white paper and a coffee cup filled with plastic spoons. She asked if anyone wanted to register for the slam. At least ten people took forms and in return received a numbered plastic spoon.

"When your number is called, you're up," Purple Hair called out. "After you slam, give me the spoon and I give you free coffee. Got it? Takers? Anyone else here to slam?"

I raised my hand. She passed me a form and spoon number twelve. I scratched my name and the number assigned to me in the spaces provided on the paper and waited for things to start. Nerves swirled in my belly and I rinsed the growing dryness in my mouth with the last of my cool, sweet coffee.

It quickly became clear this first Slammin' Sunday wouldn't follow a traditional format. The first poet didn't slam at all, but rather read in nervous tones from a well-worn volume by Elizabeth Barrett Browning. The applause was lukewarm. Numbers two and three were fairly forgettable. By number four the crowd started to get into it, and the slammers got more creative. Some read from notes, others ad-libbed. One young girl even sang and rapped, which brought her crowd of friends to their feet.

As participants gave up their poetry and plastic spoons, the reality that this place was a far cry from Dennie's classroom started to sink in. I debated dumping that number-twelve spoon into the trash and bolting. Gulping back shyness, I looked around at the crowd. The woman whose legs I'd avoided earlier was looking at me. Right at me. Was she there to listen or to slam?

Lanky stared, her expression compelling me to smile back. The crinkles around her eyes were gentle, the gap between the two front teeth delicate. I grinned but looked away. If I didn't let myself hope that she was flirting, then I wouldn't be disappointed if she wasn't, right?

Purple Hair called number twelve. I rose from the stool and scanned the room to see how many sets of eyes were watching. A lot. In fact, most of the people packed into Q's—even the people in line for coffee who probably had no idea there was an event—turned when I stood. A thrill rose in my chest. I was ready for this in a way I hadn't expected. More than ten years after Dennie's supportive looks allowed me to open up and speak out, I resumed that comfortable posture. I could do this. I turned to the earmarked page in my notebook and stood taller so my voice would project.

"This is an original poem I wrote a while back," I said. "It's called Closeness."

I drew in a breath and paused.

Years ago, the poem had been a way to vent the loss of an ex who I'd known wouldn't stay. In that coffee shop, my voice tripped with emotions as vivid as they'd been when I felt her absence in sheets that felt cold even as she slept beside me.

> Snow is falling
> sagging the arms of tired pines.
> We are curled together
> beneath covers, a cashew,
> my ecstatic saliva swirling
> on the whorl of your breast.
> Copper owls tinkle with the flurrying winds,
> regret collects in corners,
> muddies, hardens.
> Eyes close, disembodied lamps,
> the poof of soot from a candle.
> Between us, desire like white embers
> the taste of unwashed carrots.
> The room is overtaken by the red-dial hour.
> We awaken beneath blue soap.
> Unfamiliar sheets, impressionable down
> traces of cork in your mouth.
> Glass fruit at the bedside
> is cold to the touch.

I whisper how long I've wanted this.
You listen,
holding snow in your ear.

With those eyes on me and so many ears tuned to my voice, I felt the way I imagined Dennie must have during a performance. Singing allowed her to make an offering of herself to others in a way I felt I now understood. Her lyrics and my lines touched strangers with the sudden intimacy of a first kiss. The café was quiet. Even though I hadn't been reading, I closed my notebook to convey that I was finished.

Then, the 'I hope she's flirting' woman gave a loud, "Yeah!" With that, applause barked off dozens and dozens of palms. I blushed. Purple Hair took my spoon and handed me a free coffee.

The slam ended after the fourteenth poet and Purple Hair drew for the gift card. The winner—the half-singing, half-rapping girl—screeched and her friends thundered to the counter.

I gathered up my messenger bag, notebook, and my full, free coffee. I had to pee and the thought of wading through the crowd to the single-stall bathroom appealed as much as dancing through a pit of snakes. I always carry the key card to my office, and security on the weekends was light. I could definitely hold it. I was almost to the door when the woman from the floor cushion touched my arm.

"Hey."

She was quite a bit taller than me. She wore a thin, white tank top and faded black skinny jeans.

"Hey," I said.

"Are you, um, getting out of here?"

"I was planning on it, yeah."

"Mind if I walk a bit with you? I promise, I'm not a psycho. I just really loved your poem."

I scanned her face, as if crazy were as obvious as a mole or a unibrow. Her smile accentuated the space between her teeth in a way that charmed me. Her cheeks were flushed, and a star scatter of freckles drew me into her warm, welcoming orbit. I held the door open for her.

"Let's go."

We walked for several blocks, chatting about the slam.

"So what was that you said in your poem? The something of your breast?"

"My ecstatic saliva swirling on the whorl of your breast."

"That's fucking hot." Her grin was enthusiastic.

I laughed.

"Thanks." My body tingled when she said breast. "Whorl, by the way, is kind of stretch."

"How so? I don't even think I know what that means. How do you spell it?"

I spelled it and she nodded, indicating that she knew the word.

"Whorl is really like circles, you know, a spiral kind of pattern almost."

"I get it, yeah."

I remembered that she was the one who'd given me that same word of affirmation at the end of my slam.

"You do?" I tilted my head to gauge whether her face matched her words.

"Hell, yeah, it's sexy and I can really see it," she said. "So give me the line again?"

I repeated it and she nodded.

"It's so clear, like the breast, you know, the nipple, the movement and the circles. I can picture a hand gratefully tracing the breast and, like, happy saliva. Happy because of what the mouth must have been doing to leave the saliva there. Yeah, fuck, that's good."

I laughed again. Maybe it was how closely she walked to me, but I felt as though the cold I'd been braced against suddenly had turned mild. I breathed a little deeper and relaxed my shoulders.

"What's your name?" I asked.

"Casey. Well, I go by Casey. After about 3rd grade, Cassandra didn't really fit. What about you, Slammer Number Twelve?"

"Eryn. With a y."

"Huh. Vowel stereotype just blown. Poetic spelling for a poetic woman."

I'd never thought of it that way. I liked her.

As we covered the blocks between the café and my building, I debated telling Casey that I had to work or that I needed to go home. Should I try and ditch her and get on with my day? I really, really had to pee, but bringing a stranger into the place where I work?

As we walked, Casey adjusted her pace to my shorter steps. She leaned toward me, her elbow brushing my arm. She hovered a hand above my forearm, barely touching me when the walk light turned from white to amber.

My building was a few paces away, which meant more time with Casey or a decisive good-bye. A tug in my belly forced me to decide—safe or bold?

"I work right there." I pointed. "And I really need to pee. Do you want to go in with me? Maybe we can grab lunch or something after?"

I noticed then that she had light eyes, not quite blue, but a soft grey. Her eyes evoked the feeling of a nap under light covers in a sunny room.

Casey squinted toward the building. "I'm not gonna be shy about it, I would love to spend more time with you." She chuckled. "And I really have to pee too."

While we rode the elevator, the energy between us changed from polite, still-strangers into something more, something connected. How it could happen so fast, I didn't stop to ask. When we reached the fifth floor and I stepped into my familiar, dreaded workspace, I waited for her so we could walk side by side, together. She touched my back, her fingers resting between my shoulder blades.

"Lead the way, poet."

— ✦ —

After we'd taken our bathroom break, I gave Casey a tour of the floor. It was deserted and quiet—the energy was still the same, though, as if the papers and extra sweaters and chairs held onto the tension and sluggish inertia of the staff.

"Where would you like to go?" she asked, absently poking buttons on the multi-function printer. The building operated on a low-energy system on the weekends, so the common areas were fairly dark and the large machines, normally buzzing with work, were not just still, but powered down.

"I would say I know this great coffee shop nearby…"

Casey laughed. "I think I've had plenty of coffee." She stepped closer and lifted a length of my hair from my shoulder. She tugged my curl through her fingers, pinching the end of the strand with her thumb and index finger.

I remembered something else Dennie taught us.

"When you aren't sure how to tell the truth, tell a lie," she would say. "If you lie just right, the truth will come through."

I told the boldest lie that I could. "I don't think we should do this here."

"Okaaay…" Casey stuffed her hands in her pockets and stepped away from me.

"Emphasis on *here*," I stressed. "Let's go to a conference room."

I chose a windowless conference room at the far end of the floor. On the off chance someone did come in to work, it was unlikely anyone would go to a conference room, but I chose the least appealing space on the floor just in case. I shut the door behind us and left the lights off. The room was dark, but a strong ray of late morning sun slipped past the cracks where the wood met the metal jamb. As my eyes adjusted, I could make out the contours of Casey's face and body, but not the details.

I dropped my messenger bag on the floor and pulled off my sweater. I could hear Casey take a few tentative steps toward me. Her hand reached for my waist. I fit myself against her.

"Whorl," she whispered, taking the weight of me in her palm.

"Ecstatic," I said.

Our mouths met in the dark and our first kiss wasn't tentative—it was ravenous. I opened my lips and Casey's tongue teased and plunged against mine, the taste of our coffee mingled on our breath. I reached for the back of Casey's neck. The soft stubble of her haircut tickled my fingertips as I scratched my way from her neck to the gentle curve of the back of her head.

Casey leaned her weight against me, my back pressing up against the closed conference room. She slid one leg in between mine, and my knees admitted hers. My hands trembled as I touched the length of her arms, the points of her elbows. I was delighted in a way that rivaled the high I'd experienced performing my most personal poetry just an hour ago. I laced my warm fingers through hers.

I drew rapid breaths to bring the sweet smells and tastes of her deeply into my mouth.

Casey trailed long, slow kisses along my jaw. Her teeth teased my skin. I felt her lips taste my earlobe as though I were so delicious she wanted to savor even the smallest parts of me. Her moans against my ear quivered the hairs on my arms.

"Casey." I panted her name, fumbling with the button on my jeans. "Touch me."

She tugged at my waistband and slipped her fingers inside my pants to stroke the front of my satin panties.

"Eryn." Her breathlessness mirrored mine. "You're so wet." Her fingertips traced a poem over the damp fabric. She kneeled in front me and tugged my jeans down around my ankles.

I slipped off my Vans and stepped out of my jeans. Cool air seeped into the space between us.

Agonizing strokes saturated me with need. Casey teased her way into my panties. She pressed her thumb to my clit as she swept her fingertips against my drenched folds. Thought faded into feeling as my consciousness centered on Casey's gentle probing.

Gone were words or hopes or my performance high. My awareness became as focused as a pinpoint of starlight in a black night. Casey. At her touch, my body grew from a concentrated throb to a pulsing need as large as a planet.

Just as I found her predictable orbit, Casey withdrew her fingers and offered her hand, wet with my juices. I sucked her fingers, swallowing my own metallic taste. Casey's tongue swept mine. Our moans met in the space our mouths formed when we opened to each other.

"You taste amazing," she breathed.

"Please…" I begged. I wanted to go back to that place where her touch was a galaxy of lights in the darkness.

She obliged, fucking me with strokes as rapid as my racing pulse. Her mouth never left mine. I crumbled against her, my strength focused on the tempo building in my core. I rode her fingers until I came, my cries of pleasure dissolving against her smile.

"Your turn" I whispered. "Conference table or floor?"

"Whoa," she said. "So I take it I need to lie down?"

"Please."

"I choose floor." She carefully sat on the rough carpet. I kneeled next to her and felt for her in the dark. I could make out her long and slender shape. I grabbed my messenger bag and put it beneath her head.

"Thoughtful." I heard gratitude in her voice.

I lifted her tank top and nibbled her lean belly. I scratched my fingers along the sides of the soft skin of her waist. Kissing from her ribs to her waistband, I used the tip of my tongue to tease the intimate place below her belly button, the edges of her ribs, and up toward the flat, smooth bone between her breasts.

Her tank top bunched over her small breasts, Casey inhaled deeply as my kisses traveled up her chest. Her soft, high gasp conveyed that she would welcome a rougher touch, but I wasn't quite ready to move past teasing and tender. I tugged the tank top past the elastic band of her athletic bra with my teeth. Emboldened by the speed of her breathing, the panting that had a small audible coo at the end of each sigh, I pushed the bra toward her collarbone and took her hard nipple into my mouth.

"Eryn." It wasn't a command but a prayer.

I sucked her harder, steadying myself with my hands. Casey started to writhe just as I grew impatient to feel her, more of her.

"Off," I pleaded, reaching for her belt. She lifted her hips so I could pull down her jeans. I slipped a finger under the snug waistband of her boxer briefs and placed hot kisses against her pussy through the fabric.

Casey bent her knees and tangled her fingers in my hair.

I pulled her underwear down Casey's hipbones, slow as a caress. The faint smell of her musk hovered in the warm room.

"You're so fucking hot, Casey." I kissed from her belly button down. When I finally opened her pussy, my fingertips dappled every bit of her trimmed mound. Casey's lips were sticky with want. I explored her until her legs shook and her back arched against the conference room floor. I slid two fingers in a V-shape along the length of her drenched pussy, feeling the swell of her clit between my knuckles. Casey's orgasm bucked against my drenched hand.

After she stilled, I helped her into a sitting position. We kissed, our tongues mingling our ecstatic saliva.

She stood and pulled up her boxers and jeans. I smoothed down her bra and top.

I can only imagine how we looked as we walked out of that room, our eyes dazed by the sudden light, our hair mussed, her come drying on my palm, mine on her fingers.

We walked to the elevator in easy silence, and when the doors opened, Casey drew me in to her arms and held me, her head resting on top of mine. We had no need for words.

When the elevator reached the lobby, Casey released me, and we walked out into the city.

"Enjoy the rest of your Sunday." I squeezed her, a reluctant good-bye. I whispered in her ear.

She listened.

Casey pulled a neon-green flyer out of her back pocket. She tapped me with the announcement from Café Q, a gesture that conveyed closeness and an unspoken promise. "I can't wait to hear what you write for next Sunday, Number Twelve."

"Save me a cushion," I said.

PARADISE REWRITTEN
BY EVE FRANCIS

THE SNAKE'S TONGUE SLITHERED IN and out of its mouth. Livia walked up to the tank and bent down, peering inside the glass. Zoe watched the silhouette of the snake's body against the heat lamp and Livia's fingers spread wide against the barrier.

"What's its name?" Livia asked.

"I don't name the pets. It makes it harder to get rid of them."

Zoe folded her hands on the counter. Her gaze darted up to the clock with a grimace before she shut down the rest of the cash register. She slid the bag of money under her arm, ready to go back to the manager's room. But she stopped by the snake tank again, waiting for Livia to follow her.

"Are you ready to go?"

The hot June sun had just begun to set outside. The blinds that protected the puppies and the other pet store animals during the day were drawn. Most of the animals were asleep now, knowing that it would be another little while before nine a.m. came again and there would be someone there. Everything was asleep but the snake; they were nocturnal creatures, feeding off the energy of the night. Sometimes, when Zoe didn't want to be at her rathole apartment with too-thin walls on the other side of the noisy city, she'd study late into the night at the pet store counter, the blinds drawn and nothing but the glow of her laptop computer. It was easier to work at the pet store, especially when she was studying to be a vet. The air conditioner—and relative privacy—also helped.

Zoe watched, along with Livia, as the snake's tongue moved back and forth, sensing the ground. Zoe wondered what it would be like to sense things that way, to feel and see things through that organ above all else. How disorienting, she figured, especially when her wandering eyes had already gotten her into trouble with Livia once this semester.

Livia didn't move from the tank. Her pink tank top had ridden up, exposing her back and the ink from a tattoo. Zoe tilted her head to try and get a better look at the mark, only to pull away when the freckles on Livia's back threatened to draw her in more.

"Are you ready to go?" Zoe asked again, her voice insistent. "We're running late."

Livia laughed as she took a step back.

"I like him," she declared. She put her fingers on her mouth to reconsider. "Is it a him? It may not be. Do you know?"

From her years studying biology, Zoe knew that snakes' sex organs were inverted, kept hidden inside. You could only tell visually if a snake was male or female by context: a female's tail was thinner, not as long as a male's. From what Zoe saw of the snake next to Livia's hand against the glass, she figured they were looking at a female snake. But it was only a passing thought.

More than anything, Zoe knew from the Bible and from growing up in the South just how tempting those snakes were—no matter what was held underneath the scales. Snakes were either tempting Eve for knowledge in the Bible, or their brightly colored scales and low hisses were drawing Zoe in as a child. She had been warned, from a young age, to always wear boots when she went outside into her backyard. *Snakes don't bite above the ankle*, she heard her mother's voice in her mind often, so much that the first month she worked at the pet store she wore her combat boots without question. Now she had become comfortable with always having snakes around—probably too comfortable.

"No," Zoe said, looking up at Livia again. "I don't know. What does it matter?"

"Okay, okay," Livia said, flipping her hair to the side. She turned away from the tank, leaning her back against the counter and the warm light from the snake's cage. She smiled, her eyes rolling back in her head as she appreciated the heat on her back.

"This place must seem like an oasis to the animals. All their needs are met, and people come in to worship them day in and day out."

"I don't really think the animals have much existential angst," Zoe said. "I also don't think they really have that good of a life here. It's hardly worship if you're kept in captivity."

95

The two of them began to walk towards the back. Zoe shut off the lights as she went and programed the alarm for the front door. Some of the cats paced in their cages, while others merely stretched their legs with their eyes still closed. A guinea pig with brown and orangey red patches all over its body chomped down on its metal water feeder and made a clanking sound that Zoe had gotten used to. Livia jumped at the sudden noise.

"Yeah, sorry." Zoe stood just outside the manager's door. "I keep telling Gabrielle to get plastic water bottles, but she resists. You get used to it."

"It sounds like a typewriter," Livia yelped with an amused smile. "A million guinea pigs and maybe they'll produce Shakespeare!"

"Maybe," Zoe said with a roll of her eyes. She dug into her pockets for the keys, balancing everything under her arm. "I'm almost done. Just give me two secs."

"It's okay, Zoe," Livia said with another sly smile. "We have all night, remember?"

Zoe swallowed. She shoved her key inside the manager's door and flicked the lights on. She spotted the black safe at the back and the receipt binder. She flipped through the old, thin paperwork as Livia leaned against the small shelf where the employee manuals were kept, along with basic biology text books. All the texts were out-of-date editions. Zoe was pretty sure the local California high school had gotten rid of them in the Dumpster at the side of the road, but one of the former cashiers had brought them in for resources. The textbooks probably still had sections of Creationism in them, or parts where they discussed how evolution was still 'just a theory'.

Zoe opened the safe and put the money inside, verifying several times the numbers on her receipt. The number *666* stared back at Zoe as the final tally of the day. Livia appeared over her shoulder, her breath hot on Zoe's neck.

"The number of the beast, huh?" Livia hissed. "Seems appropriate."

"Don't be so superstitious," Zoe said, filing the receipts away and then shutting the safe door.

"Why not? Seems like the most appropriate place, since I'm feeling lucky to finally see you again," Livia said, her eyes locking strongly on Zoe. "It's been a long time, Zoe. I've hardly seen you all semester."

"I've been busy."

"Uh-huh. I can see that. But you hiding away in this little Eden has only made temptation that much stronger. And I miss you. Do you miss me?"

Zoe blushed. She turned away and closed the safe. "I haven't thought about it much."

"Oh, sin number one: lies."

"I mean," Zoe corrected, lip trembling. The thought of sin in any kind, even if Zoe had renounced God and all of her Baptist upbringing, still made her flinch. Sin was the worst insult, the highest threat. Zoe felt her skin bristle with heat, as if already scorched.

The air conditioner rattled on. Zoe breathed a sigh of relief as she saw Livia's eyes flash away from her, allowing Zoe a small reprieve. Livia liked toying with Zoe. She didn't believe in sin, let alone Eden, any more than anyone else from California. But right from the start, Livia had zoomed in on Zoe's religion neurosis. Even without talking about their childhoods, Livia had sensed her weak spot like it was an Achilles heel.

"Come on," Livia said, stepping closer. "Did you miss me?"

Zoe clenched her jaw. This close, Livia was a few inches taller than her. Zoe's small shoulders and tiny hands made her look younger than her twenty-five years. Livia was twenty-nine, though she seemed to hold onto her youthful years as if they could never end. Zoe was convinced that Livia had only gone back to school to feel young again. According to Livia, she had spent so much of her adolescence and early twenties working crummy jobs across the country as her family moved that she had really had no "youthful" experiences. Moving to California and registering in a college class was her form of teenage rebellion—ten years later.

"Yes," Zoe finally admitted. "I did miss you. It was easier to study bio with another person around."

"So I could be your good example?"

"So we could share some of the reading burden. They assign so much, and with all the work I had to do here…"

"It was nice to have a friend. Sure, I get it."

Livia backed up a couple steps. Though she appeared to be letting the issue go, Zoe knew that nothing was ever so simple with Livia, who now folded her arms over her chest, making her cleavage deeper in her small tank top. If Zoe got any closer, she could look down her shirt. Zoe knew that even that was part of Livia's grand design.

"Well, I guess you're ready to go," Zoe stated. "Where are we heading tonight?"

"How about… Johnny's? The bar over on…"

"I know where it is."

"Oh, good," Livia said, her eyes bright. "I was thinking you had forgotten."

Zoe sighed. No, of course not. Biology class at the local college was not their complete origin story. Johnny's Bar, the one where frat boys hung out, was the real beginning. It was there, after recognizing one another from the bio classroom, that they did the unthinkable: they made out for free shots.

At first, Zoe thought their make out session was something that she did to survive; going to school wasn't cheap. She wanted to be a vet, and it was one of the few jobs in the medical industry that really didn't have a high return on the initial investment. Caring for animals was not like being a brain surgeon, as far as money went. Zoe had student loans. She had a car with an insurance deductible and ridiculous medical bills from her mother's cancer to contend with. When Zoe was able to go out, she couldn't afford drinks. She could barely afford time away from this shitty job at the local pet store where she knew some kids were buying hamsters just to blow them up around the corner for shits and giggles. She hated this life, but she thought Livia was okay and pretty enough. Livia's hands on the small of her back at the bar had made Zoe feel safe, so when the offer was put on the table, she couldn't help but nod along.

And so, at the crowded bar, when the lights were really hot and the men were cheering them on, Zoe had made out with Livia. But she had thought that would be it. She had never expected herself to enjoy it and then want to do it again, but without frat boys cheering her on. She wanted to do it again, with just her and Livia, and see what could happen.

But Zoe was busy. She had tried to put the event from her mind and get on with her life. Then, about a month ago, Livia had walked by the pet shop window and spotted Zoe from outside. Even on that first visit, Livia had moved towards the snake tank as if it was the only creature in the room.

Even though Zoe was no longer in school, Livia had still found her, randomly, in this pet store. But it didn't feel random; it felt like fate, fate like that which must have befallen Eve in the Garden, surrounded by beautiful creatures that were ultimately trapped.

Livia took another step forward and placed her hands on Zoe's waist. Zoe swallowed hard, not backing up.

"Or maybe we could stay here," Livia suggested. "There is no one here to watch us. Just the animals. Just the snake."

Zoe felt her body warm around Livia's hands. Soon, Livia began to run one of her fingers over Zoe's skin. She touched the collar of Zoe's black uniform shirt, loosely buttoned over a tank top. At first, Zoe thought Livia was caressing the logo of the pet store embroidered on the fabric. But the way she traced her fingers lightly, Zoe knew it was her clavicle that Livia was after. She moved her delicate fingers over the bone, then down, over each one of Zoe's ribs. She touched her bones over her skin and fabric, whispering the names of the ribs in between small touches.

Zoe stood frozen. She felt herself being made; her body turned to putty and then became hard again.

"You know, they say Eve was made from Adam."

"Yeah," Zoe gasped. "And?"

"I think that's a lie."

"No kidding," Zoe said with a small laugh. "You're a biology major too, Livia. You should know that's just a story. As much as people want to believe, science involves real, empirical evidence. Like the kind you get through clinical trials and lab reports. Even a history major is lost to a time before words existed on paper. Everything they piece together is like a bad game of broken telephone. The stories aren't real. They're just..."

"Restricting," Livia said with another smile. "Are you done your little rant, Zoe?"

"Um. Sorry. I didn't realize I was..."

"It's okay," Livia said. "I like it when you talk. You've been so quiet the past little while that I was pretty much relishing the sound of your voice."

Before Zoe could respond, Livia was speaking again, her eyes turned towards the animal cages. "But I suppose you're right in some way. I know that these stories aren't real—not in the scientific sense. But people still treat them like they are real, and that's where I want to come in. I want to mix up their expectations a little bit, you know?"

Zoe swallowed hard. She had dealt with expectations her whole life. She wasn't sure how much wiggle room there really was. As much as she wanted Livia, there was still the outside world to contend with and what people would think. Zoe liked to spend her nights in quiet reflection alone in the pet shop for that very reason. To have anything else beyond that seemed like a dream.

"Sure," Zoe finally mumbled. "I guess."

Livia narrowed her eyes at Zoe before she took a step towards her. Livia ran her thumb along Zoe's ribs, following the curve of her body until her hands rested on Zoe's lower back, pulling her close again. "You need to relax."

"I'm fine. I just want to go."

"Why would you want to leave here?" Livia asked. "You have everything you ever wanted."

Livia kissed Zoe's neck then, soft and supple. She threaded one of her hands through Zoe's hair, pulling it back gently to expose more of her neck. Zoe trembled. She felt the slow pecks of Livia's dark lips. They were gentle, as if she had never touched her before and was sure she would break. When Zoe did feel Livia's tongue against her skin, she swore it was forked.

"There is no one here watching us." Livia whispered again, just by Zoe's ear. "No one but the animals."

Livia pulled back from Zoe and looked directly at her lips. Zoe could still feel the heat of Livia's whisper on her skin as she moved in for a kiss. Zoe opened her mouth almost instantly. She felt a great heat start from the center of her body and move outwards, overwhelming her. Livia's body against hers was like Eden, like the beginning of her life. And yes, she confirmed, as their tongues moved together: she was absolutely positive Livia's was fork-like. Zoe knew she would give into temptation again and again.

"What were you saying?" Zoe pulled away for a moment. Their foreheads touched, mouths panting frustrated breaths. "About Adam and Eve?"

"Right. I don't think Eve came out of Adam."

"All right. Was it the other way around?"

Livia smiled then, her eyes wide like saucers. "No. I think it was always two women in the Garden, always two women who brought the earth to life."

Zoe thought about this. It had been a long, long time since she had gone to Bible school and learned all the origin stories. She soon remembered that Adam's first wife was Lilith and that she was cast out of The Garden after refusing to lie down and submit to Adam. Maybe it could have been Eve and Lilith, all along, then. Most Bible stories did feel like gossip and like watching soap operas on TV. There was a dream like logic to all of it, spliced together with symbols and vignettes that were supposed to mean something.

But if there was one thing Zoe did know for sure from the Bible, it was how alluring paradise was. And how addictive the feeling of pleasure, in and outside of the body, could be.

"Maybe," Zoe allowed. "That's an interesting theory."

"But just a theory. Nothing important or permanent."

Livia winked. She backed away a little bit as she reached for the light in the manager's room. Silently, she lifted her eyebrows and offered to shut it off. Zoe nodded, feeling herself relax again.

Going, Zoe thought. Okay, good, we're really going this time. Anything more, and she feared she would explode.

The quiet overwhelmed her as they walked out of the manager's office. Through the slatted blinds, Zoe could see the sun setting. It was still a long way off from night-time, and the bar's atmosphere would be mediocre right now. Not too many people, just the pathetic ones who spent their Friday afternoons and paychecks on stools, wishing for a better life. The air conditioner came on again and reminded Zoe of how hot it was outside the glass doors.

I want to stay, she thought suddenly. I want to stay inside of paradise.

"What are you thinking?" Livia asked, looking behind at Zoe. "You've got a look to your eye."

Zoe smiled. "Nothing."

"Liar. You can't lie to me. Not anymore. I know you too well in here. You are yourself here."

Zoe sighed. She slowed her pace as she walked, running her hands along the edges of some cages around them. A rabbit stared out, along with a couple hamsters and rats. Cats and dogs paced, some mewling quietly. They all silenced themselves when Zoe's eyes met their trapped gazes.

"I was just thinking that all creatures need to be taken care of. All creatures desire life."

"Including us," Livia said.

Livia stopped in front of the pet store door. She turned around slowly, a sly smile on her face. Zoe paused too, knowing what this meant. She didn't flinch this time when Livia's hands moved to her waist. Instead, she relished the touch and savored how fiercely her fingers moved. From her waist, Livia's hands soon moved to Zoe's ass, gripping her and pulling her forward.

Zoe moved with it. She allowed herself to pull Livia's dark hair over her shoulders, exposing her tanned neck in the same way. She had only planted two careful kisses on her skin when she heard Livia laugh.

Zoe turned to see the snake behind them, up from her rock, watching them through the glass cage.

"The final temptation," Livia said. She clasped Zoe's hand in her own, and tugged her towards the tank. They stood by one another, looking down as the snake's mouth parted and its tongue moved forward.

"Too bad paradise was made by men who believed women should be punished."

There was a hitch to Livia's voice, long and mercurial, that made Zoe lean closer.

"And what are you suggesting? What's the solution?"

"Don't rebel against the story. Rewrite it."

When Livia raised her eyes from the snake, Zoe understood: if you didn't like your surroundings, change them; believe in something different. If Eve didn't come from Adam's rib, maybe she sprung up out of the water, fully formed, and walked into The Garden of Eden. There, maybe she found Adam's first wife, Lilith, and together they ruled. What if it had been two women in the Garden—would they still be tempted by the snake?

Livia leaned down and tapped on the cage. "I always wondered what they would feel like, you know? If their tongue is what they use to smell and sense, how would they feel me? What would I feel like to them?"

"Take her out. Find out," Zoe said.

Livia looked back at her, her eyes wide. "So it is a she?"

Zoe hesitated for a second before she nodded. She still wasn't quite sure if the snake was male or female, but she had never been more sure in that moment that what she believed, what she truly wanted, could be true.

"She won't hurt me?"

"No," Zoe said. She looked back at the snake's green and black skin. A common garter snake. Something that most people drove out of their tulips during the spring, that the store kept safe and sold for $4.99. "No, she's benign. She only looks scary."

"You sure?"

"Yes," Zoe said, a smile on her face. "I've read enough about her to know the real story."

Livia nodded. She removed the barrier, reached her hand in, and allowed the snake to writhe between her two fingers before she lifted her up. Livia's mouth opened, gleeful and happy at the sensation. She held the snake in two open palms before she placed her around her neck. Livia took a step closer to Zoe, placing her hands on her hips, as the snake rested over her body.

"What do you think?" Livia asked. "Do you trust me?"

Zoe nodded. She barely took her eyes off the snake's body, before she pressed her lips against Livia's again. She tasted sweet, not bitter like she had when they had made out at the bar. Everything was softer, easier now. Zoe moved her body closer, touching their hips as her mouth remained open and their tongues remained urgent. Zoe felt the snake move from Livia's body to hers, wrapping around her tightly. Zoe knew the snake would not suffocate them. If anything, she felt like the snake was protecting them.

"Do you hear her?" Livia asked. She pulled away only slightly, her lips still touching Zoe's trembling ones. "I hear her."

"What does she say?"

"Listen for yourself."

Livia combed a hand through Zoe's hair, and then placed the head of the snake close by her ears. Zoe could hear the dry hum and hiss of the snakes from her backyard in her mind and her mother's old warning. But the snake here in her hands was quiet and calm. Zoe felt the snake's tongue touch her skin and laughed. She felt so much joy radiating inside of her as she stared at Livia, and the snake continued to move.

They were alone, she realized. Truly, this time. No one was watching but the snake and the animals who circled their cages. The guinea pig bit its water bottle, making loud typewriter sounds, and Zoe imagined he was rewriting their origin story. The snake hung close by, over both of their shoulders now, pulling them closer and binding them together.

Slowly, they begin to kiss again. As she felt Livia's tongue inside of her, she felt the same way a snake did: Zoe felt as if she could understand the entire world with their bodies, and in a way, that was right. For the night, they would remain perfectly safe. Away from smog and light pollution, away from LA traffic, and student debt. It was just them. It was just the animals. And the beginning of something new.

"Take off your clothing," Livia whispered. "I want to taste every last bit of you."

Zoe moved the snake from between their bodies and placed her on the counter. The snake slithered between the open biology textbook near the register. Its body rested inside a few crumpled bills, her skin green like the cash. Zoe was not worried about the mice or hamsters. It would take too long for the snake to reach them. Instead, she would explore the machines and the books, as if she were an emblem of the new world order.

Zoe watched as Livia slid her skinny tank top straps down her shoulders. The pink fabric moved effortlessly, only getting caught on her breasts. Livia arched her back, knocking the fabric off them with only the slightest effort.

She was wearing a thin bra, one that left very little to the imagination. Her nipples were hard, her skin pale through the bra.

"Come here," Livia said.

Zoe obeyed. She cupped her hands around Livia's breasts, touching her thumbs over her nipples. She saw the beginning of a floral tattoo on Livia's side; a cherry blossom tree wrapped around the small of her back and part of her hips, marking her skin pink and beautiful. Zoe's fingers moved over the ink before she touched Livia's breasts again.

"Take everything off," Livia demanded as her hands moved towards Zoe's waist. She slid a hand between her thighs, rubbing against Zoe's clit through layers of unwanted fabric.

"Come on," Livia repeated. "Show me what you want. Show me what you like."

"Silence," Zoe said, placing her lips over Livia's mouth. She kissed her, allowing their tongues to touch only briefly before she pulled away. "I like silence more than anything. In the Garden, with only one another, there was no need to speak."

Livia grinned. She bit her lip and nodded. In her mind, Zoe could hear a faint nod of *as you wish* under Livia's tongue, like a fairy tale. But everything was muted. Everything became focused on the edge of her own tongue as she ran it from Livia's clavicle towards her breasts, sliding off the bra as she went.

The room throbbed. The hearts of animals sounded inside Zoe's ear like a steam engine, like something she could not control. Zoe continued to suck on Livia's breasts, hearing her heart beat slower than the animals'. Livia's skin broke out in gooseflesh as Zoe left a small trail with her tongue. Her hand spread out over Livia's body, as Livia's hands found the edge of Zoe's shirt and began to tug. She continued to taste Livia's fair skin, sucking the nipples and smelling the soft scent of her cranberry lotion before Zoe relinquished some control and allowed her shirt to be taken off.

Livia's breasts bounced with each movement. She was thin, supple, and yearning for more. As she removed Zoe's shirt, she smiled, showing off a perfect mouth and great teeth. She made silent *O* formations with her lips, and then discarded the shirt on the ground.

"You're beautiful," Livia said, and bit her lip. She mouthed the same words again.

"You too," Zoe mouthed back. She stepped forward, renewed and energized. Sliding a hand around Livia's back, she grabbed her ass for stability as she began to undo her pants. When there was enough room, she slid a finger deep down. The heat was welcoming—then the wetness was too. Livia gripped onto her arm, overwhelmed by Zoe's fingers suddenly moving against her clit.

Livia breathed and moaned into Zoe's ears. And Zoe allowed her fingers to continue working, egged on by each utterance. The body was so easy to explore, and Livia was so beautiful to touch. Zoe still wore her bra and her pants, but she felt naked next to Livia's skin.

Livia only lost herself for a few moments in the caress. Then, as she opened her thinly lidded eyes, she spotted Zoe's breasts. She slid a hand forward, kissing Zoe's neck as she did, and pushed her breasts free. Zoe's pert nipples felt cool in the sudden air. She let out a low groan at the back of her throat, and tried to keep moving as she ran another finger next to Livia's clit. She longed to find the right angle to go inside and really make Livia beg. But the sensations in her own body overwhelmed her.

Livia bent to her knees, hissing as her bare skin hit the tile floor. She tore away the rest of Zoe's bra and slid her own pants down as she moved. She looked up at Zoe as her hands moved around Zoe's waist, undoing her pants.

"Like that?" She mouthed the words.

"Yes," Zoe said back. "Like that."

Livia looked up at Zoe's now-visible black underwear, a smile forming on her face before she slid those down too. A small flash of red, almost copper, pubic hair emerged, along with Zoe's gasping breath. Livia kept her eyes on Zoe as long as she could, even as she began to tease her by touching her clit. Zoe moaned. She closed her eyes as she felt Livia's tongue over her.

"Fuck-fuck-fuck." Livia was exploring her with precision; she must have done this before; she had to have. There was no way someone could hit all the right spots without careful practice. Zoe opened an eye as her thighs were spread wider, Livia inserting a finger as she worked. She was focused, keen, and aware, but she also trembled as if with slight nerves.

No, Zoe thought. This has to be the first time. They have both just been so utterly dissatisfied with life all around them, that suddenly turning towards one another rewrites all past history. Yes, she told herself again. This is the first time. Zoe felt the cool flick of Livia's tongue over her, sucking her, and felt as if she would fall. She could lose her balance completely, and then crash down on the ground, losing paradise as she went.

Zoe opened her eyes and spotted the snake watching them, her tongue firing out of her mouth with the same beat and precision that Livia did. Zoe swallowed and grasped Livia's shoulders.

"Move," she said. "We should move."

"Where?"

"The counter," Zoe said. "I want to see you too."

They scrambled only for a moment. Zoe stepped out of her pants completely, and then as Livia's back was turned, Zoe approached and helped her slide off her clothing. From behind, Zoe ran her fingers along Livia's clit. She rubbed her with sudden fast movements and welcomed Livia's ass pressing into her body, warm and strong.

"Fuck," Livia said. Zoe moved her fingers faster. She kissed Livia's neck, sucking hard on the skin as she willed her fingers to move even faster. Livia panted, and Zoe smiled into her skin before she let her go.

"Fuck," Livia said again. She turned around, ready to attack Zoe with more kisses and touching, but Zoe was too fast. She had already slid a finger against her own clit, her palm rocking into her hips.

"Go on," Zoe encouraged. "I want to see you."

Livia smiled, nodding slightly as she went over and sat atop the counter. Naked, she leaned back on her elbows. When Zoe approached, she spread her legs again. Zoe placed her hands against her chest to prevent her breasts from hitting the cold counter as she placed her face between Livia's legs. She spread Livia's thighs more with the palm of her hand. Zoe sucked and licked, feeling Livia's wetness against her neck. She could hear the slow hiss of the snake in her mind, and again, Zoe advanced towards Livia's body like it was a vast desert plane and they were in the middle of the Mojave.

"Fuck." Livia moved her hands through Zoe's hair, tugging on her in moments of extreme duress. "I'm going to come."

Zoe pulled away after giving her another small suck. Livia let out a low groan, angry at what was just cut short. Her annoyance left as she watched Zoe climb onto the counter too.

Zoe's legs moved to either side of Livia's body, straddling her as she looked down. Livia reached up and ran a finger over Zoe's clit. Zoe allowed herself to get close to orgasm before she backed away. Livia's green eyes moved wildly, looking excited and ravenous as she watched Zoe.

When Zoe turned around, her face between Livia's legs again and her pussy over Livia, there was only a moment's gap before they both understood. They began to work again, taking the other with tongue and fingers. Livia moved her hands over Zoe's sides, occasionally moving her fingers to spread Zoe wider so her tongue could tackle more. Zoe lost herself in the wet heat of Livia and how she felt against her tongue. Sometimes, Zoe bit Livia's thigh. Softly, subtly, as if it were a forbidden fruit itself.

When Zoe looked up, she saw the snake watching them. She was over towards the front of the window, where the blinds were tightly shut. A small crack let light inside, and it pooled at the front where the snake had kept herself. Towards the hottest part of the building, the snake would rest happily. Zoe only had a moment to think before she felt her body being brought closer and closer to orgasm.

"Fuck," Zoe murmured against Livia's pussy—and she heard "fuck" murmured against her own. Zoe moved her hips against Livia's tongue, and then moved her tongue against Livia. Forwards and back, they rocked as they continued to pleasure the other. Together, their bodies made the Ouroboros, a snake eating itself at the head and tail, no ending and no beginning. Zoe relished this thought as her body shook with orgasm and wetness trailed her thighs.

Even as Zoe came, hard and fast, as Livia's tongue worked, she didn't feel sad. She pressed her tongue into Livia and brought her to orgasm short and quick.

"Fuck," Livia echoed. Her hands squeezed Zoe's skin and then let go. Together, both women panted and waited in stasis until their hearts evened out. The guinea pigs chomped down on their water bottles, the cats mewled, and the snake started to hiss. Everything inside the pet store, even the two women on the counter, seemed back to normal after only a few seconds.

Zoe turned around and looked at Livia, bringing their lips together.

"How was that?" Zoe moved her light hair over her head and tried to lie next to Livia on the counter. They balanced precariously on the edge, hands linked.

"Not bad for a first time." Livia smiled. She traced her finger over Zoe's lips and then pulled at her chin. They kissed, bodies moving even closer together on the counter.

"We can go again," Zoe said with a smirk. "It'll only get better from here."

Livia laughed. She seemed to see the dark spark in Zoe's eyes, because she became serious once again.

"Of course. I wouldn't dream of it any other way." Livia placed her lips over Zoe's again, her tongue tracing a new pattern against her skin. "But let's put the snake back first."

THE LONGEST NIGHT

BY RONNIE WILLOWS

TWENTY-FIRST OF DECEMBER. THE LONGEST night. Darkness reigns and light fails, however briefly.

It was the darkness Lacey craved. The night wrapped around her like a cloak made of lust, desperation, and onyx sensuality. She needed it so badly, it would have brought her to her knees. But that position was for later.

She entered the seedy leather bar, knowing full well how rarely women went there, and the kind of woman she wanted was rarer yet. But surely on the longest night, her luck would hold.

Lacey made her way to the bar and smoothed down her tight leather skirt, barely long enough to conceal the fact that she didn't have on panties. She noticed a slight scuff on the toe of her stiletto and grimaced inwardly. She wanted to be perfect tonight. She'd decided not to flag, in the hopes that someone, a special someone, would ask instead of simply deciding they weren't interested in her chosen Crayola. With the black sheer top and the black skirt and heels, she hoped that flagged enough.

The rough leather of the barstool was cold against the back of her thighs, and she shivered in anticipation.

The hairs prickled on the back of her neck. Yes. She could feel her, could feel her staring. The one Lacey wanted was here tonight. She steadied herself and settled in to wait.

After ordering her Sex on the Beach, she turned to scan the room. Mist from the fog machine provided for a modicum of privacy. She saw mostly shadows dancing in vapor, silhouettes shrouded in an erotic embrace. She breathed in deep, sucking the scent of sweat-laden desire and well-worn leather into her soul. Taking a sip, she let the citrus flavor mingle with the sense of expectation on her tongue.

A hand slid over her lower back, the touch firm, sure. The cologne was somewhere between musky and spicy, and she instantly began to salivate.

"I can feel your need bleeding off you."

The voice. Laced with sex and the promise of agonizing pleasure.

"How do you know it's mine and not from one of these other people?" she asked more bravely than she felt. Hot breath tickled the hairs on the back of her neck as the stranger breathed her in like a fine wine.

"Am I wrong? Tell me I am, and I'll leave you alone."

The firm hand began to slide away, and she nearly lost her poise. "No. You're not wrong. I just wanted to know."

The hand returned, and she gave a quick, silent thanks. This wasn't a game she wanted to lose.

"It doesn't matter. I can." The stranger's hand slid up her spine to the back of her neck. "You're not flagging."

It wasn't a question, so she didn't answer. She simply raised an eyebrow and shrugged slightly. She still hadn't turned to face her, but she could feel her stare.

The hand squeezed her neck, and she sucked in a quiet breath. The stranger chuckled.

"That's a dangerous game. At least tell me right or left."

"Does it matter?"

The hand squeezed tighter. "Tonight it does. Tomorrow, maybe not."

"No tomorrow. Just now."

"Even so."

She took a risk and turned to face the stranger. What she saw was a wet dream made flesh. Tall, but not too tall, encased in a tight black tank and tighter black jeans, her muscles straining against the fabric. Perfect lips grinned at her over small straight teeth. Her eyes were hidden by the dim lighting, and all Lacey could see in them was lust.

"Figure it out," she said, tilting her head and breathing deep to push her cleavage forward.

Long fingers dug into her exposed neck, and the other hand slid from her thigh to her calf. "I don't have to." Her fingertips caressed the kanji tattoo on Lacey's inner ankle. "I know what it says. But the placement puzzles me."

Busted. The slave tattoo usually passed by unnoticed. That the stranger not only recognized it but also knew it was on the wrong ankle impressed her. "Maybe it's meant to. Maybe things aren't that simple."

The stranger gave her a cocky grin, and her nails scraped along Lacey's collarbone. "Then tonight, I decide. I'm Devon, by the way." With a tug, she pulled her from the stool and led her from the bar by the back of her neck. In the parking lot, they stopped next to a large black-and-chrome bike. It made Lacey think of the kind of thing a demon would ride. Devon reached into her saddlebag and pulled out a choke chain and leash.

"Kneel."

She did, dropping to the cold gravel as gracefully as she could. The cold chain slipped over her head, and the icy metal burned against her neck. The click of the leash sounded like thunder in the empty night. Devon handed her a helmet. "Don't want anything happening to that pretty face."

Lacey slipped it on and hoped it wouldn't mess up her hair too badly when she took it off. "Where are we going?"

Devon tugged on the strap under her chin to make sure the helmet was tight before she closed her hand gently around Lacey's throat. "Does it matter?" She looped the leash handle over her wrist and turned to get on the bike.

She shook her head, though Devon hadn't waited for an answer, and climbed onto the bike. The tug and pull of the leash and chain connected directly to her pulsing clit. No, it didn't matter. She wanted whatever this woman had to give, and she'd be damned if anything would stop her now. Whether it was a soft bed or an empty warehouse, she'd gladly follow. She climbed onto the back, her legs open, her skirt pulled high and tight. The vibration of the bike combined with anticipation and desire, and she felt a momentary bit of guilt that she was going to get the seat messy. But as soon as they took off, the guilt was quickly replaced by deep, longing need. She wanted to be craved, devoured. Lacey wanted someone to look at her as though they needed to crawl under her skin, make her scream with pleasure from the inside. She wanted that look of pure lust aimed solely at her. Most of all, she wanted to submit. To be used to the point of being undone, body and soul.

She felt the flat stomach muscles contract under her hands as Devon maneuvered the bike deftly down empty streets. She pulled up in front of a brick building, keyed in a code to open the wire fence, and drove around the back. Lacey climbed off, biting back the smile that threatened when she saw the wet patch on the bike's leather seat. When Devon got off and hung their helmets from the handlebars, she wiped the wet patch with her palm, then turned and clamped it over Lacey's mouth.

"You got my bike dirty. Not that it hasn't happened before with plenty of other women, but usually it's while I'm fucking them. Not before I even get there. Dirty bitch."

The slight smile around Devon's eyes let Lacey know she wasn't overly serious, which put her at ease. She realized just how alone—and vulnerable—she was. And while that added to the excitement of it, it also added a genuine flutter of fear. Devon tugged on the leash and led her into the building. *I need this. I'm not going to run scared.*

The heavy metal door opened soundlessly, and she followed Devon inside, noting the small tight ass and perfect shoulders. Strong. This woman looked strong and capable.

Once inside, Devon turned to her. With a tug on the leash, she pulled her to her knees. "Stay." She looped the leash handle to a hook in the wall.

Lacey bowed her head in acknowledgment, the wood panel flooring smooth and unforgiving under her knees. Devon walked away, and Lacey could hear lights being turned on, doors opening and closing. She'd been left in a hallway with beautiful black-and-white photos of nudes on the walls. There was a door directly in front of her and one a few feet to her left. The door in front of her opened just as her knees began to complain, and she caught a glimpse of a cozy but classy living room. The door closed, and all she could focus on were the heavy black boots.

A tug on her leash brought her to her feet, and she followed Devon through the door on her left. Steep stone stairs led down into a dimly lit basement. At the top of the stairs, Devon turned to her and cupped her face in her hands.

"If you want to stop, now would be a good time to say so. Once we're down there, I won't be listening to anything but your body."

Any lingering doubt or fear fled, replaced with overwhelming lust. "Please," Lacey said, leaning forward to brush their lips together. Devon's soft groan preceded a sharp pull on the leash, and she led the way downstairs. At the bottom, Lacey was allowed to stop for a moment to take it all in. Her knees nearly buckled in amazement.

Serious BDSM equipment covered the room. Stocks, a rack, a cross. Fucking machines, sawhorses, leather-topped benches of various sizes. Chains attached to pulley systems hung from heavy wood beams. And in the corner, a small, intimate space with couches sat next to a little kitchenette.

She heard the soft laugh and realized she'd been gaping. She instantly lowered her gaze respectfully, although she wanted nothing more than to run around the space like a fat kid let loose in a candy shop. Devon led her to one of the couches, and Lacey felt a moment of disappointment. Had she changed her mind? She knelt at Devon's feet and waited for what seemed eons before Devon spoke.

"Tell me why."

She glanced up. "Why? Why what?"

"Why are you here? Now. What do you need?"

Thrown by the question, she just shrugged.

The leash handle made a cracking sound as it hit her left breast. She gasped and jerked forward.

"Not acceptable. Answer."

She thought for a moment. "I need to submit. It's this part of me, this element that has to come out. I need to hand over control and get used. Not sex in the vanilla world. Sex in the give-me-pain-and-make-me-beg-for-it kind of way. I need to feel someone's focus and need to match my own." She stopped for a moment, overwhelmed by the sudden desperate emotion overtaking her. "I need to be wanted. Truly wanted. As though I'm the only person who can possibly satisfy, the only person capable of taking it all." She blinked back the sudden appearance of tears. "I want to feel someone taking me, filling me, using me, all because they want to, not because they feel they should do it out of obligation."

Devon's head was tilted as though she were seriously considering the answer. "Okay. And what do you like?"

Lacey swallowed past the lump of embarrassment she always got when that question came up. "Everything you want to give. I want to take what someone actually wants to give me. I've got a high pain threshold, and I particularly like floggings, and beatings in general. And deep, hard fucking." She took a deep breath to try and stem the burning in her cheeks at saying the words out loud. "No body fluid exchange or electricity. Pretty much anything else goes."

She saw Devon's eyes darken and her breathing quicken. "Safe word?"

"Sherbet."

Devon laughed. "People's safe words always amaze me. Okay, ice cream girl. Ready?"

"More than I can say."

She gasped as she was jerked to her feet and pulled to the cross. Devon quickly stripped her down to nothing but her heels, and then placed Lacey's ankles and wrists in thick leather cuffs, which were then attached to the cross.

Spread eagle, at the mercy of a top who clearly knew what she was doing, she felt herself relax against the polished wood. So many nights she had lain awake imagining something just like this. Or a version where she was the one in charge. Regardless, it was a fantasy, and as the first lash of the flogger sent silver slices of pain through her back, she'd never felt so free.

Lash after lash rained down on her back, ass, and thighs. When she began to get too high, when she started riding the magnificent waves of pain, a harder, deeper strike brought her back into the room. Just when Lacey thought she couldn't take anymore, Devon gently brought her down from the cross, only to lay her on her back on one of the high benches. She hissed as the hot welts met the cold leather. Her ankles were quickly attached to the bench legs, and her wrists were pulled high over her head and attached to something she assumed was on the floor.

"As you know, it's my needs I really want met tonight. If I manage to meet a few of yours, then that's a bonus. But right now, I want to fuck you. I've wanted to fuck you since the moment you came into the bar. And I'm tired of waiting." Devon unzipped her jeans and released an eight-inch black-and-white-marbled dildo. "I'm guessing you've been fucked with something big before, and I can see you don't need lube. I want to hear you scream for me." She pushed it into Lacey's pussy, sliding it all the way to its base with one firm, hard thrust.

If she could have arched her back, she would have, the pleasure ripping through her was so intense. But tied as she was, open and firm, all Lacey could do was feel every inch as she was fucked hard and deep. When she thought she was going to come, Devon slowed, and then rammed into her with hard, slow strokes.

"Please. Oh God. Please. Please let me come."

"Do it. But be aware I'll be fucking you all night long, so if you're one of those women who can only come once, I suggest you hold off, or it's going to be a rough night."

Lacey came with a long, low moan, squeezing tight around the enormous cock inside her. Devon squeezed her breasts, twisted her nipples, and the orgasm seemed to go on and on.

Once they'd both caught their breath, Devon slid the cock out, grinning at Lacey's moan of pain and disappointment. "Don't worry. You'll be getting more than you hoped for later." She quickly untied her and moved her so she was bent over a spanking bench. Once again her ankles were tied to the bench legs, but this time her wrists were tied to her ankles, essentially folding her in half over the bench. She saw the tails of a braided cat drag along the floor under her, and she closed her eyes.

She felt Devon's fingers slide inside her, and she moaned. Then the tails of the cat connected with the welts from the flogger, and she cried out. Over and over the cat came down on her shoulders, but Devon's rhythm fucking her never faltered. The combination of intense pleasure and pain was intoxicating, and she pushed back as much as she could against the fingers inside her. The pain turned into unbearable pleasure, and she couldn't stand the thought of it ending. When it finally did, Lacey was so high on endorphins, she barely whimpered.

"Time for you to give me mine, little one."

Devon unhooked her from the bench and carefully moved her to a kneeling bench with two metal steps on either side. Her wrists were chained to her ankles, and once again the leash was in Devon's hands. She watched as Devon removed her jeans and the strap-on, revealing tight microfiber shorts. When she pulled them off, Lacey was transfixed by the hard, muscular thighs and lightly trimmed pubic hair. Devon moved onto the metal steps, and the angle told Lacey exactly what was expected of her. The smell of hot arousal wafted from Devon's pussy, which was right at perfect mouth height.

"I think you know what to do."

Lacey leaned forward eagerly and slid her tongue over Devon's drenched pussy, stopping to lick firmly at the engorged clit. She licked and sucked, altering her motions with the moans coming from above her. She'd dreamt of being tied down and forced to suck a woman off, and now that it was happening, it was better than she could have predicted.

Devon's hips began to buck, and her hands closed hard on Lacey's head. She came hard, the juice dripping from Lacey's chin. Devon stumbled slightly as she stepped off the plates and leaned against the wall to take a long drink of water. She took another swig, then grabbed Lacey's hair and pulled her head back. She pressed their lips together and slowly fed Lacey sips of water.

"Okay?" she asked.

Lacey nodded, unable to speak through the haze of satisfaction pulsing through her.

"I'm going to make you comfortable, and then I've got something to take care of. I'll be back in a minute."

Lacey felt a moment of anxiety at the thought of being left tied down. But Devon tied her to a bolt in the floor in front of her with her hands attached to her ankles. If she really needed to, she could unhook herself. She relaxed and settled in to wait as Devon loped up the stairs.

She floated in the sex haze, feeling the welts, the throbbing of her sore pussy, the heavy weight of the cuffs, the warm metal chain around her neck. It was all so perfect. The door opened above, and as she tried to focus past the state of bliss, she realized there wasn't just one set of footsteps. She tensed even as a new wave of excitement ran up her spine.

Behind Devon, attached to a thick black leash, was a beautiful woman. Also in cuffs, she held herself with pride, even with her eyes downcast. Her hair was nearly the color of the cuffs, and her firm breasts were made to be sucked. When Devon stopped beside her, the woman instantly dropped gracefully to her knees, her head bowed, her hands on her thighs.

"This is Mia, my house slave. I thought you might enjoy getting to know one another. And I'll enjoy watching you do so." She tugged on Mia's leash. "Say hello to our guest."

Mia leaned forward, her back straight, and captured one of Lacey's nipples in her warm, inviting mouth. She sucked expertly, and Lacey was immediately captivated. Mia was tugged away, and she resumed her original position.

Devon unhooked Lacey from the bolt on the floor and moved her to another bench. Once again on her back, this time a spreader bar was placed between Lacey's ankles, holding them open. A piece of rope around each thigh attached her firmly to the bench, and she nearly moaned. When her wrists were attached to the bench legs, forcing her body as open as a book, Lacey gave in and sighed happily.

Mia crawled across the floor and knelt between her thighs. Her body was beautiful, seductive. She moved like someone who knew exactly how to get the greatest effect.

"Now Mia's going to give you a proper welcome. And I'm going to show you both what you are."

Mia's mouth was hot on her pussy, and Lacey moaned as Mia dipped and licked, sucked and bit lightly all along her slick wetness. When the riding crop came down on her stomach, she was almost too stunned to react. A millisecond later, the pain blossomed, and she cried out. When the crop came down on Mia's shoulders, her cry was muffled by the pussy in her mouth. Devon alternated, hard strikes, soft strikes, Mia, then Lacey. Breasts, thighs, stomach, back, shoulders. Nothing was safe. And through it all, Lacey got higher and higher. She came under Mia's practiced tongue, and there was a sudden deafening silence. Mia seemed to hold her breath.

"Did you just come without asking?"

The tone was one of anger and delight, and Lacey shivered. "I'm sorry. She's so good…"

"Surely you know better than that? Well, I'll teach you right now."

Mia scuttled out of the way as Devon dragged Lacey, without taking off the spreader bar, over to the low sawhorse. After securing her to it, Devon dragged over a thick padded box, which sat just below her face.

"Mia."

Mia crawled over quickly and lay faceup on the box, her pubic hair close enough to tickle Lacey's lips.

"Apologize to my girl for coming in her mouth without my permission. Do it well, and don't stop until I tell you to. Start."

Lacey began, and when the first strike of the cane flashed a line of fire across her ass, she screamed into Mia's pussy, an action which seemed to spur both of them on. Mia pushed harder against her mouth, and the cane blazed across Lacey's ass and thighs. Stripe after stripe had her screaming incoherently, even as she tried desperately not to stop sucking on Mia's sweet pussy. The fire stopped, and she let the tears fall against Mia's thighs, though she didn't stop.

Lacey moaned when she felt the head of the huge dildo press against her pussy.

"Make my girl come."

As Devon began fucking her hard, so hard it was slamming her forward on the sawhorse, Lacey sucked hard on Mia's clit. The combination of being fucked so hard while restrained and allowed to lick another slave's pussy quickly brought her to the edge. But with her mouth full, she couldn't ask permission to come. Lacey squeezed her eyes shut and tried desperately to control herself. She didn't think she could handle another round with the cane.

Mia began to beg to come, her thighs tight against Lacey's face.

"Do it."

Devon fucked her even harder, and as she cried out, Mia came hard, her hips rising from the thing she was lying on, pressing her clit hard against

Lacey's lips. Devon wound Lacey's hair around her hand and yanked her head back. "Do you want to come too?"

"Yes. Fuck, yes."

"Ask."

Devon was grunting, her thrusts brutal.

"Please may I come?"

"Yes."

She did, and as she did, she felt Devon buck against her as though she'd come as well. The thought of Devon coming from fucking her that way made Lacey's orgasm that much stronger, and she nearly sobbed with the release.

Devon pulled out slowly, allowing her to feel every hard inch. She released Lacey's hair and snapped her fingers. Mia moved languidly off her perch and crawled away. Devon unhooked Lacey from the sawhorse and walked to the stocks. She knew she was expected to follow, and she crawled behind Mia, mesmerized by the sway of Mia's perfect ass.

Devon pulled Lacey to her feet by her hair and locked her into the stocks in a kneeling position. Once again, she felt Mia slide between her legs. This time there was no instruction. She felt the flogger come down on her back and ass again, and Mia's mouth was clearly intent on getting a result. But even as Mia sucked her clit hard, she felt the rhythm change, and Lacey knew Mia was getting fucked the same way Lacey'd been fucked only moments before. Mia's moans vibrated against her clit, the flogger came down hard and fast, and within moments Lacey was already begging to come again.

"Hold it. You don't come before my slave does."

She gasped and ground down against Mia's mouth and felt Mia's body jolting from the pounding she was taking.

"Now."

She came at the same moment Mia did, their cries mingling as did the jerking of their bodies.

They all came down slowly, and this time when she was moved, it was to a large kneeling pillow with the leash snapped to a bolt in the floor. Devon moved a high-back chair to the middle of the room and motioned to Mia. As Lacey watched, Mia climbed onto the massive dildo and began to ride. The easy rhythm, the sway of her body, the way Devon held her hips but allowed her to set the pace was possibly the most sensual thing Lacey had ever seen. Sated, however, her body feeling as light as cotton candy, she simply enjoyed it rather than wanting to be a part of it.

After receiving permission, Mia arched her back as she came, her onyx hair cascading like a waterfall behind her. Devon buried her face in it as they held one another for a long moment.

"Head upstairs. I'll be with you after I've dropped her off."

Mia nodded, looking beautifully sleepy, and crawled slowly up the stairs.

Devon came and unhooked Lacey, taking the cuffs off and massaging her wrists. "You okay?"

"Perfect. Thank you."

Devon nodded and gave her a tired smile. "I'll take you back to your car."

"If you'll call me a cab, I'll just head home and get my car tomorrow. If that's okay?"

"Sure. No problem. If you want to grab a shower, there's a bathroom at the back behind the rack."

"Thanks. I'll do that."

Lacey gathered her clothes and headed for the shower. Once in, the hot water stung the many, many welts covering her shoulder to ankle, and she smiled. She hadn't felt so sated, so complete, in a long time. When she made her way back into the room, Devon smiled and waved at the door. "Your yellow chariot awaits."

She gave Devon a kiss on the cheek. "Thank you. Really. I don't..." She shrugged, unable to find the words.

"Believe me, I get it. Anytime."

Devon held the door open and Lacey headed into the night. The sky was just beginning to give way from onyx to silver, and she took in a deep breath. The longest night had been just long enough.

DOCTOR'S ORDERS
BY N.R. DUNHAM

SHE WAS NOT GOING TO get involved. Absolutely not, Kate told herself, even as her waitress dabbed at bloodshot eyes for the third time. Even while listening to her voice quiver as she confirmed that the retiree by the window would absolutely get extra tomato on his BLT, no problem. Even as the waitress dropped her pen in the middle of jotting his order, reacting as if she'd let go of a live grenade instead of a writing utensil.

Kate cringed, half at the woman muttering shaky apologies across the room, half at herself. The woman. The waitress. Julie, for God's sake. Not much use trying to distance herself now, after being on a first-name basis with the shapely redhead for over a year.

Julie was pale as she approached, missing that subtle glow Kate had come to associate with her.

Glow. Honestly. If her colleagues could read her thoughts, they'd assume she'd been pilfering drugs from the hospital stores, getting high as she read cheap romance novels.

Still, Julie's skin, fair on the best of days, was unnaturally pale. And her smile, usually so easy and genuine, was painfully false. "What can I get you?" she asked.

Kate twisted and pulled at the napkin on her lap, worry deepening. No "What's up, Doc?"—that tired old joke she heard every day of the week. No batted eyelashes as Julie inquired about the cute guys she'd "played doctor" with that day.

Kate glanced at her menu, forcing a light tone. "How about we stick with tradition? Chicken sandwich, Diet Coke."

She'd meant it as a tension breaker, but Julie didn't seem to take it that way. The next few seconds contained a rush of words and a lack of pauses for air that might've been impressive under different circumstances.

"Oh, jeez. Duh. Like you haven't ordered the same thing every time. Sorry. Really sorry. I'm not...I guess I'm not thinking today. Clearly."

"Julie. Hey. Relax. It's not a big deal."

Julie stopped talking, delicate shoulders hunched.

Kate shook her head. Julie was biting an already-swollen lip, which looked as if she'd been doing that a lot tonight. It also looked hot, or endearing, or both, and neither was acceptable.

Julie rushed off toward the kitchen, and Kate tracked her across the diner. She cut a familiar figure, one Kate had grown quite fond of. Pink socks trimmed in white lace peeked out above plain, white canvas sneakers. A glint of gold hit Kate's eye as the light touched Julie's tiny anklet, adorned with x's and o's. Long, athletic legs led up to the hem of a formfitting, pink skirt that stopped at mid-thigh. And then there was the tight, white shirt that showed off more than it concealed. Julie had worked here a long time, said that before Kate started coming in, the shirt had featured bright pink lettering proclaiming the words "Tasty Treats" right across the chest.

Families had complained, and the uniform was altered. Kate wished sometimes that she'd found this place earlier, before the change.

In an effort to keep from destroying her napkin, she ran a hand through dark hair, as much as she could with it tied back in a ponytail. A throb built behind her temples, but the too-tight hairband had nothing to do with it.

When Julie returned with the old man's food, she seemed marginally better, not so close to tears. Her legs shook, though, minutely, and Kate noted that she was favoring the hand holding the plate. Their gazes locked for half a second as Julie retraced her steps to the kitchen. The smile she dredged up was more painful than reassuring.

When Kate saw her next, Julie came bearing food, drink, and another look that was probably meant to be cheerful. "Sorry about that, Doc," she said, setting plate on table. "Blonde moment."

Kate's eyebrows went to her hairline. "Blonde jokes?" she asked, going along with Julie's try at their usual banter. "Aren't those a little beneath you?"

"Hey. Long night, Doctor. Quit with the judgment, huh?"

Julie said this lightly enough, but Kate thought she heard something underneath. She hesitated. She'd just worked twelve hours straight. There was a warm bed a few miles down the road, ready and waiting for her to fall into.

There was also Julie, who reached over to place Kate's soda on the table.

Screw it. What was ten minutes added to twelve hours?

Before her overly analytical mind could process the action, Kate took hold of Julie's hand. The iced beverage had chilled Julie's skin, but the jolt that came with contact wasn't about cold. Kate did her best to ignore it. "Hey. If there was something wrong you could...you could talk to me about it. If you needed to. If...if you thought that would help."

God. She'd have to survey her patients next week, find out if her bedside manner was always this horrendous.

Tired eyes widened. The mouthy waitress stayed silent, then held her gaze on their joined hands.

Kate let go, flashing on the memory of a practical exam gone wrong, and the stitches she'd needed after. She was supposed to demonstrate her ability to make smooth, even surgical cuts. The instructor she both loathed and feared had been standing over her shoulder, waiting for her to screw up. And she had, suffering a nervous spasm and a deep gash in her palm. She'd dropped her instruments, yanked her hand away fast. Only slightly faster than she had just now. "Sorry."

"Why? No. I... Why do you ask?"

At least they were both fumbling with words, and it wasn't just Kate embarrassing herself. "I have eyes and ears, for one."

"That's two, Miss Valedictorian. Thank God you got the anatomy bits right, anyway."

Julie still looked vaguely terrified, but the gentle teasing had some real feeling behind it. "Yeah. Anatomy's kind of a biggie in my profession," Kate said, taking progress where she could get it. "So. You want to be serious for five seconds and tell me what's up?"

A jumble of emotions rushed across Julie's face in an instant. "It would take more than five seconds."

Kate decided she thoroughly hated that measured, guarded tone, resolving to get rid of it as soon as possible. "Sit down, then." She indicated the empty space across from her.

Julie's gaze shot from Kate to the kitchen entrance, then back. "I'm on duty, Doc."

"Yeah," Kate said, drawing out the syllable. "You look swamped." The man by the window was all they had for company, and he was engrossed in his sandwich and a book of crossword puzzles. Kate doubted he'd notice if Julie chose to clear off the table and throw her on top of it.

And for an instant, her mind flashed on exactly that: Julie grabbing the lapels of her suit jacket, pressing her down on the table. The redhead's breasts against hers. Their lips coming together in a heated kiss as Julie's soft hand slid ever so slowly up her nylon stockings until disappearing under her tailored skirt.

Kate shook her head to clear the image. She needed sleep. That damn waitress uniform did weird things to her when she hadn't had enough sleep.

"I'm already in hot water with the boss."

Julie's words pulled her back to purer thoughts. Kate hated the note of defeat in that normally upbeat voice. "That why you're so jumpy?"

Heaving a sigh, Julie settled in on the other side of the booth. "Thanks for caring. I mean it. And I'm not trying to be difficult."

"That's a first."

Julie chuckled and mouthed something obscene. The levity didn't stick. "Marty, my boss, he's kind of pissed at me right now."

"Why?" Kate asked, genuinely perplexed. Julie was good at her job. Kate had certainly been here often enough to know.

"I missed some time today. Had to file a police report, got in late from my break."

Kate sat forward, fighting a reflexive tightening in her gut. "Police? What happened? Are you all right?"

"At ease, Doc," Julie said, though she wasn't following her own advice. She folded her hands together on the table, a vain attempt to hide that they were shaking. "You can see I'm still in one piece. I just…" She paused for what felt like a long time.

Kate bit her cheek to keep from pressing for answers, terrified of what Julie might say. She beat the urge to demand a response, but not the one that sent her hand to rest against Julie's folded ones.

Julie didn't pull away. She smiled, a thin, wavering expression. "My landlord, he likes getting paid in cash. Checks bounce, checks get cancelled; he's one of those. So I walk to the bank during my break this afternoon, before he has time to yell about the rent. I damn near emptied my account, Kate. A few bucks left plus tonight's tips, that's all I have."

Kate. It was rare, hearing her name on Julie's lips. Doc, Doctor, and occasionally, "the pretty one," those were Julie's go-to titles for her. That they weren't being used now only confirmed Julie's distress. "So what happened?" Kate asked, already having an unpleasantly clear idea.

Julie shook her head. "I couldn't believe it, honestly. Broad daylight, people on both sides of the street. I'm walking back from the bank, and this guy, out of nowhere, he just snatches up my purse."

"And no one helped you?"

Another headshake. "He was fast," Julie said, talking from the side of her mouth and shooting the old man across the room a cautious glance. "I'll give the bastard that much."

Kate had other gifts in mind. A surgery without anesthetic, perhaps. "What did the police say?"

"Nothing I wanted to hear." Julie paused again, head bowed. "He took everything, Kate. My ID, my credit cards. I don't know how I'm going to pay my rent."

The fingers under Kate's were trembling again. Kate searched for comforting words, but found nothing that didn't seem trite. She focused on what came easier, on the odd stiffness in Julie's right side when she pulled her hand back and covered her mouth with it, faking a cough. "The son of a bitch *hurt* you."

Julie blinked and let her arm drop. "One piece, Doc, I told you."

"That wasn't a question. You're babying your right side, been doing it all night," she said, thinking of the way Julie's hand shook as she served the other customer his food.

"Didn't know I warranted that much attention."

"Well, now you know." It wasn't what she should've said. Something easy, generic about how she was trained to notice these things. That would've been better. Or maybe not, because Julie smiled. Nothing dazzling, not the way Kate was used to, but a genuine look of happiness, broken only when Julie opened her mouth to speak.

"You worry too much, but it's nice. In an annoying way. I had my purse over my arm, across my shoulder. When the guy ran up he just"—Julie made a small motion with her right arm, winced, then settled for a vague hand gesture—"pulled on it weird. Something's a little out of whack, but it's no big deal."

"You can't know that. Did you go to the hospital, have it X-rayed?"

"Yeah, that's exactly what I did. Since this place has such an awesome insurance plan. Not that I'd need it if my fifty bucks extra cash and all my credit cards hadn't been snatched."

Kate flinched away from the bitterness in Julie's voice. The typical sass had morphed into something else. Kate was familiar with that more biting brand of sarcasm; she'd seen Julie use it a time or twenty before. Against high school kids who tipped five percent, her neighbor with the dog that wouldn't shut up, motorists who didn't grasp the right-of-way concept.

None of that sharp-edged frustration had ever been directed toward her, though, and Kate was more hurt than she'd care to admit by the new experience.

"Oh hell," Julie muttered, pinching the bridge of her nose. "Sorry, Kate. Didn't mean to go all poor, pitiful me on you." She made a face. "I hate people who do that. God, what's happening to me?"

"An exceptionally bad day?" Kate offered.

Julie rolled her eyes toward the old man's booth. "That would be the PG version, minus all the adult words I can't use in this professional environment, but yeah. Still, didn't mean to take it out on you."

"And I didn't mean to let the doctor part of my brain shut off the rest of it."

Julie waved that comment off. With her left hand. "It's nice that you worry. Even though you do it too much, and now I'm probably contributing to that ulcer you've got to have."

"No ulcer," Kate promised, happy the awkward moment had passed. She had so few of those with Julie, making the exceptions harder to deal with.

"There'll be one if you keep eating here, not that I'd ever say that about such a fine culinary establishment. Not on the record, anyway."

"I'll take my chances. But you shouldn't be lugging around trays with that arm. If you've sprained something—"

"I'm fine, Kate. Gotten worse bumps and bruises from a night at the gym. You know, during those two weeks in October when I went to the gym."

As if she needed it. The thought nearly became more than that, Kate barely catching herself from making it so. "Come back to my place."

Julie's mouth dropped open as her eyebrows rose.

Kate wished quite fervently that she could slam her head on the table. "I'd like to check on that arm," she added, lacking a better alternative.

Julie rolled her eyes, the shocked expression softening. "Thanks, good doctor of mine, that's sweet. But I really don't need a house call."

"How about a drink? Might you need one of those?"

The redhead grinned, flashing white teeth. "I'm listening."

"We'll go to my place, open some wine, hide out from your landlord."

"You're a sweetheart, Kate, really. But you don't owe me anything, least of all a pity party."

"You wouldn't get it," Kate murmured, being sure to hold Julie's gaze. "You'd never have pity from me. Just sympathy. And friendship. We are friends, right?"

"Of course we're friends. I love seeing you here every day. And in all that time, I never once thought about spitting in your food."

Kate snorted back a laugh. "True friends, then. Honestly, though. Come over. We'll watch a stupid movie, decompress."

"And you'll look at the arm," Julie said flatly.

"Yes, but we'll also switch jobs. I'll wait on you for once."

"You sure you wouldn't mind the company?"

"Positive."

Julie shot a glance across the room. "I can't leave until our pal over there finishes up, and he likes to get his money's worth. We could be here a while. I keep telling Marty to get rid of the free refills, but he's not the one babysitting the cheapskates, so what does he care?"

Kate smiled. The complaints about her boss indicated an improvement in Julie's mood. "I don't mind waiting. Really."

"Really," Julie mimicked. "So, free medical care, sanctuary, wine, and movies?"

"Along with some general pampering, yeah, that about covers it."

"Well," Julie waggled her eyebrows, "if you can rustle up something stronger than wine, I will gratefully avail myself of your hospitality."

"I think I can manage that."

"Then I'll see you after my shift ends, Doc. Just give me five minutes to change into my outside clothes," she indicated her waitress uniform with an expression of long suffering, "and we can get out of here. Whenever the place finally empties out," she added, glancing at the man by the window.

"Good," Kate said. And it was. She wanted to help Julie out, in some small way. The woman was funny and kind, a constant breath of fresh air. The arm did need checking. Julie would keep working until it fell off, if given the chance.

Kate's motives were pure enough. She worried; it was that simple. Still, part of her regretted that Julie wouldn't be wearing the uniform for the duration of the night.

She really, *really* hadn't needed those two weeks in the gym.

Kate behaved herself when the crossword puzzler ordered two more refills of coffee, but when he took a last sip and prepared to wave Julie down for another, she decided an intervention was needed. She stood up quickly, smoothing her hand down the front of her blouse, and approached the man's table. After a backward glance to confirm Julie was still busy cleaning in the back, she withdrew a hundred-dollar bill from her wallet and placed it in front of him. "This is yours if you leave now and get that next cup at Starbucks. Without asking questions."

He gawked, then grinned, pocketing the money and his crossword puzzles with more speed than he'd shown all night. "Nice doing business with you, lady. Have a great night, huh?"

"Same to you," Kate replied as he scurried out the door. He hadn't bothered to pay his bill or leave a tip. With a sigh and a bemused smile, she fished in her purse for a twenty and slid it under the coffee mug before returning to her own booth.

"You sure he was okay? He split pretty fast. If an older guy like that got food poisoning—"

"He seemed fine to me." Kate avoided Julie's gaze as they stepped into her apartment. "Probably just remembered an errand or something."

"At eight in the evening?"

Shrugging out of her coat, Kate shut the door behind them and held out an arm for Julie's jacket. "People forget things."

"You're too kind," Julie said, handing over the garment.

Kate smiled. Though she missed Julie's uniform, she'd hardly complain about the snug jeans her friend wore now. She also had no problem whatsoever with the green and gray flannel shirt. It brought out all the darkest hues in Julie's brilliant hazel eyes. It took effort to still her hand, keep it from stroking at the soft, inviting fabric. Kate shook herself. Julie was her friend, nothing more. Friends didn't pet and paw at each other's clothes.

"I still say it's fishy. That guy's come in before, and the only thing he seems to forget is that it's not 1925. Now, all of a sudden, he's overtipping?"

Kate busied herself with hanging their jackets on a hook by the door. "Maybe he looked at a calendar. Or it's karma. Small repayment for the day you've had."

Julie made a noncommittal noise. When Kate turned to face her, she was studying their surroundings with a frown that was both adorable and worrying.

"Problem?" Kate asked.

"No, why?"

Kate smirked. She walked through the large living room to the open kitchen, switching on lights as she went. "Tell me. If you start censoring yourself for the first time since I've known you, I'm going to worry even more about what happened today."

"Are you asking if I got knocked on the head?"

"Unless you have a better explanation for the sudden shyness."

Scoffing, Julie followed Kate into the kitchen and pulled up a stool by the island. "You swear you won't throw me out?"

"Sure," Kate replied, uncertain but amused. "Something stronger than wine, you said. Bourbon work?"

"Bourbon's great. Seriously, promise you won't shoot the messenger?"

"Do we need to pinky swear? Is this a pinky swear situation?" Julie gave her a sour look, and Kate straightened up, setting down the glasses she'd grabbed from an upper cabinet. "I promise I won't get mad."

Releasing an audible breath, Julie tapped her fingers against the marble countertop. "All right. So this place is huge. Really nice. It's just…kind of the nicest *waiting room* I've ever seen. There's nothing personal, you know? It's very…"

"Sterile?" Kate suggested.

"You don't sound surprised. Or pissed."

Laughing, Kate took the bourbon from its place in the pantry, an enormous walk-in affair that was totally unnecessary. She smiled ruefully as she surveyed her home. The epitome of modern, everything glass and straight edges, as clean and bare as the day she'd bought it. "My ex wanted the place; I leased it with her. We broke up not long after, and somehow I got stuck here."

Kate paused, gauging Julie's reaction. If she'd considered it too much, she'd never have mentioned that "she" bit. But she seemed to be doing a lot of not-thinking today, and aside from a brief, unreadable look, Julie didn't react to the word.

"I've thought about brightening it up," Kate continued, bolstered by an encouraging nod from Julie. "But with my shifts at the hospital, there's not much time for decorating. And I'm hardly ever here anyway, except to sleep."

"Maybe you'd want to be here more if you found the time to make it yours. Like that space over there." Julie indicated a patch of white wall in the middle of the living room. "If you just put something there, something you liked, it would be an anchor for the whole room."

"That's the thing," Kate replied, heading to the fridge for ice. "I want something that really speaks to me. Not just whatever I can find in the few hours I have to go shopping. If I'm going to spend money on something I'm rarely going to see, I want it to be worth it. And I haven't found anything I just need to have, you know?"

"So." Julie flashed a mischievous grin. "You're really picky. That's what it comes down to, right?"

"In certain areas of my life, yes." Kate passed Julie her drink. "Anything to say about that?"

"Nope. Some people have every right to be picky."

Julie raised the glass in her direction, and Kate did what she was supposed to, clinking their tumblers together. When she felt Julie's gaze on her, she willed back the blush that wanted to heat her face.

"Okay I'm thinking, from what you described and how you were carrying yourself tonight, that the shoulder's just strained. If the tissues were actually torn, I doubt you'd have been able to finish your shift without dropping a lot of plates."

"Right. So, no problem. Isn't that what I said in the first place?"

"Yes, problem, and I still have to check. If it is a strain and nothing worse—"

"You and your positive thinking."

"I'd like you to take some over-the-counter pain relievers tomorrow," Kate said, ignoring the muttered interruption. "To help with the soreness you're pretending not to have. Unless you want to take something now, keep the booze down to one glass?"

"You're kidding, right?"

"I figured," Kate said with a laugh. "Leave the medicine for tomorrow, then. You don't have any drug allergies, do you?"

"Not a one. Other than this damn shoulder, I'm all good."

That didn't need to be stated. Kate turned away before her blush could grow. "You'll have to take your shirt off so I can get a proper look at your shoulder. You could—" She stopped short. When she returned her gaze to Julie, she instantly zeroed in on the burgundy silk bra peeking through the gap in Julie's shirt. Despite Julie's earlier shakiness, half the buttons were already undone. "I...I was going to tell you there's a bathroom around the corner. You could have undressed there."

Julie started to shrug, then winced at the movement. "No worries, Doc. I've been looking for a reason to take my shirt off in front of you for a while," she said, a sexy smirk on her lips.

"You're incorrigible." Kate couldn't very well admit that Julie didn't need an excuse.

"I thought that was one of the things you liked about me?"

"Did I say it wasn't?" Kate took a step forward before Julie could retort. They'd be at this all night otherwise. Which she wouldn't have minded if Julie didn't need medical attention. She put on her best doctor face, needing to refocus them both. "Turn around, please."

She'd treat this like any other examination. She would. So she kept telling herself as she ghosted her fingers over Julie's flesh.

Julie jumped at the first touch.

"I'm sorry. Did that hurt?"

"No, Doc. Your hands are a little cold; that's all."

Murmuring an apology, Kate took her hands away from Julie's smooth skin and rubbed them together to chase away the chill. She wondered idly if the heat wasn't being stolen from her hands while other parts of her body overheated. She took an extra moment to blow on her fingertips before bringing them back to settle on Julie's neck.

Touching her ignited all sorts of feelings in all sorts of places. The only way to get through it was to focus solely on the practical. She had Julie lift her arm and rotate the shoulder as best she could. "You know, the shoulder is one of the most mobile parts of the body. It's also very prone to injuries." She talked to ground herself as her hands traveled across the tops of Julie's tanned arms and across the blades of her shoulders, comparing temperatures and textures. "There's a bit of edema and—"

"Edema? Is that bad? It sounds bad."

"No, sorry. Fancy word for swelling. We can fix that with some ice. Twenty minutes on, twenty minutes off. That'll take care of the bruise as well. It would be best if you could take some time off from work."

"Yeah, that'd be great. And if I could use Monopoly money to pay my rent, I'd be all for it."

"Yes, I know." Kate picked up Julie's shirt from the back of the chair, stealing an extra moment to enjoy the softness of the flannel before relinquishing it. "You can put this back on, then make yourself at home on the sofa. I'll get you an icepack."

"And another drink?" Julie added with a hopeful expression.

"Of course."

"Hey, Doc. Can I ask you a personal question?" Julie asked once Kate had returned and they were settled comfortably in the living room.

"Might as well do it while I'm prepared." Kate indicated the drink she'd put on the coffee table.

"You and the ex. Why didn't that take?"

"Probably because of me. *Mostly* because of me." Kate sipped at the bourbon. "She said I wasn't there enough. Story of my life."

Julie frowned. "Yeah, the hours suck, but she knew what she was signing up for, right? And as far as excuses go, saving lives seems like a pretty good one."

Kate sighed. "Maybe, but it's still an excuse, and she got tired of hearing it. Tired of waiting up for me."

"Is that when you started eating at the diner every day, after you two broke up?"

"Yes, actually. Like I said, I had no particular reason to be here, especially then."

"Well," Julie said after a beat of silence. "Some people are worth waiting up for."

"Some people, huh?" Kate echoed, a smile on her lips as they clinked glasses again.

It was amazing what you could learn about a person when there wasn't an interruption every five minutes, someone demanding extra napkins or more ketchup. They'd covered anything and everything over the last couple hours, sitting together on the couch that rarely saw any use. For her part, Kate knew she should be exhausted after the shift she'd put in, but the tiredness she'd initially felt at the diner had ebbed away, replaced by something else entirely.

After a minor battle, she had convinced Julie to kick off her shoes and get comfortable. Kate had traded her skirt and blouse for black leggings and a scoop neck, sapphire sleep shirt, letting her long hair fall loose around her shoulders.

She caught herself smiling too much, sure she looked foolish. But Julie was in her home, totally at ease, in that comfy flannel shirt that must've been so soft against her curves. Those damn curves.

"I didn't always want to be a waitress, you know."

Julie's voice forced Kate out of her thoughts, which was for the best. "No?" she said, sipping from her drink before setting it back on the table. She didn't particularly want the alcohol, had already spent too much time watering it down with club soda, but the glass gave her hands something to do.

"Nah." Julie tucked one leg underneath her as she faced Kate more fully. "I was into art, if you can believe that. Still am. Marty yells at me all the time for sketching things on napkins instead of wiping down counters."

"I've never seen that," Kate said, transfixed by the way Julie's eyes gleamed as she spoke.

"I only do it when I'm bored. Not bored when you're around."

Kate smiled. "Good to know. But you light up when you talk about this. Why not do something with it, if it's what you really enjoy?"

"Professionally, you mean? What makes you think I'd be good enough? You've never seen my work."

"I can't imagine you not excelling at anything you're passionate about."

Julie actually blushed at that, and Kate was too busy finding it adorable to worry about tipping her hand.

"I did take classes for a while, after high school. Then my mom got sick, and making pretty pictures got put on the backburner."

"You dropped out to take care of her?"

"Yeah," Julie said with a shrug. "Anybody would've."

"No, they wouldn't. Trust me, I know. You're a good person. And you should try to get back into the art. You deserve to do something you like."

"Well, I haven't given it up completely. I still paint when I can. I've even sold a couple online, not that I made much." Julie laughed wryly. "Maybe if I can get rid of all of them in the next two days, I'll be able to pay my rent."

Kate bit her tongue. She'd give her the money in a heartbeat. She also knew Julie would turn her down just as fast. "You have a site?" she asked instead. "I'd like to see it, see what you can do."

Julie grinned wickedly. "I just bet you would."

"I would," Kate said, the seriousness of her tone derailing Julie's teasing.

"Maybe another time,"

"You really think there'll be a better one?"

Julie sighed audibly. "What if they're not good?"

"What if they are? Besides, you've got them online for everyone else to see. Does it really matter if I do, too?"

"Yeah, Kate. Because you're not everyone else."

Kate swallowed. Hard. Julie had begun tapping a nervous rhythm against her own thigh, and it took all of Kate's resolve not to reach out and caress the denim-clad muscle. "You're a tease," she said, not as lightly as she'd intended. "If you didn't want me to be interested, you shouldn't have shown me this whole new side of yourself."

"I never said I didn't want you interested, but I've got to hold back some things, keep you interested. More than that, I never wanted you to think of me as just a waitress, you know?"

"No, I don't. I could never think of you as 'just' anything."

Kate watched, mesmerized, as Julie pushed a strand of hair behind her ear, flashing that megawatt grin as she did. It would be so easy for Kate to bury her hands in those gorgeous, silky tresses, see what that bourbon tasted like when it was on Julie's lips. Put the hard seam of those jeans to good use.

And then she caught herself. Kate wasn't oblivious to the spark that'd burnt between them all evening, but Julie was at the end of a traumatic day. And she'd been drinking. Not a lot, just enough to give Kate the excuse to chicken out. After forcing a deep breath, she cleared her throat. "We...we should really look at that arm."

She looked away fast, avoiding Julie's reaction.

There was no joking this time. Julie simply stood, fumbling with the buttons of her shirt.

"Do you need—?"

"I got it," Julie said.

Kate rubbed her hands together, warming them so there wouldn't be a repeat of last time. Julie sat in front of her, at the very edge of the couch, torso bare except for her bra. Kate took a breath that was too shaky as she fingered the strap covering the injured shoulder. "Tell me if I hurt you." At Julie's stiff nod, she eased the thin piece of fabric down, exposing the bruise. Carefully, she touched the darkened skin with the pads of her fingers. "Doesn't feel as stiff," she said, trying hard to be clinical about it. "Does it feel like the ice made a difference?"

"Yeah. Yeah, I think it did."

Julie's voice was very small, the way it had been when she'd tried not to cry at the diner, but not like that at all. Her hands were at either side of her, gripping the sofa. As if she were bracing for impact. She shivered under Kate's touch, gasping in the large, silent space.

Immediately pulling her fingers back, Kate noted the gooseflesh forming over Julie's skin. The room wasn't that cold, even without a shirt. "You okay?"

"Yeah. Wasn't that kind of gasp."

"Oh. Good."

"Good," Julie repeated. She turned her head to the side, just barely catching Kate's eye. Reaching back, she found Kate's hand and placed it on her shoulder blade, above the bruise. She didn't let go. Slowly, very slowly, she brought the hand to her lips, kissing the fingertips first, then palm, then knuckles.

Holding perfectly still, Kate closed her eyes as she felt Julie's breath on her skin.

"You going to kick me out now, Doc?"

Kate pulled her hand free, using it to tilt Julie's face toward her. She thrilled at seeing a desire there that matched her own. The smile Julie wore was all the encouragement Kate needed. She brought her thumb to the corner of Julie's mouth, enjoying the suppleness of pink lips as she traced them gently. Touching wasn't enough. Kate wanted to taste, *had* to taste. Her lips settled on the spot her thumb had just abandoned. The sound of Julie's soft moan spurred her on. Kate's bottom lip brushed against Julie's top lip, nudging them apart. The kiss was slow, exploratory. Julie's tongue against hers sent a jolt of pleasure straight to her clit. They breathed the same air for a while. Kate lost her sense of time.

When the contact broke, she placed a series of butterfly kisses along Julie's shoulder, up her neck, along her jaw. Her free hand covered Julie's hip, drawing absent patterns. Her mouth stopped at Julie's ear, breathing into it, sucking the lobe into her mouth. "I'd never kick you out," she murmured in a voice she hardly recognized. "But I need to ask you something first."

"Ask whatever you want, Doc, but do it quick. I can't really think when you're doing what you're doing."

Kate barely kept herself from skipping the talk altogether. She had to know, though; it was too important. Julie was too important. "Would you want me doing this if you hadn't been mugged?"

Julie's chuckle was low and throaty as she glided a hand through Kate's hair. "I've wanted you every day since you started coming in. Is that answer enough?"

Moaning, Kate licked and sucked at the sensitive skin of Julie's neck. "Yes, it is. And I didn't keep coming back for the chicken sandwiches."

Julie laughed and gasped as Kate's mouth moved against her. "I fucking told Marty he wasn't that good of a cook."

Grinning, Kate made quick work of Julie's bra, tossing it aside with the abandoned flannel. With Julie squirming against her, Kate cupped her breasts, testing their weight, squeezing experimentally. "You do know that the uniform barely covers these."

"I always hoped you'd notice."

"I noticed," Kate whispered, kneading Julie's flesh, playing with the nipples until they pebbled in her hands. It happened remarkably fast, but apparently not fast enough.

"Come here," Julie said, voice low and rough as she moved against the hand that grasped her hip. "Either come around here or let me turn, Kate. Need to look at you for real. See all of you."

Dusting her shoulder with a final kiss, Kate released her hold on Julie's breasts and stood up. Whether she'd been teasing Julie or buying time for herself, she didn't know. She did know that she wanted this to be right, would never be able to face Julie again if it wasn't.

The slightest frown pulled at Julie's lips as Kate came around to face her. "You nervous, Doc?"

It was something approximating Julie's normal tone, and Kate appreciated that as she knelt in front of her. "Been a while," she said, playing at casual.

Nodding, Julie caught Kate's hand and again brought the knuckles to her lips. "Me too, but I wouldn't worry about it. We've already established how good you are with anatomy."

Kate smiled and caught Julie's lips in a soft, tender kiss. It wasn't that she didn't know bodies in general; she didn't know Julie's. Kate admitted this while her tongue teased at Julie's mouth.

Pulling back, Julie framed Kate's face in her hands, their foreheads brushing together. "So, fix that. Start studying. I'll tell you if you're on the right track."

"You promise?"

Julie laughed and bumped her nose against Kate's. "Have you ever known me to keep my mouth shut?"

"I guess not," Kate said, reassured. With one last kiss to the mouth in question, she sat back far enough to run wide, lazy circles over Julie's thighs, loving the play of muscle, the feel of denim against her fingers.

Julie used her left hand to pull at her nipples, alternating between them.

Kate had to freeze in the process of unzipping Julie's jeans. "You're gorgeous," she said, raw emotion backing her words.

Julie caught her breath, right hand lifting shakily to stroke Kate's cheek. "You kidding? All those shifts staring at you, now you're on your knees for me? *That's* gorgeous."

Smiling, Kate eased Julie's hand away from her face, conscious of the bad shoulder. "Rest that," she said and placed it at the edge of the couch. "And I did tell you that I'd pamper you this time. If that puts me on my knees in front of you, there are worse things." Many worse, very few better.

With a bit of help from Julie, Kate got the jeans off, leaving her all but naked. Kate fixated on the white lace panties.

"If I'd known I'd get this far tonight, I'd have made sure they matched," Julie said, glancing at the burgundy bra on Kate's floor.

"You're gorgeous," Kate repeated. She trailed Julie's inner thighs with licks, kisses, and the occasional bite.

"Watch what you're doing. That damn uniform isn't going to cover much if you mark me up," Julie teased, her momentary self-consciousness gone.

Kate smirked, deliberately leaving a love bite near the apex of Julie's thighs. Tomorrow, she'd smile behind her coffee cup, knowing what that skirt concealed. She halted at Kate's underwear and hooked her thumbs beneath the fabric.

"Off. Want them off."

Kate obliged, easing the panties down toned legs. She froze again on seeing what lay underneath. Julie was visibly slick, hips trembling. "Do you have any idea how wet you are?" Kate whispered into Julie's folds.

A low, desperate noise escaped Julie. With her left hand, she stroked through Kate's hair, massaging her scalp. "Happens whenever I see you."

Kate shuddered. All those times, Julie soaked under that skimpy fucking uniform. Julie's hands, soothing and arousing all at once as they petted her hair. Those hazel eyes, so much darker than Kate had ever seen them. "Jesus," she murmured, spread Julie open, and pushed her tongue into wet heat.

Kate did what Julie asked. She studied. Swirled her tongue along Julie's center, learned the places that made her breath hitch, the hand in Kate's hair tighten. She lapped at Julie's clit, varying speed and pressure, and felt it harden under her tongue. Her hands kept Julie's legs apart, nails raking lightly over her thighs.

And Julie, always so witty and talkative, was reduced to quivering gasps, sounds that came loud and high as Kate mapped her out.

Kate loved Julie's voice, loved the near-constant flow of words. She hadn't imagined it would feel so glorious to render her speechless.

A particularly forceful jerk of Julie's hips against her mouth had Kate looking up.

Julie was braced against the couch with her eyes closed, gripping the cushions hard enough to turn her knuckles white. She bit her lip, a hopeless attempt at stifling the moans.

Kate watched, rapt. "You're amazing." She breathed the words against the bud of Julie's clit. "You *taste* amazing."

Hazel eyes opened. Julie's tongue peeked out to worry the abused lip. She smiled down at Kate. "Do I? Prove it."

Kate grinned back and shifted. Planting her palm where her mouth had been, she moved enough to pin Julie's lips in a deep, needy kiss. Julie's hands locked on Kate's shoulders, holding her in place. Kate swallowed her cries with pleasure, would've kept at it if Julie hadn't pulled back.

"More. Your fingers. Inside."

She gasped the plea into Kate's neck, making her shiver. As Julie smothered her throat and jaw with kisses, Kate adjusted the hand massaging Julie's clit. She stretched her out with two fingers, relishing the sensation of Julie clenching down on her.

She found a rhythm quickly, synced herself with Julie's movements, discovered a particular way of twisting her fingers that made her scream. After kissing her once more, Kate returned to a kneeling position, sucked Julie's clit into her mouth, and fucked her with her fingers.

Julie grabbed at Kate's hair with both hands when she came, not tugging, just holding her in place. As if Kate would stop before Julie wanted her to.

She smiled, watching and feeling Julie come apart against her tongue, her hand. Julie's cries echoed in the too big, too empty apartment, and for once, Kate absolutely loved being there.

She nuzzled at her folds as Julie came down, dropping gentle, soothing kisses. She was careful about regaining the use of her hand and held Julie's gaze as she eased free.

"Come here," Julie said for the second time that night, her voice trembling nearly as much as her body.

Kate did, stretching Julie out along the couch and draping her body on top of hers.

Julie held tight while Kate kissed her mouth, her cheek, her forehead.

"Well," Julie said a few minutes later. "That finally happened."

They both laughed at that, Kate recovering first. "It did," she said. "And it answered a long-standing question of mine."

"Which was?"

"If we ever got around to this, I wondered whether you'd call me Doc or Kate when you came."

"So you've thought about this. Before now. Often?"

"Very. Sorry if I didn't make that clear."

"You're not allowed to apologize to me. Possibly ever again. And about your title, you weren't wearing the white coat. If you had been, I might've said something different."

Filing that statement away for later consideration, Kate shook her head and gently pinned the hands that were pulling at her shirt.

"Come on, Kate. You're way overdressed. Off with the clothes."

"You really love giving me orders for a change, don't you?"

"Yeah. And?"

"And," Kate said, tangling their fingers together, "I said that tonight was about you. And that you needed to rest the shoulder."

"So I won't use my hands," Julie countered. Her tongue roamed deliberately over her lips.

Kate closed her eyes, stifling a groan. It took several deep breaths to get her need under control. "You're going to rest," she said, using her professional voice. "You're going to come to bed with me, and we're going to sleep. *Just* sleep, because we've both worked a few too many double shifts. And tomorrow, you're going to show me your art."

Julie opened her mouth, closed it, shook her head. "Is this how you talk to your patients?"

"The difficult ones, yes."

Shrugging her good shoulder, Julie smiled. "Sure, you've already seen everything else. But if you don't like them—"

"We've been over this. Not liking them is a non-issue. And when I see them and fall in love with all of them, you'll help me choose which one goes there." Kate nodded at the blank space they'd discussed earlier. "How much do you charge?"

"Depends on the piece. What the buyer's willing to pay."

"How much is your rent?"

"Kate, no. You'd have to buy twenty of my finger paintings to—"

"One, don't call them that. Ever. Two, I've got lots of empty walls here. An equally empty office. But if you insist on haggling, we'll do it tomorrow. I've got a day off, first one in weeks, and I'm spending it with you."

"You don't know how much I want to hole up with you and return the favor. Repeatedly. God knows you deserve it, making my worst day ever into one of the best. Thing is, I don't have a day off tomorrow."

"Yes, you do. We're going to handle your rent, fair trade. Takes care of the immediate problem."

"Right. And what do I tell Marty?"

Kate smirked and touched her lips to Julie's. "I'll write you a doctor's note."

Julie laughed long and hard at that, her body shaking under Kate's. "Okay," she said finally. "So, you want to go check out all the blank walls in your bedroom, get ready for tomorrow?"

"I think that'd be great."

"Great. But when we get there? Lose the clothes. You're still overdressed, and if I can't have you tonight, I at least want a preview."

"Fair enough," Kate said and smiled in a way she knew looked ridiculous. "I did say that it was your night."

"Some night." Julie flashed a crooked smirk. "If I'd known that a mugging was all it would take to have a sleepover with you—"

"You can have anything you want with me," Kate said. "All you ever had to do was ask."

"Yeah?" Julie murmured, voice low and throaty. "I'll hold you to that, Doc. Better get writing on that note."

ROCKET TO YOU

BY SAMANTHA LUCE

"Damn." The word drifted out on my surprised breath. Just a moment before, I had heard the front door open and bumped my head on the cabinet I'd been trying to squeeze under. Through the cracks between the cabinet and its top I glimpsed long, tan legs, black and silver four-inch heels, and a naughty-but-nice hemline that fell an inch above the knee. Then, as I climbed back to my feet, I took in the whole picture. If I'd have been a cartoon character, I'm certain my eyes would have bugged out like a pair of retractable binoculars.

"That's an interesting way to greet a potential guest." The tall redhead shook a few droplets of rain from her thick mane. There was a hint of a smile on her wine-colored lips, leading me to believe she was only mildly perturbed by my swearing. She continued forward into the small reception area. Her designer shoes echoed on the polished checkerboard floor.

A hint of jasmine teased my nose. I cleared my throat, struggling to remember the key parts to moving my mouth and making words come out.

It had been a decade, but I'd know those long, soft curls, the intense sea-blue eyes, and high cheekbones anywhere. They had fueled many a fantasy when I first allowed my brain to explore my attraction to women. How many nights had I drifted off wondering what she would taste like? How she would react if I sucked her nipple, then followed that with a gentle bite? Would she be as wet as I was at only the thought of her hand grazing my clit?

"Are you all right, hon?" Her eyebrow arched. "You look a bit flushed."

Oh God. I swallowed. Transparent, that's my name. I brought my hand to my cheek. "I'm fine. I got a little dizzy from being scrunched under that counter for so long. I was trying to fix a short in one of the wires running from the cash register to..." I trailed off. She had no interest in my excuses.

She had always been direct. Efficient. No wasted time from this beautiful ginger. "Never mind." I made myself take a breath, then smiled. "Mallory Roarke, you look amazing. I never thought I'd see you again after you moved away."

A few small laugh lines became visible when those penetrating eyes narrowed on my face. She looked as though she was about to tell me she had no idea what I was talking about. My hopes were just about to smash on the tile floor when she set everything right with a warm smile. "Jade Summers! Look at you. All grown up. I bet my son wouldn't complain for a second if you offered to sit with him now."

"You mean he didn't want me to babysit him back then?" I pretended to pout.

"He was seven. He thought he could do everything all by himself. Come to think of it, he hasn't changed much since then." She laughed softly. It sounded magical. Low and full of promise. "On the other hand, you certainly *have* changed." Her vibrant blue gaze traveled over me. "No more braces or glasses. I see you've grown out of the baggy clothes look, too."

I laughed and held out my hands in a "ta da" gesture. "And you haven't changed at all." *You still make my mouth dry and my pussy wet.*

"I know what I look like." She laughed again, her right hand fingering a silvery lock of hair between her crown and her temple. The streak only added to her allure. She had had it since I could remember. "You don't have to fib to get me to pay whatever your bed-and-breakfast is charging," she said. "I'm desperate."

"Oh, I'm sorry. There's a rocket launch scheduled in just a few hours. Between that and the spring break stragglers, the whole town is booked. Let me call around, see if—"

"No," she cut in. "Sadly, I've already been through all that. You were my last hope. I'm only here for the night. I thought I would catch the launch for old time's sake, then head back to LA. Have all your reservations arrived? Maybe I could wait a bit and see if there's a cancellation." Her face seemed to light up with hope.

I hated myself for having to dash that optimism. "Everyone's here. This is the best time of year to get ahead of the game so I rent out everything, including my own room." My words chipped away at her cheerful expression until she looked positively deflated. "Hey, I've got an idea. It's kind of out there, so feel free to pass. I'm sleeping in the restaurant. It's been gutted

141

for a big renovation. A real mess. No TV or Internet, but the back office is workable. I've got some essentials in there. It ought to be a smidge better than sleeping in your car."

The spark returned to her eyes. "Are you sure you wouldn't mind?"

"Not at all." I smiled. "I've got about an hour left before I can shut down the lobby. I'll give you my key. It might look a little scary going in, with the plastic covering everything. Just stick to the walkway. It'll lead you right to the office. There's a couch and a shower. I've had a big batch of pasta fagioli simmering in the Crock-Pot all day. Make yourself at home."

Her fingertips brushed my palm when she took the key, setting off a warm tingle that traveled the length of my arm. It took an effort to hold back the whimper tickling the back of my throat. My gaze flitted back to hers, and she looked unaffected. My lip twitched in a half smile. I was relieved she hadn't seemed to notice I was practically drooling for her, while at the same time disappointed she wasn't sharing in the attraction.

A turtle in quicksand would have gone by faster than that last hour. Other than a few callers checking to see if we had any vacancies, it was pretty quiet. I spent the whole time reminiscing about Mallory. The hot single mom had moved to Water's Edge during my junior year in high school. Fresh off her Jane Drew win for innovation in architecture, she had been commissioned to design an exploration tower. Her days and nights were spent dreaming up ways to stay on budget while still giving our town the centerpiece for its state-of-the-art, space-themed resort and playground. My nights were filled with dreams of us lying in her queen size bed, my body wrapped in her arms as her silky hair fanned out all around us.

I licked my lips and smiled at the empty lobby before I turned off the lights. Perhaps tonight I would observe enough to fill another ten years of fantasy about the auburn-haired MILF. I grabbed my jacket and hurried out the back door onto the cobblestone walkway leading to the shell of the restaurant.

A sleek black BMW was parked in front. I laughed to myself. What a step down for Mallory, stuck spending the night in the disaster zone I temporarily called home.

The scent of slow-cooked vegetables, garlic, and rosemary wafted toward me even before I opened the door. I hoped it did the same thing to her insides as it was doing to mine.

Mallory had changed from her sexy black dress to jeans and a formfitting, ice-blue Henley that made the intensity of her eyes damn near electric. Her hair was damp. It looked darker, giving her a shroud of mystery. The smile she flashed me was big and warm. "Thank you again, Jade. I hope you don't mind I borrowed your shower. I needed to do something to distract myself. Your soup smells incredible. It took a lot of self-control to make myself wait for you."

"You didn't have to wait."

"Yes, I did. If it tastes anything close to how good it smells, then it has to be shared. It's always more fun when you experience something heavenly with someone else rather than on your own. Don't you think?"

I think I have forgotten how to think. I gave my head a shake. I was studying her lips. The way her mouth moved as she spoke. I barely registered what she had actually said.

"Have I done something wrong?"

"No, not at all. I'm sorry. It's just been a long day." I checked my watch. "We have a couple hours before the launch. I have a loaf of Italian bread and a restaurant full of wine. Let's get this party started."

Her laughter filled the room. "I like the way you think."

I like everything about you. I bit my lower lip to keep the words inside.

"Have a seat." She pulled out the leather office chair and waved her hand invitingly like a hostess. "You've been my hero tonight. You're providing shelter, delicious food, and good company. The least I can do is pamper you a little bit." She leaned in close enough to whisper once I was seated, her hand skimming up my arm and across my shoulder. "I spotted the wine earlier. I even found a couple of glasses, bowls, and a few other necessities." A cloth napkin appeared in her hand. She gave it a snap before draping it over my lap.

My breath caught. I watched in silent admiration as she selected a bottle of my favorite wine. The short sleeves of her shirt allowed me to admire the contours of her toned arms as she expertly fitted the opener on top and released the aroma. I was pleasantly surprised to see her pick up a clear decanter. Not everyone knew a wine couldn't breathe properly until shifted from its original bottle to a new container.

Her jeans fit her snugly. She had kept her perfect figure. I couldn't help admiring her physique as she busied herself ladling soup, tearing bread, and pouring bottled water into tall glasses. I tried to tell myself not to stare. Yet each time I looked away, I was drawn back, the way it happens when I'm on a diet and I know there's an emergency chocolate bar hidden behind the healthy cereal box. Then that cereal box is suddenly the only thing I can focus on when I walk into the kitchen.

"How is Scotty?" I asked, trying to keep myself focused on something other than getting my guest naked.

That sweet, soft laugh floated on the air again. "Oh, don't let him hear you say that. He hasn't gone by Scotty in years. It's Scott now." She was beaming when she sat down across from me. "He's doing very well. I am so proud of him. He's dual enrolled, majoring in design. I think he wants to take over my firm. It's a dream come true."

"That's wonderful." I dipped a piece of bread into my soup. "I'm happy for you both."

She dipped her own piece and brought the moistened bread to her mouth. She chewed for a moment, then swallowed. "This is amazing." Her pink tongue peeked out as she licked her lips. "You could sell this. You would put all those other soup companies out of business."

I'm sure I blushed. "My mother handed down the recipe to me. She says it's been passed around in my family for at least four generations. I could tell you the ingredients, but then…"

"You'd have to kill me?" Her lips quirked as she gently cut me off.

"Nah, you'd just be bored if I babbled on about the details." I dabbed the napkin to my mouth. "I remember you too well. I've always admired your directness."

"If you say so." Her eyes twinkled. "What about you? How did you go from earning extra cash as a babysitter to running a bed-and-breakfast?"

"Luck, good timing, smart parents who taught me the value of savings, and hard work. Oh, and no social life," I said with a laugh, her warm gaze prompting me to blurt out that last embarrassing bit of truth.

"No social life?" she asked. "How can that be? You have such beautiful dark hair and brilliant green eyes just like the jewel your parents named you after." She grinned. "And that killer smile."

I couldn't help but grin back. "Well, gotta thank my parents for that, too," I said, wishing we had opened the wine sooner. It needed time to breathe, but so did I. "They paid a small fortune for it."

"Worth every penny. You're stunning."

I nearly choked on my water. "I hate to break it to you, Mallory, but you may need glasses."

"Nonsense. I have a mirror in my bag. I could get it, but I honestly don't want to tear myself away from this. Best meal I've had in a long time." She dug in with her spoon and pursed her lips to cool the broth.

Thanking her for the compliment, I glanced at my water and wondered if pouring it over my head would cool me down. I had a feeling it would just boil on my skin. I took a few more bites and watched her do the same.

We settled into a comfortable rhythm, trading snippets of our lives during the past decade between bits of bread and soup. Then I noticed the distinct lack of a ring on her finger. Suddenly the food and small talk weren't doing their job as distractions. I needed something tangible to put a lid on my lust. "So, I'm sure you've remarried by now. Where is the lucky man?"

"That's a good question. I wish I knew the answer." She reached for her wineglass and twirled it by its stem, the deep red liquid swirling and clinging to the glass. She shut her eyes and inhaled its bouquet.

I wished I could read whatever thoughts were traveling through her mind, a desire I'd nurtured for over a decade.

She kept her eyes closed as she took a healthy sip. Her cheeks puffed out just a tad when she moved her tongue to swish the wine over every surface.

I've attended wine tastings in the past. Mostly I found them educational, sometimes boring, and occasionally delicious. Finding them erotic? That hadn't happened before. Not until Mallory walked back into my life.

Her head tilted back when she sipped. The muscles in her neck stretched gracefully. The look on her face was decadent. No exaggeration. There was no other word for it, at least none that I could think of at that moment with my hormones on overdrive and my brain on standby. The reactions I was having to her every movement made it impossible for me to savor the flavor or the scent. It was a waste. I knew it. Still, I had to have a hit. I needed a buzz to dull the craving. I picked up my glass and chugged it, then reached for the container to refill it before I had even finished my last swallow.

Mallory chuckled, azure eyes alight with mischief. "I don't think you're supposed to guzzle wine like beer, Jade."

"It's a new technique. Frat guys love it," I quipped.

"Been hanging out with a lot of frat guys lately?" A wicked smile crossed her lips as she tipped her glass toward me for a refill.

"Guys aren't my thing." I answered too quickly, with no time for rational thought. I felt a blush rising from my cheeks to my scalp. I poured the remainder of the wine into her glass and got up for another bottle.

It had looked so easy when Mallory opened it. I had taken classes, and I still had issues lining up the corkscrew and keeping it moving in a straight line. The levers never popped up as easily as they did for everyone else I'd watched, and they certainly never closed evenly. This time I did fairly well—only a slight slant, but the cork was long. It hadn't been completely extracted. I sucked in a breath and pulled with everything I had.

"Here, allow me." Mallory seemed to have teleported behind me. Her warm hand lightly grasped my elbow.

The hairs on my arm stood to attention. A trail of gooseflesh soon followed. I jostled the wine and nearly dropped the bottle. In my fumbling attempt to hang on, I pulled it to me like a wide receiver with a football, hugging it to my chest. The liquid sloshed upward, making me an unwilling participant in a wet-shirt contest.

"I'm so sorry." Mallory came around me. Her gaze landed only briefly on my wet chest before darting back to my eyes. "You seemed a little...jumpy. I only wanted to help."

"It's okay." I pinched the front of my shirt and held it away from my skin. "You're right. I am jumpy." Arousal plus a splash of wine in an already chilled room made my nipples far too prominent beneath the damp fabric.

"Is it me?" The smile that had kept her features so light throughout the night suddenly faltered. "Am I making you uncomfortable?"

"No, of course not." Uncomfortable wasn't the right word for it. Not at all. *You're making me hot and bothered. That's all.*

"I always liked you, you know." Her words felt careful, measured. "I thought you were so smart. A real go-getter." She glanced around the room. "Proved me right, didn't you? You have what I'm sure will be a highly successful authentic Italian restaurant and a sold-out bed-and-breakfast. What you've done here is nothing short of amazing."

I opened my mouth to downplay her compliment, hopefully with a modicum of grace. She was quicker, deftly keeping the conversation on point.

"I know it's been a long time, but when we used to talk after I'd return home from work, we always got along so well. At least I thought we did."

"Yes, we did." I smiled. "I mean, we do get along." Too well. Hadn't that always been the crux of the matter? I filled my glass and gulped another half of its contents down. "I know you appreciate it when people are straightforward. There's something that I've wanted to tell you for ten years. I don't know if

I'll ever get the chance again. I just hope what I'm about to say won't make you uncomfortable."

"Whatever it is, I'm sure it won't. Out with it."

"I look at you and I forget to breathe."

The right corner of her mouth curved up, and her eyes narrowed as if she was trying to grasp a not-so-funny punchline.

"Looking at you makes me weak." I blurted out another inept line.

The remnants of her smile faded quickly, replaced with a puzzled frown. "So-o." She stretched the word until it sounded as though it had more than one syllable. "Looking at me makes you sick?"

"Oh, no, that's not what I meant at all. God, I'm an idiot." I prayed for a lightning bolt to split the roof and strike me dead. I took a moment to swallow the last of my wine. I couldn't meet her gaze. "I want you, Mallory. I've wanted you practically since the day I first saw you."

"What?" A surprised laugh drifted on the air on between us. When I looked up, she was shaking her head. "You can't be serious."

"I've never been more serious about anything in my life."

"But I'm old enough to be your…" She trailed off and cleared her throat. A muscle near her eye began to twitch. I remembered that happening whenever she was stressed. "At the very least I could be your older sister."

"Age is just a number. It doesn't define you."

She ran her fingers through her hair and released a shaky breath. "You really mean that?"

"Yes, I absolutely do. It doesn't matter, though. I know you like guys. I'm sorry I've ruined the night. I'm a dumb—"

"Jade," she cut in, stepping forward until our breaths mingled. "You're right. I do like guys, sometimes." Her flirty grin grew wider. "And sometimes, like tonight, I like women. A lot. You know, I used to have a mantra I said to myself on the nights you left my house after sitting for Scotty." She brought her hand up and cupped my cheek. "Would you like to know what it was?"

I swallowed hard. The smell of shampoo and bodywash had me thinking of her standing naked in my shower. Water sluicing over her curves. Every bit of her wet and glistening. Words were too far out of reach. It was all I could do just to nod.

"'She's only seventeen.' I used to whisper it over and over, trying to get you out of my head," she said. Her mouth a hair's breadth away from mine. Her crystal blue eyes somehow even more hypnotic up close.

"D-d-did it work?"

She smirked and drew me to her. Her lips met mine. A good, firm, breath-stealing kiss. She gave me her breath in return, her tongue sliding the length of my smile.

My lips parted on her tongue's return path. I sucked it inside, enjoying the pleasant intrusion. A girlish giggle from her mouth to mine was my reward. I embraced her tightly, and her taut muscles yielded under my touch.

"More," she panted, peppering kisses in a trail from my chin to my neck. A soft nibble against my throbbing pulse elicited twin growls from both of us. She clasped my hands, dragging them to the hem of her shirt.

I grabbed hold and pulled it over her head, then tossed it away. Every schoolgirl fantasy paled in comparison to the actual sight of her creamy breasts encased in sheer, black lace. Just as I was dying to beg for a taste, I felt her hands at the back of my neck, urging my mouth back toward hers. Her fingers twisted through my hair. Our mouths merged in a kiss that was long, deep, hard.

My fingers traced designs on the smooth flesh of her back until I found the clasp of her bra. I had her freed in a blink. I wanted desperately to get a look at her, but her hands were still tangled in my hair. Two sets of lips blended into one. Our breathing was ragged, chests heaving as our bodies desperately ground against one another.

Drowning in the sea of Mallory, I couldn't imagine a sweeter way to go.

She must have sensed my need for more air, though. Her mouth reclaimed my neck. Fingers settled on the buttons of my blouse. She pulled and tugged until the fabric came undone. Once my shirt was freed of my pants, she slipped it past my shoulders to puddle on the floor. The tips of her fingers set fires in a zigzagging trail from my collarbone to my breasts. Her magical tongue soon followed the path, stoking the flames.

"Mmmmmm," she murmured. Her swirling tongue and warm lips captured my nipple. "The wine is delicious. Almost as good as you."

"Aw, hell," I groaned, attempting to back away. "I forgot about my spill. I could go shower."

"Not a chance." She nibbled softly. "It's been ten years, girlie. Don't expect to go anywhere anytime soon."

"Wouldn't dream of it," I whispered.

"Good. Glad we're on the same page, because I like you just as you are." She emphasized the point with another lick. Her soft, skilled fingers touched me all over, achingly slow. Her knee bent, demanding a place between mine.

My legs opened wider to her, my whole body pressing back against every velvet touch of hers, seeking relief. Finding none. The contact only stirred up more intense needs.

She went back to sucking my jaw, her tongue thrusting in time with my heartbeat. The wine was back in her hands, and she poured it over both our mouths. Messy. Wet. Delicious.

I cupped her cheek, stroked her bottom lip with my thumb. She caught me off guard when her lips parted and she sucked it deep within her searing mouth. The room began to spin. The joints in my knees became mush.

Mallory steered me to the couch, where she eased me down. I pulled her with me so that each of her knees hugged my hips.

Pushing my fingers through her hair, I drew her mouth to mine again. I found the button on her jeans and unfastened it only to find another in my path. "Button-fly jeans?" I groaned. "Are you trying to make me crazy?"

She laughed, tugging at the button on my pants. "You saying I'm not worth the trouble?" She clenched her thighs, adding a slow grind against my pelvis.

It was one of those rare moments when I was at a loss for words. Every move she made unraveled me. From head to foot, every single nerve was set aflame with want. I arched against her, allowing the slow removal of my pants by expert hands. Her sharp intake of breath and Cheshire cat smile set me more at ease.

"You're so fucking beautiful it hurts." I had found my voice. It was strained and much quieter than I intended, but still I managed to get the words out.

Her laughter danced on the charged air between us. "Such a dirty mouth," she teased, then helped me finish unbuttoning her jeans. She brought my hand to her mouth, slowly sucking the first three fingers in.

I bit my lower lip. Watching and feeling her talented mouth at work had me hovering on the edge. By the time she took my hand and guided it past her jeans and lacey underwear, I was drenched and on the brink of coming. Slick, moist heat met my questing fingers. She whimpered at the first caress, before her breathing became slow, shallow pants.

Together we worked her jeans and panties off. My fingers never broke contact with her wet pussy. I alternated between feather-light and firm strokes, drawing sounds of pleasure from her. When we were both so close that everything ached, I sat up to get a better angle. I slid my knee between hers, welcoming her wetness on my thigh. My hands reached up to grasp her soft breasts as she ground herself against me, drenching me in her juices. Her pointed nipples poked my palms.

"More, now," she panted. It sounded somewhere between a plea and an order.

Our lips came together in another scorching kiss. She grasped my hand and dragged it lower, keeping it against her hot flesh as she did so, until I reached her bare mound. Her legs moved farther apart, accepting my thumb rubbing her clit and two fingers tracing her lips, spreading them but not entering. I reveled in the soft noises she made and the quickening movement of her hips.

The hand she had behind my neck worked its way into my hair. Her other hand teased my nipples mercilessly. Her eyes were hooded when she pulled away minutes later, and her face was red, her lips swollen from demanding kisses. She looked absolutely gorgeous. "If you don't fuck me soon, I think I'll die," she said between gasps.

"Direct *and* dramatic," I murmured, loving the power I had over this woman who had always seemed so far out of reach. My fingers slid through her wetness, not stopping until two were deep inside her. My thumb pressed against her clit, drawing new sounds from her lips. The sound of rushing blood filled my ears. Our heavy breaths mingled. Mallory rose and fell in pace with my hand.

When I felt her clenching my fingers more tightly, I changed their position, bending them so I was teasing the spot that made her shudder and shake. The curses that left her mouth made me laugh. Who knew the single mom and upstanding citizen had such a dirty and inventive mind? She leaned forward until her head rested between my neck and shoulder. I kept my hand moving all through her quakes, not stilling until she did.

"I think I'm a bad influence on you, Mallory," I whispered while her breathing gradually returned to normal. I slipped my fingers out and brought them to my lips, inhaled and smiled. I moaned at the first taste. "You were saying some words that would make Samuel L Jackson blush."

She gave my shoulder a gentle bite. "I like your influence, very much." Her mouth found mine again, her lips and tongue working me back into a frenzy. "And I fucking love the way you kiss." Her soft hands skimmed up and down my sides. Short nails grazed my skin on the last trip down, raising goose bumps. She nudged me backward until I was lying flat on the couch.

My heart beat like the guy's in that Edgar Allan Poe story. I felt it pounding in my ears. I surrendered to her completely as she explored me with fingers and tongue. Desire swelled within me until I thought I would implode.

Mallory was relentless, not letting up even when I begged for release. Her kisses were maddening and fierce. Fingertips danced across my skin until her palm finally landed between my thighs.

I arched up and rubbed myself against her, trying to convey with my eyes what my mouth was no longer capable of saying.

She ducked her head lower. Two fingers stretched me open, withdrawing only to be replaced with her tongue. She was gentle at first, and I melted into her touches. Then her repeated licks, flicks, sucking, and pumping became hard and hungry, leaving me gasping. My whole body stiffened. Every muscle tightened at once until I finally gave her my release.

We lay there spent, Mallory tucked in behind me, warm arms snuggling my back against her lovely front. We were content just to breathe each other in, our legs tangled in a most delightful way.

While my own tremors were still dying down, I heard a low rumble. The windows began to rattle. "Oh, shit. Mallory, I'm so sorry. I made you miss the rocket launch."

"Shh," she whispered. Her tongue traced my outer ear. She made me gasp when she sucked the lobe into her mouth. She moved it back and forth the same way she'd maneuvered my clit just a short while ago. Her hand snaked lower, fingernails lightly tickling along my underwear line. "You've just taken me higher than any rocket ever could."

Who knew the no-nonsense, unflappable Mallory Roarke could be so corny? I sure didn't. The woman never stopped surprising me. If I had anything to say about it, she never would. I wondered what else I'd learn about her when I took my next vacation in LA.

SOUND BITES

BY T.M. CROKE AND T.M. BALLION

IT WAS CLOSING NIGHT OF the Centre City Theatre's sold out run of *Sunset Boulevard*, and I still couldn't believe I had got this gig. When the call had come offering me the sound tech position, I was ecstatic. Their resident stage manager, Abigail "Abby" Donahue, was the most feared and revered in the city, and you did not get a call to work with her unless you came highly recommended.

Since day one of rehearsals I had spent most of my time in the tiny sound booth above the back row of seats, mastering the cue calls and watching the cast sort out their onstage production. Once the play was up and running, I spent all the major sound lulls with my feet up, constructing sexual fantasy scenarios in my head which starred me and Ms. Abby Donahue.

I couldn't help myself.

For weeks, on a nightly basis, her voice slid into me with a sharp and commanding tone. There was never conversation, just cue calling and the occasional secondhand chatter through her open mic. Her wish was my command, and one of my fantasies had her wishing for much more than cuing sound five.

I found it odd that despite how often my colleagues had spoken of Abby, her stunning and wonderfully distracting appearance never came up. It surprised me to discover that her demanding work expectations and disengaged manner were encased in a sensual exterior. The combination elicited an ongoing swirl of excitement and anxiety in my gut since the day I first saw her.

This, however, did not stop me from introducing myself to her after our first technical production meeting. I was shy and a little on edge as I approached her, but I really wanted to thank her for the opportunity. On that night as on every other, she was dressed in basic theatre-tech black, but the way the material clung to her body drew my attention to the subtlety of every curve underneath. A pair of low-slung trousers hugged her hips and a long-sleeved V-neck shirt stretched seductively across her pert breasts. That all-familiar stirring twisted in my gut at the sight of her. Her raven hair was pulled back in a high, tight ponytail. Dark-framed glasses accentuated her icy blue eyes, which locked with mine as I drew near. The venom in her stare was not at all inviting. She was a stage manager interrupted, with absolutely no interest in meeting the help.

"Hello, Ms. Donahue," I peeped. "I'm Jameson, your sound tech. I wanted to thank you for the—"

Abby interjected with a strict, but surprisingly soft tone. "Well then." She paused, her gaze blanketed my body as it wandered down, then up, taking me in. "You're sound."

With a voice as sexy as the body from which it came, she was irresistible. I was confident I could be anything this woman ever wanted.

She continued, "As you know, opening night is in nine days. I don't expect to see much of you over the next few weeks, but you'll certainly become well acquainted with my voice. If you need anything else, I'm sure my assistant can handle whatever it is."

With a smooth, but abrupt turn she walked away leaving my mouth agape. *I better not fuck this up.*

That proved to be the one and only time I engaged in a "conversation" with Abby Donahue and I was hooked. From that moment on I could not get her out of my head.

Rehearsals had been a little scratchy at the beginning. The first night I had gotten my cues confused, and instead of a siren in the distance, the cast was treated to a monkey's screech. Abby roared into my headset and I was sure not to make that mistake again. By the time the show opened, every aspect of the production had fallen into place. Things had been going very well. I was managing my nerves like a true professional and here I was: closing night.

I arrived much earlier than usual, using the extra time to quietly wander about the theatre and take in as much as I could of what was left of this experience. As the cast and crew eventually streamed in, the air was filled with a wave of closing night energy. Everyone was in good form and a little more relaxed and cheerful than usual. The Centre City closing night parties were legendary in the local theatre community, and we were all looking forward to congratulating ourselves on a job well done.

After making my usual checks with the other technicians, I headed back to the sound booth for the beginning of the show. As I began my ascent up the ladder and through the latch into the sound booth floor, I was startled to find myself face to feet with a pair of black leather shoes.

"Hey," I said as I lifted my body into the dark and tiny booth. "I'm the sound tech, anything wrong up here tonight?"

As I found my footing and my eyes adjusted to the low light, I saw that the person before me was Abby.

"Oh, sorry, Ms. Donahue, I didn't realize it was you. I'm usually up here alone, as you know." Her presence in my booth amplified both the tininess of the space and my heart rate.

"Yes, of course I know that, Jameson. And please call me Abby."

It was the first time she had used my name. Even I had begun to think my name was "Sound." I was silent and frozen in place.

"Have you enjoyed your time here with us, Jameson?" she asked.

"Yes, I have."

"When I first hired you, I didn't know you were going to be a girl." She grinned. "Jameson is a rather interesting name. Were your parents hoping for a boy?"

A quiet laugh issued from my lips at this familiar question. "Yes, yes, they were, but in a fortunate turn of events they got a lesbian instead."

Her response was a curt, obligatory smile as she held my gaze, not unlike she had at our first meeting, but without the venom. I expected her to say something, but instead she turned to leave. The room was narrow, which meant she had to squeeze by me to move. In the process her ass brushed my pelvis, sending a shiver down my spine as she maneuvered to exit through the floor door. She tilted her head and grinned. "Enjoy tonight's show."

I reached for my headset and took my seat in front of the board.

What just happened?

I inhaled deeply. The scent of Abby hung in the air, and I hoped it would linger until the sound lull for tonight's final fantasy.

Placing the set on my head, I adjusted the band and situated the mic. The usual banter of backstage noise rustled through the earpiece. Technicians calling for marks, looking for props, and even holding faint conversations about what people did the night before.

And then Abby.

"James. James? Are you there?"

I gulped. I didn't quite know if she was talking to me or someone next to her.

"James?" The way she shortened my name sent goose bumps across my body. "Are you there?"

"Ye...yeah, I'm here," I stammered. I needed to get a grip. My breath caught in my throat and my heart hammered in my chest.

"Okay then. Get yourself together, they're about to open the doors. You'll know when I'm ready for you."

I had been listening to her voice in my ear for weeks, but suddenly it took on a seductive, playful lilt. I closed my eyes and sighed.

"Sure thing," I replied, and was sure I heard a faint chuckle across the line. It may have been Abby, or perhaps someone passing by her open mic, or just my imagination.

Abby cued the house music as the ushers directed patrons to their seats.

Okay, time to get serious.

As the house lights dimmed, my finger hovered over the slider in anticipation of her command.

Abby's voice filled my ear. "Sound, cue one."

I slid the fader up to start the opening music. Shortly the curtains lifted and my night began.

Having heard this show for weeks, I settled in, knowing Abby would interrupt my daydreams when the time came to do my job.

The first half of the show went by smoothly, and before I knew it we had reached the first major lull in the performance. I swiveled in my chair, cued the next sound bite and sat back. I wouldn't get another cue for twenty minutes.

So far, so good.

I tilted my head back and closed my eyes.

"So, James, do you ever leave your booth during this segment?" It was Abby.

My eyes shot open. Was she really making conversation with me?

When it came to this point in the performance, Abby was usually here with me in my head, but she had never engaged me in any form of conversation. My breath hitched and I shivered. "Not usually," I sputtered.

Why was I so nervous? I shook my head. Because Abby made me nervous.

"So what exactly do you do up there....all...alone?" The cadence of her voice made me blush. Heat spread across my chest, up my neck, and into my cheeks. I was grateful I was alone. She had never affected me like this before. My lips ached to press against hers.

"James? Are you still there?" She let out a quiet chuckle.

"Yeah, sorry." I tried to sound nonchalant but there was still a nervous squeak to my voice. "I usually just..." Just what? What could I tell her? That I sat back and fantasized about her? No, I couldn't do that. "I usually just think," I spat out.

"And just what do you think about?" Again, her tone was seductive and alluring. Was she baiting me? I was terrified and turned on at the same time.

I would love to tell you what I really thought about.

She filled the silence with, "I think about a few things myself during this break. I can tell you what they are, if you like?"

My thighs clenched.

"Sure." The word stumbled out of my mouth.

"Well, tonight I was thinking that's an awfully small space you have up there."

I found myself nodding. "Mm-hm" was mumbled from my lips.

"It was a rather tight, or should I say, cozy, squeeze for just the two of us."

I tried to keep my cool, but my breathing grew fast and erratic through the earpiece.

"If I were you, up there now with a little time on my hands, do you know what I would do?"

"N-no." I rubbed my sweating palms against the coarse material of my cargo pants.

"I'd sit back, close my eyes and think of *me*."

I gasped and bolted forward. *What the fuck?*

I let the shock run through me and sat back. A breathy "Oh" was all I could muster as my eyes slid closed and Abby was all I could see.

"Do you know why I was up there, this evening?"

"No."

"I wanted to get a feel for you in that space. I wanted to see how much room we'd have for what I want to do to you." Her voice caressed my skin, and I shivered as her words inhabited my space.

"And what would that be?" My imagination was good, but I desperately wanted her to spell it out for me.

"I'd push your chair against the soundboard, my hands on your shoulders, pinning you. My face brushing yours as my breath sweeps across your cheek. You want me to kiss you, don't you?"

"Yes," I whispered.

"But I'm not going to, you're not ready yet."

I gasped. I wanted her lips against mine so badly.

"Can you feel me, James? Can you feel the warmth of my mouth against your neck, the want of my tongue?"

Of course I could feel her. My hips rocked forward, trying to rub against her.

"Yes," I squeaked.

"Picture me straddling your thighs," she whispered into the line.

My ass shifted to the end of the seat and my legs parted as if I was bracing myself for Abby. I frantically pulled at the crotch of my cargo pants, easing the seam away from my sensitive clit.

"Mm," Abby vibrated through the mic. "I can taste the salt in your skin as my tongue runs down your neck, nipping at your soft, delicate flesh," she purred. "Your shirt is in my way. Unbutton it."

Without question, I did just that.

"Describe what you're wearing underneath," Abby instructed.

I let the fabric of my shirt hang open, exposing my breasts.

As my hands smoothed over the surface of my bra, my nipples hardened under the fabric. "It's...black. Soft. Satin."

"Take it off," she half-growled, half-whispered. The hoarse command travelled down my body, fueling the fire between my legs. Did I dare? I was alone in my attic, but still, I was at work.

Compromising, I shoved the cups of my bra up and gripped my nipples firmly between my fingers, groaning as she spoke again.

"We're face to face now, your lips only a fraction from mine. I want to kiss you, but I'm still not sure..."

"Please," I begged. "Kiss me."

In my mind I created the perfect kiss. Abby's plump, sensual lips captured mine, her subtle taste playing with my senses. The tip of her tongue, warm and wet, skated along my bottom lip, urging me to open for her.

"Ugh." I grunted and bit into my lower lip.

"I squeeze your nipples, pinching and teasing them. They're so hard." Her words tugged at me.

"Uh-huh." I was pulling at them, arching toward Abby's voice. I rolled them back and forth, feeling them harden. Jolts of pleasure traveled through my body and I trembled at the exquisite torture she induced. "Please..." I pleaded. "More…" I wanted her to touch me, all of me, to run her fingertips over every inch of my body and then do it all over again.

Her voice dropped an octave. "Feel me squirm in your lap, grinding my pussy against you. I reach between us and scrape my nails down your stomach to the waistband of your pants."

The muscles in my abdomen contracted and I gasped at the tightness in my stomach.

"I want those pants off." Her command was low and exacting in its authority.

I loosened my belt, warring with wanting to touch myself and the thin thread of control I had left.

My want won out.

I let the leather slide free of the buckle and undid the button. As I fumbled with the zipper, the sound of it cut through the quiet rush of heavy breathing. A sharp intake of breath came across the line. "Oh."

There was no going back now.

"Oh yes," she moaned. "I slide my hand into your pants, brushing over your hard clit. Are you wet, James?"

I shoved my hand under the waistband of my pants and briefs into my drenching depths and groaned. "Very," I replied.

My fingers slipped between my slick folds, coming in direct contact with my eagerly swelling clit.

"You're soaking. So hot for me." She exhaled a long breath.

The sound of her blowing against my ear made me shudder. A fresh flow of wetness trickled between my legs as I squeezed my thighs together hard around my hand. I couldn't believe what she was doing to me.

"Mm, I love how wet your pussy gets for me. I can't wait to taste you, to slide my tongue against your clit and drink you."

I nearly came off the chair. "Yes." I squeezed my clit and jerked forward, my legs parted to give myself room. I was going to come soon.

"I slide off your lap to pull your pants down around your ankles and spread you wide. I have to have you," Abby murmured in my ear.

"Oh God," I cried. My vision clouded with my own personal fantasy, featuring Abby descending to the floor, nestled between my legs. Her hooded crystal-blue eyes looked up at me and that full, sensuous mouth nearly set me off. My hand stilled and I concentrated on her staccato breathing across the line.

"I part your lips, feeling you slip against my fingertips, and run the flat of my tongue along you."

My clitoris twitched beneath my fingertips as I circled lightly at the throbbing flesh. I was near shattering and needed to come soon.

She was killing me. Slowly, but definitely killing me.

I looked down at the movement of my hand, and the image of Abby again came into view. Darkening eyes looked up over the rim of her glasses as her mouth latched onto my clit.

"Please, I need you to suck it." My breathing was coming in fits and starts. I wanted those lips around me, sucking me hard to a climax.

"Yes, I'm going to make you come in my mouth," Abby's words pierced through the headset. "But not yet."

"Oh God." My eyes rolled in my head, and my tongue snaked out to wet my dry lips. My hips pumped a slow, steady rhythm. I slid my fingers on either side of my clit, squeezing slightly.

"You taste amazing, James. I'm going to suck you until you squirm and explode all over me."

"I'm going to come soon. Please," I begged her. I couldn't take much more. I wanted her mouth to bring me off at the same time my fingers did.

"Mm. I can feel you throb under my tongue. Your clit's so firm. You're ready to explode, aren't you, James?"

"Uh-huh." I was near whining as I continued my ministrations.

"My hot, wet mouth is tugging at your clit, my tongue flicking you hard."

"Oh God, I can feel it." I gritted my teeth, trying to draw out the pleasure for as long as I could.

"That's it, James. Touch yourself," Abby groaned. "I can feel how hot you are for me."

My breathing was staggered and rough. I massaged the length of my clit, avoiding the tip of it. If I rubbed there, I would go off in less than a few strokes.

Abby's tiny whimpers were doing more for me than my own fingers. Was she touching herself in a dark corner backstage, too? The sounds flooding my earpiece told me Abby was into this as much as I was. I imagined her hand tucked firmly in her trousers, jerking back and forth as she told me everything she wanted to do to me.

My moans came louder and my hips flexed as my fingers eagerly slid back and forth.

"Oh fuck, you're so wet. I love the taste of you in my mouth. You're so close, James, aren't you?"

"Yes," I hissed between my teeth. "S-so close." My whole body was trembling. The sounds coming from my mouth were gibberish at best.

I needed to come. I wanted to come. I wanted to come for Abby. I circled my clit hard and fast. My hips completely lifted off the chair. My thighs stiffened. Sweat drizzled between my breasts. The sweet burn between my legs rose with urgency.

One more stroke.

I grunted as my fingers and Abby's imagined mouth took me to the edge.

"Oh, James," Abby moaned.

That did it.

My breath was sucked from me. I came in one mind blowing explosion, flooding my hand and crying out into the mic.

Everything faded from my vision as I fell back into the chair, my hand still stuck in my cargo pants. I released the breath I had been holding and started panting heavily as my heart pounded in my chest.

"Shit. Shit. Shit. Cue five. Damn it!" Abby's voice echoed sharply in my ear. For a brief second I couldn't comprehend what she was saying, and then the realization of where I was and what was going on hit me. I ripped my hand from my pants and tripped toward the board.

I reached forward and remembered that my arousal still clung to my fingers. After briskly wiping them against the leg of my pants, I flipped the switch.

The cue went off and the audience roared with laughter. Despite having sat through the show for weeks, for the first time my sense of where we were in the play was lost.

Within moments my attention was redirected to the task at hand and my body cascaded back into the chair as I slowly came down from one of the hardest orgasms I had ever had. I inhaled deeply. The room was stuffy and the smell of sex lingered.

I shook my head before lowering it into my palms, my own scent permeated my senses.

Damn. Abby. Is she still there?

I was almost afraid to ask. The silence coming across the headset was deafening.

"Abby?"

Dead air.

She was there. It was her job to be there.

"Abby?" I asked again, my stomach churning with uncertainty.

"Be ready for the next cue, sound."

And there it was, the cold, monotone, professionalism I had been hearing for the last couple of weeks. Gone was the seductive purr of the woman I had been listening to for the last twenty minutes.

I closed my eyes. My clit still pleasantly throbbed and I squeezed my legs together to enjoy the last memories.

It was back to business, with no soothing sentiments in the wake of afterglow, just detachment. I let out a deep sigh, my heart easing into its regular pattern.

Abby's voice only penetrated the silence to call for the next series of cues. That one brief moment we shared was over and gone. The show ended with a standing ovation, regardless of our little faux pas.

I didn't want to leave the safety of my enclosure, not wanting to face the crew, or worse, Abby.

Running my hands through my hair and straightening my clothes, I realized I couldn't hide up here forever. Whatever mistakes I made tonight, I knew overall, I did a good job.

With a deep sigh, I opened the hatch and backed my way down out of the little room, jumping the last two steps to the floor.

Embarrassment shrouded me as I made my way backstage where the crew was mingling, celebrating the end of the show.

"Did you fall asleep during the monologue, Jameson?" Tanya, a short blonde runner, called with a smirk.

I flushed. "Something like that," I threw back.

Everyone around me chuckled. I laughed along with them, my shame still colouring my face.

From behind, a voice called, "What the hell was that?"

I stiffened. It was Abby and she was not pleased.

"How could you forget that cue?"

Ultimately, it was her responsibility to call the cues, but she was the boss and who was I to argue?

I turned to face her. Her hands were firmly planted on her hips. She was sexy before, but riled up, she was the epitome of hot.

"What were you doing? Playing with yourself?" she yelled at me. To those around us, she was giving me a royal chewing out, but I caught the glint in her eye.

Everyone scattered awkwardly, mumbling about seeing us later at the wrap party. I nodded in acknowledgement before turning back to face Abby. I had no idea what she would say or how she would react.

She didn't say anything. The heat in her eyes scorched the length of my body as she studied me.

I tried to swallow around the dryness in my throat and shifted from foot to foot.

She tilted her head to the right, and the opposite corner of her lip turned up in a smile. "See you at the wrap party....and maybe after." She winked and turned to leave.

I smiled at her rear end sashaying down the dark corridor. It might be my last night working here, but if I played my cards right, it would not be the last night I heard Abby's voice in my ear.

BIRTHDAY GIRL

BY MEGHAN O'BRIEN

THEY WERE DEEP INTO A session of toe-curlingly erotic foreplay when Lucy forced them to stop. "So, now that you're turned on…"

Alice whimpered, trying in vain to guide Lucy's head back to her nipple. "I've been turned on all evening. Less talking, more sucking." After dinner at her favorite restaurant with her stunning wife, followed by a port and dark chocolate pairing that whetted her appetite for all of life's pleasures, how could she *not* be? The port had loosened her muscles and inhibitions, leaving her ready for intense, prolonged birthday sex—the wilder, the better—so as to negate her mild despair about turning forty. Who said her best years were behind her?

Laughing, Lucy ducked out of Alice's reach. She sat and took Alice's hand between both of hers. "Wait. I have a potential gift for you."

The sight of her wife looking so serious did nothing to cool her ardor, but curiosity allowed her to set it aside for the moment. "A *potential* gift?" Alice ran her gaze over Lucy's shapely form, hoping that the timing of this offer was significant. "If it involves your beautiful body, yes, please."

Lucy lifted Alice's hand and kissed her fingers, one by one. "I would be there."

Alice waited for more, but Lucy just kept kissing around the inside of her wrist, up the length of her bare arm. Wanting her to expand on that intriguing statement, Alice said, "What does that mean?" Lucy reached her shoulder, then grazed her neck, causing Alice to shiver. If she wasn't careful, Alice might lose interest in birthday presents until morning. "*Honey*, what gift?"

Lucy drew back wearing a mischievous grin. The same one that made Alice fall in love with her twenty years ago. One that let her know that *this*—whatever birthday surprise she had planned—was big.

Thirty minutes later, they were in a cab.

Alice couldn't believe she'd agreed to leave their bed. Not just because she was so horny it was painful to walk, but also because, as perfect as Lucy's gift was, she would need every ounce of her courage to enjoy it. Grateful for her mild intoxication, she whispered in Lucy's ear. *"Where* is this party?"

"Not far. At the house of a woman I met while researching an article."

Alice wondered which one. As a freelance writer, Lucy had authored various pieces about different sexual practices. Their own sex life was active and never vanilla, albeit private until now. More than once, Alice had read Lucy's stories about taboo subcultures and secretly wished to dip her toes into the waters of sexual adventure. Or perhaps not so secretly. Over the years, she'd overcome her innate shyness to share a handful of dirty fantasies with her confident, uninhibited wife. Apparently, Lucy had taken notes.

Exhaling at the thrill of what she knew—they were attending a lesbian sex party—and the suspense of what she didn't—how many women would be there, what they would do, and how it would feel to be touched by someone other than her college sweetheart—Alice held tight to Lucy's hand. Murmuring so the cabbie wouldn't overhear, she said, "Will you know everyone there?"

"I've met them all at least once." She gave Alice a reassuring squeeze. "Everyone loved that photo I took of you at the beach. Believe me, I had no trouble finding volunteers for tonight."

Alice blushed at the thought of strangers assessing her. At the same time, it comforted her that the other guests knew what to expect. That they might honestly be excited about her inclusion in tonight's festivities was intoxicating, to say the least. That's when Lucy's words registered. "Wait, volunteers?" Everything clicked into place. *"You're* throwing this party?"

Lucy's eyes sparkled under the passing streetlights. "Yes. It's *your* party, based on *your* fantasy."

Alice was too stunned to recall which fantasy that might be. "My... fantasy?"

"You're the guest of honor." Lucy nibbled her neck, leaving her more distracted with each press of hot lips against cool skin. "And also the entertainment."

Gasping, Alice closed her eyes as she recalled a years-old desire, every bit as enticing now as it was when she'd shared it with Lucy during their late twenties. "This is dirty," she'd warned in case her kinky wife somehow didn't approve. "But I've fantasized about going to a party where I'm stripped naked and used by all the guests. Never knowing who's next, or what they'll do, or want me to do to them." Alice shivered now just as she had when first confessing her secret desire, and, as she did then, willingly curled into Lucy's warm embrace. Holding her close, Lucy rubbed her back in a soothing rhythm.

Quietly, Lucy said, "We can still go home. I won't be upset. No one will. If I cancel, I'm sure everyone will find *some* way to entertain themselves."

Alice chuckled, noting the stab of disappointment she felt at the prospect of skipping out on her own birthday gang-bang. Would she ever forgive herself for turning down this opportunity? Wishing she felt braver, she asked, "You'll be there?"

"If you want me."

Touched that Lucy was apparently willing to leave if that was what her fantasy required, Alice nodded. "Stay with me."

Lucy nipped her lower lip. "You're lucky I'm a voyeur."

She considered what Lucy had engineered for her birthday. "I'm lucky for lots of reasons."

<hr>

When they arrived at their destination, Alice nearly asked to turn around and go home. The cabbie parked in front of a nondescript ranch style home three blocks from their dentist's office. For some reason, this proximity to everyday life spooked her. But then the front door opened, emitting a warm, honeyed glow, and a voluptuous redhead who breezed outside and sauntered down the front walkway. She wore a broad smile that eased Alice's anxieties, and when she opened the passenger door and offered her hand, Alice was confident enough to take it.

"Alice," the redhead chirped, kissing her fingers as she guided her onto the sidewalk. "You're even lovelier in person."

"Thanks." Alice glanced back, desperate for her wife to act as a social buffer. But Lucy was still paying the driver, and the longer Alice waited for rescue, the more awkward this introduction became. Being shy was silly, anyway. If she planned to let this woman fuck her tonight, small talk should probably come first. Turning, Alice forced a smile. "Sorry, I'm still processing Lucy's surprise."

The woman pulled her into an embrace that crossed the line from friendly to intimate in many subtle ways. One of which was her body's reaction to the other woman's ample curves inviting her to linger in the embrace. Soaking in the sensuality, Alice shivered when the woman's hand grazed her breast before reaching to press between her shoulder blades. "I'm Audrey, and no apology necessary. It's a lot to process, I'm sure." She shot an admonishing look over Alice's shoulder. "You *just* told her?"

"I wasn't sure she'd go through with this if the anxiety had too much time to build." Lucy approached from behind, sliding an arm around Alice's waist. "But I'll say it again, if you want to leave, whether it's right now, in five minutes, or in five *hours,* just say the word. We'll leave."

Alice glanced at the cab, then at Lucy, then finally at Audrey, who stood so close their breasts touched. Scared or not, she wouldn't turn back now. "Let's stay."

Audrey led her by the hand to the house, while Lucy walked at her side. Audrey spoke over her shoulder to Alice, "I promise that everyone is *very* nice and *very* eager to meet you. When Lucy contacted me about arranging this get-together, I thought it was such a delicious idea. My friends agreed. We've been told you're incredible in bed, but a little shy when it comes to sharing your fantasies, let alone acting on them." Showing them into an empty foyer, Audrey hung back to lock the front door. Despite knowing she was perfectly safe, the *click* of the deadbolt made Alice's stomach swirl with a confusing mixture of fear and excitement.

Feeling the need to respond lest she appear socially inept, Alice said, "Weird, I know, a woman like Lucy married to someone as shy as me."

Tightening the arm around Alice's middle, Lucy steered them toward a loveseat in the front room. She barely had time to wonder where the other guests were before Lucy pulled her down onto her lap. Once they were seated, Lucy nuzzled the spot behind her ear that always made Alice erupt in goose bumps from head to toe. Lucy murmured, "Not weird at all."

Audrey sat beside them on the narrow loveseat, so close that Alice could feel the heat pouring off her body. And what a body it was—curvier than Lucy's, more substantial, absolutely thrumming with passion. Audrey's blue eyes smoldered as she caressed Alice's face. "Shy can be *very* sexy." She scooted impossibly closer, briefly meeting Lucy's gaze before cradling the back of Alice's neck in her hand. "We just don't want you to be *too* shy."

Alice wasn't certain whether Audrey kissed her or vice versa. It probably didn't matter. Suddenly there was an unfamiliar tongue in her mouth, one that didn't move like Lucy's, or taste like Lucy's, or feel like Lucy's in any way. It was new and different and strange and fantastic. She couldn't predict what Audrey might do next, and her body reeled to take in the unique sensations. Despite being seated firmly on Lucy's lap, Alice's knees wobbled and she felt as if she might fall down.

Audrey pulled away to reveal a smile that was even brighter than before. "You okay?"

Alice glanced at Lucy. *Were* they okay? Based on her wife's hooded gaze, her heaving chest, and the hand that palmed her ass in a way that signaled familiar arousal, it seemed they were fine. Maybe even embarking on a new kink together. "Did you like watching her kiss me?"

Lucy groaned, licking Alice's exposed collarbone. "Very much."

She shouldn't be surprised. Lucy had never been shy about what got her off. Voyeurism had always played a starring role in her wife's fantasies, but beyond a live BDSM show they once attended as spectators, they'd never had the chance to indulge that desire. Jealousy didn't seem to occur to Lucy, so watching Alice with another woman was pure pleasure.

Happy that this truly was mutually beneficial, Alice mustered all her pluck and turned to Audrey. "Kiss me again." When Audrey raised an eyebrow, ostensibly impressed by her boldness, Alice dissolved into a blush. "Please."

"My pleasure." Audrey leaned in, teasing her with gentle licks along her upper lip, then the lower. As she attempted to initiate a proper kiss, Alice didn't notice the hem of her dress being raised above her knees until her panties were exposed. When cool air breezed across her upper thighs, she gasped. Audrey finally slipped into her mouth, swallowing her exclamation by kissing her deeply. A hand landed on the inside of Alice's thigh above the knee. It didn't feel like Lucy's. Not that she cared. Heart pounding, she closed her eyes and fell deeper into the kiss.

Lucy's voice, soft, almost dream-like. "She likes a gentle touch, especially at first. My delicate little flower...literally." A second hand covered the one that had been tracing distracting patterns on her inner thigh, sliding it higher and higher until both hands rested atop the soaked crotch of her panties. "She gets *very* wet."

Lucy removed her hand and Audrey broke their kiss, still cradling her intimately. She waited for Alice to reluctantly meet her gaze. "Is this all right, Alice?"

She *really* didn't trust her voice right now. Nodding, she leaned against Lucy's solid chest and spread her legs. At this point she was up for almost anything, as long as it ended in wet, glorious pleasure. When it became clear that Audrey wouldn't proceed without verbal consent, she managed a tremulous, "Yes."

Audrey used her blunt thumbnail to stroke Alice's clit through the lacy fabric. She kept the contact light at first, applying additional pressure intermittently. Her index finger probed the material covering Alice's vagina, hinting at penetration. "Lucy suggested we ease you into tonight by introducing you to me first. Let you get used to being touched..." She paused to slide her finger beneath the elastic band of Alice's panties, pulling the material aside so she could resume her caresses directly on bare flesh. "And fucked, by one stranger first. Before the rest join in."

Alice felt poised to explode right then and there. Between the sound of Lucy's increasingly ragged breath and the exquisite sensation of Audrey so carefully and tenderly stroking her, it was a wonder she hadn't come apart already. Only her desire to prolong this moment prevented her from succumbing to the thunderous pleasure that beckoned. Reaching out, Alice sighed with relief when Lucy caught her hand and squeezed, providing an anchor to keep her grounded for at least another few minutes.

Lucy brought her free hand up to tease Alice's nipples through her dress. "Do you want Audrey to fuck you with her finger?" She licked Alice's earlobe, then whispered, "I hope so, because I *really* want to see her sliding in and out of your beautiful pussy."

Audrey's sly smile made it clear she'd heard every word. "It *is* beautiful." She used her free hand to tug at the waistband of Alice's panties. "Why don't we take these off?"

Alice lifted her hips and allowed Audrey to strip her bare. As if underscoring that thought, Audrey placed her hands on the inside of Alice's thighs and pressed them apart, exposing Alice's ridiculously aroused sex to both their hungry gazes. The reactions were visceral. Lucy groaned, hips shifting and rolling with the obvious desire to fuck. Audrey whimpered, fierce desire written over her face as she drank in the sight. She glanced at Alice, then Lucy.

"Mind if I lick her first?"

Alice shivered, then reddened as she experienced a surge of arousal that left her as wet as she'd ever been. As though sensing her self-consciousness, Lucy dropped her roving hand to rub Alice's belly in slow, calming circles.

"Audrey loves the taste of pussy. The messier, the better." Lucy's hand shifted lower, the fingertips brushing across her swollen labia. "Will you let her kiss you here?"

Alice cleared her throat. "Yes."

Audrey sank onto the floor in front of them as Lucy spread her legs—and by extension Alice's—to allow her to kneel in the space between. She bent to kiss the inside of one knee, then the other, but instead of continuing to her goal, she straightened instead.

"Hold yourself open for me, darling. Show me how pretty you are," Audrey said. When Alice hesitated, Audrey bent again to place a soft kiss directly over her clit. Her mouth came away shiny. "Don't be shy."

Exhaling, Alice used her fingers to spread her outer labia open. She knew that to take the next step and join the party proper, she would have to embrace the idea of vulnerability. This fantasy involved subjecting herself to the whims of others. That was, in fact, the entire point of the scenario. Her difficulty with letting loose with anyone who wasn't Lucy was precisely why this fantasy was so enduring and intoxicating. It required her to do exactly that. Based on the way her body was reacting so far, reality might actually live up to her imagination.

Finding her voice, Alice said, "Lick me, *please*."

Audrey smirked and Lucy squeezed her around the middle, chuckling. Then Alice watched in slow motion as Audrey's sexy mouth—lips smeared with red from their kisses—descended upon her. A pink tongue poked out to lick a trail from her opening up over her labia, ending with a flick to her swollen clit. Alice arched against Lucy's chest and inhaled swiftly. Not only had that felt divine, the visual stimulus alone could make her come. *That's not my wife* echoed through her head, generating shock and mild anxiety and deep, primal exhilaration. Audrey licked her again, angling her head to make it clear she was performing for Alice's benefit.

Eager to participate more fully, Alice lifted a hand to finger a lock of Audrey's stunning red hair, then to caress her jaw. She closed her eyes when Lucy kissed the side of her face, whispering, "Beautiful, isn't she? I know you've always liked redheads."

The feeling of Audrey smiling into her wetness prompted her to reopen her eyes and enjoy the show. Lucy was right, this woman seemed to enjoy getting messy. Face buried between Alice's thighs, she licked and sucked and probed teasingly, bringing her right to the edge without ever settling into one rhythm long enough to push her over. Stroking the crown of Audrey's bowed head, Alice said, "She's incredible."

"I'll bet." Lucy kissed the edge of her ear. "Happy birthday, sweetheart. Come in her mouth for me?"

Almost as soon as the question was uttered, Audrey surprised her with the gentle pressure of a single fingertip pressed against her opening. Nodding at Audrey's unspoken request, she answered both women with a breathy, "Yes." When Audrey hesitated, perhaps unsure to whom she was responding, Alice clarified. "Yes, fuck me."

Audrey drew away, eliciting a sharp cry of protest as Alice's crescendoing pleasure faltered, then stalled with the loss of her hot tongue. But then she realized that Audrey was simply giving her—and Lucy—a better view of her excruciatingly slow penetration of Alice's vagina. Alice and Lucy released twin, pleasure-filled moans at the sight of the disappearing finger, which made Alice giggle until Audrey pulled out and then re-entered her with two. Pleasure overwhelmed her, tearing a strangled cry from her deep in her chest.

Lucy resumed her caresses of Alice's still-clothed breasts. "That's it. Come for us."

Audrey winked saucily, her perfectly coiffed hair now sexily askew. "All over my face, darling. I want to feel it, so don't hold back." She lowered her mouth to Alice without breaking eye contact, lapping her clit with the tip of her tongue while watching Alice watch her. The further knowledge that Lucy was watching *all* of this—and enjoying it, if her heavy breathing, undulating hips, and roving hands were to be believed—created a complex loop of mental and visual stimulation that brought her right to the edge.

"I'm almost there," Alice warned, gratified when Lucy tightened her embrace and Audrey doubled down on the rhythm she'd established. Her fingers and tongue picked up speed, driving her toward the inevitable explosion. And then what? Would she be passed to the next stranger so the process could begin again?

That thought spiked her fear and arousal and sent her flying apart. She arched her back and groaned, trembling as Audrey continued sucking and fingering despite the wild motion of her hips. No longer shy, Alice grabbed Audrey's hair, hoping she didn't mind having it pulled. The moan Audrey released assured her that no, she didn't mind at all. She held Audrey tight against her clit until she couldn't take any more, then carefully but firmly tugged her away. Laughing, Audrey again kissed the inside of one knee, then the other, before rising to rejoin them on the loveseat. She pulled Alice onto her lap, kissed her deeply, then turned her to face Lucy, who stared at her with palpable hunger.

"Did that feel as good as it looked?" Lucy kissed her before she could answer, sampling the juices Audrey had left on her mouth with her tongue. "Sure tastes good."

Alice shivered when Audrey teasingly stroked between her legs before pulling the hem of her dress back down. As though her modesty was still within reach. "It felt wonderful."

Lucy seemed genuinely thrilled to hear that. "So shall I call a cab, or do we go downstairs and start this party for real?"

Alice's confidence lasted until they reached the door to the basement staircase. For the first time since they'd arrived, she heard the indistinct murmur of women's voices. Multiple women. Alice put a hand on Audrey's wrist to stop her from turning the knob. "How many are here?"

Audrey and Lucy shared a look. "Six. All with their own proclivities and desires."

Alice swallowed. *Six* women? So there would be eight total, not including her? The idea of being the center of attention for that many hands, mouths, and who-knew-what-else made her hesitate. "Wow."

"I let everyone know your personal limits, what you like, don't like." Lucy pulled her close. "I promise nobody will do anything you won't enjoy. But if you *aren't* enjoying something, all you have to do is use our safe word and it stops."

Alice nodded. Logically she knew that Lucy wouldn't allow anything bad to happen. It wasn't as though she was particularly worried about not enjoying whatever happened next. She'd just always gotten nervous in big groups, especially at parties. Was that what had attracted her to this particular fantasy in the first place? Maybe she was a masochist. "Okay."

Audrey stepped in front of Alice and held her gently by the shoulders. "It takes a lot of courage to overcome your anxiety in service of your fantasies. I know that, and so does everyone else here."

Lamenting her rising embarrassment, Alice said, "They know I'm shy?"

"They not only know, they're out of their minds excited about it." Audrey rubbed her upper arms. "We wanted everyone to be sensitive to the fact that you might need a soft touch. It's been a long time since most of us have been with anyone even remotely shy. They're all dying to bring you out of your shell."

"Among other things," Lucy muttered, good-naturedly.

Alice exhaled. Despite its strength, her orgasm with Audrey hadn't quenched her need. On the contrary, it had sharpened it, hinting at the rich possibilities ahead if only she went along for the ride. She loved the idea of living out her fantasy, especially with Lucy watching. The encounter with Audrey had turned both of them on. She couldn't wait to see what an entire night of watching would do to her sweet voyeur. "Okay, let's go."

Audrey went first, then Alice, with Lucy providing support by maintaining a firm grip on her arm. When Alice stepped off the bottom stair into a surprisingly well-furnished space, the room erupted in raucous applause. Coming to a dead halt, she allowed Lucy to pull her into a loose embrace while she struggled to process the sights and sounds of a party well underway. A rustic table sat in the center of the room, where glasses and bottles were arranged in a haphazard cluster. The clapping women mostly stood around that table, their drinks abandoned, except for a handsome butch of Asian descent who whistled from her place on the room's only bed. "Happy birthday!" she called out, then stood to reveal small, perky breasts atop a bare, well-muscled chest. "Welcome to your party!"

A chorus of feminine voices joined in the enthusiastic greeting. Names floated through her consciousness, barely connecting with the women to whom they belonged. Lin. Maggie. Lakshmi. Teresa. Jasmine. Sam. Each one was uniquely beautiful, running the gamut of age and skin tone and body type to offer a full spectrum view of the splendor of womanhood. Speechless, Alice accepted hugs and handshakes until the first woman who'd greeted her, the butch whose name she actually remembered was Lin, boldly cut through the chatter.

"I hope you don't mind that I won the privilege of going first." Dodging an elbow from a lithe blonde, she bowed politely. "Well, second, I'm guessing." She winked at Audrey. "Yummy?"

"Perfection." From seemingly out of nowhere, Audrey produced the black, lacy panties Alice had been wearing and held them aloft. A titter of excitement passed over the small group, but instead of being embarrassed, Alice felt empowered. Every woman there was clearly eager to be with her. Both the immaculately attired black woman—who she thought had introduced herself as Jasmine—and her apparent companion, Lakshmi, a young lady at least ten years her junior, actually patted Lucy on the back as they congratulated her good taste. The others watched her anxiously, waiting their turn.

Lin, whose hair was shaved so close that only a bare shadow remained, touched Alice's arm. "Believe it or not, this is us at our most restrained."

Alice smiled at her gentle attempt at humor. "I believe it."

Taking her by the elbow, Lin led her to the queen bed. Despite the fact that the woman was topless and stunning to behold, Alice felt relatively comfortable in her presence. All things considered. Away from the crowd and no longer the center of attention, she could relax a bit. At least until Lin gestured to her loose-fitting pants, drawing Alice's attention to the obvious bulge they concealed.

"So, I brought you a present." Lin shared Alice's laughter at the predictable, cheesy line. "But, um, you'll have to reach into my pants to get it." She wiggled her eyebrows, smirking. "Your wife assures me it will be perfect for you."

Intrigued—despite knowing *exactly* what was hiding in Lin's pants—Alice tentatively rested her palm over the firm lump. "This?"

Nodding, Lin raised her hips to encourage Alice's hand to slide along the length of her hidden cock. "Why don't you pull it out and stroke it?"

Alice glanced back at the crowd of women and caught Lucy's gaze. Lucy nodded, then mouthed, "*Go for it.*" Resolving to surrender to this experience completely, Alice turned to Lin with a deliberately bashful smile. "Okay." She fumbled with the strings on Lin's pants, at first because she sensed it turned Lin on, then because she couldn't stop staring at the bare chest on display. "You're really sexy."

Lin leaned back on her elbows, content to let her work for it. "Likewise."

Freeing Lin's cock from its confines, Alice was thrilled to discover it was the same one she and Lucy used when they played. That meant it would be a snug, but pleasurable fit. Appreciative of all the ways Lucy had tried to make tonight good for her, Alice shot her wife a pleased smile before bending to kiss the tip.

Lin inhaled noisily. "Hello." She tangled her fingers in Alice's hair. "Not so shy anymore, are we?"

Contradicting the words with her heated blush, Alice took the condom Lin offered with a one-shouldered shrug. "I like your cock."

"Good, because I'm about to fuck you with it." Lin lifted her hips, gesturing for Alice to put the condom on. "That's what you want, right?"

Lin obviously drew great pleasure from her red-faced modesty. Unable to meet her gaze, Alice said, "Yes."

"Then take off your dress. You won't be needing it anymore." Lin stripped off her pants, then kicked them away from the bed. Now completely nude except her harness and cock, she didn't seem the slightest bit self-conscious. Across the room, more than one woman cheered. Gripping the cock in her fist, Lin assumed a triumphant pose before dissolving into good-natured laughter.

Alice used the momentary distraction to attempt to shimmy out of her own dress. Nerves made her clumsy, but Lucy materialized at her side before her frustration hit peak levels. "Let me," Lucy murmured. The dress disappeared in a flash, followed by her bra. Which…meant she was nude. In front of everyone.

As though foreseeing her panic, Lin knelt on the edge of the bed and reached for Alice's hand. "You're even better than I imagined." Kissing Alice's knuckles, she asked, "Lie on your back for me?"

She obeyed more out of necessity than anything else. It was too difficult to keep standing, anyway. Scooting to the center of the mattress at Lin's urging, she rolled onto her back and let her legs fall open and tried to remember to keep breathing. In her peripheral vision, she saw Lucy pull up a chair to watch. Would everyone watch?

Alice thought she might die from anticipation. Lin settled between her thighs, nestling the cock snugly against her labia. Alice relished the foreign sensation of a body taller, leaner, and harder than her wife's, hopeful that Lin's weight would somehow keep her from shattering into pieces. Kissing her gently, Lin teased Alice's lips with her tongue. "Open wider so I can put it inside."

Eyes closed, Alice opened her legs as far as she could. The mattress moved as Lin shifted position, first to use the slick head of her cock to rub circles around Alice's aching clit, then to carefully probe at her opening, a promise of what was to come. "Does she always get this wet?"

Beside her, Lucy chuckled. "Always. Sorry to disappoint, but it's not just for you."

"Oh, well." Playfully, Lin said, "I'm going to stick my dick in your wife now."

"Please do."

A finger tapped her chin. "Alice, look at me."

Confused, Alice struggled to meet Lin's heated gaze. The finger tapped again, more forceful this time. "Up here, sweet thing." Unable to refuse, Alice raised her eyes until she was looking directly into Lin's. "Good," Lin praised, then sank into her with a groan even louder than the one she tore from Alice's aching throat.

The cock was a perfect fit, all right, but that didn't mean it wasn't big. Lin kept her movements careful and deliberate, easing Alice into it slowly. She held eye contact the entire time, and whenever Alice threatened to close hers or look away for too long, a sharp rap of Lin's fingers on her chin refocused her attention. Lin murmured to her the entire time, asking her if she liked it, how it felt, whether she wanted it to stop. Occasionally she addressed Lucy, praising Alice's body, her obedience, the precious, shy countenance hiding the wanton slut that clearly lurked within. All the while Alice's pleasure built, keeping her poised on the edge of orgasm for what felt like hours.

"Your wife loves feeling my cock slide in and out." Lin growled as droplets of sweat beaded on her forehead. Staring into Alice's eyes, she murmured, "Don't you? Tell her."

"I love it." So close she could taste it, the surprise appearance of the couple she'd observed earlier—Jasmine and Laksmi— caused Alice to swiftly tumble over the edge. Lin kissed her hard, swallowing her moans without ceasing the steady motion of her hips. A moment later she stiffened and quaked atop Alice, then collapsed, spent.

Without hesitating, Laksmi leaned down and slapped Lin's ass. "Time's up. We're next."

Lin grumbled as she carefully extracted herself from the tangle of Alice's useless limbs. "A little patience?"

"Not when you're threatening to use her all up before we get ours." Laksmi shot Alice a sultry smile, offering a hand to help her sit. "Lucy said you like eating pussy." She gestured at Jasmine, who was unbuttoning a perfectly pressed blouse. "My girl loves being eaten. So do I."

Alice watched in a daze as the two comely women undressed. She waited on her knees, too overwhelmed to move, and tried to imagine how a pussy that wasn't her wife's might taste. The thought of sampling two at once staggered her.

Jasmine and Laksmi knew exactly what they wanted. Positioning themselves side-by-side on their bellies, they rose onto their knees and thrust their butts in the air—one soft and round, the other firm and muscled—to await the first touch of her tongue. When Alice hesitated, uncertain where to begin, Jasmine glanced back sharply. "*Go.*"

"Yes, ma'am." The ease with which she wielded authority allowed Alice to ignore everything except the task at hand. Kneeling behind Jasmine, she placed a hand on each cheek, then pressed her face into slick, aroused labia, and her tongue deeper still.

A single hitch in Jasmine's quiet exhalation betrayed her pleasure. "That's acceptable." She backed onto Alice's tongue, rolling her hips and coating her face with wetness. "Make sure to lick all over."

"And don't forget the girlfriend," Laksmi interjected moments later. "My turn."

Leaving Jasmine, Alice shifted her focus to Laksmi's swaying sex. Literally dripping, she was an easy feast to dive into. Though Lucy remained her favorite flavor, she enjoyed the contrasting sweetness and spiciness of Jasmine and Laksmi—so much that she forgot to feel bashful about perching on her hands and knees while going down in front of an audience. When Jasmine suddenly pushed her away with a firm hand on her shoulder, Alice took a moment to return to reality.

"New position," Jasmine told her, then dragged Laksmi atop her body so that her lover's back rested against her chest. Laksmi turned her head to kiss Jasmine heatedly as their legs fell open, entwined.

Granted access to both of them at once, Alice lay on her belly and wrapped her arms around Jasmine's strong thighs. She ducked low, lapping at Jasmine's dripping sex, then raised her face to suck Laksmi's clit. Back and forth she went while the two women lost themselves in each other. The sounds of their kisses and moans set Alice aflame; the delectable marriage of their flavors left her ravenous for more. Soon it was painfully clear that her earlier orgasms hadn't been enough to sate her out-of-control libido. Shamelessly, she set her knees apart on the mattress, arching her back in a not-so-subtle invitation. No need to be shy at this point, right?

Within seconds, a gentle hand touched the back of her upper thigh. She startled, then grinned into Jasmine's abundant wetness. Licking tight circles around the clit in her mouth, she resisted the urge to look back and identify the woman caressing her ass, the backs of her thighs, her stomach—everywhere except where she was slick with need. It wasn't Lin, because she could hear her sharing sordid details over by the beverage table. Switching to lick Laksmi just as Jasmine threatened to come, Alice used her peripheral vision to confirm that her wife hadn't moved from her chair. So it wasn't her, either.

Whoever touched her did so deliberately, drawing a path down the backs of her thighs, then up to the cleft of her ass, *almost* but not quite brushing her labia. Alice moaned into Laksmi and wiggled pleadingly. She would give *anything* for more. At this point she didn't care what—the mystery woman could kiss her, slap her, lick her, pinch her, bite her, *fuck* her. So long as she did *something*.

Suddenly empathetic toward Jasmine, who *had* been close, Alice pressed a finger against her entrance and awaited permission. The kisses above her cut off so Jasmine could issue a terse, "Do it."

Alice slid one finger into Jasmine, then two. She angled her wrist so she could rub the swollen clit with her thumb, satisfied when each stroke caused Jasmine to contract around her. A light touch swept along the length of her own labia, aided by her abundant wetness. Pressure teased her opening briefly before disappearing. Frustrated, Alice redoubled her efforts. She gave Laksmi's clit a hard suck, unleashing an adorable mewl and a hot rush of wetness to coat her chin. The sound of Laksmi's pleasure clearly affected Jasmine. She tightened around Alice's fingers and, after another thrust, came all over her hand.

The mystery woman rewarded her by slipping a hand beneath Alice to toy with her clit for maddeningly brief seconds. Hoping that Laksmi's orgasm was the key to her own pleasure, Alice batted the flat of her tongue against the hard clit between her lips. Then she sucked until she elicited a different mewl, and more wetness, and finally a quivering, full-body orgasm that filled her with pride. With her mouth still on Laksmi, she sobbed in relief when the hand between her legs flattened, then ground into her labia. She tended to both women until they pushed her away with grateful smiles. Easing back onto the hand fondling between her thighs, Alice sat up to let her happy guests disentangle and make room for whoever might want to take their place. They left her with kisses on her cheeks and murmured "Happy birthday"s before strolling away arm-in-arm.

The hand between her legs withdrew, and then another hand curled around the back of her neck and forced her face down against the mattress. The mystery woman said, "Birthday spanking."

Does that mean she actually plans to smack me forty tim—

A firm slap sent pleasant vibrations to her clit, leaving her suddenly unconcerned about the answer. The second slap was just as pleasurable as the first, skirting the boundary of pain without stepping over the line. The third was somehow even better, and made her clit jolt with searing pleasure. Maybe forty wouldn't be so bad after all.

After twenty-four increasingly intense blows, Alice realized that the rest of the partygoers were counting aloud, some whooping gleefully after every stroke. She was certain that Lucy's voice was the loudest. Smiling through the stinging pain, Alice endured the humiliating ritual by reflecting on everything her wife had accomplished. She wasn't just fulfilling a long-held fantasy, she was gifting Alice a lifetime of sexual experience over the course a single, surreal night.

By the time she received her last five smacks, Alice had to grip the bedsheet to keep from squirming away. Her ass stung, the skin hot and undoubtedly rosy, but her dominant concern was her pussy, which was dripping and needy in ways she'd never thought possible. "Forty!" a chorus of voices shouted as the mystery woman delivered the final blow, before the room erupted into wild cheering.

The hand covered her pussy, the palm hot from its repeated contact with her backside. Rubbing sensuously, the woman said, "Make yourself come."

Simultaneously, a hand touched her shoulder. The blonde who'd admonished Lin earlier was there wearing a hopeful smile and nothing else. "Hi." She gestured at the spot Jasmine and Laksmi had vacated. "May I take a turn?"

"Please," Alice said. She welcomed the distraction. Though she was already rocking against the disciplinarian's hand, the reminder of her audience had left her feeling slightly inhibited. Pushing up onto her hands, she waited for the blonde to get into position without ceasing the motion of her hips. "I'm sorry, what's your name?"

Settling against the headboard, the blonde smiled as she ran a suggestive hand between her legs. "Maggie."

"Nice to meet you, Maggie." She scanned the toned length of the young woman's body, tempted to follow up by asking her age. Looking to be in her mid-twenties, tops, Maggie was bright-eyed and full of youthful vigor. Alice wasn't sure whether to feel triumphant or old as she leaned forward to lick the tip of one impossibly perky breast, then the other. "Tell me what you want."

Blushing—and thereby immediately putting Alice at ease—Maggie actually seemed tentative to ask. "Say no if you want. This never came up during our discussions about limits..."

Both charmed and intrigued, Alice bit Maggie's nipple hard enough to cut off her speech. "Ask me."

"Will you lick my ass while I touch myself?" Maggie blurted out, then blushed even brighter. "Totally a fantasy of mine."

Nothing about burying her face in this pretty young thing's firm, round butt sounded unappealing in any way. Especially if it fulfilled a fantasy. "Absolutely. Turn over."

Maggie didn't hesitate to get into position. Ass in the air, she rested the side of her face against the mattress and used her right hand to rub her clit in small, fast circles. Then she brought her other hand back to hold herself open to Alice's hungry gaze. Thrilled to feel fingertips begin circling her own clit, Alice bent to lick the tight ring of muscle nestled between Maggie's shapely cheeks. An excited whimper inspired her to lick harder, then faster, then finally deeper. She could feel the vague vibrations of Maggie's self-pleasuring as she feasted, mirroring the increasingly bold caresses on her own clit. As it turned out, the faster she moved against the mystery woman, the firmer her touch became. Soon Alice was humping her hand like a mindless animal, but she couldn't stop and she didn't care.

Maggie came first, Alice following mere seconds later. Losing track of where Maggie's pleasure began and her own ended, Alice kept licking until she literally couldn't anymore, then collapsed along with Maggie in a heap. The mystery woman withdrew, leaving her sated and yet still curiously bereft. Rolling onto her side, she grinned at the sight of her wife, still watching. Lucy's hand was in her jeans and she looked out-of-her-mind aroused. Alice reached for her, but Lucy shook her head.

"One more."

Alice had no time to ponder her meaning before a hand clapped around her ankle and dragged her onto her back. A dark-haired beauty stood over her holding a large vibrator. "You're not done yet, birthday girl." She sat on the edge of the bed and ran her hand over Alice's thighs. "Open your legs."

Submission came easily. It always had. Despite her exhaustion, Alice parted her thighs. Her gaze flicked behind the woman's shoulder, landing on those who'd already had their turns. The crowd watched with interest. Polishing off her wine, Lin cupped a hand to her mouth. "Get it, Teresa!"

Teresa's mouth quirked as she flipped on the vibrator. Leaning down, she brushed sweaty hair away from Alice's forehead. "I love forcing a woman to come until she can't stand it anymore." She nipped Alice's earlobe, whispering, "Remember your safe word."

All rational thought fled when Teresa touched the rounded head of the vibrator to her clit. Her climax was swift and violent, shattering her with its impact. At least that's how she felt, like a limp puppet jerked around by the strings of her involuntary muscular contractions. Clutching at the sheets, she tried to writhe away from the buzzing, but Teresa followed her, eventually pinning Alice's thigh to the bed with her hand. The safe word flashed through Alice's mind but she hesitated, certain she could withstand a *little* more.

Teresa looked at Lucy and...winked? Alice couldn't focus on either of them, too overwhelmed by the agony of sustained orgasm to keep her eyes open for more than a second or two. Teresa waited until she had Alice's attention before pulling the vibrator away. Blissful relief rolled over her even as she kept shuddering with aftershocks. Teresa said, "It stops when your wife comes."

The vibrator touched her clit again, making her squeal and reach out desperately. "Lucy..."

The mattress dipped as Lucy appeared at her side. "I'm here."

Alice slipped a shaking hand between Lucy's thighs, glad to find her bare. "Baby, come, sit on my face." She jolted. "Please. Please. *Fuck.*" Teresa turned the vibrator up a notch, destroying her ability to speak. She attempted to curl onto her side, but Lucy pressed her shoulders to the mattress and swiftly moved to straddle her face.

"This won't take long, I promise." Lucy spread herself with her fingers as she settled herself over Alice's open mouth. "But if you need Teresa to stop, just pinch me hard and she'll stop." She hesitated to make contact with Alice's outstretched tongue. "Nod if you understand."

Alice nodded, then grabbed Lucy and forced her down onto her mouth. She didn't want to cheat or change the rules. She wanted to end both her torment *and* Lucy's while finishing with her head held high. Mindful of her goal, Alice disassociated from the riotous sensation coursing through her body. She became nothing more than a mouth and hands—roaming, stroking, tweaking. Lucy filled her mouth, pulsing perceptibly, moving with such enthusiasm she left Alice's entire face slick with her juices. After years of mastering Lucy's body, Alice knew she was close. That knowledge empowered her to keep going, just a *little* longer.

Inspired, Alice gripped Lucy's buttocks. Recalling decades of dirty talk, she spread Lucy's ass apart so that anyone watching could have a good, intimate look. Clearly affected, Lucy hastened her movements in a clear push for the finish. Alice obliged by sucking her clit harder, drawing out a full-throated cry that made her shudder in sympathy. A wave of tranquility rolled over her as the vibrator disappeared, this time for good. Relaxing, she carefully coaxed every last bit of pleasure from Lucy's wonderfully familiar body. Licking and sucking gave way to loving kisses, until Lucy couldn't take anymore and moved off her face to collapse at her side.

Panting, Alice rolled over just as Lucy did, and they entangled themselves with practiced ease. Taking a furtive glance around, Alice realized they were alone. The others gathered around the table, except for Jasmine and Laksmi who were locked in their own heated embrace on a couch across the room. Alice shook her head, unable to believe how she'd just celebrated her fortieth year. "How am I supposed to top this when your birthday comes around?"

Lucy giggled. "You liked it? Not too much?"

"Let's see...a lifetime of sexual fantasies fulfilled in one night, courtesy of the woman who knows me best." Alice pretended to think, then pinched Lucy's hip. "It was incredible. The perfect way to keep me from feeling like my best years are behind me."

Snorting, Lucy said, "Don't let Sam hear you talk that way." At Alice's questioning look, she pointed out the androgynous, gray-haired woman standing with the other guests. She was the only one Alice hadn't met face-to-face, which meant...

"The disciplinarian?"

Lucy guffawed. "I'll have to share that nickname with her. But yes, the woman who spanked you turned sixty-five last month and she's obviously still going strong."

Reaching back to touch skin that was still warm to the touch, Alice said, "Very strong."

"Point is, you're only as old as you feel." Lucy pulled her close and peppered kisses across her face. "And darling, you feel *damn* good to me."

Infused with renewed energy, Alice pushed Lucy onto her back and climbed on top. "Let me show you exactly *how* good."

Lucy gasped as Alice entered her with a single finger, then laughed at the accompanying outbreak of applause. "And the crowd went wild."

SECRET ADMIRER

BY ANDI MARQUETTE

"Ladies and gentlemen, put your hands together for…*Niki St. John!*"
Erin started clapping as I entered the coffeehouse part of the bookstore.

I took my leather jacket off, slung it over one of the three empty chairs
at the table, and slid into the chair next to her. We leaned over to do our
requisite double air kiss. She pushed a cup of coffee toward me, and I took a
sip. Americano, splash of cream, tiny bit of sugar. Erin rocked.

"I can always count on you to make me feel good, E. And that is some
damn fine coffee."

"Only the best for you, my partner in whatever trouble we can get up to."

The whole front wall was windows, so I looked out across West End Avenue
toward Centennial Park, where I could just see a bit of Nashville's full-scale
model of the Parthenon. Several people strolled through the late October
chill, a few with dogs. Closer to the bookstore, goths and hippies wandered
past, mingling with Vanderbilt students who frequented this establishment.
Some of those goths and hippies were probably students, too.

Erin sipped her latte. She arched one eyebrow, regarding me with a
question in her eyes. "So what's up, *mujer*? You were all mysterious in that
text message."

I reached over to the adjoining chair and pulled a white business-length
envelope out of the right-hand outer pocket of my jacket and handed it to her.
She looked at it, puzzled.

"Read what's inside."

She set her cup on the table and pulled the piece of paper out, leaving it
on the table where I could see it, too. One sheet, plain white. A typewritten
note:

Oct. 22: Knowing that you're probably holding this paper and reading this note puts butterflies in my heart and stomach. I can't stand it anymore, and I have to let you know how I feel. I can't get you out of my head. Thinking about you some days drives me crazy, since you don't know me like that. I wish you did. I wish you could. I'm taking a chance here, because you're probably thinking that this is insane or that I'm insane. I don't care. I'm a woman on a mission, and I hope you'll take a chance. This Saturday, go to the back side of the Parthenon. 11 PM. Please, Niki. If you never do anything else in your life, grant me this.

Erin let her breath out. "Holy shit." She turned the page over, then looked at me, dark eyes wide. She grinned like a wolf. "Where the fuck did you find this?"

I laughed. Erin has a potty mouth almost as bad as mine. That doesn't always go over well in the South, but neither of us cares. Erin's from San Diego, and I'm from Phoenix. People swear out there.

"Windshield of my car."

"You are so shitting me." She set the paper on the table between us.

"I found it last night after I left the lab."

"Girl! You have a secret admirer. It's about fucking time."

"So tell me, Professor Gallegos," I continued, "how one hooks up with a secret admirer." I picked the paper up and pointed at the elegant calligraphic heart near the bottom. "But it could be some freaky psycho serial killer."

"Let's dust it for prints," Erin said, teasing. "Ms. Forensic Anthro-type. You could turn *this* into your dissertation project. Do you think Vandy would go for it?"

"I already did check it. It's clean," I retorted, joking.

She reached over and punched me lightly on the arm. "This is amazing. Can I switch *my* dissertation topic to your secret love life?"

"Seriously? This is, like, stalker shit." I sipped my coffee.

Erin sat back, an enigmatic expression in her eyes. "You have got to pull your head out of your damn work and have some fun, *mi gringita dulce*." Her tone became serious. "I mean, lately, you've been—I don't know. Not yourself. And I know you've got some personal shit going on, but really. I'm worried about you."

"So you approve of me meeting some freaky psycho serial killer at the ass end of the Parthenon at eleven p.m. on a Saturday night?"

Erin laughed. "When you put it like *that*—"

"Exactly." I refolded the piece of paper and slid it back into its envelope.

"Okay, look. Let's be all logical, since that's how you like it." She reached into her giant woven Ecuadoran bag and took a pen and small notebook out, becoming very official. "Now then, Ms. St. John. Let's go over what we know."

"Jesus, Erin—"

"Ms. St. John, I don't think Mr. Christ is part of this investigation."

I laughed again. "Okay," I said, playing along. "Whoever it is knows my first name, at least, and how to spell it. And she knows I spend a lot of time on campus. She knows what I drive, since that's where she left the envelope."

"Very good, Doctor Watson. That's a start." Erin pretended to scribble in her notebook. "So by extension, can we assume that she might know your campus schedule?" She tapped her chin with the end of her pen. "Why, yes, let's assume. My guess is"—she tapped the table with the end of her pen—"another student." She said it like she had just revealed that the butler did it in a bad murder mystery.

"That narrows it down to thirty-five thousand."

She shot me a mock glare. "We're not through yet. Have you noticed anyone in the program paying particular attention to you lately? Oh, bad question. You wouldn't know someone wanted in your pants if she undid 'em and went down on you in a parking lot."

"*Erin!*" I glanced around, completely embarrassed.

She grinned. "You know I'm right."

"Well, okay, but you don't need to *say* it."

"Niki, *mi amiga especial*, you live in your books. And if you're not living there, you're in your lab work. Or your research. And on days I can't find you there, you're in your head."

I opened my mouth to say something, but she put her hand up, cutting me off. "I know that you do that to deal with the bullshit of the program, and

186

lately I know you spend more time in all of those places because your stepdad has developed a major midlife crisis."

"He's a ho," I muttered.

"Regardless, I know that's stressing you and I know your mom is calling you for therapy through the divorce. And"—she cut my retort off again—"I also know that your assorted dating travails over the past year have left you more cynical than usual." She smiled sweetly. "Which is why this situation is so cool. It's perfect to get you out of your rut."

"I'm in a rut?" I looked at her, feigning indignation..

She reached over and patted my hand. "It's a cute rut. Like you. So what about Amy Griff?" Erin tapped her pen on the table again.

"In the lab? Not a chance."

"Why not?"

"She only has eyes for Mel over at the library."

"Hmm. True. Okay, what about that new chick that came in last semester? From Ithaca?"

"Sue," I mused. Tall, granola. Nice enough. "I never see her. She's already dissertating."

"Lauria from Romania?" Erin rolled the R and tried a fake accent.

"She's not queer. She's Ro-*mahn*-eee-ahn." I responded in kind, which made Erin laugh.

"Let's keep assuming it's someone you've come into contact with. What about at work?"

"Nah, same thing. You know them. All men, except for the boss."

Erin snorted a laugh. "Oh God. No. Definitely not her. Though how funny would that be?"

I grimaced. Grad students called her Doc Ock because she looked like the character in the second *Spiderman* movie. Not very sporting of us, but it gave us gossip over beers. "Nice, Erin. I thought I'd at least warrant a Sue or an Amy."

She glanced at me. "Please. You warrant fuckin' Angelina Jolie. You are *such a babe*." She put the pen and tablet down.

"I'm so glad I have you to tell me these things," I said with long-suffering emphasis.

"For real, Nik. You don't see it because you're always up here"—she poked me gently in the head—"but when we go out, the *mujeres* follow you around the room with their eyes." She dropped her voice, slipping into a Mexican accent, which wasn't hard since her grandparents on both sides of the family were from that country. "They long for you, señorita. I can see it. And I wonder, too. Why does Niki not see this admiration? *¿Porqué esta su cabeza en su recto?*"

I shot her a withering glace. "You think my head is up my ass?"

She smiled sweetly. "Look at you. You work out, you have great hair—girl, don't get me started on your eyes—a sense of humor. And you're nice. You're a genuinely nice person."

"So how come I can't land someone like that?"

Erin smiled, expression soft. "You don't trust yourself. You think you're not worth that. But you are. And someone"—she gestured at the envelope—"realizes it."

I scoffed.

"C'mon, Nik. You're always talking about adventure and romance. I think this is cool. Somebody has the hots for you. What have you got to lose?"

"Besides my life?"

Erin rolled her eyes. "Okay, Ms. CSI. The Parthenon is reasonably public, and I know you can outrun anybody chasing you. If it's freaky, you can call the cops. Or call me and *I'll* call the cops. But if it's not..." She grinned. "How fucking romantic is this?"

"Whatever." But I was smiling. I stood up and reached for my jacket. "Come on. We'll be late for the department meeting." I had two days to talk myself either into or out of the rendezvous.

———— ✦ ————

"So, mujer, have you decided?" Erin and I were walking across campus toward the parking garage. Friday evening, and we'd both had tons of shit to do that day. I had worked in the lab all day and e-mailed my prospectus to my committee chair, who was in Guatemala until the end of the month.

"Not sure."

Erin stopped, jerking on the shoulder of my leather jacket. Her expression was serious. "Go. Meet her. If she's freaky, you can run and dial 911. If she's not your type, you can—"

"Run and dial 911."

Erin snorted with laughter. It was cute. "No. You'll say, 'Um, thanks, but I'm way too obsessed with my bones in the lab right now to consider a serious relationship. I really appreciate you taking the time to meet me like this, but please check back in about five years.'" She smiled innocently.

"Come with me, E. Scope it out. Please?"

She took my hand and squeezed it. "You know I would, but my brother's business partner is in town, and Mike wants me to come along to make it a nice double heterosexual date."

I wrinkled my nose. "*Qué tú haces para tu familia.*"

"Sí. Scary, huh?" She continued walking to the parking garage. "Here's my schedule, if it makes you feel better. I'm going out to dinner at J. Alexander's on West End at eight thirty. Then we're supposed to go see someone at Third and Lindsley play. I'll have my phone on vibrate, but I'll check it constantly for you."

We approached her car, a sporty blue Toyota sedan. It had seen better days. She stopped and handed me her bag as she dug for her car keys in the pocket of the barn jacket she was wearing.

"Jesus, Erin. This thing is heavy. It'll give you arthritis. Get a real backpack."

"*¿Perdón?* Are you dissing my heritage, *mi amiga*?" She opened her car door.

"No, because you're Mexican, not Ecuadoran."

"Ah. Well, fine." Her eyes were sparkling, and I smiled. "See?" she said. "You look so much better when you're cheerful. Hey, meet me later tonight at the Lipstick. I'll buy you a drink."

"Okay. What time?"

"Ten." She hugged me suddenly, kissed me on the cheek, and stepped back and looked at me critically. In a fake New York accent, she said, "My little girl is growing up. She's got a date. I just hope it's with a doctah."

I snorted and squeezed her arm. "I'll see you later." I tossed her bag onto the backseat of her car. She blew me a kiss and got in. I watched her back up and head down the ramp, and I wanted so badly to—to what? Ask *her* to meet me? So not a good idea to be lusting after your best friend. I shoved my hands into my jacket pockets and crossed the parking lot to my own car, a nondescript Mazda four-door that had seen better days than Erin's. I sat in it for a minute, clenching and unclenching my teeth.

So I had the hots for Erin. But who wouldn't? She had everything anybody could want. Great hair, great face, awesome lips. Athletic, but not too skinny. Cheekbones to die for. Super smart and articulate, two of the myriad reasons

I liked her when I started the grad program here. She came in the same time I did, also on fellowship. And she was from the West, like me. So we had bonded, and we'd stayed tight for the last three years.

Except lately, I'd been wanting much more. But how the hell did you approach that? *"Hey, E., I've been thinking. Would you mind if I kissed you? Or maybe we could get naked together?"* I lowered my forehead to my steering wheel. *I have no class. None. And absolutely no chance.* Sighing, I started my car and backed out of the space.

I spent Saturday reading through articles I had collected for my dissertation and taking notes. I had started the heinous process, as Erin and I called it, using the available facilities at Vandy. I'd already done four semesters of fieldwork toward this project, so now began the "evidence coagulation," as my advisor termed it.

I stacked the articles on a half-empty shelf in my bookcases and flopped onto my couch, staring at the ceiling, tired and cranky. Why the hell was I even considering meeting a stranger late at night? The thought of someone watching me and learning my habits without my knowledge kind of creeped me out. I rearranged one of the throw pillows behind my head. But on the other hand, I felt a thrill, too. I mean, who *wouldn't* want a secret admirer, right? But then again, maybe this was just some kind of elaborate joke.

Erin had called earlier, and I had voiced my misgivings for the hundredth time. And she had said, "Where's that fine sense of adventure you used to have?"

She had a point. It had been a while since I'd cut loose. School and family life had consumed a lot of my energy this past year, and I hadn't been on a date in a long time. Unless goofing around with Erin counted.

I sighed. It did to me. Every second I got with her counted for something. Maybe this situation at the Parthenon was just what I needed to snap out of my limbo with her. I closed my eyes, trying to relax. I didn't remember falling asleep, but clearly I did because when I woke up, it was dark and nearly ten o'clock. A knot of anticipation tightened in my gut and I checked my cell phone. Erin had called at seven. Why hadn't I heard it? Oh. My ringer was off. Her message wished me luck. She sounded way more upbeat than usual, signing off with her *"muchos besos"* line. And way more positive than I felt, though in a really twisted way, it was exciting, this whole thing. Even though

I was still a little leery, Erin was just a phone call away and Centennial Park was near enough to civilization that if something got weird, I could make a run for it.

I changed into a clean pair of faded Levi's. Erin always said my ass looked *really* good in this particular pair. I slipped on a black long-sleeved T-shirt and tied the laces on my battered Doc Martens. I wasn't much for super-fashion, especially not at 11:00 p.m. at the Parthenon. I grabbed my leather jacket as I headed out the door. I could not believe I was actually doing this. I checked the ringer on my phone as I slid into the driver's seat of my car. Holy shit, I was actually doing this. I started the engine.

I made it to the Parthenon at ten thirty. A few other people were around, but since the evening was chilly, most were making their way back to their cars. Park staff had turned the lights on, and the structure was splashed light green. Though totally faux and built for an exposition in the late nineteenth century, the smooth, elegant lines of the architecture did evoke the real deal on the Athenian acropolis. Underneath the Nashville version, someone had thought to build a gallery where different artists showcased their work.

The temple proper included an interior gallery as well that was open during the day, and at the butt end, a massive statue of Athena stood, painted in bright, garish colors that made her look more like a Victorian drag queen than a classic Hellenic goddess. The first time Erin and I saw it, soon after our first semester in the program started, we both stared slack-jawed, then burst out laughing. At that moment, I knew we'd be friends.

I parked in the lot next to the structure and sat, waiting. My palms were sweating. I half-expected this to be a big joke, with some of my other friends showing up and having a good laugh about the whole thing. On some level, I was hoping that was the case. Otherwise, I'd have to get out of my head, which meant *feeling* stuff, and that was kind of scary these days. It was so much easier for me to just stay focused on my grad work.

Finally, with about ten minutes to spare, I headed for the Parthenon and climbed the stairs so I could walk around the colonnade, the wall of the interior gallery on my right, the massive columns on my left. I was the only person here. Even my footsteps sounded lonely. I reached the back side and saw in the weird green light another envelope leaning against one of the pillars. I looked around, then checked my watch. Eleven sharp, and no sign of anyone. *A joke. It's just some weird joke. Maybe a scavenger hunt or something.* I felt my shoulders relax, felt the adrenaline rush pour out of my gut. I guess I'd been looking forward to this more than I admitted.

I stood looking down at the envelope. Might as well finish this out so whoever it is can have a good laugh. I picked it up and opened it. Something soft and dark was within, along with another sheet of paper. I carefully took the sheet out, leaving the other object inside, and unfolded it. The lighting was dim, but if I held the paper at a certain angle, I could read it. Another typewritten note:

You've come. I'm watching you."

I stopped reading and looked around, the hairs on my neck standing up. No one else nearby. Just some guy walking his dog out on the grass, and I seriously doubted he was involved. I cleared my throat nervously and continued reading:

Please put the blindfold on. I can't reveal who I am yet because I don't know if you'd understand. Leave it on until I'm gone.

I looked in the envelope at what I now knew was a strip of black cloth. Blindfold? I'd always wanted to do something like this. Hell, I was enjoying this. I looked around again and pulled the blindfold out and stood contemplating it for a long moment, reminded of Erin's piñata parties. I waited for a huge crowd of people to suddenly appear playing mariachi music, but nothing happened.

I put the cloth to my eyes and tied it behind my head. As I did, I heard something behind me. Somebody moving? I knew someone was nearby because I felt a presence, and I fought my instinct, which was to rip the blindfold off and throw myself down the steps and take off running through the park. Instead, I forced my feet to remain on the concrete as whoever it was moved closer. I heard someone breathing, and then I smelled jasmine. Just a hint, just enough to keep me here. Whoever approached didn't say anything but—she?—moved even closer, and goosebumps raced up and down my arms and legs.

And then I felt hands on my shoulders. They squeezed gently, making the leather of my jacket creak. The hands worked their way up my shoulders to my neck where fingertips lightly brushed my bare skin over the collar of my tee, sending shock waves rolling down my spine. The fingertips moved and gently traced my lips, startling me because I couldn't see. My heart was pounding so hard it almost hurt my chest. A woman. This was definitely a woman.

"Who—" I started to say, but the fingertips interrupted my question and softly pressed my lips closed. Whoever this was slid her hands under my arms to my back. I was shaking a little. A hand returned to my face, caressing my cheek, and then I felt her breath on my lips. Hot. Rapid.

Her hand slid inside my jacket to the small of my back, and she pressed full-length against me, her body heat washing over me and the very inviting curves of her body fitting mine in a surprising intimacy. From our positions, I guessed she was a little bit taller, but that thought went nowhere fast because I felt her lips close over mine very slowly, very softly in an utterly delicious brain-melting kiss. Sensuous. Un-fucking-believable. And I'm not sure why, but I kissed her back. She eased her tongue into my mouth, gently exploring, and I welcomed her, sliding my tongue across hers and kissing her a little harder. Fireworks went off in my skull, and I put my arms around her, working them inside her coat. She moved again and pushed me against the cold, ridged pillar, but I didn't care because my entire body was on fire.

Her lips worked their way along my jaw to my neck, and her hands were on my hips, holding me against her as well. The throbbing between my legs increased exponentially as she kissed me deeper. I lightly bit her lower lip, and she moaned softly, sending a bolt of lightning down my thighs. Her hands moved to my abdomen, stroking, then traveled to my neck so she could hold my mouth to hers. My legs shook. Hell, every part of me trembled. I moved my right hand from her waist to her shoulder, and from there, I found her face. I tried to read her features with my fingers. Strong jaw. Full lips. Her hair seemed to be pulled back.

She caught my hands in hers and moved them back inside her coat to her hips. She wore what I guessed were jeans and a wide leather belt. I ran my hands along her waist, felt her body heat through my fingertips. Christ, I couldn't think anymore. All I knew for sure was her hands on me and mine on her, the heat and wetness in my jeans, and her lips on my mouth. I was totally ready for her to undress me and have her way with me. *Jesus fucking God*—and then she stopped.

A moment later, she held my face and kissed me gently on the cheek, then pulled away. I heard the rustle of paper, and she opened my jacket, slid something into the inner pocket. She squeezed my hand and left. I listened to her footsteps putting distance between us. A few moments later, I untied the blindfold. Her kisses still burned holes through my guts. I held the cloth in one hand and pulled the envelope out of my pocket with the other. I waited for my eyes to adjust to the dim lighting and looked around. No one. I checked my watch. Eleven forty-five. I opened the envelope and pulled the piece of paper out with the now-familiar typewritten note:

> Niki, you've made me the happiest woman in the world tonight. I have to see you again. I'll be in touch.

Who the fuck *is* she? I put the note and the envelope back in my pocket and headed to my car. Once inside, I sat for a bit, trying to clear my head.

Erin would want to know what happened and she'd be worried about me. I speed-dialed her on my cell.

"Well?" she answered.

"I can't talk. I'm floating."

Long pause. "You're okay, though, right?" She sounded concerned.

"Yeah, I'm fine. Brunch tomorrow?"

"Definitely. You have to tell me everything that happened. My place, though. My brother's leaving tomorrow morning, and I want to see him off."

"Okay. See you then."

"Sí, señorita. Now please go home and lock your door. Thank you for calling me. I was...okay, I was worried."

A pleasant warmth sank into my bones at that. "Thanks. Do you want me to call you when I get home?" I said it with mock innocence.

She made a disgusted noise in her throat. "Don't make me feel like *tu madre*, mujer. But I *am* glad you called. And tomorrow you'll tell me everything."

I laughed. "You know I will. I can't resist you."

"Not so far. Ciao."

"Later."

I hung up and started the car. The clock on the dash registered midnight. I felt weird but euphoric. And guilty.

I sat with that thought for a few minutes. I felt somehow like I was stepping out on Erin. I'd just been kissed to a state of mind-blowing intensity by a woman with some of the best lips on the planet, and I was worried about Erin. I drove home, both aroused and freaked out.

"You are so kidding." Erin was staring at me over the rim of her glass. It was fresh-squeezed OJ, which I always brought. That, along with flowers every time we had brunch. Erin loved fresh flowers and fresh OJ.

I shook my head. Erin looked really good this morning in her faded and torn jeans and men's white V-neck tee. I still felt weird. It made me nervous to think this, but I really wanted my admirer to be her. God, she looked so hot sitting there with her knee up on the chair and her easy smile. So hot.

"She fucking kissed you and you didn't see her?"

"Uh, blindfold?"

"And you did it?" Erin put her glass down. "You didn't even *try* to peek?"

"No." I took a sip of coffee. It was as good as the bookstore's.

"I cannot believe you had a major mac-session at the Parthenon while you were fucking blindfolded, and you do not even know who she is."

I shrugged. "I was in the moment. You're always telling me to try it." I took a bite of omelette stuffed with avocados and tomatoes. Erin was a really good cook.

She leaned back. "So would you have gone further?"

"Than what?"

"Just kissing."

"I don't know. Maybe."

She raised her eyebrows. "Maybe?"

"It's kind of a fantasy, I guess. A secret admirer. Me wearing a blindfold. It'd be really sexy for a scenario like that to go further."

"Oh? How much further?"

I shrugged, a little uncomfortable, even though we'd talked quite a bit about sex in the past. "As far as I could, I guess. And I wouldn't mind a little bit of restraining," I admitted.

"The control freak giving up control?" she said, teasing.

"Whatever. It'd be hot, don't you think?"

"Very. And it has been a while since you were seeing anyone for those purposes."

"Thanks for the reminder." I gave her a fake glare.

She laughed. "It's only a matter of time. And I'm jealous."

"Of what?"

"Of *her*, asshead." She stood up and faked a big drama queen pose. "I can't *live* without you, Nik. And off you go, secret rendezvous all over Nashville. I'll just stay home. Watching telenovelas and eating bonbons."

"You forgot the cucumber face mask and hair curlers."

She threw a dish towel at me. I caught it and grinned. "Erin, you're my best friend in the world. No matter what happens, we are the two freakin' musketeers. And don't you dare forget I said that, once you find your next flavor of the month."

She slid back into her chair and pretended to pout, and it only added to her hotness factor. I was having seriously carnal thoughts about my best friend.

"Nik, it's not like I sleep with everyone I date." She sounded hurt.

"I'm just teasing. I know you don't." I took another bite, glad that she wasn't currently seeing anyone. "This is so fucking good. You should get married, have a bunch of *niños*. You're, like, the June Cleaver of the Latina world."

She flicked orange juice on me. "*Tú estas una pindeja*, San Juan," she said, Spanishizing my last name, too.

I raised my eyebrows, pretending to be shocked. "*¡El lenguaje! ¡El lenguaje en esta casa!*"

She laughed. "So what's next?"

"I don't know. She said—or rather, wrote—that she'd be in touch."

Erin stood and grabbed my empty coffee cup. She filled it at the counter and put it back on the table next to me. Erin's kitchen mimicked her favorite grandmother's. It had a retro 1950s feel to it, with a cool chrome table and chairs padded in red vinyl. It was like we were eating in an Americana diner. The rest of Erin's apartment, which occupied the second floor of a refurbished Victorian, was like a Mexican hacienda. She loved really bright colors, and she had some great folk art and Mexican-style furniture. I loved her place. It felt like home.

"And you don't know when?"

I looked up at her. "No. Maybe she'll leave another note on my car or something." And maybe this whole thing was over.

"You know you have to tell me when she does."

I looked at her. "*If* she does."

She started clearing dishes. "She will. This is too good not to."

"Maybe it was all a joke," I said as I helped her. She got my hopes up, this mystery woman, but on the other hand, I still couldn't shake the weird feeling that I was going behind Erin's back.

"That's just mean, to pull a joke like that."

I made a noncommittal noise, and we were quiet for a while, washing and drying. She put leftovers in a container for the fridge.

"She'll contact you again," she announced quietly. "I have a feeling about this. I mean, think about it." She put the lid on the container, looked at me with an odd expression. "What did you feel when she kissed you?"

I flushed, remembering. "God, amazing. It was un-fucking-believable. I have not ever been kissed like that."

"Really? Never?"

"No. Never."

She smiled. "Well, there you go. If it was a joke, do you think she could have done that?"

I pondered that for a few seconds. "I don't know. Maybe. Maybe not. Maybe she's a film studies major working toward the Oscar."

Erin splashed water on me from the sink. "Would you get the fuck out of your head and *feel* for once? What was that Robin Williams movie? Where he says 'Carpe diem. Seize the day.' Nik, you only live once."

"Okay, so I seized it and now she may be done."

She sighed with extra-heavy emphasis. "She wouldn't have gone to all this trouble to just cut you loose. That's not logical."

"Oh, so who's the one in her head now?"

She splashed more water on me. "Just let me know when she contacts you."

"You'll be the first I tell."

"Stick to that, San Juan."

"How could I not? You won't let me do anything else."

She was still laughing when I left.

I saved the document again in three separate places because it would suck to lose a huge chunk of my dissertation notes. The clock in the upper right corner of my monitor registered 9:32. Friday night, and here I was, still on campus in my cramped little office space, still working. The mystery woman had contacted me again, but not for another meeting. She'd left me a note on Wednesday saying she missed me and was thinking about me, but she'd see me soon. I thought I might miss her, too, but only if I imagined she was Erin.

I took the most recent note out of my backpack and read it again. No clues to her identity. The only thing handwritten was that little heart in a neat calligraphic style. The clock on my monitor registered 9:41. A couple of my other friends had invited me out for drinks, but I wasn't sure I felt like going, and Erin was busy with something else.

I was about to start typing again when a soft knock on the door pulled my attention there. "Who is it?"

In reply, a piece of paper slid under the door. I stared at it like it might bite. Finally, after a few shocked moments, I picked it up.

Will you trust me?

She'd added the heart. I reached for a pen on my desk and wrote "yes" under the sentence and slid the paper back under the door, heart pounding. I didn't even know her. Why did I say yes? Another sheet of paper appeared under the door. She'd prepared answers ahead of time because this one, too, was typewritten and included the heart.

Open the door.

I read it several times before I got up the nerve to unlock the door. I swallowed hard, took a deep breath and let it out, then opened the door. A large manila envelope lay on the floor in the hallway, right in front of the doorway. I glanced around, but saw and heard nothing. I picked up the envelope and flipped it over. It was unsealed, so I looked inside. Another piece of paper and a familiar black strip of cloth. My mouth went dry, and I read the note.

Please trust me.

"Okay," I said aloud. She had to be nearby. I knew she'd hear. I retreated into my office and set the envelope and the note on my desk before I sat down and tied the blindfold around my head. My heart continued to pound, and I was pretty sure I was shaking a little. I sensed someone enter, and then the door closed. Oh God. What was I doing?

Footsteps. I smelled jasmine, and then I felt her hands on mine. Every nerve I had fired in anticipation. She pulled gently, and I stood, not sure what would come next but wanting it. She touched my face and lips, and then her arms were around me, and her lips were at my ear. She lightly bit my earlobe, and I made an involuntary noise as arousal surged to my core. And then she was kissing me, and I was drunk on her lips and tongue and only vaguely aware that she had worked her hands underneath my T-shirt until the warmth of her palms seared that fact into my awareness.

Was this okay? Did I want it? What about Erin?

I wasn't dating Erin, unfortunately.

But this felt really, really good.

Her hands found the front clasp of my bra, and they undid it. We both stopped, breathing hard. Her hands didn't move from right below my breasts.

"Yes," I said, and she gasped and it sounded like a sob and her hands stroked the flesh just beneath my breasts, and then slowly, her palms engulfed me and I groaned and pressed against them and she was squeezing and stroking, and I was having a hard time standing up beneath the onslaught of her lips and hands. I didn't even care that I couldn't see her, and I didn't know who she was. I just really needed her.

She undid my jeans, and I got my hands inside her shirt. Touching her skin almost made me come even as I felt one of her hands slide inside my underwear against my ass. I cupped her breasts through her bra, and she moaned. The sound made me even wetter. She pulled her hand out of my underwear, much to my disappointment, but it moved to the small of my back, and her other hand pulled at the front of my panties, easily accessible now that my jeans were undone. I was totally ready for this unknown woman to fuck me right there in my office.

She pushed me gently, and I took a step back in response. She kept pushing until I felt the wall against my back, and then her hands were in my shirt again and her lips were on my neck and she was nipping and sucking my throat. And then one of her hands was at my crotch. She cupped me through

199

my jeans, and I couldn't breathe as she gently squeezed. My clit throbbed so hard, I was sure she could feel it.

I found her belt buckle with my hands and worked her belt undone as her hand entered my jeans. She cupped me again, and I knew she could tell how wet I was from the dampness of my underwear. She moaned again and worked her fingers past my underwear. Oh yes. I moved to make it easier for her, and she slipped two fingers in. I groaned, long and low, and she started thrusting with her hand, and my whole body was on fire. And then she used her other hand to pin both of mine to the wall above my head while she fucked me.

"Yes," I said through clenched teeth as her fingers slid in and out. I was so close. So close.

"Niki," she said softly near my ear. "Oh God."

And somewhere in my sex-crazed haze, I heard it. Heard her voice, heard the words, and I froze.

She stopped, too.

"No," I said, the heat of lust and excitement fading in realization. "No way."

She pulled out, and I felt her step back. I reached for the blindfold, and I heard her moving away. I had it off just as she reached for the doorknob.

Anger and confusion overrode everything else. "Erin, what the fuck?"

She turned toward me. "Niki—"

"Did you think this was funny?"

"No."

"Then what the hell is wrong with you? Why the hell would you do that?" I was shaking again.

She stared at me, and it looked as if she might cry. "I wanted to."

"You wanted to mess with me like that?"

"It's not about that."

"Then what the fuck *is* it about?"

She opened the door.

"Don't you fucking walk out of here after this."

"I can't—Niki, I'm sorry. I'm so sorry. I thought—I hoped—"

"What? You thought what?"

She lowered her gaze. "That maybe you felt like I did. I'm sorry. This was a really bad idea. I should have just told you how I felt about you. I'm really, really sorry."

How she felt about me? A thousand different thoughts collided in my head, but she was in the hallway before I could stop her, my anger replaced by fear that I'd lose her for good.

"Erin," I rushed to the door. "Dammit, don't go." I heard her running down the hall. "Erin," I called after her, but she didn't stop. Less than a minute later, I was out the door with my things. Maybe I could catch her in the parking lot. But as I got closer, I saw her car pull onto the street. Even as I jogged to my own car, I called her, but she wasn't answering her phone. Where the hell would she go? I threw my backpack on the front passenger seat as I got into the car. Seconds later, I had pulled out onto the same street, going the same direction.

"Erin, open up."

No response.

I leaned my head against the metal of the external security door to her apartment. "I know you're in there. Come on." I texted her. "Pls open door. Want 2 talk."

Still nothing.

"Erin, please? It's really late, and I'm about to embarrass you in front of the neighbors. It involves singing."

The interior door opened, and she stood, waiting. She'd been crying. Any residual anger I might have had disappeared.

"Can I come in?"

"I said I was sorry," she said.

"I am, too."

She waited.

"I reacted—it was bad. I'm sorry. I was confused. About your motives."

"Jesus, Niki."

"I know. Can I come in?"

She took her keys out of her pocket and unlocked the security door, then stepped back so I could enter. She locked it behind me and shut the interior door. I studied her for a few moments, taking in the baggy flannel shirt and the ripped, faded jeans and the bright yellow socks. Totally adorable. And sexy. Really fucking sexy.

"Why didn't you just tell me?" I asked.

"And risk losing you?"

"So you were going to…what? Keep pretending I had a secret admirer? How long did you think I'd do that?"

"I don't know. I didn't think it through. I wanted to tell you tonight, but things got a little out of control." She stared at the rug under her feet. Its bright designs complemented her socks. "I've had feelings for you for a long time. I wanted to take it further, but I didn't think you'd ever do that with me as myself." She looked up at me. "I'm so sorry. I hate that I hurt you. This—it was dishonest. I really fucked up."

"So what would have happened if I got really into Little Ms. Unknown?"

"I had it all planned out. I'd start leaving clues that pointed to me."

I laughed, and it eased some of the tension between us. "Seriously?" That was so Erin.

"You would have figured it out. Eventually."

"As dense as I am about these things."

"You said it. I didn't." She finally smiled.

"Okay," I said. "It was a little fucked up and maybe dishonest, but it was coming from a good place." I moved closer to her. "And it was really hot." I caressed her cheek. She stared at me, uncertainty in her eyes. "And I so wanted it to be you." I leaned in and kissed her, and she sighed against my lips and wrapped her arms around me, and it was un-fucking-believable because I knew it was Erin this time, and every fantasy I'd ever had about her rocketed down my spine to my crotch.

I pushed away after a bit, as hard as it was, and pulled the blindfold out of my jacket pocket. "Finish what you started." I said it with a challenge as I tied it around my head. I didn't have long to wait. She pushed my jacket off my shoulders, and I let it fall, and then she was pressed against me, kissing me again, a mixture of soft and deep and hard and hungry. She had her hands in my shirt and she undid my bra again, and I groaned as my breasts pressed against her palms, and she squeezed, gently, and pushed me back against the door, shoving her thigh between mine as she kissed me.

My hands found their way underneath her shirt, but she grabbed them, and I felt her smile against my mouth as she slowly pushed my hands out of her clothing. And then she pulled my T-shirt off and brushed my bra straps off my shoulders so that it, too, fell and I was suddenly aware of the cool wood of the door against my skin.

"Don't move," she said softly near my ear, and I obeyed. I heard the rustle of clothing, and then she was pressed against me again, this time without fabric between us. The soft heat of her naked skin made me ache, and I ran my hands up her back, something I'd been wanting to do for months, and she sucked and nibbled my earlobe, which sent sparks right to my clit. Still kissing me, she undid my jeans and slowly worked the zipper down, the throbbing between my legs increasing with every movement.

She stopped kissing me, and I felt her hands on mine, and she pushed my arms above my head and held my hands there, touching each other, against the door. She moved one of her hands while the other kept both my wrists pinned. Her free hand stroked my nipple, and I arched, every nerve on fire. Then she nuzzled my neck, and I felt her teeth close gently on my earlobe.

"*Te quiero*," she said before she moved again and put her lips on my nipple. I moaned and trembled, not sure I could stay standing.

And then her hand was in my pants and she was cupping me, squeezing gently, stroking through the fabric of my very damp underwear. She moved again, and her breasts pressed against mine. I could have moved my hands, could have broken the hold she had on my wrists with her one hand, but I didn't want to.

"*¿Qué tanto me deseas?*" she asked, voice husky.

"I want you in the worst way," I managed between gasps. Just talking to me like that was going to make me come. "Can't you tell?"

She slid her hand inside my underwear, and I gasped when she entered me. I couldn't breathe for a few moments, couldn't think, couldn't do anything but grit my teeth. And then she was thrusting, deep and slow, her tongue on my nipple matching the pace of her fingers in my pussy. The grip she had on my wrists with her other hand tightened, and I wasn't sure I could break free now, even if I wanted to.

She stopped working my nipples and returned to kissing me, her fingers still thrusting, picking up speed, and it felt so good I forgot to breathe again, forgot where I was as a massive wave of sensation broke deep within and rolled across every nerve I had. I sagged, trembling.

Erin released my wrists, and I slowly lowered my arms until they rested on her shoulders. They tingled because they'd been in one position too long. My back was still against the door, which was good because I didn't think I could stand without support. She carefully pulled her fingers out and rested against me for a long moment before she took the blindfold off. I blinked in the light.

"Pretty sure I got out of my head," I said.

She laughed and pulled me close. I leaned into her and rested my hands on her hips. She smelled like jasmine. And sex. I smiled.

"I'm hoping you'll stay," she said after a while.

"You're joking, right? After that? You won't be able to get rid of me."

She pulled away so she could look at me while she traced my jaw with her fingertip. "Good." She kissed me again. "I'm so glad you took a chance."

"Me, too. But"—I gestured at the blindfold—"it's way hotter knowing it's you on the other side of that."

She laughed again, all the way to the bedroom.

A HEIST TO REMEMBER

BY ANA MATICS

THE JOB WAS SUPPOSED TO be simple.

Ash flicked her cigarette away into the pouring rain. She was standing outside her hotel, the city a looming black mass of shadows and mist above her. It was cold. She shivered, drawing her long wool overcoat more tightly against her thin frame. The dress she wore underneath, a gray sheath meant more for the distraction it caused than the warmth it provided, did little by way of protection against the whipping wind that swept up the street.

Outside meant escape; outside was a moment to clear her head before the next step in her plan. She had to find Dick Firsch and get his keys before he realized what her game was. The only problem, however, was that Dick Firsch knew her face and was uninterested in playing her games.

"Ashleigh Lowe, international woman of mystery," Ash muttered. She dug in her pocket for another cigarette, staring out into the neon glow of the city, her lips twisting into a scowl. "Some mess you are." She bent to light the cigarette, hand cupped against the wind and rain.

The door beside her opened. Ash glanced over her shoulder, forcing her teeth to stop chattering. A woman had emerged from the party inside, her breath fogging in the cold rain. She wrapped her arms around herself despite the thick, gray wool coat that descended past her knees. She stood there, fingers rubbing up and down her coat sleeves, hissing at the cold. The sound was pretty, coming from lips painted red and a face framed with dark red hair tumbling artfully from an updo that must have taken hours.

"You got a light?" Her voice was accented in that blandly neutral way that placed her as being foreign, without specifying any particular homeland. She approached Ash with a steady click of stilettos on pavement, coming to stand beside her.

Ash held out her Zippo with a pleasant smile. Her own hair, swept back in a fishtail braid that had taken Miguel—her tech guy—close to an hour to do, was starting to frizz a little. She brushed her long bangs away from her forehead as the woman took the lighter and cupped it to the cigarette at her lips.

"Thank you."

"Anytime." Ash plunged her hands back into her pockets; her coat was now open to the wind and the rain. "Are you here for Firsch's party?"

"Yes," came the reply, an exhalation of smoke and misty breath. "Marcella Palliet." Marcella held out her hand.

"Ashleigh Lowe." She took Marcella's hand and was surprised by her grip. Ash's face was a blank mask, but inside, the panic rose. She had given her real name, not the alias she was using for this party. *Stupid, stupid....*

She was here to steal Dick Firsch's keys so that she could get into his office above the hotel and have a look at his computers. He was accused of stealing a series of blueprints and patent applications for a new type of wind turbine that was supposedly silent running. If he succeeded in proving that he held the patents, his company would stand to make billions in clean energy.

Ash plastered on her best smile, all teeth and predatory. "But the people here call me Lana Underlowe." She spoke in a quiet undertone, not fully trusting that Marcella wouldn't react badly to her having an alias for this event. She'd messed up, and now she was scrambling, trying to cover her ass.

Marcella's laugh was like a bell chiming in the distance, pleasant and full of mirth. "And why do you have two names, Ms. Underlowe?"

Ash glanced down, forcing her smile to appear sheepish. She sucked on her cigarette. "I'm a reporter, doing an exposé on Firsch's business practices."

"Oh?" Marcella leaned in, eyes soft and friendly in the neon light from the marquee above them. "What sort of business practices are you looking at?"

"Patents, he's recently applied for about fifty of them at once. Even for an innovator, that's a lot. It raised some red flags at work." If work was to mean Ash's front of a legitimate business. She maintained an office in a strip mall in Philadelphia, advertising herself as a private investigator for tax purposes. Ash was a thief, first and foremost, but having an office attracted some of the clientele that Ash occasionally enjoyed helping out.

This particular client, however, was not one of those Robin Hood scenarios. Jack Medincort was the head of security for a well-known engineering firm in New York who had approached Ash on behalf of his employer, the CEO of AllTurn Technologies. They had recently submitted that a series of patent applications had gone missing on their way to be filed, and Medincort was all but positive that Firsch had stolen them. All he needed was proof and for Ash to acquire the original applications and blueprints so that they could prove ownership in court.

Ash liked Medincort, they had worked together before on a similar snatch and grab. She kept urging him to tighten his security, to employ private couriers to deliver his applications, and to stop being such an easy target for robbery. "Firsch and his ilk are sharks, Jack. You gotta be more careful," Ash had urged him when he agreed to pay her fee.

Now though, staring out at the wind and the rain, Ash wanted to be anywhere but at Dick Firsch's stuffy party full of society page guests. He made her feel dirty even standing outside the event in her too tight dress and too high heels.

"Hummm," Marcella drew out her thought. She exhaled smoke like a dragon, the neon light from above casting her red hair almost black with fire to complete the image. She looked dangerous, beautiful. Ash wanted to get to know her better. "That sounds horribly boring, if you don't mind my saying so."

"Why do you think I'm out here?" Ash raised an eyebrow.

"Touché."

They lapsed back into silence, two women smoking under a marquee that seemed out of place in this upscale hotel. Ash's mind was racing. She had to get back inside before Firsch ducked out of the party early, as he had a habit of doing. Leaving Marcella, this beautiful woman with her charming accent and hair like fire, who had happened upon her and who was content to share, as so few people seemed to be, the silence of togetherness.

"You know..." Marcella leaned in. Her perfume smelled of rich taste. Ash inhaled deeply, tasting her scent. "Your company is far more enjoyable than Mr. Firsch's. Perhaps I'll have you tonight instead."

Ash choked on the smoke she was inhaling. She spluttered, bending over slightly, hacking up smoke and ash and her own surprise. "Were...were you planning on having Firsch?"

Marcella grinned cheekily at her. "Not like that, my dear Ms. Underlowe. My firm is debating extending our services to Mr. Firsch, and I have been dispatched to feel him out, as it were."

"He's a gross old man."

"And you're an attractive young woman. The decision really is an easy one."

Smiling shyly, her composure recovered, Ash extended her arm. Marcella would prove a good cover, an easy way to get close to Firsch without him noticing her true intentions. She would have to get away from Marcella eventually, to steal upstairs and get the patents back, but the evening could prove far more fruitful than she had initially intended. "Shall we go inside then, Ms. Palliet?"

Marcella flicked her cigarette down onto the ground and stubbed it out with the toe of her obscenely expensive shoe. The look of her leg, long and encased in a silk stocking which ended in a garter at midthigh underneath her black dress, made Ash's mouth go dry. Ash wanted her; she wanted her badly.

"We shall."

They walked back into the hotel and grand ballroom that Firsch had rented out. The whole party was a sham, a self-aggrandizing exercise in expensive taste meant to impress those who would be afraid of the man. Ash hated it.

She hated everything about the opulent lie that Firsch was selling in this illusion of glittery lights and beautiful people. The only thing that felt real at all was Marcella, fingers curling around her arm, leaning against her after they dropped their coats off at the door. The lighting inside gave Ash a good chance to get a look at her, and her dry mouth from before they had gone inside returned with a vengeance.

Marcella was beautiful. Her hair was a deep auburn, and her pale skin was brushed with freckles, littering her skin like stars and disappearing down into the hefty pull of her cleavage, hidden before by her long jacket. Her dress was sleeveless, black, and beautiful, and it dipped low in the back to reveal that the freckles did not stop at her chest.

Ash licked her lips and looked down at her own feet. Her heels were just as tall as Marcella's, and they were probably the same height barefoot. Marcella appeared taller, her hair done up on top of her head.

She leaned over, fingers splaying across the small of Ash's back. She was so warm, this close. "Why don't you go speak to Mr. Firsch and I'll get us some drinks?"

Swallowing, Ash nodded stiffly. She had to get her head back in the game, if she was going to be able to pull off this ruse. She stood for a moment, watching the sway of Marcella's hips as she sauntered off toward the bar before raising her hand slowly and tapping her earpiece to life. "You there, Miguel?"

"*Si*," came Miguel's thick Spanish accent, loud and clear. "You're running out of time Ash, he's going to be leaving soon."

Ash scanned the room, her attention focusing in on Firsch. He was surrounded by a gaggle of smiling women in skimpy clothes. Ash's lip curled. It was just the way he liked it, taking advantage of all the attention money could garner him. "I see him." Her lips barely moved.

"Your kit is in the third bathroom stall from the door, in the tampon bin."

"Gross."

"Where the hell else was I supposed to put it?" Miguel demanded, irritated. Ash shook her head and smoothed her dress down flat. Miguel had gone silent in her ear. Show time.

Dick Firsch was a round, portly man with jowls on top of his jowls and a shiny bald head crowned with bleached blonde hair. Ash hovered at the edge of his periphery for a few minutes, watching him, waiting until he saw her and drew her in.

The trick with marks like Firsch was to let them drive the action, until such a time that control could be easily stripped from them. Ash was good at this; she could usually grift without needing to add too much sex appeal into the equation. Older men tended to like her because she seemed up and coming, but not opposed to the idea of sleeping to get ahead. It worked well in her favor.

Soon enough, Firsch gestured for Ash to approach. He was smiling at her, he knew her face from other events, from times he had employed her services. "Ms. Underlowe." His voice was slippery, oozing over Ash and making the hair at the back of her neck stand on end. "What are you doing here?"

Ash smiled politely at him. "Casing the joint." It wasn't a lie, but he laughed anyway. She did too, the pressure of the situation aching at her temples. "In all honesty, Mr. Firsch, I'm here to enjoy the party. Your office sent me an invite after the thing in Paris."

"Ah yes, Paris. I am glad that worked out." Firsch extended his hand, and Ash took it, letting him pull her in and press kisses, continental style, to her cheeks. She pulled his keys from his pocket. "It's lovely to see you again."

"Likewise."

Marcella slid in beside them, two glasses of champagne in her hands. She smiled politely at Firsch and turned, leaning down to whisper in Ash's ear. "You're *not* flirting with him."

Ash turned, mouth open and all fake scandalized, the keys sliding easily into her purse. It was a window that Marcella had given her, a chance to slip the keys away before they were noticed. Had she seen? Did she know? All Ash could see was the playful arch of one of Marcella's dark eyebrows over her twinkling blue eyes. Marcella was just flirting, she hoped.

Holding out a glass, "Champagne?" Marcella's lips quirked upwards into a warm smile. Ash's knees felt weak, and she tucked her clutch under one arm. Marcella's fingers lingered on her own for longer than was strictly necessary. Her skin was warm, and her expression was so carefully neutral that Ash could easily read through the lines to the want barely hidden beneath the bland mask.

She was everything Ash could ever want.

Firsch's booming laugh broke Ash's thoughts before she could think any more about how she wanted to pin Marcella up against the wall like the piece of art that she was. He clasped Ash's arm and smiled lasciviously at Marcella. "I see you two know each other."

"We do," Marcella answered smoothly. Her fingers spread out over Ash's hip, pulling her in close. Ash felt possessed, owned, a prize that had been won. Need started to build within her. She had to get away, and soon, because she was losing her ability to maintain her composure and her grip on what little self-control she still possessed.

"Carry on then ladies, carry on." Firsch waved at them, drifting off to engage in conversation with some other young woman who was not otherwise attached.

Ash turned to Marcella. "One would think you possessive."

"I am possessive of what's to be mine." Marcella leaned in, her breath hot on Ash's ear, her lips mouthing gently at the sensitive skin as she spoke. "And you are, aren't you Ashleigh?"

Her brain was clouded. She had to get this done before things got out of hand. "I need to use the ladies," she said quietly. Marcella's lips brushed against her earlobe and it was all Ash could do to not cry out at the feeling of it. "And that isn't a suggestion of meeting me up there, okay?" She stepped half a step away from Marcella and opened her clutch. She pulled out her room key and handed it to her. "Let me say my goodbyes here and then I'll meet you upstairs—room eight twenty-four—in ten minutes."

Marcella sipped her champagne. "And what if I want to have you in the bathroom?"

Swallowing hotly, Ash tried, and failed, to prevent the flush from coming over her skin. She exhaled, her composure growing more and more difficult to rake in. "I want you in a bed, with nothing but those stockings and shoes."

"But darling…" Marcella leaned in, lips close, so close. Her breath smelled of expensive champagne and danger. "You haven't even seen what I'm wearing up top."

"Your dress is backless."

"Exactly my point."

Marcella leaned in, lips pressing full against Ash's own, slightly parted ones. Her skin sang as painted red lips sank into her bottom lip and tugged gently, smearing Ash's lipstick and tasting of sin. Marcella pulled away before Ash could say anything more, and stepped back into the gaggle of people they still stood amongst. "Ten minutes."

"Ten minutes."

Ash all but ran for the bathroom, heart pounding in her ears. Firsch's keys jangled in her clutch as she counted three stalls down and ducked inside the thankfully clean and empty stall. She was beyond screwed.

True to Miguel's word, the copy kit was hidden where he said it would be, thankfully mess free. Ash sat on the toilet and cracked the resin kit that would fuse to make the polymer and create an identical copy of the key. Her hands were shaking. When the hell was she going to do this if not tonight? Firsch was sure to know that she was up to something. Her mere presence at this party, while totally legitimate, was enough to tip him off that she might be up to something. She had to play her cards carefully now.

She squeezed the tube of polymer out into the mold and counted to fifteen, gathering her things quickly and staring down at Firsch's keys. Perfect. She tossed them into the air and caught them, flushing the toilet and heading out of the bathroom. She cut directly down to coat check, collecting both her coat and Marcella's, and then slipping Firsch's keys into his overcoat pocket from where it hung next to her own.

"Miguel." She tapped her earpiece as she headed toward the elevator. "I'm going to do it tonight, late. Be prepared to receive the files."

"When is late?" He sounded tired over the com.

Ash jammed the button on at the bank of elevators. "I don't know…later."

"Does this have anything to do with that leggy redhead? Because seriously Ash, you should che—"

211

"Goodnight, Miguel." Ash pulled the earpiece from her ear and set it neatly in her purse, taking the elevator up to the ninth floor and exhaling. She had Firsch's key, he was none the wiser. She would have her fun and slip away in the night. It would be perfect.

A hum of excitement reverberated through her body as she made her way up to the ninth floor. Ash fluffed her hair in the elevator and fished out her lipstick, smearing more of the same cool shade onto her lips. She was lucky the elevator had a mirror, or else it would be back down to the lobby and into Firsch's grasp once more.

This plan was going to go off without a hitch.

She paused then and pulled her phone, with some difficulty, from her clutch. She had to make sure she did not miss her window of opportunity to make off with both the blueprints and the patent application proof. She had copies of the blueprints in her room, provided by her employer so that she could verify the copies Firsch had in his office. It was good, too, an excuse to have more in her room. Hopefully Marcella would not think to ask what they were for, although she had bought Ash's story about working on an article about patent applications.

She programmed her alarm for three o'clock in the morning and stuffed it back in her bag, just as the elevator dinged its arrival.

Ash slung both of their coats over one arm and stood before the door, her palm resting on cool, fireproof metal. Her heart was hammering in her chest. It had been too long since she had done this, since she had lived so dangerously and had a woman like this. Marcella was all that she could have possibly wanted, beautiful and utterly charming.

She knocked, feeling foolish even though it was her own room.

The door opened, Marcella was still in her dress, a far-off look in her eyes. She glanced down at the coats in Ash's arms. "I was wondering what was keeping you." She stood aside and let Ash into the room.

Sheepishly, Ash draped both coats over a chair. "It took a while to convince the coat check guy to let me take your coat."

"Did he think you were stealing it?" Marcella sauntered toward Ash, her expression distant. Her fingers pulled pins from her hair one by one. Ash's breath caught in her throat, watching as her dark red hair fell softly around her shoulders. She took half a step forward, their bodies so close but not yet touching, and raised her hands to touch Marcella's hair. It was soft, smooth under her fingers.

Marcella leaned forward, her lips pressing to Ash's in a kiss that had been coming all night long. Her hands came to rest on Ash's hips, while Ash buried her hands in Marcella's hair. There were no more pins, nothing to keep her from touching every last beautiful strand of her hair.

The kiss was long, searing. It burned Ash in its intensity. Marcella's teeth and tongue lingered, ghosting over her lips and forcing through the barrier. It felt as though Marcella was trying to devour her, to eat her soul out through her mouth in this blissful kiss that felt so damn good.

It was over soon though, Marcella pulling away to turn, her fingers plucking at the zipper at the back of her dress. Ash tugged her own over her head, lips swollen and desperate for more. "He didn't think I was stealing it..." she started to explain.

Marcella laughed. Her dress pooled at her ankles leaving her chest bare. A smattering of freckles drifted across her breasts and Ash's mouth felt dry just looking at them.

"Those are magnificent." She sounded like a teenager, but she didn't care. Reaching forward, pulling Marcella to her once more, Ash pressed her palm firmly to Marcella's breast. The other rested at the small of her back, just above her garter belt and underwear. Her nipple was hard, pressing against Ash's palm. She swallowed, her fingers squeezing gently, and let Marcella kiss her once more.

This kiss was different, hungry. Ash could feel Marcella's racing heart under her fingers as she let her fingers relax and drift to touch only the raised nub of Marcella's dusty pink nipple. It grew harder still under her touch and when Ash pinched it gently, Marcella shuddered in her arms.

They stumbled backward, both still in heels that were a little too high and both feeling a little too drunk for this sort of an encounter. It felt dangerous, wanting. Ash kissed Marcella like she was salvation from a poorly led life, a trick of the light and the blessing of the night. Marcella kissed back, moaned as Ash's fingers wandered over her breasts, and let her approval of every touch Ash left on her skin be heard.

The bed connected with the back of Marcella's legs and they tumbled down in a heated mess of bodies. Ash landed on top, her hands on either side of Marcella's head, spread wide to break her fall. Marcella's hips canted up and Ash stared down at red hair fanning out on the crisp white of the bedspread, a low hum of approval at the back of her throat.

Ash dipped her head, pressing her lips to the tight muscle at Marcella's neck. She nibbled at her earlobe, enjoying the feeling of Marcella wriggling beneath her. She kissed her way to Marcella's collarbone, lingering, her tongue drifting into the hollow there, flicking across the constellations of freckles before dipping down. Her body ached to be touched, and for all that Marcella was the aggressor in this liaison, this was what Ash wanted. She wanted to bite, to touch, to fuck, and then to let Marcella have her way.

This was her way of winning.

She scraped her teeth over the soft, sensitive underside of Marcella's breast, enjoying how Marcella's hands flew up to grip her head and hold it to the nipple Ash now had caught between her teeth. Her free hand shifted, her weight was on one elbow, tweaking and squeezing the other, reveling in how Marcella enjoyed this.

"Scoot up," Ash said. She kicked off her shoes and wriggled out of her bra and underwear before coming to rest between Marcella's legs. The scant bit of fabric she was wearing as underwear was dark with Marcella's desire, and Ash licked her lips slowly, watching Marcella watch her, her nipple caught between one of her hands, the other half open above her head.

"I could tie you up." Marcella's tone was casual, but the proposition sent a white-hot jolt of desire down Ash's spine. Her neglected cunt ached and Marcella's smile grew. "I could tie you to this bed and fuck you until you don't remember your own name."

Ash tugged at the tiny scrap of fabric covering Marcella's sex. She unclipped the garters that held up Marcella's stockings and threw the underwear away somewhere behind her. "Let me fuck you first."

"Where's the fun if this isn't a power struggle?" Marcella asked. Her entire body surged upward, but Ash held firm. She smiled down at Marcella, sitting up slightly, her fingers resting on the garter belt around Marcella's hips.

Her nails bit into the skin there, as Marcella fell back, acquiescing this round. Ash leaned up and kissed her gently on her lips. "I'm going to eat you." Her lips were a hair's breadth away from Marcella's. "And then I'm going to hold you there."

"You wouldn't."

"Would I?"

Ash would too. She kissed her way down Marcella's flat stomach, past scars and a strange knot of tissue that looked suspiciously like a bullet wound. She was too focused on her task to ask where it came from, her fingers digging into Marcella's hips, her lips brushing against the soft skin of her sex. She smelled aroused, and she was so wet. Ash buried her face in Marcella's cunt, licking a solid, steady line from her clit down to her opening, her tongue dipping inside and Marcella's hands flying down to grab Ash's head and hold her there.

Smirking, Ash set to work. She twisted her tongue around Marcella's clit, and when she was certain that Marcella was not going to try and fight her for control again, she pulled one hand around to push in under her chin. She bit at Marcella's outer lips, her fingers curving up to find that spot, the one that Ash knew would make her cream her own underwear just hearing Marcella's reaction. She was so beautiful as she started to come undone.

Marcella humped Ash's face, her hips jerking upwards uncontrollably. It was all that Ash could do to keep her still. She wanted to fuck this woman, to have her and to own her until she couldn't bear it any more. She dragged her teeth along the engorged surface of Marcella's clit and sucked it more firmly into her mouth. Ash rocked with Marcella's rhythm. Her body felt like it was shaking, her entire being was concentrated on this moment, on having Marcella.

"Come up here." Marcella tugged on Ash's head. Her fingers were warm and her pull was insistent. Ash moved up, her hand still trapped between them, and kissed Marcella gently on the lips before letting her head fall to the damp skin at her neck. Ash leaned on her elbow, her hips thrusting behind her fingers into Marcella.

She felt, rather than saw, Marcella's hand slip into her own underwear. Marcella's fingers were long and manicured. They dipped once into the wetness that had pooled between Ash's legs and drifted out, slipping easily over the sensitive skin her underwear still hid. Ash gasped, her hips coming down and the heel of her palm grinding against Marcella's clit.

"Fuck." Ash panted. Marcella quickened her pace. Ash tried to keep time, but she was losing focus, too concentrated on the pinching, flicking, beautiful sensation of Marcella's fingers on her clit. "Fuck, fuck, fuck."

"You like that then?" Marcella asked. Her free hand was wrapped around Ash, pulling her closer with every thrusting rock of Ash's hips. "You like being played like a fiddle while you're supposed to be in control?"

"Oh God." Ash groaned. Marcella's fingers were like magic. They were slick and gentle, yet firm, and moving with the practiced ease of one who has perfected this art. She twisted her wrist, just as Ash's hips came down, and Ash saw white. Her entire body went tense. Her thighs trembled, and her heart raced. Her hips flopped listlessly against her wrist. She kept moving her hand, chasing Marcella over the edge. She had to, she had to prove she could.

Marcella was still moving, her hand never slowed. Ash's body felt like it was on fire, relaxing and falling right back into the familiar build of orgasm. She shifted, looking into Marcella's eyes. Her own were wide, she felt a little bit frightened.

"Did you need a break?" Marcella asked, her lip curling.

"No." Ash ducked her head back down and twisted her hand so her thumb could swipe across Marcella's clit.

It was not long then, the pull of her thumb, caught and slippery in Marcella's arousal, shifted, and Marcella moaned loudly, her nails digging into the small of Ash's back. Her body shuddered underneath Ash and then went still. The hand that was still in Ash's underwear fell lifelessly to the bed.

Ash let herself curl into the crook of Marcella's arm. "You're good."

"You too."

She could barely cover her yawn, stifling it behind her shoulder as she curled downward to pull her underwear from her body. Ash tossed them to the floor. "I'll be good for round two in a bit, just let me..."

And for a while, all Ash saw was the darkness of sated sleep.

Her phone buzzed. Marcella rolled flat on her back and threw an arm over her head. "Who is it?" she mumbled. Her accent was more pronounced when sleep and sex sated.

It was just an alarm, but Ash sat up and gathered her dress from the floor. "My editor," she lied. She was playing a journalist, after all. "It's after deadline and I didn't check in. I'll go down to the lobby and take this, okay?" She leaned over, pressing her lips to Marcella's shoulder, the back of her dress half-zipped. "I'll be back in ten minutes."

Marcella stared at her, eyes half-lidded in the blackness of the hotel room. "You'd better be."

Ash leaned over, phone pressed to her shoulder, and kissed her cheek. "Promise." She grabbed her clutch and the keycard from where Marcella had left it and slipped from the room. "Hey, Mr. Sanderson," she spoke into her phone after she silenced the alarm. "Hang on, let me get to where I can talk."

Showtime.

Dick Firsch's office was ten floors up. Ash took the elevator after slipping her earpiece back into her ear and ensuring with Miguel that the cameras would go black.

They were focused now, one being. He guided her using the cameras that he had looped to their advantage. Ash sucked in steady pulls of air as he unlocked the door using the remote transceiver in her phone. Miguel explained what Ash was looking for on Firsch's computer and Ash found it easily. She downloaded the files and riffled through a few filing cabinets before she found the blueprints in question. Sure enough, the logo on them was not from Firsch's company. Ash honestly wasn't that surprised by this development. Firsch had always been dirty.

Still, there had always been this nagging feeling of doubt about this entire job that Ash couldn't shake. The swell of smug vindication was enough to propel her into action once more. She stole out of the room, leaving it just as she had come. The key she wiped down and tossed onto a discarded room service tray, two floors down. They would never find it before it hit the garbage chute in the morning. It really was the perfect plan.

When she got back to the ninth floor, Ash checked the hallway for onlookers before slipping into the room once more. She stood in the dark and stripped off her dress, laying it and the blueprints flat next to each other and hoping beyond all hope that Marcella would not ask too many questions. It was too late to deviate from the plan now. She and Miguel would just have to regroup about how it went down afterward.

The bed was warm. Marcella had curled under the covers, her body was wrapped around a pillow and she started when Ash touched her. "I didn't hear you come in," she said sleepily.

Ash leaned over and kissed her. Her body was pressed flush against Marcella's side. Her hand found the juncture between Marcella's legs and glanced over her clit, warm and still wet. Ash smiled as Marcella made a sleepy noise of contentment. She shifted so her legs were spread wider, and turned. "You're a charmer," she whispered.

"Maybe we should do this again sometime."

"Mmm, if you keep doing that I'll keep you on retainer." Marcella threw her head back, her lips parted in a breathy moan. She was beautiful in this half-light. Her body was tense under Ash's fingers and she let herself be touched as Ash wanted her to be touched, gently, reverently. She was a beautiful woman and Ash wanted to make sure she knew it.

She shifted, leaning into Marcella's neck. Cigarettes and sex hit her nose and pooled in her abdomen, warm and comforting. She smelled of expensive perfume and beautiful women splayed out over a bed, Ash's fingers buried deep inside them—a thousand encounters, this the only one that mattered. "You're beautiful," Ash babbled. Her teeth nipped at Marcella's ear and Marcella groaned. Her body arched up into Ash's dancing fingers, and Ash withdrew.

Marcella's eyes flew open. "What are you doing?"

Ash smiled, slow and easy, shifting so she was straddling Marcella's hips once more. Her hands rested on Marcella's breasts. They caressed her pert nipples, but never really touched, never lingered longer than they had to. "I want you on the edge."

Hips thrust up, asking for Ash's touch. "It's three-thirty in the morning, I'm in no mood for games." Marcella's pout was so alien on her face that Ash had to bend to kiss her. Their exchange, no more than a touch of lips, was gentle and lingering. Ash let her hips drop, grinding hard against Marcella and feeling the moment when she groaned into the kiss. Ash leaned forward then, resting on her elbows and began their dance anew.

It was slow. Getting off this way was not easy. Ash liked the dance of it. The push and steady pull, the feel of friction as her sex ground against Marcella's. Ash sucked lazy patterns into Marcella's neck, marking her, biting at her skin, knowing she could not play the game she so desperately wanted to play with her. There was no time; Ash had robbed a man tonight.

Marcella's hands were in Ash's hair. Ash's braid had long since started to fall out, and Marcella's fingers worked through the rest of Ash's hair. Nails scraped at Ash's scalp. Ash shifted, resting all her weight on one elbow and pushing her fingers into Marcella.

The hiss of pleasure that escaped Marcella's lips was beautiful, and Ash pressed her thumb against Marcella's clit, her own needy sex dragging against Marcella's thigh as their position shifted. "That's it," Ash muttered. Her head was down, resting in the crook of Marcella's neck. "Take it all in."

"I'm—" Marcella started, but words were choked back in a sob as Ash held her at the edge. She lingered there, Marcella's orgasm at her fingertips. It was an obscene feeling, powerful and grandiose. She liked it, but she knew it could not last. It was with a smug smile and a gentle kiss that Ash pushed her over. She went, tumbling into bliss. Her arms and legs wrapping around Ash as best they could as Ash rode Marcella's thigh to her own, shuddering release.

Boneless, their breath still struggling to gain purchase in their lungs, they fell back onto the bed. Ash curled around Marcella, one finger lazily circling her nipple. "Am I ever going to see you again?" she asked. Her eyelids were too heavy to keep open.

Marcella pressed a kiss to Ash's forehead. "That remains to be seen, I think."

For a long time, all Ash knew was dreams.

She woke up bathed in sunlight. The bed was cold, she was alone. The room was silent, and it rang in Ash's ears as she forced herself to sit up. Her entire body ached. There were scratches on her skin, running down her arms and breasts, and a blossoming bruise on her breast from where Marcella had kissed her for far too long.

Across the room, her dress lay draped over the desk chair and Ash frowned. She was fairly sure she left it on the floor. She had used it as a cover to hide the plans.

The plans.

They were gone.

The desk was empty of anything that could have resembled a wind turbine blueprint. Ash let out a low groan rubbing at her face. "Fuck," she muttered. "Fuck, fuck, *FUCK*."

Her phone rang on the bedside table. Ash leaned over and picked it up.

"What?" she growled.

"Hello, darling."

Anger rose in Ash's stomach, chewing at her insides and making her want to lash out. "You fucked me."

"Yes, I believe I did."

"You know what I mean." Ash let out a frustrated growl, pounding her fist into the sheets pooled at her waist. "Where are they?"

"Where are what, darling?"

"The blueprints, where are they?"

"On their way to their proper owner. You were played, Ashleigh. AllTurn Technologies never designed those turbines. A small firm in Sri Lanka did. I've sent them back to their proper owners; your conscience can thank me later." Marcella chuckled into the phone. "We really must do this again sometime, you were a wonderful distraction."

"Go to hell." Ash growled. She hung up and threw the phone down on the bed. Her mind was already racing, trying to figure out how she could see Marcella again.

THE DUPLEX

BY L.M. PERRIN

ONCE UPON A TIME, A fifteen-minute walk would not have left Beatrice breathless.

When she was younger, Beatrice's mother had warned her about getting old. "That weight around your middle doesn't come off when you're forty the way it does when you're twenty," she'd said.

Well...score one for her mother.

In the last ten years or so, a hefty plumpness had accumulated across Beatrice's stomach and thighs that refused to budge. Beatrice remembered when she was twenty, when looking good in a bikini had taken a month of running and that was it. Now it took a yearlong commitment just to wear a tank top.

Beatrice took a deep breath in an attempt to calm her racing heart. She brushed her hair from her face and squinted against the sun, trying to gauge how many horrible steps it would take before she reached her duplex. Hazel, her tenant, was stretched out on the thick cement banister on her side of the duplex's front porch. Her feet were bare, and she was wearing shorts and an old T-shirt she'd cut the sleeves off of, exposing her long, tan limbs. She was sketching, making long strokes across a pad of paper, but she glanced up when she noticed Beatrice approaching. She brushed her short, sandy-blonde hair out of her eyes and lifted a hand in greeting.

"'Lo, Beatrice," Hazel said when Beatrice began climbing the steps. She smiled and the scar under her left eye crinkled.

"Hi, Hazel," Beatrice said, trying her hardest to not sound out of breath. "How's your day?"

Hazel pointed at the clear sky with her nub of charcoal. "It's nice out. So, good. You?"

"Fine."

She was always fine. And even though she knew Hazel would listen if one day she admitted she wasn't fine—that her job was boring on a good day and frustrating on every other—a part of her didn't want Hazel to know. She was the stereotypical nine to fiver—unfulfilled by her work and wishing she'd focused on what she'd loved instead of making money. Hazel, in contrast, was a twenty-something college dropout who was pursuing an art career with a single-minded determination that Beatrice envied.

"I got some of your mail again," Hazel said, stopping Beatrice before she could make the turn toward her half of the house. "Hang on, I'll get it." She set the sketchpad down and swung herself off the banister.

"You know you can just drop it in the mail slot," Beatrice said. It was a conversation they'd had before, but Hazel had yet to take the offer.

"I know. Have a seat. I'll be right back."

Beatrice dropped onto one of Hazel's metal patio chairs, grateful to be off of her feet. She pointed her toes and rolled her neck.

Hazel returned with two glasses of water and Beatrice's mail tucked under her arm. She turned, offering the mail to Beatrice. The armpits of Hazel's T-shirt had been stretched and ripped almost to her hip, revealing more skin than it covered, and Beatrice caught sight of the ever-elusive rib tattoo peeking out from behind Hazel's arm. Beatrice pulled her mail free before Hazel caught her staring.

"Just what I wanted, Hazel. Pizza coupons."

Hazel grinned and set the waters on the small table next to Beatrice's chair. She sat as well and dragged her chair closer with her heels.

Beatrice took a sip of her water. "What are you drawing?"

Hazel shrugged. She rubbed one foot over the top of the other. "People. Whoever walks by. Lots of joggers, lots of little old ladies walking their dogs."

"No painting today?"

It was what Hazel usually did—what she was trying to do for a living. She'd shown Beatrice some of her work once, shyly, and only after a year and a half of living next door. Beatrice would be the first to admit she didn't know anything about art, but she'd been impressed nonetheless.

Hazel shook her head. Her hands were wet from the sweat of her glass and she rubbed them together, smearing the charcoal from her fingers across her hands. She dragged her hands down the front of her shirt, leaving behind dark grey streaks. "Not today. I've got to switch it up, otherwise I get bored and do nothing."

"Can I see?"

Hazel leaned forward, not quite standing but stretching out far enough to snag the sketchpad by the corner and pull it from the banister. She handed it to Beatrice.

Beatrice gave a low whistle, impressed. "That's a really good Mrs. Allen."

"She's easy," Hazel said. "I have her face memorized. It's the people who I see for a split second that are the hard ones." She drummed her fingers against her knee. "I'm trying to teach myself to pick out major features and get them down quickly. Not so good at it, though."

Beatrice snorted. Hazel's "not so good" was light-years better than anything she could do. She pointed to a man's face in the upper-right corner. "This is the mailman. Right?"

"Let me see." Hazel leaned over. Beatrice could feel the heat radiating off of Hazel's body, pushing up against her own. "Yeah."

"It's good."

Hazel gave her a lopsided smile. "Thank you."

Beatrice turned the page. For a moment she wasn't sure what she was looking at—not a face, more like—

Breasts. Those were breasts. And legs.

Blood rushed to Beatrice's face. She inhaled sharply. "Oh." She tried to turn the page back quickly but Hazel had noticed.

"Yeah." Hazel cleared her throat. She sounded as embarrassed as Beatrice felt. "That...that didn't walk by today. Sorry."

"No, it's okay." Beatrice laughed self-consciously, willing the color to leave her cheeks. "Just surprised me."

Hazel ran a hand through her hair, pushing her bangs out of her face and making them momentarily stand on end before they flopped across her forehead again. "I wouldn't be an artist if I didn't draw naked women," she said, though she sounded more apologetic than teasing. Beatrice handed her back the sketchbook.

"No. I guess not."

They sat in awkward silence. Hazel fiddled with the edges of her sketchbook and bounced her leg. "So," she began slowly, "I'm going to have a party Friday."

Beatrice traced the rim of her glass with her fingertip. "Okay."

"Nothing big," Hazel said quickly, as if she were afraid that Beatrice would protest. "Just some friends."

"What's the occasion?"

Hazel ducked her head. "Sold a painting," she mumbled. She was trying to hide her smile.

Beatrice sat up quickly. "You did?"

Hazel nodded, a slow grin splitting her face. "Yeah. I did."

"Hazel." Beatrice stared. "That's awesome."

"Thanks."

"I'll make myself scarce, then. You can get loud and not worry about keeping me up or anything."

"No, uh…" Hazel bit her lip. She fidgeted. "Actually, I was going to ask if you'd like to come."

Beatrice blinked. "Oh."

"Yeah."

Beatrice hesitated. "I can't remember the last time I went to a party," she said carefully, building up to a polite refusal.

"So?"

"So you should have a party with your friends, not the old lady who lives next door."

Hazel's smile faded. The look in her eyes turned serious. "Aren't we friends?"

"Of course we are. Just…" Beatrice didn't understand her own logic. "Different friends."

"Friend is friend, Beatrice." Hazel said. "I like you. I like talking to you." She fixed Beatrice with an earnest stare. "Please, I want you to come."

Beatrice sighed. "You won't be mad if I leave before midnight to go to bed?"

Hazel shook her head, her scar crinkling again. "Not at all."

"Okay," Beatrice said after a moment. "I'll think about it."

It was stupid, how indecisive she was being. She put less effort into dressing for work. And this was a party barely five feet from her own front door.

Beatrice brushed her hands over her sides, hating how the shirt clung to her middle. She felt fat and uncomfortable and unattractive, but it was one of the few shirts she owned that felt appropriate for socializing outside of work. When she lifted her arms to adjust her hair the shirt rose past her belly button.

That wasn't happening.

She ripped the shirt over her head and flung it back toward her closet. She had a three-pack of V-necks—all different shades of blue, all technically men's shirts—that were comfortable and made her feel…if not sexy, then at least not completely repulsive. Maybe they weren't skin tight and stylish and maybe the sleeves were a little long, but at least they didn't accentuate every part of her body Beatrice wanted to hide. She pulled the lightest of the three over her head and shut off the light in her room before she had a chance to look at herself in the mirror and change her mind again.

Music filtered through her walls as she descended the stairs. Hazel's porch lights were on and Beatrice locked her front door, feeling more than a little self-conscious when a woman with dreadlocks and a man with a massive beard climbed the front steps and turned toward Hazel's unit. It figured that Hazel's friends would all be artistic types as well.

Hazel's front door was open, the screen door the only thing separating the porch from the foyer. Beatrice always felt awkward walking into Hazel's half of the duplex. Everything was the same but it was all reversed, as if she'd stepped into an alternate reality, and it took Beatrice a moment to orient herself in the space. She studied the people standing around the living room. She'd been right. She was by far the oldest person there.

Beatrice moved in the direction of the kitchen, scanning for Hazel among the young people milling from room to room, but it was Hazel who found her first. She squeezed Beatrice's arm from behind. Beatrice jumped.

"Sorry." Hazel grinned. "Hi. How are you?"

Beatrice smiled in return. She still felt out of place, but Hazel's eyes were warm and she looked genuinely happy to see Beatrice. "I'm good."

"I'm glad you came," Hazel said. Her eyes traveled down, taking in Beatrice's T-shirt and dark jeans. "You look nice."

It wasn't true—it couldn't be true—but the compliment pleased Beatrice anyway. "Yeah?"

Hazel nodded. She leaned back, her eyes sweeping over Beatrice again. "I never see you outside of your work clothes." She reached out and twisted the hem of Beatrice's T-shirt between her fingers. "I like it."

Beatrice opened her mouth, not sure if she was going to tease Hazel for her lack of fashion sense or thank her when Hazel let the hem go and slid her open palm across Beatrice's hip. Beatrice's mouth snapped shut. A tingling feeling started in the hollow of her throat.

Hazel glanced up. "I—"

A pair of arms wrapped around Hazel's middle, interrupting her. A woman's pale face appeared over Hazel's shoulder. "I found you," she announced in a singsong voice. She pulled Hazel back sharply, jerking Hazel's hand from Beatrice's side.

Hazel's expression lost its warmth. She grimaced and then glanced over her shoulder as she extricated herself from the woman's arms. "Alison. Hi."

"Hello to you, too, Picasso." Alison smiled and leaned forward. Her hands fluttered over Hazel possessively.

Hazel stepped to the side and gestured to Beatrice. Alison's blue eyes followed the movement. When her gaze landed on Beatrice, she squinted suspiciously.

"Alison," Hazel began, "this is—"

"Let me guess," Alison interrupted. She stuck her hand out. "You're Beatrice."

Beatrice took the offered hand. She smiled nervously. "Guilty."

Alison didn't smile back. She held Beatrice's hand for a moment and looked her up and down. One eyebrow rose. She did not seem the least bit impressed. She glared at Hazel. "Really?" she demanded.

Hazel didn't answer. She was very carefully looking at anyone that wasn't Alison or Beatrice. Alison shook her head with obvious disgust and dropped Beatrice's hand. She turned away, still shaking her head, and walked away.

Beatrice felt her cheeks go hot. "What was that about?" she asked, trying to sound casual. She could hear the strain in her own voice.

"Nothing," Hazel said, but she said it too quickly and she wouldn't meet Beatrice's gaze. "It's nothing." She licked her lips. "I think I should see if anybody needs anything." She moved toward the living room, leaving Beatrice alone, and Beatrice tried to ignore the confusing mixture of jealousy and disappointment she felt creeping. She stayed put for a moment, half hoping Hazel would return, and then, irritated with herself for standing and pining like a school girl, Beatrice found herself a bottle of beer.

After her second drink, Beatrice stepped outside. Alcohol had never succeeded in overpowering her self-consciousness. She felt tipsy and obvious and no one else had even looked buzzed. She didn't need to be the drunken woman at the party who was old enough to know better.

All of Hazel's chairs were gone, moved to the backyard, and for a moment Beatrice considered climbing onto the banister and sitting the way Hazel did when she was sketching. The mental picture of drunkenly toppling over the side and onto the sidewalk stopped her. Her own chairs were still on her porch, and Beatrice slowly made her way to her side of the unit. She took a second to make sure she'd end up on chair, and not on the ground, before lowering herself onto the seat. She closed her eyes and tilted her head back, breathing through her nose. The porch felt as if it were rolling under her feet. Beatrice opened her eyes again.

"Does this mean you've gone home?" Hazel asked.

She was standing in the doorway, one hand holding the screen door open, the other holding a bottle of beer.

Beatrice rolled her head back and forth slowly. Too fast made the world spin. "I needed fresh air." She smiled. "I'm a bit buzzed."

Hazel let the screen door go. She crossed to Beatrice's side of the porch and pulled a chair close to Beatrice's. She sat and crossed her long legs at the ankle.

Beatrice lifted her hand and tapped the side of Hazel's arm with her index finger. She wanted to touch her, even if it was just a finger, and her inhibitions were at an all-time low. "You're missing your party."

Hazel scoffed. She twisted the beer bottle back and forth between her hands. "It's not my party," she said, and then paused. "I mean, it's for me, but you're actually the only person I invited."

For some reason the admission made Beatrice smile. "Really?"

Hazel nodded. She tilted her head, gesturing toward the house. "Those people in there... They're my friends, I guess. I mean, they say they are and I say they are, but...they're barracudas. They're all artists trying to sell that painting. And I'm the one who did it, and now they're pretending to be happy for me and proud and the whole time they're thinking 'my stuff is better than hers.'" Hazel took a deep breath and then shook her head. She smiled apologetically. "Sorry. I think I'm buzzed, too."

"You do deserve it," Beatrice insisted. "Your paintings are beautiful."

Hazel glanced at her. "You know, you're the only person who says stuff like that to me who doesn't make me feel like I'm supposed to say it back."

Beatrice grinned. "Why would you? I don't paint."

Hazel laughed. "No, I mean...fishing for compliments."

Beatrice snorted. "Why would I fish?" She spread her arms. "What is there to compliment?"

Hazel's smile was gone in an instant. "You don't mean that."

Beatrice didn't answer. She stared across the street at nothing and scratched her thumb against the arm of her chair.

"No, really Beatrice." Hazel sat up and leaned toward her. "You don't mean that, right?"

Beatrice sighed. "No. I suppose not."

"What does that mean?" Hazel pressed.

Beatrice smiled humorlessly. "It means I know I'm not supposed to think that."

Hazel was silent for a moment. "But you do?" she asked.

"Oh, for—" Beatrice rolled her eyes, not sure if she was irritated with herself for letting the conversation move in this direction or with Hazel for pretending she couldn't see what Beatrice was talking about. "Look at me, Hazel. I'm 42. I have a shitty job, no family—I don't even have a dog. I'm old, I'm fat—"

"No, you're not," Hazel interrupted.

Beatrice laughed bitterly. "You have a house full of beautiful, not-old, and not-fat people. And I am definitely not one of them."

"You're not old and you're not fat. I think you're beautiful."

"That's very sweet of you, Hazel."

"But you don't believe me." It wasn't a question.

Beatrice twisted her lips. "I own a mirror," she said. It came out harsher than she'd intended, more hurt, and Hazel stood.

"Don't move."

Beatrice squinted up at her. "Where are you going?"

Hazel held up her hand, gesturing for Beatrice to remain seated as she moved toward her unit again. "I'll be right back," she promised.

Beatrice tilted her head back and closed her eyes, upset with herself for her apparent inability to deflect while intoxicated. A moment later she heard the screen door slam. Something flat and hard slid across her lap.

"Here," Hazel said.

Beatrice opened her eyes. She lifted a leather bound notebook from her lap. It was tattered and well worn, held shut by a thick rubber band "What is it?"

Hazel would not look at her. She sat. "Open it," she mumbled.

Beatrice slipped the rubber band off and opened the book. The first page held Hazel's name and phone number. The second page was a charcoal drawing of a woman, her head propped in her hand, smiling happily. Beatrice turned the page. The same woman was sitting in a chair, her knees pulled to her chest, her arms wrapped around her shins. The same woman was on the third page, and again on the fourth.

"Are these..." Beatrice flipped back to the front of the sketchbook. "Are these me?"

"Yes," Hazel said. Her cheeks were red. She picked at the label of her beer bottle. "Please, don't think I'm creepy."

Beatrice traced the edge of the first drawing with her index finger. This wasn't her. She wasn't this beautiful. She shook her head. "Hazel..." She didn't know what to say. *These are really good, but, sorry, they don't look anything like me?*

Hazel saw the doubt in her eyes. "That's you," she insisted. "That's... It's not how I see you, I don't want you to think they're idealized, but that's... you." She bit her lip. "You're not weirded out, right?"

"No, I just..." Beatrice shook her head again. "I don't know why."

"Why?" Hazel let out an incredulous laugh. "Because..." Hazel paused. She reached out and touched the page, her eyes fixed on the sketch as if drawing strength from the paper. "Because I see you when you come home from work," she began, "and you're exhausted. And you look so tired, and then I say 'Hello' and you brighten right up..." she trailed off, searching for the right words. "Like it's the best part of your day." She looked up, finally meeting Beatrice's gaze. "Like a million people stepped on you and you got back up just so you could hear me say hello."

Beatrice blinked. She looked back at the drawing, at the easy smile on the woman's face. "It's the best part of my day," she admitted quietly.

"Mine, too."

Beatrice let out a shaky breath. "Hazel..."

"I like you, Beatrice. I really like you."

Beatrice closed the sketchbook. She handed it back. "Hazel, you don't want somebody like me."

Hazel's forehead furrowed with confusion. "Why not?"

"I'm old—"

"No, you're not," Hazel said.

"I'm old enough to be your mother."

"My mom is 54."

"Still." It made Beatrice feel hollow, establishing that barrier, telling Hazel no, that this was not going to happen. "I'm closer to 54 than I am to 25."

"So?"

"So…" Beatrice shrugged. To her it was self-explanatory. She was too old for Hazel. There were millions of twenty-somethings in the world, all of them with full lives ahead of them. She had nothing to offer. No matter how badly she wished that weren't true, it was, and this was for Hazel's own good.

"Do you really think about our age gap that much?" Hazel asked, gesturing between them. "When you come home and sit and talk to me, do you think about the twenty year age difference?"

"No," Beatrice admitted.

"So why does it matter now?" Hazel sounded hurt. Not angry, just hurt, and Beatrice would almost have preferred anger.

"Because this is different."

"It's exactly—"

"Hazel?" The screen door slammed and Alison stepped onto the porch. She stopped and stared before fixing Beatrice with a venomous glare. "What are you doing?" she asked Hazel. "Everybody's looking for you."

"You should go inside," Beatrice said softly, and she wished she didn't sound as if she meant it.

Hazel glanced at her, her mouth pinched in a firm line, her face hard. "I don't want to."

"Hazel. It's your party."

"You're going to leave, aren't you?" Hazel asked, a hint of desperation in her voice.

Beatrice lifted a shoulder. She gave Hazel a small smile. "It's past my bedtime."

Hazel opened her mouth to argue.

"Hazel!" Alison shrilled.

Hazel shoved a hand through her hair and whirled on Alison. "Wait!" she snapped.

"No, it's okay." Beatrice stood. "I'm leaving. It was nice meeting you, Alison." She glanced down to say 'good night' to Hazel and froze. Hazel was staring up at her with open desperation, her lips parted as if she was trying to argue and couldn't find the words to do so. She looked wrecked, as if Beatrice walking away would destroy her.

Beatrice couldn't remember anyone ever looking at her that way.

Against her better judgment Beatrice leaned down to kiss Hazel on the cheek. She felt Hazel turning her head, felt the soft touch of Hazel's mouth against the corner of her lips, and Beatrice felt something deep in her stomach clutch. She pulled away quickly. She'd meant it to be a congratulatory kiss, a kiss goodnight, but the tension she'd felt coursing through Hazel's body when she'd leaned close had made anything innocent all but impossible.

"Sorry," Hazel said, misreading the shock Beatrice knew was etched into her face. "I shouldn't have—"

"Don't." Beatrice shook her head. "Don't apologize." Something had clicked, something missing had fallen into place when she'd touched Hazel, and the argument she'd clung to all night—that Hazel couldn't want her because Beatrice couldn't envision herself being wanted—evaporated under the intensity of Hazel's gaze. Her face was hot, her lips buzzing as she stared at Hazel.

Hazel reached for her. Tentatively, she dragged her fingertips across the inside of Beatrice's arm, her eyes certain and focused. Beatrice turned her hand and trailed her fingers across Hazel's wrist.

"I don't want you to apologize."

Hazel blinked, and Beatrice knew she'd seen the uncertainty evaporate from her eyes. The corner of Hazel's mouth turned up in a slow, hesitant smile. "Can I come in?" she asked.

The question made Beatrice's heart trip. She was mildly aware of Alison still standing on the porch, glaring daggers at her, but she couldn't care less. She closed her hand around Hazel's wrist firmly and pulled. "Yes."

Hazel rose from her chair followed Beatrice to her front door, smoothly adjusting their hands so that their fingers were entwined. The feeling of Hazel's cool fingers pressing between hers left Beatrice light headed. She couldn't remember the last time she'd held someone's hand. Maybe not since college.

Hazel bent her head and pressed her nose and mouth against Beatrice's shoulder as she fumbled with the lock. She exhaled, her hot breath seeping through Beatrice's cotton shirt and scorching her skin. Beatrice shuddered and bit back a giddy laugh as she opened the door. She heard Alison begin to say something else, something that sounded an awful lot like "Are you kidding me?" and Hazel shut the door behind them. She turned and Beatrice took her hand again.

A bemused smile lifted the corners of Hazel's lips. She stuffed her free hand into her pocket and rocked back on her heels. "Do I get a tour?"

Beatrice shook her head. She pulled Hazel forward, backing toward the stairs, and Hazel's eyes went dark.

"I meant what I said outside," Hazel said. She placed a foot on the first step. "I like you. And I want—I don't want this to be a one-off thing."

Beatrice studied her—studied the strong line of her jaw, the soft fall of her bangs across her forehead, the sharpness of her collar bone above the soft swell of her small breasts. She watched Hazel's jaw clench nervously. Beatrice nodded, a slow warmth unfurling in her stomach. "Okay."

Hazel grinned. She took another step. "Really?"

Beatrice felt her lips curling upward in response. "Yes. Really."

Hazel surged forward and Beatrice met her lips eagerly. A punch of arousal hit her, driving away the last of her inhibitions. She tilted her head as Hazel's lips moved against hers, soft and searching, and draped her arms around Hazel's neck. Hazel's hands were at Beatrice's waist, pulling her close, and when Beatrice opened her mouth to gasp, Hazel's tongue brushed against hers. Beatrice groaned with pleasure and pushed back.

Hazel's mouth was hot and foreign, a delicious non-taste that made Beatrice shake. She tipped her head back to take a breath, to chase away the buzzing in her ears that demanded oxygen, and Hazel pulled gently on her bottom lip with her teeth. Beatrice groaned and Hazel laughed. She moved her lips to the point of Beatrice's chin and then down the front of her neck, peppering Beatrice's throat with hot, open-mouthed kisses.

"Oh, Jesus." Beatrice leaned against the banister and shut her eyes. Her hands twisted in Hazel's hair. She exhaled shakily; if her breathing were any faster, she'd need a paper bag. Her body was positively humming—every stroke of Hazel's tongue, every press of her searching fingers increased the pressure building in Beatrice's groin. It had been a very long time since she'd been kissed and even longer since she'd even considered physical intimacy with someone, and Hazel's touches were quickly sending her nerves into overdrive.

Hazel's fingers dipped under the hem of Beatrice's shirt and danced across the skin of her lower back. Beatrice whimpered. She pushed at Hazel's shoulders and Hazel lifted her head from Beatrice's neck.

"What's wrong?" Hazel asked, genuine concern in her voice. Hazel's lips were red, her pupils large, and Beatrice felt a spike of pleasure at the wanton look in Hazel's eyes. She was making Hazel short of breath and fuzzy headed just as much as Hazel was having that effect on her.

Beatrice brought her hand up and traced the edge of Hazel's jaw. "Nothing," she whispered. The desire to touch her, and to never stop, was so overwhelming Beatrice was amazed she'd ever kept it contained. Hazel turned her head and kissed Beatrice's palm. It was easy and affectionate, the most natural thing in the world, and Beatrice's stomach swooped again. "I don't want to do this on the stairs," she said. "And you're…making that very difficult."

The admission visibly delighted Hazel, but she stepped away with obvious difficulty. Beatrice leaned involuntarily, her body seeking contact with Hazel's again as if it were a magnet. She blinked and forced herself upright, then inclined her head in a 'follow me' gesture.

It was strange to be moving again. She was entirely distracted by Hazel's presence behind her and the ample amount of wetness already coating her inner thighs. She stumbled up the stairs, clinging to the rail as if it were a lifeline. Hazel placed a hand on Beatrice's back, just below her shoulder blades, and the thought that Hazel was having a hard time keeping her hands to herself as well inflamed Beatrice even further. She didn't think anything could top it, but the sight of Hazel standing in her bedroom, her cheeks flushed with arousal, was an even headier aphrodisiac.

Beatrice kicked off her shoes and Hazel cupped Beatrice's face in her hands, framing her ears with her fingers, and kissed her again. Her lips were hungry and searching and Beatrice made an indelicate noise of approval. Her fingers found the button of Hazel's jeans. It was an uncharacteristically bold move, but she was too far-gone for meekness. The desire to see Hazel's naked body, to touch her, to press herself up against Hazel's lean frame was all consuming. She felt the button give beneath her fingers and began pushing Hazel's pants from her hips.

Hazel shook her legs, trying to help as best she could, without moving her lips from Beatrice's. She lifted one foot free and kicked and Beatrice heard the jeans thump against her closet door. She smiled against Hazel's mouth and Hazel's breath hissed out of her nose in a silent laugh.

Their hands collided at the hem of Hazels' shirt. They pulled the shirt up and off together, Hazel lifting and Beatrice guiding the shirt over Hazel's head. Beatrice's eyes were fixed on Hazel's body, committing the reveal of Hazel's bare skin to memory—the way her belly button stretched when she lifted her arms above her head, the way the space between her ribs hollowed and filled with each ragged breath.

Hazel's breasts were small and she didn't wear a bra—a fact Beatrice had always been painfully aware of whenever Hazel was not wearing a cutoff and bikini top—and seeing her naked chest was almost enough to short-circuit Beatrice's brain. Beatrice took a half step back. Hazel stood before her, all clean lines and lean muscles, her hair mussed, her chest heaving, and Beatrice watched as goose bumps swept across Hazel's skin. Her small, light pink nipples tightened. Hazel watched her, waiting, her nostrils flared. She was vibrating with excitement.

Beatrice reached out one trembling hand. She touched the tip of her index finger to Hazel's left nipple and Hazel went rigid. She made a keening noise in the back of her throat and leaned into the touch. Emboldened, Beatrice stepped close again. She closed her thumb and forefinger over Hazel's nipple and rolled it between her fingers. Hazel let out a shaky breath and dropped her head forward, pressing her forehead into Beatrice's shoulder. Beatrice could feel her shaking. She opened her hand and stroked her palm over Hazel's breast, pushing up and squeezing and repeated the gesture when Hazel gasped. Hazel's reaction to her touch was intoxicating. She made Beatrice feel powerful and attractive, two things Beatrice hadn't felt in a very long time. She dipped her head and took Hazel's nipple into her mouth.

"Beatrice," Hazel said and whimpered.

Beatrice moaned at the sound of her name on Hazel's lips, and Hazel cried out. Her long fingers wrapped in Beatrice's hair, stroking it away from her face as Beatrice swirled her tongue around the turgid nipple. Beatrice bit down gently, experimentally, and then circled her tongue again. Hazel swore. She moved her hands to Beatrice's chin, fumbling and frantic, and pulled Beatrice up for another searing kiss.

"Naked," Hazel said. Her hands were already working beneath Beatrice's shirt, fighting the clasp of her bra. "Now."

Beatrice wiggled her hips free of her jeans. She felt the straps of her bra go limp and then Hazel ripped her shirt and bra off over her head. She flung them toward the corner of the room and dragged Beatrice to her. And then they were pressed together, skin on skin, Beatrice's bare breasts pressed against Hazel's chest as Hazel drank her in. She heard herself make an uncharacteristically lustful noise, felt her hips roll against Hazel's of their own volition. Her underwear was soaked, probably ruined, and Beatrice didn't care.

Hazel backed her toward the bed. Beatrice hadn't realized how badly she needed to sit until her legs hit the mattress. She sighed gratefully and reached to pull Hazel down as well, but Hazel knelt quickly between Beatrice's legs and pressed her mouth to the smooth skin above Beatrice's belly button. She ran her hands along the outside of Beatrice's thighs in a gentle caress. She lifted her head, unadulterated desire shining clearly in her eyes.

"God, you're beautiful," Hazel breathed.

A delighted laugh bubbled up out of Beatrice's chest. Ten odd years of telling herself she wasn't even pretty anymore, and Hazel swept it all away with one fevered whisper. Beatrice ran a hand through Hazel's hair, marveling at its downy softness. "I haven't done this in awhile," she admitted. Despite Hazel's obvious ardor and her own body's desperate humming, there was still a niggling uncertainty about her ability to perform.

"Could have fooled me," Hazel said. She dipped her head again and trailed a path of kisses down the center of Beatrice's chest. Beatrice dropped her head back.

"Maybe..." She took a series of short breaths, trying to focus, "Maybe you just bring it out in me."

Hazel growled in agreement. She wrapped her hands under Beatrice's legs and pushed, guiding her further onto the bed. Beatrice sank into the mattress and watched through half-lidded eyes as Hazel crawled after her. Hazel's legs brushed the inside of Beatrice's, and Beatrice bent one knee, creating space for Hazel and encouraging her to come closer. Hazel bent her head. Her hair brushed Beatrice's stomach as she kissed the skin above Beatrice's underwear and Beatrice whimpered. It was the part of her body she was most self-conscious of, but rather than make her uncomfortable Hazel's attention drove a spike of pleasure through her. She shifted, desire making her restless, and Hazel dragged a hand gently across Beatrice's soaking center. Beatrice's hips jerked. She bit her lip and slammed her eyes shut.

"Jesus." Hazel groaned. She pressed her lips to Beatrice's stomach again and kissed her fervidly, her hot breath washing over Beatrice's skin.

"Hazel." Beatrice pressed a hand to her forehead. She wasn't going to last long, and if Hazel wasn't careful just the feel of her between Beatrice's legs—just knowing what she was planning to do—was going to set Beatrice off. "Please."

Hazel hooked her fingers in the elastic of Beatrice's underwear and pulled. The cool air that washed over her soaked and aching tissues took the edge off, but only just. She still shook with need, clenched with anticipation, and when Hazel slowly lowered herself between Beatrice's legs, the visual was almost too much. Beatrice's breath caught in her chest. She clenched her teeth.

Hazel fixed her mouth to the inside of Beatrice's thigh, tasting the wetness that had spread from her soaked sex. Involuntarily, Beatrice's knee jerked and tipped inward, pressing her leg against Hazel's head. Hazel groaned. Her lips came away from Beatrice's skin with a wet pop. She wrapped her hands under Beatrice's hips and pulled her closer. Even though Beatrice knew it was coming, even though she'd had Hazel's tongue in her mouth and on her skin already, nothing on earth could have prepared her for that first gentle stroke.

She writhed. She cried out. Hazel paused, waiting for Beatrice to settle, and then repeated the gesture, stroking from back to front with the flat of her tongue. Beatrice slammed her fists into the mattress.

"Fuck," she choked the words out.

Hazel made an appreciative noise of her own that ripped through Beatrice as if an electric wire had been touched directly to her clit. She pressed closer, opening her mouth to fasten it over as much of Beatrice as she possibly could. There were no more careful strokes, just a reckless, hungry movement of lips and tongue.

Beatrice was distantly aware of her hips rocking, thrusting against Hazel's mouth, of the quiet noises escaping her throat whenever she managed to gather enough breath to vocalize. It was all secondary to the burn growing between her legs. She'd known she wouldn't last long, but she'd been unprepared for just how sharp the pleasure would be. It was more than the night's tension clamoring for release. It was years of pent up sexual frustration that Beatrice had thought she'd done just fine relieving on her own and was quickly discovering that was not the case. If she didn't pass out, she'd be amazed.

Hazel's tongue flicked left to right across her clit and Beatrice gasped as her upper body curled up off of the bed. She started to fall back again and Hazel sucked her clit into her mouth.

Beatrice slammed upright. Her hips jerked once before her orgasm washed over her, fast and powerful. She felt her muscles go tight. One hand clenched the comforter, the other found the back of Hazel's head. She cried out as the pleasure ripped through her, more intense than she'd thought possible. Her vision went blurry and she dropped back to the mattress, gasping for air. Hazel's tongue stroked her again and Beatrice felt herself pulse against Hazel's lips. Her temples were damp with sweat and her ears were ringing. Hazel pressed a tender kiss to Beatrice's engorged flesh and she felt herself spasm.

She tugged at the back of Hazel's head and Hazel slipped up Beatrice's body, a pleased smile on her shining lips. Beatrice captured Hazel's face between her hands and kissed her, tasting her own saltiness on Hazel's lips. Hazel groaned and shifted so that she was lying half on Beatrice, half on the bed. She wrapped her left leg around Beatrice's and Beatrice felt the soft play of Hazel's fingers through her pubic hair. A solitary finger pressed against the hood of her clit, and Beatrice moaned appreciatively.

"Yeah?" Hazel smiled down at her, her cheeks flushed. Beatrice nodded, distantly amazed at her own quick turnaround, and Hazel slipped her finger inside.

Beatrice had forgotten how it felt to have someone inside, touching her deepest parts. She rocked her hips and bit back a moan when she felt Hazel's finger brush against her walls.

"You're so wet," Hazel whispered in her ear. She salved the skin beneath Beatrice's ear with quick, wet kisses and thrust her finger slowly.

Beatrice whimpered. "More," she said brokenly.

Hazel withdrew her finger and Beatrice experienced a moment of emptiness before Hazel pressed back in with two fingers, stretching her, filling her until her palm was pressed against Beatrice's pubic hair. Beatrice ground her hips against Hazel's hand and Hazel pressed her face into Beatrice's shoulder, moving her hand slowly. She didn't thrust. She moved her palm in slow circles, brushing her fingers against Beatrice's walls pressing against her clit. She curled her fingers inside and Beatrice's eyes snapped shut. She could hear her wetness as Hazel rubbed, slowly bringing her back to the edge.

A wave of heat crossed Beatrice's face. Her pulse was pounding in her temples but Hazel's control of the pace meant she could only grit her teeth and wait, and Hazel seemed all too interested in the skin of Beatrice's chest to be in a hurry. She licked and sucked her way down to Beatrice's left breast and then stopped. She lifted her head and made eye contact, then slowly extended her tongue toward the tip of Beatrice's nipple. She froze a millimeter from contact and Beatrice held her breath, the hand between her legs all but forgotten in favor of this potential new pleasure.

Hazel's tongue curled. For the briefest of moments she brushed Beatrice's nipple, barely wetting the engorged flesh before retreating again.

Beatrice pressed her head into the mattress. "You're a tease," she said with a groan.

Hazel grinned. She poked her tongue out and dragged it over Beatrice's nipple. Beatrice arched her back and Hazel took the hint, swirling her tongue in slow circles over the sensitive skin and sucking it to a peak. Beatrice clenched her eyes shut, abandoning herself to the sensation of Hazel's mouth and fingers working in tandem. Heat crept up her neck. Her breathing had shallowed again, and when Hazel curled her fingers inside at the same time she pressed her hand down against Beatrice's pubic bone, Beatrice felt the first jolt of another impending orgasm.

"Yes," she said, panting desperately. Hazel repeated the motion and Beatrice jerked, her legs kicking and then falling open, trying to force Hazel deeper. "Oh God, Hazel, right there." She tilted her hips, trying to generate friction.

She felt Hazel's arm shift and then her fingers slid deeper than ever before into Beatrice's aching wetness. Hazel rose up onto her elbow, staring down at Beatrice, her eyes hooded with desire. She began thrusting quickly, her palm slapping wetly against Beatrice's clit. Beatrice pumped her hips, meeting Hazel thrust for thrust. She wrapped her arms around Hazel's neck, needing to touch her, needing something to ground her. "Yes," she mouthed, "yes, yes, yes."

Hazel drove her fingers home. Beatrice felt herself contract around them once and then her orgasm crashed through her. Her hips rose from the bed and Hazel pressed her palm against Beatrice's clit and rubbed, doubling the pleasure racing through Beatrice's body. She cried out and thrashed weakly, her heels slipping against the comforter as Hazel drew out the last vestiges of her orgasm.

Beatrice fell back to the mattress, a shuddering, shaky mess. Her chest and forehead were drenched in sweat, and when Hazel kissed her, her lips felt heavy and slow to respond.

"Good lord," she said hoarsely when Hazel pulled away, and Hazel smiled. She brushed her lips across Beatrice's neck again.

"Perfect," she whispered in Beatrice's ear. "You're perfect."

Beatrice dragged her fingertips across Hazel's back and up her ribs. An hour ago she would have laughed if Hazel had said that to her, but Hazel's enthusiastic lovemaking left very little room for disagreement. She made Beatrice feel perfect. And beautiful. And desirable. And a million other adjectives that Beatrice had long ago set aside as belonging to other people, but was now tentatively reclaiming them for herself.

"Do I get to return the favor?" Beatrice murmured. "Or are you going to nibble on my neck all night?"

Hazel's deep laugh against her throat made Beatrice's skin buzz. She propped herself up on one elbow and quirked an eyebrow. "You don't like nibbles?"

"I love them," Beatrice said. "I just thought you might want to be nibbled on for a change." She slid her leg over, pointedly pressing her thigh between Hazel's legs. She watched the joint in Hazel's strong jaw clench, watched her nostrils flare and her eyes darken, and that settled it. Beatrice rolled herself on top of Hazel and kissed her. A different kind of desire was making her head fuzzy. She wanted to touch Hazel, wanted to feel Hazel's body go tight under her hands, and know that it was all her doing when Hazel came. She pressed her hips forward and Hazel exhaled against her lips. She kissed Hazel's chin and slid down, pausing only to press her lips to the tattoo on Hazel's ribs that had taunted her for so long—an odd bird looking thing made of thin black lines. She traced the lines with her tongue and Hazel jumped.

"Ticklish?" Beatrice asked. Hazel nodded.

The edges of Hazel's pelvis jutted prominently, providing Beatrice with a pair of very convenient handholds when she wrapped her arms around Hazel's waist. She pressed her nose into the soft, dark blonde thatch of hair between Hazel's thighs and inhaled. Hazel's scent filled her head, a clean velvetiness that made Beatrice's mouth water. She glanced up. Hazel was watching her, her arms crossed over her forehead, her mouth parted with anticipation. Never in her wildest fantasies had she ever even entertained the thought of Hazel looking at her like that.

Beatrice tucked her chin and lightly touched her tongue to Hazel's swollen folds. She was sweet, sweeter than anyone else Beatrice could remember, and she drove her tongue forward again in earnest.

"Shit." Hazel's arms fell over her eyes. She pulled her bottom lip between her teeth and tilted her hips slightly, giving Beatrice better access, and Beatrice took it.

She didn't know if she'd ever been particularly proficient at cunnilingus— no one had ever complained, but no one had ever exactly showered her with praise, either—but she did know she'd never put as much effort into the act as she did with Hazel. Every jerk, every small twitch of muscle was silent motivation to suck a little harder, to press her tongue a little deeper. She wanted to drink Hazel in, wanted to keep Hazel from thinking straight.

Hazel pushed Beatrice's hair out of her face, her fingers shaking, her breathing shallow and ragged, and when Beatrice looked up, Hazel's eyes were so dark they were almost black.

"I'm going to come," Hazel choked out the words.

Beatrice hummed and fluttered her tongue. Good. She wanted Hazel to come—maybe more than she'd wanted to come herself.

Hazel's head dropped back. Her body went stiff, and she spasmed once, twice, completely silent, before she collapsed against the bed. A rush of air left her lungs and Beatrice gave her one final swipe of her tongue before she kissed her way back up Hazel's body.

Hazel's eyes were still closed, one arm thrown over her head, when Beatrice reached her face. She kissed her lightly on the corner of the mouth, and Hazel turned her head weakly to kiss her back. Beatrice dropped back and settled her chin on the hard line of Hazel's sternum and smiled up at her. Hazel pried her eyes open. She blinked blearily and then smiled as well.

Suddenly there was nothing more important than making sure Hazel knew just how grateful Beatrice was for making her feel wanted. How grateful she was that Hazel hadn't accepted her excuses on the porch when her own insecurities had threatened to take control. "Thank you," she whispered.

Hazel drew a lazy hand through Beatrice's hair, letting it fall between her fingers. "We're far from finished," she promised. Beatrice laughed.

"I know—I mean, good, but I meant…" Beatrice shook her head. "Really. Thank you."

Hazel's gaze grew serious. She nodded and pulled Beatrice up for a gentle kiss. "Thank you back."

Beatrice started to roll to the side but Hazel stopped her, wrapping a firm arm around Beatrice's shoulders.

"I'm heavy," Beatrice protested as Hazel reached for the throw blanket they'd almost kicked from the bed.

"You feel good," Hazel said. She pulled the blanket over Beatrice's body and dragged the inside of one foot up Beatrice's calf before twisting their legs together. Beatrice sighed and settled against her, her cheek pressed to Hazel's chest. Hazel's body was long and warm, and a heavy looseness permeated Beatrice's muscles.

"I wanted to make you come again," Beatrice muttered.

Hazel kissed the top of her head and Beatrice knew she was smiling. "Next time," Hazel said. A delighted thrill ran through Beatrice and she squeezed her arms against Hazel's sides.

Next time.

A BEAUTIFUL KNIFE

BY VALERIE ALEXANDER

SUMMER EVENINGS AT THE LAKE went blue at dusk. As the daytime roar of boats quieted, the birds in the lilac bushes began to sing and the stilled water became a mirror of the darkening sky. That was my favorite hour to stand on the balcony and watch the lights come on across the bay. At sixteen, that was where I wanted to be—on the fun side of the lake, where cars cruised along the main strip of restaurants and bars that lined the beach.

My grandmother's cottage was on the Bluffs, the quiet side of the lake where the only action was old ladies visiting each other for bridge and cocktails, or golfing at the country club across the street. My older sister and her friends went to the cottage every weekend, and I tagged along. Every night, they would drive to the strip to hunt down the local studs. Because our grandmother's bad hips wouldn't allow her to climb the stairs, the second floor—particularly the massive Blue Room with its French doors opening to the balcony—became the perfect place for them to smoke and exchange vulgar stories.

Whitney and her friends were nineteen. They were sorceresses in bikinis, pursuing conquests with ruthless calculation, and sometimes trading them like baseball cards. Mostly they were looking for older men, but there was one woman who dominated their conversation. Her name was Jax Whitworth.

A twenty-one-year-old bartender, Jax was the ultimate conquistador on the lake. She was tall, rangy, and butch, according to their descriptions, and notorious for seducing and discarding girls with ease. Her name tended to be followed by "and she's into all that twisted sex stuff"; Jax tied girls up, Whitney explained disdainfully to me. She used them in all kinds of perverted ways. She was such a *dyke*, with her cocky swagger, a heartbreaker who left a trail of crying girls in her wake. That was why they couldn't stand her.

And why they kept talking about her.

At night, when they went out, I'd linger on the cottage balcony, looking across the lake and imagining how it would feel to be naked and bound and under the control of an older, butch woman. I was a teenage virgin then, with guilty, feverish dreams of being dominated by faceless figures. I wanted someone dangerous to control me, to master me, and that someone never had a gender until that summer. And, though I'd never seen her, Jax Whitworth made those dream figures acquire a certain form. Boyish girls. Laconic butches. Women who were just hard enough to make me feel soft.

One night, an unfamiliar motor came down the road, followed by giggles filling the night. I went outside to hush them before they alerted Mrs. Rathbone, the next-door neighbor who liked to sit on her porch with a drink and a cigarette. A black car was parked on the road; my sister was on all fours in the moonlight, getting sick in Mrs. Rathbone's bushes. And there, helping another girl stumble across the lawn, was a tall, lanky figure with short, dirty-blonde hair. She was the hottest thing I'd ever seen, and I knew who she was before she spoke.

She jerked her chin at me. "Whitney's car is on the strip," she said. "I drove them here. I'm Jax."

I was too amazed to think of acting older than sixteen. "Claudia."

Her mouth twisted in a downward, skeptical smile. "What are you, someone's little sister?"

Busted.

Whitney lurched toward us like a drunken zombie. "Inside," she said, snapping her finger at me as if I were a dog. And then to Jax, "She's in high school, you perv!"

"I was just telling her about your car," Jax said.

"You need to go. Now."

Without another word, Jax walked to her car.

I hoped she would return the following weekend, but there was no following weekend. Mrs. Rathbone informed my grandmother of the drunken commotion waking her every weekend—the boys beneath the balcony at three in the morning, the empty vodka bottles in her hedges, the condom wrappers on her lawn. And, most recently, the *gay girl* who'd been there over the weekend. And Whitney was banned from the cottage for good.

School started and the memory of Jax should have faded, but it didn't. I never stopped replaying her dirty-blonde hair and her twisted smile, or thinking about her taunting me as she tightened the ropes around my wrists and stroked my clit until I begged her to fuck me. I knew she would break my heart if we met again, and I was okay with it. After all, that was what she was born to do.

This is what teenage femmes learn—butches are ultimately unattainable. The way she saunters down the hall, scarcely looking in your direction after making out with you behind a convenience store, the way she hooks up with your friend despite seven consecutive weeks of after-school sex with you, the way she fails to call after theorizing, vaguely, about the two of you seeing her friend's band; you learn that this detached indifference is the hallmark of the species. And so a flash of her smile becomes like manna from a god to a devotee starving for acknowledgement.

I went to college, dated more girls. No women to speak of, at least none who knew how to do what I wanted. None who would push me over a table and rip off my skirt, or tie me up and take control. None who treated me as if I were the whore-princess who needed to be fucked and cherished and dominated, all in one wet, skin-slapping encounter.

When I was twenty, my grandmother died in the spring. My father hired me to pack up her cottage in July and prepare it for sale. "She's going to stay there *alone?*" my sister said, aghast, but I liked the idea—painting and cleaning by day, prowling the lakeshore strip by night. And, of course, there was Jax. I was a woman of the world, not a sixteen-year-old virgin anymore, but she still dominated my dreamlife in a variety of scenarios, which started with a faceless figure, then melted into her unzipping her jeans and biting my neck as she fucked me.

Jax was twenty-five that year, but she hadn't faded into social obsolescence like other summer legends. Through my sister and some Facebook spying, I knew she ran the busiest bar on the strip. I made some plans, you could say, plans to lure her into my bed, where she would ignite my fantasies like some exotic, risky powder keg of a drug.

When I arrived at the cottage the first night, the electricity hadn't been turned on yet. I set up a small, battery-operated camping light as the stifling heat closed around me like a tomb. Mrs. Rathbone had sold most of the furniture for us, but in the shadows I could see stacks of magazines, old decks of playing cards, ceramic figurines, and boxes of paperback mysteries. The paint was faded, the carpet dotted with cigarette burns, and the faint smell of mildew mixed with dust hung in the silence.

The oppressive enormity of the task ahead washed over me. To escape, I changed into my green bikini and then ran to the lake.

Diving into the cold water served as a slap back to life. I swam to the raft that was anchored offshore, climbed up and looked across the water. The pale-gold lights of the strip twinkled just beyond the ghostly-white boats of the marina. Shivering in the night air, I felt both romantic and predatory.

A few boats cruised along the lake, and eventually, the lights of one drew close. A girl called out, "Dena!"

"Not Dena," I called back.

With a loud click, I was bathed in the white glare of a powerful flashlight. I squinted and pushed my wet hair back, but the light dropped just as abruptly to illuminate the boat—a brunette with a suspicious face and a lanky woman next to her. Her dark-blonde hair was disheveled, and her expression changed to surprise.

"I know you," she said.

No. It couldn't be this easy. Or this fast.

"You knew my sister," I said. "You came to our grandmother's cottage once, years back." Despite the anguish on her date's face, I added, "I'm living here this summer, by myself." It was a blatant invitation I wouldn't normally issue in front of another girl. But it was Jax, and for me that changed all the rules.

She nodded a few times, not taking her gaze off me. The girl snapped, "We need to find Dena." And she turned off the light, powered up the boat, and roared off.

My heart hammered like an idiot's. I plunged into the water and swam to shore. This time the heat of the cottage wrapped around me like a blanket. I stood dripping in my bikini, almost numb with disbelief that I had seen Jax so soon. I knew I should go upstairs and unpack, because it wasn't as if she was coming over tonight. Or any night, probably, despite my drawing her a map. She was on a date, possibly with her girlfriend.

There was a knock on the door.

Jax stood, outlined against the starlit yard like an incubus. *Don't let her in*, said a voice. *You fuck her tonight and then you're stuck here alone for weeks with nothing to look forward to. Because you know she's not coming back.*

"Come on in," I said. The long-ago reports of Jax and her BDSM sex life echoed in my head.

She followed me into the mostly empty living room. The weak battery-operated light cast long shadows around the empty room, but she wasn't looking at the piles of junk. She was looking at me.

"What happened to your girlfriend?" I asked.

"Oh, she's just a friend. I was helping her look for her roommate."

"Ah." I didn't believe her for a second. But her speed in coming here validated my four years of love-struck pining.

Jax leaned back on her heels. Her jeans were too loose and hung off her hipbones, exposing a band of tanned abdomen below her T-shirt. Her dark-blonde hair was still disheveled and her expression intense. Her hazel gaze didn't leave my face for a second. After all my dreams, it was like having an actor step through the movie screen and stand before me.

"So, how old are you now?" she said, her mouth twisting in that downward smile. "You were jailbait before."

"I'm twenty. All grown up and legal."

And then, because I was a smitten fool who'd been waiting my entire life to be dominated by the woman who stood before me, I reached behind me and released my bikini top.

Her gaze went right to my tits. But her face didn't change. My stomach was a jumping knot as I stepped out of my bikini bottoms and stood naked before her, awaiting appraisal.

She studied me for about a minute. Then she said, "Get on your knees."

I knelt on the threadbare carpet. The cottage was so quiet that all I could hear was my pounding heart. It felt like the dead of the night.

She walked behind me and gathered my light-brown hair. She wound it so tenderly into a knot, I thought all those reports of her brutal ways were wrong.

Then she gripped the knot and pulled it so hard that I toppled backward, sprawled at her feet.

She lifted her boot and put it lightly on my stomach. "You're just a little slut, aren't you? Inviting me over and taking off your bikini."

I nodded.

She took her foot off and pushed me onto my stomach. Kicking my legs apart, she put the cool leather of her boot against my sensitive, inflamed cunt. "I think we need to establish some ground rules."

Suddenly she was sitting on the carpet and I was over her lap, already feverish with the need to feel her hand inside me. Instead she spanked me once. "I'm going to lay down the rules and if you accept, you thank me. Understood?"

"Yes, thank you."

"I'm not going to stop until I've fucked you and used you and dominated you and turned you into my slave. If you need me to stop, you say your safe word, which is…" She spanked me to prompt me.

"Bluff. Thank you."

"I won't truly hurt you, but you may acquire bite marks or rug burns." Another smack.

"Thank you."

"You will trust me and submit to me at all times." Her hand connected to my now-flaming ass.

"Thank you."

I waited breathlessly for the next rule, the next slap. Instead her fingers moved up my thighs, felt my pussy, and then traveled up my back. It took everything I had not to squirm, not to show how much I ached for her. She played with my breasts.

"These," she said. "These need to be attended to."

Jax moved me to the floor, got up, rummaged around, and returned with a roll of packing-tape. She wound it under and over my breasts, binding them so they felt uncomfortably constricted, my nipples overly sensitive. Then she pulled off another strip of tape and smoothed it over my pussy.

I swallowed, wondering how it could adhere to my skin when my cunt was so wet. But she added layer after layer, curling around my legs until she'd effectively sealed off my pussy and clit from any kind of stimulation. Then she dropped something over my eyes—I couldn't identify what—and tied it behind my head.

With another slap to my ass, she said, "Crawl."

I hadn't been in the cottage in years. I didn't remember what was where. But I crawled through the hot, musty dark, my nipples begging to be sucked and my clit so swollen it hurt. My tactile senses were especially acute, sensitive to the cigarette burns in the carpet beneath my fingertips, the tape rubbing my thighs as I crawled. I'd never felt this naked in front of anyone.

I bumped into a wall. I turned, disoriented. The world was black and silent and I was utterly dependent on the woman looming over me.

Then her hand pushed my face into something warm—her pussy.

"Suck me," she said, "and do it well or you won't be able to sit for days."

I obeyed, sucking her clit from my position on all fours. The cottage was hot and airless, and I was sweating. I licked and tongued her cunt with all of my skill, and tried not to think about the women she'd had before. Then she grabbed my throat, just enough to make me gasp.

"Who do you belong to?" She sounded so forceful.

"You," I whispered hoarsely.

"That's right. You're my slave." She touched my nipples. "Are you thirsty?"

I nodded. Jax held a cool bottle of water to my lips. As I drank, she spanked my clit, over and over in a ceaseless rhythm until the sting spreading through my cunt became as beautiful as the cold water running down my throat.

Then she pushed me on my back and pulled the tape off my tits. They felt so full and aching; they came to life in her hands. No one had ever touched me like that before. The blindfold came off next and I caught a glimpse of that downward smile in the fading lantern light as she ripped the tape off my pussy. In another era, I would have said it hurt. On this night it felt like another electrifying slap, leaving my skin incandescent as she held me down, forced my legs wider apart and drove her fingers into me.

She fucked me against the carpet, savage and rhythmic in the heat and the dust. The battery on the lamp died. She was fucking me brutally in the silence, her hips and hands driving me down over and over into the floorboards. She bit my nipples hard, her sweat dripping on me as I spasmed in a helpless, enamored orgasm. My throat was hoarse from crying, screaming.

She grabbed my hair, biting my mouth as she came.

I drifted into a black and euphoric world. At some point, she lifted me onto her chest. "That floor's got to hurt," she muttered, holding me against her. "Sleep on top of me."

I groggily lifted my head. "There are beds upstairs."

But once we got to the Blue Room, with the balcony doors open to cool off the room, I couldn't sleep. It was almost daybreak and birds were beginning to tweet in the lilac bushes. Jax fell asleep on top of the sheets. It was my first chance to gaze at her until I got my fill, to drink in every feature, from her full lips to the tiny scar at the end of her right eyebrow. Her tanned feet, hardened at the heels, and her smooth, long navel.

My skin felt as alive and fresh as if I were in a brand new body. Watching her, something inside me lurched into unquestioning devotion. Just like that, my summer plans were blown to smithereens.

———————

"You're an idiot!" my sister shrieked. "She's going to ditch you for the next piece of ass!" Whitney was breathing so hard into the phone, I could picture her chest heaving. "It's not enough you have to be gay, now you have Jax Whitworth sleeping over *every single night*."

That intel, of course, was courtesy of Mrs. Rathbone. Once she'd ratted out my sister, expelling her from the cottage. Now, she was gossiping about me around the lake, and it had traveled home to Whitney. The circle of sabotage.

"You're just like all those other stupid girls, thinking you'll be different," my sister said. "But she's going to use you and move on, Claudia."

I already knew that. I didn't expect Jax to stay forever. My plan was simple. I wanted to absorb every crooked smile and to memorize every feverish moment. This wasn't about longevity; it was about intensity. My college girlfriends had fucked me with tenderness and solemnity, and occasionally, the rougher sex of my fantasies. Jax blew both out of the water. She strode in and pushed me against the wall as she pulled my underwear down and thrust her tongue inside me so forcefully that I ejaculated all over my shoes. She cuffed my wrists so I couldn't touch myself and then teased me until I begged with tears in my eyes to come. My nipples were perpetually swollen from being bitten and sucked, and my thighs and back were marked with what I feared might be permanent rug burns. I was drowning in an almost narcotic bliss, my submissive euphoria like a drug.

I knew Jax would grow tired of me eventually. I'd been to her bar and I'd seen all the girls who offered up their cleavage and phone numbers every night. I tried to be okay with it. I told myself I didn't need to be unique, or permanent, or the one who changed her. I figured I could be all that to someone else, later on. With her, it was simple addiction; and when she inevitably knifed my heart out, well, that was the price of admission to sexual nirvana.

On our ninth night, she came over with a TV and a loveseat on loan from a friend. "You're going to be here a few more weeks at least," she said, "so I figured, we may as well have some entertainment."

I stood very still. Furniture was a commitment. Even if Jax left one night for work and never came back, this would still be here. It was a tether. But she sat on the loveseat and pulled me onto her lap, slipping her hand into my underwear and smiling as if she wasn't skittish at all.

——— ❦ ———

On and on we fucked, exhaustive and blissful. The cottage was hot at night and we'd roll around for hours on the massive bed in the Blue Room, French doors open to the night air until the sheets were stiff with dried sweat and come. I never quite dared to fuck Jax on the balcony—not where Mrs. Rathbone could see from her nightly vigil on her porch next door. Instead, we went for walks across the country club golf course around three in the morning, after she came home from the bar and the sprinklers had shut off for the night. On the far side of the sixth-hole sand trap, we laid naked in the grass, looking at the stars and talking. I was surprised, then ashamed of my surprise, at Jax's intelligence. Whitney had referred to her as a "stupid bartender" or "dumb as a box of rocks," but not only was she smart, she listened and sought my opinions instead of just directing monologues at me.

I'd been at the lake for almost a month when my sister called again. "Dad's ready to put the cottage on the market," Whitney said in a voice that sounded like a threat. "We're coming this weekend to see what you've done with it. And you'd better not have *her* hanging around. Dad won't like knowing you've had some dyke bartender sleeping over every night."

I hung up and looked at the bed. Next week, I'd be gone and Jax would be knotting rope around some other girl's ankles. My gut clenched.

I texted Jax the news—I was going home. *That sucks. Hey, I might be a little late tonight,* came her response.

I waited for additional texts, for some sign of emotion. None came. Finally, I threw the phone on the sheets and went outside, trying not to cry. It was twilight and Mrs. Rathbone was crossing the lawn in white pants and a hennaed up-do. She had her cigarette in one hand and her cocktail in the other.

"Look at you, all this work you're doing on your grandma's house," she said, nodding toward the cottage. "Of course you've got that Jax Whitworth helping. She bartends down at the grill, right? Seems like everyone knows her."

I ignored the implication that Jax was a slut. "Right."

249

"I had a summer romance once. Jimmy Langhorn—it was magic. Swimming in the river and sneaking out to meet him at night."

I smiled with the polite respect demanded by her memory.

"Absolute magic," she repeated. "And then his number was called and off he went. Vietnam," she clarified for me.

A sense of shame washed over me. All of these years drinking alone on her porch every night. I'd thought of her as a bothersome old biddy, when really she was a woman holding vigil for her lost love.

"He never came back?"

"Oh, he came back, sure. He came back and married Patty Stone, who he knocked up that same summer when he was cheating on me." She sucked on her cigarette. "I know that's a shitty story, kiddo. But that's how they are. The ones worth screwing cut your heart out in the end." She exhaled, staring at me.

Over the following years, most of my grandmother's friends on the Bluffs died or moved into retirement communities, leaving their pearls and china sets and Life magazines to grandchildren who sold them on eBay. Most of cottages were sold to younger families and the country club across the street was turned into a school. And it burned down when I was twenty-six.

My partner and I drove to the lake out of curiosity and took pictures of the ruins. I looked at my grandmother's cottage, the windows glowing in the dusk, and decided to knock on the door.

As soon as I explained who I was, the new owners invited us inside to look around. "I bet it sure has changed from when you were a kid!" the wife said. She kept looking us up and down.

"Oh, it has. I love what you've done with it." Nothing was left of my grandmother's faded WASP museum. These rooms could have fallen out of a Crate and Barrel catalogue. I looked hesitantly at the staircase. Of course that would be far too personal, going upstairs, but I was dying to see the Blue Room.

"Go on up, look around!" the wife encouraged.

She didn't come with us. The French doors of the Blue Room were open to the damp evening air. We walked onto the balcony and it was as if I were a moony teenage girl again, watching the lights across the lake.

Jax pulled me into her arms. "Like you remember?"

"Exactly. Right now, I could be sixteen and dreaming about you." The soft melting-blue was the same, turning the lilac bushes into blurred shapes in the twilight. "I can't believe we never had sex on this balcony."

"I can't believe you thought I was going to let go of you that summer." Jax pushed her hard cock against my ass. She was packing just for me. "But I'm willing to remind you again of just how much I need you."

I arched my back, thrusting my bottom toward her. She pinned my wrists behind my back, then lifted my skirt. My cheeks burned as she pushed her cock inside me. But this time I didn't care if a neighbor was watching. I groaned, struggling not to scream from the burning joy rising inside me. The lights on the opposite shore merged into one golden-blue haze as she drove in and out of me. Memories of that summer swam through my mind, all the things she'd taught me, the nights of bondage and naked star-watching on the golf course, and then I was coming, wet and throbbing, all over her jeans.

"Oh, God." She released me, and I wiped my hair off my flushed face. "We've been up here way too long. We should go."

"Not yet." Jax hugged me against her, and we listened to the night noises of the lake. "Not yet."

ABSENCE MAKES THE HEART GROW FONDER

BY MAY DAWNEY

SARA PARKER SQUINTED TO FOCUS her impaired brain before attempting to insert her key card into the hotel door lock. She really hadn't intended to drink enough for menial tasks to become problematic. The Triple Play Realtor Convention and Trade Expo after-party always got a little rowdy, but it was the after-after party that had done her in. She'd lost track of the number of tequila shots she had taken some time after the fourth. Thankfully, she hadn't consumed enough to make her lose track of her hotel room or to need assistance getting there.

Her feet were killing her, though, and she kicked off her heels the moment she closed the door behind her. The lights stayed off. Her hair tumbled down as she released it from its clip and she shuddered happily; it was such a relief after a long day. Her handbag ended up on the double bed.

Although her mind was foggy enough to wonder about the location of the minibar, she was able to get a water bottle open without much trouble once she'd located it. As such, she estimated her drunkenness somewhere between "flirty tipsy" and "sloppy party girl." Surprisingly good, considering. With a groan, she dropped herself onto her bed and managed to keep the water contained to the bottle as she did. Yeah, she was going to be fine, with no more than a headache in the morning.

Sara wondered if she could still call Jen. This convention was the longest she had been away from her since they'd started up. Three months ago, she had sold Jen her apartment and in true lesbian U-Haul-style, Sara slept there at least four nights a week now. When Sara had left for the convention, they had promised each other an update via telephone every evening. For the past three days, Sara had kept that promise. With the after party, and then the after-after party, she hadn't gotten a chance today—until now. Unfortunately, it was two AM.

It took Sara about three seconds to decide to give it a go; if Jen was asleep or busy, she was just not going to answer. Besides, Sara missed her girlfriend. The after-after party had included a lot of dancing, and Sara's buzzing mind had readily supplied her with vivid memories of Jennifer's skill on the dancefloor. She had missed Jen's hands on her and tracing Jennifer's soft curves with her own as her girl got lost in the music. She scooted back upon the bed and settled against the plush hotel pillows before she reached into her purse with determination.

Sara squinted against the glare of the screen as she hit the power button. Blinded, she unlocked the device and turned down the brightness as low as it would go. She opened her recent calls and selected Jennifer's number. With a flutter in her stomach, she pressed the phone to her ear. The call was picked up after the fourth ring.

"Hey babe," Sara whispered happily. She could hear her own smirk in her voice.

"You're drunk, aren't you?" Jennifer sounded groggy. Still, she had picked up so she must have wanted to talk, right?

"Maybe a little." Sara grinned into the darkness of her tiny room.

"So I take it the convention ended well?"

Sara briefly wondered if Jennifer was pissed, but if anything, she sounded amused. Good. Amused was good. Her buzzing mind could deal with amused. "Yes," Sara said again. "It did. Operation successful, all good. I missed you during the dancing."

"Dancing, huh?"

Sara thought she could hear a little teasing in Jen's tone. "Yeah, I wished you were there; you're an amazing dancer." Sara got lost in her fantasies again. There was nothing better than feeling Jen's body pressed against hers from behind. To feel her hands slide under her shirt and up her abdomen. She would lean back and rest her head on Jen's shoulder for a kiss that left her lips tainted with the salt of Jen's sweat. Sara loved the sensation of hot breath against her skin as Jen pointed out that people were watching as they moved together sensually. Before Jennifer had come into her life, Sara had been rather shy when it came to public displays of affection, but she had quickly become addicted to the rush.

"I am, huh?" Jennifer answered.

This time she was absolutely sure her girlfriend was teasing her. She licked her lips. "What are you wearing?"

"Why are you asking?"

Sara tried to read her girl's voice, but either Jennifer was hiding her emotions from her, or Sara was entirely too compromised to read them properly. "Cuz...I want to know?"

"You're horny, aren't you?"

Sara blushed, but she felt a wicked smile tugging at the corners of her mouth, regardless. "Pretty much. I was thinking about you, about dancing with you...and about the way you smell."

"The way I smell?" Jennifer chuckled.

Sara moaned theatrically. "Uh-huh...like...your perfume, and maybe dancing would make you a little sweaty and then I thought about how you smell...you know...*down* there and—"

Jennifer's laugh carried through the phone line easily, and suddenly, she didn't seem half a continent away anymore.

"Oh wow, you really did get yourself worked up."

Sara nodded and licked her lips. The liquid courage coursing through her veins made this the perfect time to try and get rid of the desire building up inside of her over the last few days. "I did. So, do you want to, you know?"

"Do I want to do what, Miss Parker?"

Jennifer sounded amused, so Sara decided to push her luck. "You know... have phone sex...?" She blushed, but bit her lip in need all the same.

Jennifer was quiet a moment. "All right."

Sara's mind froze. "Seriously?" Truth be told, she had kind of expected to be turned down—they had been together for a while and they'd stayed up late, talking on the phone plenty of times but they'd never gone *there*. Besides, Sara had woken Jennifer up.

"Yes." Jennifer cut off Sara's next words. "Before we do, though, how drunk are you? If we're doing this, then I want to be sure you'll remember it in the morning and not fall asleep halfway through."

That was a fair request. "I'm a little drunk, but not *that* drunk. I'll remember and I won't fall asleep. Promise." She pinky-swore with the phone for good measure.

"All right, then. Get to it, hot stuff, before I'm the one who falls asleep."

Sara licked her lips. When she had thought about phone sex before, she had always wondered if she would know what to say—and if she would have the guts to say it. Now that she was on the cusp of fulfilling the fantasy, the words came to her slightly compromised mind without effort. "Okay, so, what are you wearing?"

"I am wearing my Fordham shirt and a pair of panties, and I am in bed, on top of the covers. You?"

Jennifer's words were fairly void of seduction, but Sara didn't care. She was feeling this for the both of them.

"Everything," she answered without conscious thought.

"What is 'everything,' Sara?" Jennifer chuckled

Sara opened her eyes to look at herself. "Uhhh, blouse, skirt, tights, jacket."

Jennifer hummed in understanding.

Sara realized she had to make the first true move. Well, she could do that. She had been thinking about Jennifer all night, after all. "Okay, I guess I walk into your bedroom… I've just come over, and I find you waiting for me in bed. The light is still on, and you look so beautiful." She swallowed as the image came to her without any difficulty: Jennifer lying stretched out on her bed, legs lightly crossed, the swell of her breasts perfectly visible in the oversized shirt. Jen's short hair looked a little mussed, and her dark eyes were a little sleepy. She must have been doing homework, must have been preparing for one of her classes, because in Sara's mind, imaginary Jennifer put a stack of books and papers away.

"I walk over to the bed as you look up at me, and without a word, I crawl on and settle over you. I wrap my arm around your waist and kiss you firmly to let you know that I have missed you and that I have been thinking about you."

Sara swore she could hear Jennifer sigh happily.

"I kiss you again and again, and then I lick your lips, hoping you will part them so I can kiss you the way I really want to." She tried to cue Jennifer that it was her turn to speak and swallowed against the arousal already drying her throat.

"I part my lips under yours and wrap my hands in your soft, long hair, pulling you close to me. I missed you, too," Jennifer confessed.

Sara's heart jumped with joy. She could feel Jennifer's hands in her hair and remembered vividly how slipping her tongue into Jennifer's mouth felt.

She didn't hide the moan that worked its way up her throat. "I slide my tongue inside your mouth, shuddering as you pull me closer. I let my hand run up your body, just brushing the side of your breast. I want to feel you shudder against me."

Jennifer gasped. "I do."

Smirking happily, she continued, "I kiss you a bit more urgently as I press my leg between yours. I love how soft you are...how good you taste." It was easy to give compliments like this—while describing the situation and not actually being part of it. She already had to use her words, so what was the harm in saying some of the things she had been dying to tell Jen but had never dared to?

"I buck into your leg with a whimper. I want to feel more of you against me and kiss you back harder. I push against your tongue until mine slides into your mouth. You are wearing entirely too much clothing, so I let go of your hair and trail my hands down to your chest so I can push your jacket down your arms."

Sara grinned; Jennifer was definitely getting into it now. Good, because she could feel how wet she was and it would suck if Jennifer stopped. "I push myself up a moment so I can pull off my jacket and take off my blouse as well. Bra too?"

"Yes." Jennifer's answer was instantaneous.

Sara fumbled with the phone while she made good on her promise. With her chest bare, she settled back down. "Okay, it's off. When I slide on top of you again, I cup my breast and bring it to your lips..." The alcohol quenched any shame she might have felt at this blatant display of her desire.

Jennifer's breath hitched. "Quickly, I open my mouth and suck your... nipple"—a note of embarrassment that quickly passed—"into my mouth and lap my tongue against it. I love your breasts, Sara. They are so responsive. They always show me exactly how much you want me."

Desire shot through Sara's body. She cupped her right breast happily and ran her thumb over the stiffening nipple in slow flicks that resembled Jennifer's favourite move. She hissed. That they were exploring new ground together only heightened the experience for her.

"You always feel so good when you do this to me," Sara admitted. She kept her eyes firmly closed. "I don't ever want you to stop, but you are overdressed, too, and I want to feel your skin against mine. I pull away from you a moment so you can take off your clothes."

"Underwear too?" Jennifer's voice was deliciously dark.

"No, leave that on for now, unless you're wearing a bra. That needs to come off. What kind of underwear do you have on?" Sara resisted the urge to touch herself where she really wanted to be touched.

"A black lace thong," Jennifer replied. "I wore it for you."

Sara heard rustling for a moment as the garment—or garments—were discarded. It didn't matter if Jennifer was actually wearing granny panties right now; in Sara's mind, Jennifer's delicious sex was barely covered by see-though material and that was enough to make her moan.

"Done," Jennifer announced.

"Good. I wait until you lie down again, and slide back on top of you. My leg presses against your panties, and I can feel how wet you are. I kiss your lips again, and then trail kisses down your jaw and neck and over your chest until I reach your breast. Teasingly, slowly, I slide my tongue over your skin. I circle your nipple, but never actually touch it; I want to hear you beg for it."

"Please, Sara, suck it."

Jennifer's needy voice caressed her ear and Sara thought she would come there and then. She decided to push her luck—and prolong her own delicious torment. "I resist a little longer, making you want it just a little more. I want to feel you push up against me, into me. I want you to take what you want from me." Sara hardly recognised her own voice anymore; like Jennifer's, it was deep and dark with desire.

Jennifer reacted to it beautifully; she whimpered in need, and Sara felt so wanted. "All right." Jen had to clear her throat before she could continue. "I wrap my hands in your hair again and push my body up into yours. I make you take my nipple into your mouth. Now, Sara, reward me for doing what you wanted me to do."

Sara clenched her legs together and licked her dry lips.

"I suck your nipple roughly into my mouth as I press my leg down against your...pussy." Okay, that was definitely awkward, but Jennifer didn't contend the word; all she could hear was laboured breathing on the other end of the line. All right, "pussy" it was.

"I lap my tongue against your nipple before raking my teeth over it, feeling you buck up harder. All I want is to make you feel good..." Sara's voice failed as she struggled with her desire.

"You always make me feel good, Sara."

Jen's need was plain to hear, and Sara's breath hitched. Arousal traversed her spine, right down to her already throbbing sex. She quickly returned to her dream scenario. "I bite down softly on your nipple as I push my leg into you—"

Jennifer groaned with such desire that Sara could immediately picture her on her bed, pinching her nipple roughly at the words. It sent a spike of arousal down to her core that was so great it momentarily dazzled her.

"Don't stop," Jennifer whispered.

The darkness in Jen's voice brought Sara back to their fantasy. "I won't." She licked her lips. "With a last gentle tug, I let go of your nipple and lick my way to the other one. I take it into my mouth and suck hard. My nails scratch lightly at your belly before my hand slides down, teasingly slowly. Then I drag it back up and do it again."

Sara could almost feel Jennifer's skin under her fingertips and her rock-hard nipple in her mouth. She was not going to last much longer, but then again, neither was Jennifer, of that Sara was sure.

Jennifer was panting now, and she whimpered with every well-placed word. She must be giving it her all, Sara mused, and once more, the image of Jennifer touching herself appeared in her mind's eye. She longed to be there, to slide her hand into warm wetness. Listening to Jennifer as she brought herself to orgasm was going to have to do until Friday—just two more days, she could do that.

"I...I slide my hands down your back and sink my nails into the skin of your ass to push you harder and faster against me. You drive me wild, Sara. I know you can't feel it—through your skirt, I mean—but I am so wet for you. You turn me on so much."

"Fuck, Jennifer." Sara shifted on the bed. "I move off of you a moment and hurry out of the rest of my clothes."

Sara quickly did as she had promised. She struggled with her tights until she finally got them off. She peeled off her skirt, and removed her panties for good measure. "Okay, done. Completely naked, I return to you, gently taking off your panties as well. I bring them up to my nose for a second and inhale your scent deeply. They are so wet. I can't wait to taste you, Jennifer. And why should I wait?"

Jennifer groaned at the other end of the line. Sara was sure she had rid herself of her last remaining clothing by now. "Licking my lips, I sit up between your legs and push them apart slowly, exposing you to me. You are so beautiful, Jen. You take my breath away. I can see how much you want me in your eyes, in the way you are breathing. I can tell by the wetness that covers your lips. You can't see it, but I am so wet for you as well. Everything you just said… you do that to me as well. I want to taste you so badly." It didn't feel awkward to say. In fact, it felt pretty damn good.

"Please, Sara, please. I want you to taste me. I want to feel your lips, your tongue. I love everything you do to me, but when you do…that, when you use your mouth on me…" Jennifer didn't finish her sentence.

Sara briefly wondered if she was already touching herself. It didn't matter; she was going to give her permission in the next few seconds anyway. "I get comfortable on the bed and lie down so I can kiss my way up your inner thigh. I bite softly the way I know you like, because you always shudder when I do it. Then I lick my way up, and God, you smell so good. I just want to taste you, so I do. I run my tongue through your slit and press against you—"

A loud hiss on the other end of the line.

Sara faltered as desire turned her already foggy mind fully to mush. She wasn't embarrassed at all now; she just wanted to hear that sound again. "I whimper as I finally taste you, and withdraw my tongue. I find your clit with my lips and suck on it. That's it, Jen, moan for me. Let me hear what I'm doing to you. I want to drive you absolutely crazy."

More and louder sounds met her hungry ear.

"I swirl my tongue over you and drink everything you have already spilled. I lap at your entrance. I love doing this to you, I love watching you when I do this to you. I know I'm completely covered in you by now and I love that, too. Again, I suck your clit into my mouth. This time, I trap it with my lips and flick my tongue over it again and again until you buck against me. I can feel your hands in my hair now, holding me close. Tell me Jen, do you want more, or should I only use my mouth on you?" Sara pressed her legs together. She was aching—aching to touch herself, aching to get stimulated. She could taste Jennifer in her mouth, could feel her against her. If she didn't open her eyes, she could almost think it was real. Jennifer's unrestrained sounds of pleasure went straight to her core and she was sure she was just as wet as she pictured Jennifer to be.

"This…is good." Jennifer took a long time answering.

Sara smiled. Jennifer really did like it when Sara got her off with just her mouth.

"Okay. Okay, then we'll do that." Sara licked her lips as she imagined how to get Jennifer off. "Sliding lower with my tongue, I thrust against your wet entrance, pushing as deeply as I can, just a little bit into you, fucking you with my tongue. Oh God. That sounded so hot. Let me hear you again. Fuck, Jen. How close are you?"

Jennifer's deep voice broke halfway through a guttural grunt that promised to be Sara's undoing. It was like music to her ears and went straight down to her own soaked pussy.

"Fuck! Sara, so close." Jennifer whimpered and it sounded as if she was restraining herself from coming already.

Well, she could. Sara wanted her to, so badly. She wanted to hear Jennifer shout out her name, hear her cry out in orgasm, hear her give in completely. "Good, that's good. I want you to come for me, Jennifer. I want to hear you come for me. I know what you really like, don't I? I know how I can make you come. I suck roughly on your clit, keeping you trapped. I know this drives you wild, because you have come for me like this before. Why don't you come for me now, Jen? I want you to come for me. I bite your clit gently, and flick it with my tongue. I'm giving you everything, so come for me. Now, baby." Sara was on the verge of orgasm. It took everything bit of willpower she had left not to slip her hand between her legs and fuck herself. She only needed a touch or two.

She very clearly heard Jennifer gasping for breath as she worked herself the last few steps towards orgasm. Sara listened as Jennifer's breath caught. When she heard the telltale signs of Jen's phone falling, she smirked. Jennifer's voice became muffled, but she could hear her gasping for breath. Jen blissfully husked her name.

Sara was feeling mightier than a queen right now; she had done that to Jennifer, all the way from Atlanta, with just her voice and her intimate knowledge of her girlfriend's body. If she thought her legs would be able to hold her, she would do a victory dance, but she wasn't going to risk it. Instead, she waited patiently for Jennifer to realize the phone had fallen down and retrieve it.

"Sara?" Jennifer sounded breathless but very happy.

Sara—still grinning like a fool—quickly reassured her. "Right here, listening to you. That was so beautiful. Seriously, thank you. Are you okay?" She could really fall in love with this one, she realized.

"Yeah, I am. I am very good, actually." Jennifer's voice softened.

Sara's grin widened; she knew her girl well enough to know she was blushing. She wanted to give Jen a few moments to catch her breath, but she didn't need them.

"You must be getting uncomfortable," she teased.

Sara snorted. She wasn't going to deny it, though; the steady throbbing between her legs had turned into a dull pain long ago and she wanted nothing more than to come.

"Why don't we take care of that?" The breathless devotion that had been in Jennifer's voice before had turned into a mischievous purr.

Sara squirmed and waited.

"Okay, I let you take your reward from between my legs before I pull you up and kiss you deeply. I taste myself on your tongue and moan against your lips. I love kissing you after you've made me come; it's so intimate and makes me feel so close to you. This is not a time to linger, though, because I really want to bring you to orgasm. I want to make you feel as good as you have made me feel just now."

Sara listened breathlessly as she pictured everything Jennifer told her. "Jen, please. Just...fuck me. I'm dying here."

Jennifer chuckled. "Okay, okay, sorry for teasing. I roll us over and settle against your side as I keep kissing you deeply. My hand slides over your breasts, giving each nipple a fast tweak before moving down between your legs. My breath hitches when I feel how wet you are for me and I waste no time, only pausing a few moments to rub your clit with two fingers. I'm finding it hard to get a grip as you are so very slippery."

Sara—who had let her hand follow the path Jennifer sketched—had to agree with her; it was almost impossible to rub herself; she was just too slick. "Then don't." She was aching to fill herself with her fingers. She just needed Jennifer to say it, to give her permission.

"I won't tease you...this time."

Sara was horrified to hear the huff she had intended to come out of her mouth transform into a needy whine instead.

"I cup your sex while I capture your nipple between my teeth and bite down roughly. At the same time, I slide two fingers deeply inside of you. It's so easy; you are so wet. I can push in and out of you without any resistance at all." Jennifer's voice was like liquid sex.

Sara was completely lost. She squeezed the phone tightly between her ear and her shoulder; she needed her hands for more important things. One was firmly on her breast, rolling her painfully stiff nipple between her fingers, and two fingers of her other hand slid in and out of her pulsing pussy. Jennifer had been right; it was so easy. Within a few strokes, Sara was on the edge of orgasm.

"J-Jen... I..." She couldn't finish the sentence, she could only move in and out of herself. Her hips met her hand with every thrust. She was already coming, no matter what Jennifer said or did now. She tried to fight it but she couldn't.

"Come for me, Sara. Let me hear you come. I push harder and faster into you and rub your clit with my thumb. I can feel your walls grip my fingers tightly. Come for me, baby."

Sara sobbed in gratitude and finally let herself go. Her body stiffened and her mind blanked in the face of the pleasure her fingers—Jennifer's fingers—provoked. For a moment there was nothing but bliss, and Sara rode the waves of it as long as she could. She whispered Jennifer's name as she passed her peak. Sara had never come like this when she was alone—but she wasn't alone, was she? Jennifer was right there, coaxing this orgasm out of her.

Sara thought she was going to pass out. She didn't, but it took a long time to recover from the pleasure she had just experienced. Her fingers continued to rub through her wetness, and she shuddered. A small voice speaking her name made her aware of her phone. She searched for it with her free hand and pulled it up with great effort.

"I'm here," she rasped. "Sorry."

"I was afraid something had happened to you." Jennifer was obviously only half joking.

"I may have had a stroke, I'm not sure. I can wiggle my toes, though, so I think I'll recover." Sara was still completely out of breath and her voice sounded like it had been dragged over gravel on the way out.

Jennifer laughed softly. "Good to hear, babe." She seemed proud of herself—and rightly so. "Why don't you go and sleep off the alcohol? I know you have an early flight tomorrow."

Sara groaned and covered her eyes with her arm in a useless effort to hide from reality. "What time is it?"

There was a short pause.

"A little past three a.m."

Sara groaned again. "I am never getting up on time."

Jennifer laughed.

Sara glared at her through her eyelids and the phone.

"I'll call you at eight and help you wake up," Jennifer promised.

Sara hummed. Her orgasm and the alcohol were taking their toll on her, even though she was still coaxing very enjoyable sparks of pleasure out of herself with her fingers. "Thanks, Jen." She struggled to stay awake. "Thank you for...you know...this."

"My pleasure," Jennifer said. "Thank you for suggesting it, even though you are drunk and probably asleep by now."

Sara frowned. "Am not."

It sounded more like a mumble than actual words, and they most certainly did not carry the accusatory tone Sara had meant to place in them. Okay, yes, maybe she was half asleep already.

"Sleep, sweetheart." Jen chuckled. "I'll be right there holding you, okay? And tomorrow, we'll be together again."

Sara yanked the covers over her cooling body with a groan and slid onto her side. After everything she had already imagined in the last hour or so, imagining Jen's arms around her came easily. She could feel her warm body against her back and her breath on her neck. Sara hummed her agreement.

"I'll be there soon," she mumbled. She was quickly losing her grip on the phone, and she stopped trying to force her eyes open.

Sara had been in love before, had felt the little flutters in her stomach, had gone over to a girl's house and had slept in her arms. She'd made love to other women, and she'd had hours' worth of discussions with them. But Jen was special. She was many miles away and yet she'd just made love to her. They had been separated for only a few days and yet Sara missed her. She missed her beautiful smile, missed the way Jen settled into her on the couch while chewing on popcorn with her mouth open. She missed the way Jen's eyes lit up when she opened the door for her.

"I can't wait. Sleep now, it'll be tomorrow in no time."

Sara didn't want to say good-bye; she wanted to listen to Jen for a little longer. But despite her better intentions, she was asleep before Jennifer got to say good-bye. She shuddered awake a moment more when the phone slipped from her hand and fell, but she quickly lost grip on her consciousness again. She dreamed of nothing but seeing Jennifer tomorrow and having her arms around her as she slept.

WELCOME TO DEEP SPRINGS
BY CASSANDRA MCMURPHY

I CHECKED INTO DEEP SPRINGS RESORT a little before lunch. Rachel wasn't in the lobby as she was supposed to be, leaving me to stand off to the side while a bunch of babbling massage therapists registered with the lady at the front desk. I wistfully watched them pick up their badges, wishing I was enough of a freeloader to ask one of them for a free massage. Lord knew I needed one.

I didn't say anything to them, though. I scooted my bag over with my foot and adjusted my cap, suddenly feeling sporty and gross next to these fashionably hippy ladies. They excitedly discussed aromatherapy techniques, draped in scarves and organic cotton tunics and trendy beaded sandals. And here I was, in my Nikes and running gear as though it were race day. I flashed a cautious smile in their general direction. One of them returned my smile with a quick one of her own.

A grin spread across my face. Perhaps a free message *was* in order later.

"Hey, Chloe," Rachel said, popping up in the lobby's entrance. "Sorry, I've been texting you—I already registered. I don't get a damn signal in this place."

I hefted my bag to my shoulder.

She smiled brightly at me, and then her face flashed with worry. "You want me to carry that, with your back and all—"

I shook my head. "Thanks, but I'm recovered. Mostly. I'll be fine," I said, as I started to follow her down the hall. At least she looked out of place too, her dark hair clearly straightened, her red lip stick practically shouting it was hip and cool and totally not organic or vegan or whatever. I usually thought she'd look better if she would, ironically, try a little less hard to be pretty, but right now I was grateful for her conventional beauty standards.

"I'm starving!" she said dramatically.

"This place has food, right?" I asked.

"Three fresh, organic vegetarian meals served daily," she said with another quick smile.

"So then lunch will be a half a raw beet sprinkled with chia seeds and raw milk?"

Rachel laughed, and it reminded me of wind chimes tinkling in a summer's breeze. I liked it. Granted, I'd liked her a laugh a lot more before I'd found out she was as straight as my eighty-year-old Baptist Grandmother, but it was still a very pretty laugh.

"Come on, Chloe, it will be good. Deep Springs wouldn't have the rep it does if the food was terrible."

"I don't know, people come here to mediate right? According to the Buddhists, life *is* suffering."

She shook her head with a low laugh and opened the door that led to the grounds, holding it ajar so I could walk through with all my crap. We'd left the reception area, which was located to the far south of the building, and headed down the wooden, eco-chic halls with their carvings of bears and deer and alligators, out into the bright sunlight and rolling emerald lawn that led to the rental cabins.

I followed her up the path to our home for the next week, a squat, stone-walled building that looked smaller than my first apartment. It probably had just as many spiders, too, if the cobwebs above the door were any indication.

The inside looked clean enough at least. After dropping my bag on the bed, I went right back out to where Rachel was waiting.

"So," she said, giving me a conspiratorial look. "You see any interesting prospects?" She gave her eyebrows a suggestive wiggle.

Snorting, I tried to hide my red face under the shadow of my dirty racing hat. "I've been here five minutes. All I've seen was a gaggle of massage therapists."

"Tantric massage?" She elbowed me in the ribs.

"The welcome banner in the lobby didn't say," I replied sarcastically.

"You should ask," she said. "How long has it been, Chloe? Eight months?"

"Eleven," I growled back.

"Well, that is a long time. I know you run, but there are better ways to blow off some steam." The eyebrow waggle came at me again.

My face felt dangerously close to spontaneously combusting. "Maybe you should take your own advice," I said.

"Maybe I will. Wait! Don't see any men here. Darn!"

I didn't see any either. The lawn was dotted with women enjoying the sunshine and open air. A yoga class was starting over by the trees, near the trail I planned to run in the morning to celebrate my recovery and return to training.

Rachel was right, though. She might be out of luck, but I was in paradise. I should keep my eyes open.

We stepped into the cafeteria, which was somehow big and functional while still having the atmosphere of some trendy Portland coffee shop. The clientele matched, too, all socks and sandals and scarves. I did see a man there, but unfortunately for Rachel, he had a waxed handlebar mustache that made him look as if he'd wandered out of an old-timey western movie.

Rachel hit the buffet line and I followed. It wasn't quite the stuff of nightmares, but still a far cry from my usual chicken breasts, pasta, and bagged iceberg salads I dined on regularly. As Rachel would say, I liked my food the opposite of my women—colorless and bland. I tried to find the most unhealthy dishes available to playfully annoy Rachel, but that ended up being some kind of cauliflower and potato casserole, a shit-load of corn, and some pita bread.

Rachel moved to accommodate me as I sat with my plate of food. I glanced up between the rows of seated patrons and my eyes happened to fall upon where the massage therapists had congregated.

One of them was glancing in my direction. I stared at her, not realizing she was staring back until the moment had gone from coincidental to *awkward*. Her pale blue gaze held mine, sharply curious. Her blonde hair caught the light of the window beside her and glowed like gold around her tanned face, held back in a loose bun. She must have been thirty-five, and was of medium height, dressed in a bright green and salmon tunic. God, her face was pretty. More than pretty. Striking.

Wrenching my gaze away, I picked up my fork.

"What were you staring at?" Rachel asked, craning her neck and turning around in her seat.

"Rach!" My voice sounded hoarse as though I was possessed by some demon summoned when my mortification reached a certain astronomical threshold. I kept my hat turned down over my face so Rachel couldn't see my burning cheeks.

Rachel continued to gawk and crane her neck like some kind of startled bird. "Were you checking out someone over there? Oh, the blonde one? She's *cute.*"

"What! Stop it now! How do you know?"

"She was still looking over here. And she smiled at me." Rachel turned back to me and grinned, her eyebrows waving at me. "Good choice, Chloe! Really, she's pretty."

"I *saw* that," I said, forcing myself to look down at my food for fear I'd look past Rachel and see the woman staring back at me.

"You should talk to her."

"Hilarious. How would *you* respond to some weirdo hitting on you after staring you down for ten minutes?"

"Well, she was definitely staring back. That's not what I'd do," Rachel said, forking a piece of tofu and gesturing with it as if she was the magic tofu fairy. "Not unless I was into weirdos."

Carefully glancing up from my food, I tried to watch the therapists from my peripheral vision. The blonde was facing the lady to her side, laughing. The whole table looked taken with some hilarious joke, which I hoped to God had nothing to do with our little impromptu staring contest.

I smeared my food around my plate with my fork, suddenly not hungry. Shit, this was a flashback to high school. The massage therapists were the cool girls, and here I was, the queer jock watching them from a different planet. Not wanting to be like them, but wanting to get with them.

No, I wasn't going to think like that. There was no use going down that road. This was a mental retreat, a place to recover from my fall during my last race. Now wasn't the time to rehash old frustrations from when I was sixteen. I was a grown-ass woman.

But I looked across the room—cautiously, hopefully—and felt crushed when I didn't meet the woman's gaze again. I didn't feel grown up at all.

Rachel and I finished our lunches and went our separate ways for a bit, planning to reconvene at the eponymous hot springs. In the interim, I unpacked my bag and tried to organize my stuff.

The living area of the cabin was a little coffin with two rusty, rickety beds stuffed inside, and the bathroom stank as though someone had locked themselves inside to chain smoke doobies for a week. Unimpressive, to be sure. Slightly annoyed at the rusticness of my new digs, I stuffed my shoes under my bed frame and then dug around in my duffel bag for my swimsuit. I found my bottoms wadded up with some old compression socks, both somehow sausaged into the pant leg of a pair of dirty pajamas, which I had accidently packed. Great. I didn't have anything to wear to bed, and I was still missing my swim top. The temperature inside the room seemed to rise with my frustration, and I started to sweat, growing irritable as I tore apart my bag. Nope. No swimtop there.

There was no way I was going to shell out a million dollars for an organic cotton swimsuit from the gift shop, so I was either going topless or wearing a sports bra into the springs. Whatever. I wasn't going to let this get me down! I was here to relax after all. Pushing aside my frustration, I grabbed my makeup bag and headed into the bathroom, and tried to stack my toiletries on the anorexic strip of a counter above the sink.

My toothbrush fell into the toilet. "Fuck!"

My sailor mouth was probably going to disturb someone's Zen. I had to get a grip on myself. This wasn't the end of the world right?

My toothbrush floated forlornly in the toilet. I plucked it out and then spent a good five minutes scrubbing my hands and taking deep breaths.

Here I was, an accomplished trail runner who weekly slogged through miles of mud and grime and moss, who had fallen and accidentally *eaten* more dirt than most people ever looked at. And yet, I couldn't handle a cabin in the woods. I didn't do meditative retreats. I liked my clothes clean and my buildings with AC, thank you very much.

Deciding my hands were finally clean enough, I grabbed my sports bra and headed out the door.

I was going to cough up the change for a new toothbrush at least. Or maybe, I thought with a silent grin, one of the more practiced patrons of Deep Springs could show me how to make one out of twigs and good vibrations.

I stalked up the path to the steam house, where the springs were. Rachel was waiting for me in the doorway and flagged me in with an energetic wave.

"You look grumpy," she cheerfully observed.

"Are you naked under that towel?" I asked, trying my hardest to shake free of my bad mood. One toilet baptized toothbrush was not going to get me down, gosh darn it!

She grinned. "You object?"

I laughed and headed inside. There was a small waiting area where I could stash my clothes. I slipped into the bra and bikini bottoms and realized I had forgotten my towel. Figures. Shrugging it off, I followed Rachel into the springs.

The springs consisted of a huge rectangle of natural stone for a floor, with six small pools ringed with built-in seats. There were several people bathing, but there was one free pool, near the front.

I dipped a toe into the water. It was indeed hot. I stepped down and lowered myself into the water.

The heat hit my back, where I'd torn a muscle almost six weeks before, and a spasm of ecstasy shot up my spine. If my back muscles could somehow drink a glass of wine, this is what it would feel like, I thought as I sank lower, relaxing into the warm embrace of heat.

Suddenly my violated toothbrush didn't seem to be such a big deal. Seriously? What was I being such a big whiny baby about? I'd walk around with a dirty mouth for a week if it meant I got to experience this little slice of Nirvana every day.

Rachel sank down next to me, her expression melting into one of pure pleasure.

"Oh, this is divine," Rachel purred, tilting her head back and closing her eyes.

"You aren't kidding," I breathed. This was *better* than wine. Or even an orgasm. Or both. Okay, maybe not the latter. But close. Then again, it had been such a long time since I had sex with anyone, maybe my memory was faulty.

"See? I told you I was a genius," Rachel said. "Never doubt the power of the springs."

I started to reply, but someone splashed down into our pool and stopped right at the edge of the seat.

I stared.

It was *her*. The therapist from the cafeteria. The steam had kinked her blonde hair into a halo of gold and condensed to a silky sheen across her tan breasts. Her nipples stood out proud and pink, I noticed, before I forced myself to look away from her nakedness and settle somewhere a little more polite.

She met my gaze and held it, and suddenly, I couldn't breathe.

I had never wanted anyone this way before. So purely. So instantly. I wanted hours to study the firm curves of her stomach, the endless miles of her legs. I wanted the chance to drink her in and savor every drop.

"May I join you?" she asked, not yet sitting. It took every shred of my willpower not to stare. My gaze betrayed me and flicked down, and I saw there were freckles on her forearms and some on her thighs, but they stopped around the gentle slope of her pubic bone.

"Sure," Rachel said for me, thankfully immune to the stupefying sexiness of this woman. She sat across from us and reached over the water to offer her hand.

"I'm Dani," she said, her voice a warm contralto.

"Chloe," I said, and shook her hand. Her grip was strong and sure, and I could feel the impression of her fingers even after she pulled away.

"Rachel," Rachel offered with a characteristic grin. "You're with the massage therapists?"

"I am. It's our yearly convention," Dani said, sitting back. The water lapped at the fine hairs around her neck, darkening them. "I have to say this is my favorite week of the year."

"You've come here for your retreat before?" I asked, finding my voice.

"We've tried a few other places for our get-togethers," she said with a shrug. "This place is always the most inviting. May I ask what brings you ladies to the springs?"

"Chloe's here to rest." Rachel said, jerking a thumb at me. "She jacked up her back something awful. You should use your skills on her."

I turned to glare at Rachel.

Dani laughed. "My *skills?*"

Rachel smiled coyly. Leave it to Rachel to be a better flirt than I was. "You know what I mean. Anyway, I'm here to make sure she doesn't overdo it."

I wanted to ask what exactly Rachel thought I was going to overdo, here, besides maybe nap and eat too much fiber. But then I thought of Dani and suddenly my imagination went a little wild.

Dani turned her piercing gaze to me. Something inside me squirmed excitedly when she did. "What did you hurt?"

"Strained my lumbar muscles. Nearly tore them." I tried to shrug casually, but in the water all I managed was a sort of soggy flop of my shoulders.

"What happened?" She seemed genuinely interested.

"I fell off a mountain," I said. Her startled look made me realize how horrible that sounded. "It was a trail, on a mountain, and I fell off the trail."

"You rolled a bit, didn't you?" Rachel said, as if I was some kind of hero for tripping over a damn rock and nearly killing myself.

"Yes," I said sheepishly. "I rolled—it's a miracle I only strained my back. I'm actually fine now, just about ready to start training again. Tomorrow is my first official day back in action."

"How long did you have to rest?" Dani asked.

"Six weeks," I said, unable to stop myself from wincing.

"I'm sorry. That has to be hard."

I felt as though I was failing because we were only talking about me, and I knew that was a poor way to make friends. "Only one more day to go though, before I am officially back in action. Rachel and I sort of came here to celebrate."

Dani smiled. "Nice. You picked a great place."

I floundered for something to say, but couldn't cook up anything. I wanted to dunk Rachel's head under water for trying to get me a free massage. Part of me also wanted to shake her hand and thank her wholeheartedly for the effort. Whatever the case, Dani had extricated herself from any obligation by deftly avoiding the question. And I wasn't about to mooch as an excuse to get Dani close to me. That didn't feel right.

Dani closed her eyes and sank into the water. I tried to do the same, taking my cue from her. But I cracked my eyes open slightly so I could watch her. The water stroked lazily between her breasts, up and down, in a slow, sensuous rhythm. I imagined my hand gliding over her skin. I ran my hands across my own thigh under the water, wondering what she would feel like.

"I need to work." Rachel abruptly popped out of the water.

"So soon?" I asked, feeling panicked to be left at this on my own.

"Yeah, I have some new ideas suddenly. You stay, Chloe. I'll see you back at the cabin."

I didn't argue with that. She crossed back toward the doors and disappeared out of sight.

Dani watched her go, then she looked at me. The water felt cold compare to the heat in her gaze. "She's nice. What does she do?"

"She's an artist," I said. "I think she's been struck by sudden inspiration." Inspiration that was perhaps, allowing me time alone with Dani, bless her. I paused, worried that Dani was interested in Rachel instead of me.

"Are you guys…?"

"Rachel and I? No. She's…she's not…she likes men."

Dani smiled softly, almost mischievously. "You guys seem to go way back."

I nodded. "Since high school, actually. More years than I care to count."
I paused. "Are you here with anyone?"

"Just my friends," she said, her eyes glittering.

God, I couldn't say it. *Are you attached?* I wanted to ask.

But I couldn't.

I was failing at this. We kept talking about me, but I needed to ask her
something about herself, anything, just to keep the conversation going.

"What's your favorite body part to massage?" I asked suddenly, and then
winced. What the hell kind of Freudian question was that?

She laughed, surprised. "That's the same as asking the teacher to name a
favorite student."

I smiled, trying to match her easy charm. "Or asking a chef what their
favorite dish is."

"You could ask me that question, too. Touching and tasting are two sides
of the same coin." she said, that same dangerous smile playing on her lips.

I felt my face flush hotter than the damn spa water. Where the heck was
this going? My brain seemed to fizzle off and short circuit. "So I take it you
don't message very many feet then."

She laughed again. God, I could get used to that sound.

Dani shifted to my side of the pool. I forced myself to remain still,
realizing I was holding my breath.

"I'll show you my favorite spot to massage," she said.

I lifted an eyebrow. "Is it your favorite snack too?"

She laughed softly as she reached through the water and turned me so my
back was to her. Her strong fingers began to knead my muscles in small, tight
circles. She focused on the spot right above my hipbone, toward my spine,
her fingers rolling in waves of varying pressure. It hurt in the best way I could
imagine.

I could feel her wet breasts as they gently brushed against my back. God,
it was torture.

"Relax," she commanded.

"I am," I lied. I was barely breathing. Her fingers pressed firmer against
me and she shifted to get a better grip. Pain that was pleasure blossomed along
my spine, spreading up through my skull. I bit back a moan.

"I see you understand why it's my favorite spot," Dani said softly into my ear, her breath making my shoulder erupt into shivers.

"That's where I hurt myself," I said, my voice unsteady.

"Oh," she said, withdrawing her hands. "I don't want to hurt you."

"You weren't," I said, leaving the rest—it not only felt good, but she was also turning me on—unsaid.

"I can keep going—"

"No," I said, too quickly. "I don't want to be a bum. I bet people ask you for freebies all the time."

"I only give them away when I want to," she said.

"Rachel made me sound as though my back is destroyed, and it's really not, it's fine now. I don't want a pity massage."

"A pity massage?" She laughed. "How do you know I'm not using you? Maybe I get more out of it than you do?"

My mouth went dry, despite the dampness in the air. "What do you get out of it?"

She went to say something, but someone shouted her name from across the pool, and she looked up toward the sound.

A shorter woman approached, waving her hand wildly. "Dani, there you are. Vera's sciatica is flaring up really bad, would you mind coming over to show her those pressure points you told her about? So sorry to interrupt, but she is in a lot of pain!"

Dani looked at me. "Would you mind? I'll be here tomorrow. We should continue this conversation."

I nodded, a fragile hope flickering inside of me. "Sure."

Dani got up, and I watched her wet, glistening body walk to the other pool, where she sat and began to talk with a cluster of older ladies.

I sat back and closed my eyes.

Tomorrow could not come soon enough.

———————— ⊷✕⊶ ————————

The next morning I awoke at dawn. Not by choice.

Someone was hammering on a prayer gong.

And I *hated* them.

Swearing, I rolled out of bed. My stomach rumbled in greeting, reminding me that I had eaten little of the steamed vegetable travesty that Deep Springs had served for dinner the night before. Rachel was draped across her bed, snoring softly. Somehow she managed to sleep through the iron thunder booming outside of our cabin.

I wasn't going to be able to fall asleep again, so I got dressed and laced up my running shoes. Rachel's borrowed pajamas found a home at the end of her bed. I brushed my teeth with my new, biodegradable, compostable toothbrush before I headed out the door.

The gong and its nefarious banger were nowhere in sight.

The grounds were beautiful though. Sunlight was just beginning to bleed over the tops of the pines, the gold and pink and blue of some hippy's flamboyant tie-dyed skirt. I headed off at a slow jog toward the trees, promising myself I was going to take it easy.

The trails were still a little dark but quickly lightened as the sun came up. The rolling green of the land was lovely, reminding me of the all the reasons I loved and had dearly missed running. My body felt good as I fell into the rhythm of the road. My shoes marked a soft beat on the asphalt, like the rhythm of a comforting song. After weeks of worrying if I was ever going to be back to normal, it was a tremendous relief. My back felt blissfully normal.

I saw birds and squirrels and startled a deer as I came around the last hill on my way back. A big, silly grin had plastered itself to my face by the time I arrived at the cafeteria.

Rachel was waiting for me there. I grabbed a tray of fruit and oatmeal and what I hoped was scrambled eggs and not some kind of mutant tofu.

The message therapists must have all been doing some group activity, because I didn't see any of them from the night before.

Rachel looked up at me sleepily.

"What's up?" I asked.

"Oh nothing," she said. "Nothing exciting going in my life right now, unlike yours." She took a drink of her coffee and leered at me over the rim.

"What are you talking about?" A smile was already creeping across my face, refusing to be denied.

"Are you really going to play dumb? Come on, Chloe, how did it go with *Dani* last night?"

I took a bite of eggs and promptly spat it into my napkin. Mutant tofu it was. "She gave me a sampler massage."

"Oh?" Rachel's brows lifted.

"Not that kind of massage," I said, but then paused. "It might have been going there though."

"You think?" She said eagerly.

"She said to find her today, but I haven't seen her."

Rachel sat back, suddenly frowning. "I heard this morning that one of the cabins had an emergency last night. One of the older ladies had to go back home due to some medical stuff, and some of the others went with her."

I felt crushed. "Shit, I wonder if she went with them." I spooned some oats into my mouth, which wouldn't have been half bad if I hadn't suddenly felt so depressed. .

"You could try the front desk for her contact info." Rachel offered.

"Hells to the no. I'd feel like an uber stalker." I waved my hand in the air at Rachel, recognizing the look in her eyes. "I'm fine, whatever. Nothing happened between us, I'll get over it."

"But you like her."

"Sure, we had chemistry." Rachel was going to hang around and try to cheer me up, I knew, and I wasn't about to make her waste her day on what might be a lost cause. I forced a smile. "Seriously. It's fine. So. What are you going to today?"

"Well, I'm going to paint more today," Rachel said. "You got plans?"

"Nah, I'll go soak some more. Read, maybe. Go do your thing."

From the corner of my eye, I saw the shorter lady who asked Dani for her help the night before in the springs. I jumped up and touched her elbow as she got in line for coffee. She looked at me, clearly confused.

"Do you know where Dani is?" I asked, realizing too late how stalkerish and crazy I sounded. Too late though.

The woman blinked. "She left last night, took Vera to the hospital."

"Oh, thanks."

"You want her number?"

I shook my head, feeling weird for being this wrapped up in a woman I had just met. I slogged back to the table and sat down.

"Yep. She's gone."

As promised, Rachel disappeared not long afterward, leaving me to my own devices. I was determined not to have a solo pity party, so I tried to keep busy. I spent an hour in the water but the weather grew hotter than I expected, and worried that I might boil like a lobster, I left the springs to go sit in the shade and fan myself with my towel. Light conversation with some of the other patrons was distracting, but it didn't yield any deep connections.

I tried to read one of the books I had brought with me, but they were so chock full of sex I couldn't tell if it was the ninety-degree heat or the book that was making me get sweaty.

When lunch rolled around, I made a plate of rice and beans and sat outside again. As relaxing as this might be, I decided that next time I celebrated anything, it would involve lots of cold beer and steak.

Rachel returned around dinner, sunburned and exhausted. She collapsed into a blistered heap on her bed and went to sleep. A cool breeze started to blow outside and I found myself energized in a way I hadn't felt in a long time. Maybe I could go for a walk. I didn't know the grounds too well, but I could at least find someone who did.

Feeling determined, I headed to the entrance and the lobby area. The desk was manned by one man. It was Mr. Mustache, complete now with an old-timey hat. The lobby was air conditioned, of course.

"There any good places to go for a walk in the dark?" I asked.

He nodded firmly "There are some good trails up around the north part of the woods. There is a gazebo up there, too, nice view."

He shuffled some papers on his desk and handed me one. "Here's a map. The massage folks were supposed to be up there tonight, but they cancelled, so it will be pretty peaceful until tomorrow morning."

"Any chance I could sleep there?" I asked excitedly. Anything had to be better than the stifling bong of my cabin.

"It's covered, and near the creek, so you might catch a breeze." He opened his hands. "If you're worried about strangers, no one else is up there, and I won't send the staff out until mid-morning tomorrow."

He gave me directions and on the way there I stopped in the cabin to grab my sleeping bag and pillow and tell Rachel where I was going. She didn't like being woken up, but I wasn't about to head out anywhere in the woods alone without telling anyone. Who else was going to call my mom if Sasquatch ate me? Rachel also declined an invitation to come with me via a series of sleepy grunts.

It was her loss. The gazebo was as he described—seated on the top of a hill surrounded by tall firs, the silver creek gurgling below. I walked the paths around it, enjoying the cool air that blew in over the water. There were lights in the gazebo too, which was handy. A few yoga mats were scattered around the floor, and I arranged them as a sort of bed and threw my stuff on it.

Sweat trickled down my back. What the hell, no one was going to see me anyway. I threw off my shirt and lay face down on my blanket. A wind picked up in the trees and kissed across my back, leaving a trail of gooseflesh. I closed my eyes, relishing the sensation.

I dozed lightly. A soft noise sounded behind me, I looked up sharply, my senses coming fully awake.

Dani stared at me over the fire, a bottle of something in hand.

I stayed down, acutely aware I was topless.

She smiled at me softly.

"What are you doing here?" I asked. "I thought you went home."

"I took Vera to the doctor. The conference isn't over though. We just got back." She paused, and I had the feeling she was studying my face. "They've cancelled our meeting for tonight and we're resuming in the morning."

"How'd you find me?" I asked, wondering if I could reach out and grab my shirt, but pretty sure it was too far away from me to do it modestly.

She rubbed her palms together, and I could see ointment glistening there. "I stopped by your cabin and Rachel said you were coming here. She'd said you'd love a visit, even this late."

I laughed. "Did she say I needed a message too?"

Dani grinned playfully. "She requested I reserve you a private appointment," she said, and came closer, kneeling beside me. Her oiled hands came to rest on my shoulders, and she started to work my muscles. I melted into her caress, unable to stop myself.

"You have nice shoulders," she said, her oil-slicked touch gliding over my skin.

"You have nice hands," I said, my voice soft and strained. Her fingers made me relax, and yet put me on edge. Her hands slid lower, to my mid back, stroking up and down the length of my spine. My hips pressed against the ground against my will.

She shifted, and along with her hands I felt a new sensation on my neck, whisper-soft. Lips. Then the hot, moist caress of tongue.

I wanted to ask, to question, to wonder. But it felt too good and I didn't want her to stop. Chills burst across my arms and legs as she drug her mouth upward to my ear, stroking the edge with the tip of her tongue. I released a shuddering breath. Her hands moved down, toward the small of my back.

Her kisses blazed back the way she had come, along my neck, my spine, her hands sliding along my ribs, tingling along the sides of my breasts. I lifted myself ever so slightly, and she teased beneath them, over them, swirling softly, taking painstaking care not to touch the nipples. I ached. I burned. A bright, hot need blossomed between my thighs and I turned my face toward her, reaching out with one hand to touch her leg.

"It's not your turn," she said, lifting my hand to her mouth and biting gently onto the cleft of my palm. Her lips curled along the calluses at the flat of my hand. I shook gently. Her warm, wet mouth opened and took the very tip of my finger inside.

I gasped. She rolled me over onto my back and I stared up at her, my heart racing, my breath a ragged tempo between my ribs.

She traced the outline of my breasts with her finger, then leaned down and followed with her mouth. My back arched and I moaned, seizing the back of her head gently in my frantic fingers.

I felt her smile against my skin, and then she crept upward. Her feather-light lips brushed the hard tip of my aching breast. Then her tongue, hot, wet, and firm, drew my nipple into her mouth eagerly.

A line of fire burned from my breasts to sex, threatening to consume me. She sucked harder and I pulled her head down.

I felt her hand on my belly, softly dragging toward my thighs. God, I was so wet. She slid her hand over the inside of my leg and down, then moved to my stomach again, before repeating the motion on the other side. She switched to my other breast and repeated the same excruciating pattern, until I was tied up in a tight, hard knot, begging her to undo me.

But she wasn't done torturing me. She kissed down my stomach to my navel. She briefly paused to remove my pants, before her hand returned to knead my breast. The other stroked along my leg, then up the inside of my thigh. I shifted my hips, trying to direct her where to go. But she wouldn't do it. She brought her mouth to my thigh, tilting it so she could kiss down the length to my knee, then creeping up the other side with slow agony.

I groaned in frustration, and right then she touched my aching cunt, her finger gliding from the top down, slipping barely inside. Her lips followed behind, then came the hot pressure of her tongue, flickering over my clit.

I made a wild, desperate sound as she began to suck and nibble at the top, her fingers swirling along the edge. She slid two fingers inside of me and began to pump in and out, matching the rhythm of her tongue. Waves of heat blasted through my body, sizzling from my toes to the top of my head. God, I was going to come! At any moment I was going burst.

She flicked her tongue faster, in time with her fingers, twisting them, plunging them as far as she could go. I made a sound that I didn't recognize, that was half-plea for release, half-growl of frustration. The fire inside of me flared brighter, hotter, until everything was lost in it. I heard myself cry out and then the blast wave carried me away from reality. I panted and whimpered and shook with pleasure so fierce my whole body seemed to fly apart, leaving me at the center of a firestorm which roared and raged inside my bones.

I came to my senses and realized that Dani was staring at me, her hands curled along my thighs, her eyes filled with satisfaction. A smile played at the corner of her mouth.

I slid my hand across her wrist and pulled her over me. I kissed her slowly, running my hand along her stomach, through her tunic shirt. I felt the soft skin over her ribs, and the satisfying fullness of her breast. I didn't have Dani's patience. I squeezed softly, listening to her gasp as I pinched her nipple between my thumb and forefinger.

My other hand slid down to her legs, then between to the warm cleft within. I stroked through the fabric, and she shivered and shuddered. God, I wanted her so badly. I eased my finger beneath the band of her leggings. I teased along the sides of her cunt with two fingers. Her breath came hot and heavy in my ear.

She jerked toward me with her hips. Maybe I wasn't the only impatient one.

I felt the dampness of her arousal and slid into her, swirling my fingers across her hard, throbbing clit. She spasmed against me. I pushed deeper and then slowly withdrew to the start.

I felt pressure on my belly and realized she was touching me again, gliding downward, into my still slick cunt. She lay beside me and stopped, reaching for the massage oil again. She gasped and dropped the bottle as I changed my strategy, moving faster with two fingers, reaching a little deeper with each stroke.

She managed to recover the bottle from where it had fallen beside me, daubed some of the liquid onto her hand, and then reached down between my thighs. Her finger returned to penetrating me, slowly, while I penetrated her, matching each other in rhythm and speed.

Then something warm and wet played at the entrance to my ass. I tensed, but her oil slicked finger swirled along the edge. Warm pleasure flowed through my thighs. My tension melted, morphing into excitement. I tried to focus on the feeling of her hot moistness surrounding my fingers, but it was too hard. She stroked me on the outside, on the inside, and her third finger opened me, teased me, made me ache for things I'd never done before.

She pressed a little deeper into my ass and I tensed. Still, she easily slid inside without hesitation. Then she swirled her finger again. God. I couldn't take it. She began to work my clit, my cunt and my ass in time with one another. I was rapidly going insane. I writhed, finding it impossible to keep touching her. Instead I grabbed at the sleeping bag beneath me with both hands, unable to cut off the cry of carnal ecstasy that escaped my throat.

I came. It wasn't fire or heat or light. But a void. I left the world for one moment, knowing only the feeling of Dani's hand touching me everywhere at once and then shuddering, breathless release.

I lay panting for a moment, unable to form a coherent thought.

Dani rested her head on my shoulder.

"So," she said, and I could hear her mischievous smile in her voice. "How do you like Deep Springs?"

WAITING

BY D. JACKSON LEIGH

I WAIT IN THE DARK FOR you.

The warm summer night flows through the open window like a velvet blanket to caress my bare skin. I've arranged myself as you've taught me. My head rests on a red silk pillow, my face turned away from the door and toward tonight's full, beautiful moon. My wrists are shackled to my ankles by soft leather cuffs, and my hips are raised for your pleasure.

I listen for the fall of your boots on the porch as tree frogs and crickets sing their night song. *Coming. Coming. Coming.* The longer I wait, the greater my anticipation and the wetter my sex grows. How long has it been? Minutes, hours since you called?

> *"Hello?"*
> *"Do you desire me tonight?"*
> *"Yes, please."*
> *"You know what to do."*
> *"Yes."*

I wait in the dark for you as a wisp of breeze tickles my pussy and cools my moist thighs. To pass the long minutes, I relive the first time I waited.

* ⚬⚬⚬ *

The thump-thump of the music vibrated my stool as I sat at the bar, watching the door the way I had most nights since I'd witnessed your power three weeks before.

I'd slipped into the bar's storeroom to avoid an ex-girlfriend and was sitting behind some boxes to plot an undetected escape when I heard you enter with another.

"Didn't I tell you to wait for me?"
"I wanted to see you."
"Then you should have waited."
"Please, I couldn't wait."

I peeked around the box to see you sit on a wood crate and bend her over your lap. You raised the hem of her dress. She wore nothing underneath. Her white cheeks were stark in the dim light.

"You slut."
"You should punish me."
"I will. But not the way you want."

I flinched when your broad hand came down with a sharp smack. Then another, and another until her ass was a mass of red handprints and her thighs were glistening with her juices. I was aroused, too, and shifted uneasily when you poked your fingers into her cunt and she moaned. You stood, yet left her bent over the crate, and unfastened your pants to unleash the tool you were packing. I watched you grab her hips and shove your cock into her. She moaned and you rocked back to drive roughly into her again, and again. When her moans turned to a keening, you pulled out, wiped your cock on her dress, and zipped up. She cried out, begging for you to fill her again and give her release.

"That is your punishment. You won't come on my cock tonight or any other night again. When I told you to wait, I meant for you to wait."

And so I'd waited for you at the bar since. I'd been lost in that storeroom memory when you appeared finally next to me, your eyes boring into mine as though you could see my every desire. Wordlessly, you held out your hand, and I gave you mine. You led me into the music and our dance began.

The bass pounded through us as we writhed together, your long, strong body calling to mine, your power filling me. I wrapped my arms around your neck and felt the press of your package against my loin. I licked your neck and made my request.

"Teach me to wait for you."

"No waiting tonight."

You led me out of the bar and down the street, through the lobby of a four-star hotel where you already had a room for the night. You put out the do-not-disturb sign and locked the deadbolt.

"Take off your clothes."

I stripped slowly as you watched, never moving to remove your own clothes. Then you circled and looked me over as if you were making a purchase. You finally smiled and stripped down to your harness and dildo. It was long and thick. You cupped my face and kissed me gently, then thoroughly. You hummed with approval when I sucked at your tongue, and you guided my hand to your cock. I stroked it a few times before you handed me a small bottle of lube to spread along its thickness. Your breath caught as it slickened, and I pumped my hand several times. Then you pushed me onto the bed, and I lifted my knees to my chest and opened to you.

My eyes closed as you stretched and filled me. You were big and it hurt a bit, but in a good way. I locked my heels behind your thighs as you rocked a few times. I raked my nails across your back. I wanted your power, not your care. You growled and rose up, your eyes bright and fierce as you drove into me hard, again and again until I screamed my climax. Then you turned me over and rode me until we both climaxed.

That was our beginning.

I wait in the dark for you and smile at the memory of how raw I was the next day, how difficult it was to walk after a full night of your relentless cock. I didn't have to wait for you that night. But my delicious lessons in waiting were soon to follow.

My first lesson was only a half hour of waiting. You bound me spread eagle and fucked me to the edge of orgasm, then left me for thirty minutes, begging before you came back to give me release.

Then you began to have me prepare for each evening with you—bathing, shaving, and douching, dressing in a particular scene-setting costume or nothing at all before you arrived.

When you would arrive was always uncertain. I would wait, wine ready to uncork, treats prepared to your liking—whatever you desired. Sometimes you came early and stayed late. Or you came early and left early. Or you came very late. That waiting seemed endless. The prolonged titillation was agony, but the ultimate climax always exquisite.

Heat spread along my chest and flushed my face as I recalled the day you added a new request to my preparations—a cleansing enema. You had me prepare, fueling my expectation several times before you ever introduced this new play into our repertoire.

It was the first time you positioned my hands between my knees and shackled them to my ankles. I felt so exposed with my knees spread wide and my hips raised to fully reveal me. You kissed and nipped my sensitive bottom and chuckled when I squirmed.

> *You like that, don't you?*
> *Yes. I'm very sensitive there.*
> *How about here?*

I jerked in surprise, then moaned when you tickled my anus with your tongue. The sensation was incredible. You lengthened the swipes of your tongue, finding my clit, probing my sex, and returning to my puckered hole. The blend of sharp, tingling, soft and electric sensations had me practically dancing on my knees.

I despaired when your tongue left me and then tensed in anticipation when you pressed against my anus with purpose.

> *Don't tense or this will hurt.*

But my muscles instinctively clenched tighter at your warning. I felt your first knuckle, then you retreated. The gel was cold between my cheeks, but warmed quickly as you spread it along my sensitive cleft and began to work it into my hole. You were gentle at first, then firm and insistent. The glide grew better and you moved easily in and out, probing deeper with each breech. You fingered my clit with your other hand until I was rocking backward to meet each invasion. It felt good.

WAITING

Good, baby. You're taking it so good. Are you ready for more?

There was more?

You abandoned my ass only to return better equipped. Thicker than your finger, it spread me very wide. I was tight and resistant. I whimpered at the pain as you pressed deeper.

Take it all for me. You can do it.
I don't think I can.
Yes, you can. Try to push it out, so your sphincter will open to let me in.

I did just as you asked when you thrust again and I felt it pop through as you stroked my clit and rocked your tool gently. I cried out in victory, exultant that I'd done this for you.

You rewarded me with your thumb in my quim and fingers on my clit as you moved behind me, fucking my tender ass, massaging my sloppy sex, and bringing me to an explosive orgasm.

My pussy and ass clench reflexively, and my hips jerk at the memory. I pant a few seconds, then draw in several deep, calming breaths. You wouldn't be pleased if I came before you arrive.

I wait in the dark for your permission.

My breath catches at the guttural growl of your motorcycle coming up long drive. I shift to get feeling back in my legs, to relieve the ache in my back from holding my position for so long. I've been waiting hours, judging by the position of the moon. I strain to hear your boots on the gravel out front, then echoing on the porch. Even the frogs and crickets have gone silent.

My sex throbs in anticipation while I listen to you take a beer from the refrigerator and open it with a pop, then I let out a sigh of resignation when I hear the television come on. A basketball game is just starting. The leather creaks on my sofa as you make yourself comfortable. Two more hours.

I wait in the dark for you.

Movement on the bed startles me to awareness. I must have drifted off to sleep.

"My sleeping beauty."

"I've been waiting for you."

"I'm pleased. Very pleased."

Your hand is warm, the calluses of your labor rough along my back and bottom. I resist the need to move and stretch after my impromptu nap, focusing only on your touch. A few inches more...but your fingers dance away from the juices that have dried on my thighs while I slept. My need flows anew, and I'm instantly slick and dripping again.

"Please. I've waited since you called."

You release my shackles, and I groan when you roll me carefully onto my back. My muscles are stiff from the long wait. You hover over me, your strong hands performing a lovely massage along my legs. You begin with a quick loosening of my tense quads, then move to my feet for a more purposeful task.

I watch you in the dim moonlight through half-hooded eyes.

You take each of my toes in your hot mouth. Your eyes burn into my mine as you lick along my arches and begin a slow, thorough massage of my calves. One hand on each leg, you work your way up, your knees between mine. I open my legs as you move higher, inviting you to survey what I'm offering, begging you to come in. You hold my gaze instead.

If only you would stretch out over me, I could find relief against the button-fly of your soft, faded jeans. You've let me do it before, as long as I come again and again for you later. I know I can. You know I will.

But you shift to my side and push my legs closed. I groan in disappointment, and you chuckle.

"Soon. But you must be patient."

You stroke your hand over my fevered breasts. My nipples are hard and tender from prolonged erection. When I press into your hand, you relent and knead them, tweaking my nipples gently.

"Yes. I could come with you doing just that."

You lower your mouth to my left breast and flick your tongue over the hard nipple, then pinch it between your teeth. I moan and jerk at the jolt of electricity that shoots straight to my clit. You stop.

"I don't want you to come yet."

I whimper. It's not a protest, but a sound of indecision. I desperately want to come, but my belly spasms with thought of prolonging this exquisite torture. Nothing compares to the buildup to that first orgasm.

I press my face into your shoulder and tangle my fingers in your hair. I love to feel the short buzz at your nape, and the long silk of forelock that drapes down to your silver-gray eyes. You capture my mouth with your Elvis lips, and I suck your tongue inside. You break off for a moment to kiss down my neck, suck my pulse, nip my earlobe and return to my mouth. I'm dying. I'm aching. My belly is heating and clenching. I push my pussy against your jean-covered leg. I want much more. I want you inside me. I want you behind me. But I'm also desperate now. It won't take much. I can't wait any longer.

Then your hand is on my knee, pushing me away. Your tongue and lips are gone. There's nothing but the warm summer night where your body was heating mine a second ago.

"I want you to wait."

I want to scream.

"Roll onto your stomach."

Hope blossoms. Yes. You are strapping the cuffs around my wrists again and raising my hips to guide my hands between my knees. I'm ready, so ready. I hope that you will ride me long and hard, through many orgasms. I smile to myself. I've prepared for you to take all of me. I've come to love it, and have laid out a selection of your favorites to signal my desire.

I gasp when your fingers test my readiness. They glide easily in, two fingers, then three.

"You're really wet. I can't wait to slide my cock into you."

"Please. I've been waiting."

"Semi-finals, my sweet. I've already missed the first half of the second game. I'll be back when it's over, then we'll have all night."

What?

"No, please. I need to come."

You stop at the door.

"What did you say?" Your tone is suddenly hard, the way it was in the storeroom the night I'd first seen you. My heart jumps into my throat.

"I'll be waiting for you."

You leave the room without another word. I listen, barely breathing, as the refrigerator opens and closes again. The leather of the sofa creaks and the sound on the television grows louder. A small part of me fears that you will leave when the game ends, leave me still waiting, still wanting. I would rather you punish me than leave me.

Who am I kidding? I'd discovered by accident that your punishment is actually reward to my randy libido. I wait in the dark for you and recall that memory to melt the icy ball of fear in my chest—fear that you will find someone else to wait for you.

You'd left me waiting for several hours, but never this long.

We'd never spoken about our arrangement being exclusive, and I doubted I was the only woman who waited for your touch. I'd found for myself, however, that other women fell too short to even bother pretending. They didn't wield your power.

And so I'd waited for you.

You'd been out of town for two weeks on a business trip. I'd counted the days and nearly fainted with joy when my phone rang mid-afternoon with your instructions. I was prepped and waiting. The hours dragged by.

The cuffs you'd given me that shackled my wrists to my ankles had a longer chain then, and I found that with some maneuvering, I could reach my clit with my fingertips.

At midnight, I was in a near frenzy. My clit throbbed. One orgasm wouldn't hurt, would it? You'd never know, would you? I held my breath and listened. No growl of your motorcycle. No crunch of tires on the gravel drive. I touched my clit and moaned. Then I stroked. It felt so good. I imagined you pumping into me, letting me touch myself. It only took a few strokes and I was gritting my teeth as relief washed through me in waves.

I'd barely caught my breath, when I heard you coming down the drive. I straightened into position and held my breath.

Your boots were heavy on the wood floors, but you wasted no time in coming directly to the bedroom. You braced in the doorway to shuck off your boots and began shedding your clothes as you walked toward me.

You are a welcomed sight. I missed you.
It's been long, but I've been waiting.
I'm pleased.

You were already wearing your favorite cock, and it sprang toward my face when you slid your jeans down your hips. It was large and black. You extracted a sizable butt plug—my favorite with the vibrator inside—from your pocket before kicking the jeans away. You put it on the bed and laid your hand on my cheek, bending to put your face close to mine. I could smell the Crown Royal on your breath, and imagined you had been at the bar having drinks while I'd been waiting naked, my ass in the air, in the dark.

WAITING

Your choice tonight. What do you need first? Do you need to come, or should I release you and reconnect for a bit?

You kissed me, then listened for my answer. I was surprised at your tenderness. I loved it, but it wasn't what kept me waiting for hours.

I need you to fuck me.

You smiled and moved behind me with a growl. You licked and playfully nipped at my bottom cheeks as you tickled my sopping pussy with your fingers. I felt you move to position your cock for entry, then freeze.

What's this?

You backed away and your breath was on my calves, your tongue tasting my fingers that rested on the bed between my shins. You lifted my hands, measuring the length of the chain that bound my wrist cuffs to my ankle cuffs.

You've been a bad girl. Waiting? I don't think so.
Please.
You've been at yourself, haven't you?
Please.
I should walk out now.
Please don't. I'm sorry. I'll do anything. I didn't mean to...
But this is partly my fault. I obviously left this chain too long.
I'm sorry. I'll do anything.
So, instead, I'm going to punish you for taking advantage of my generosity.
Yes. Please punish me. I deserve it.
Are you sure? It's going to hurt.
Yes.

You released me and went outside to your bike and returned with heavy pliers. Your mouth was a grim line, scowl ever-deepening but eyes never meeting mine as you efficiently shortened the chain on my cuffs. You didn't reattach my wrist cuffs to my ankles. Instead, you sat on the bed and jerked me across your lap as you had the woman in the storeroom.

I was startled at how much your broad hand hurt, slapping sharply against my exposed bottom again and again. The more I cried out, the faster the blows fell and the hotter the fire burned on my tortured skin. My tender breasts rubbed raw against your rough jeans, and tears wet my face as I quietly sobbed. I nearly choked when the slaps abruptly stopped and your fingers slid easily into my slick pussy. How was I so aroused by such pain? My bottom pulsed with heat, but I realized my sex was pulsing with the same need—perhaps greater—that built inside as I waited for you.

Before I could contemplate this further, I was tossed off your lap and bent over the bed. You shoved inside me. Oh, sweet relief. You drove into me hard and fast, slapping your hips rather than your hand against my abused bottom, lifting me off the bed with each forceful stroke. One hand clutched my shoulder, the other my hip as your strokes shortened. I knew you were about to come. Would you climax and leave me wanting? I despaired, though I certainly deserved it.

Then your teeth replaced your hand on my shoulder, and that hand found my clit to take me with you over the precipice of orgasm, the release of pleasure washing through me, cleansing me, restoring me, renewing me. Afterward, you lay heavy on my back—your cock still possessively buried inside me—for a long time before you spoke.

I thought you were different, that you would wait. I punish only when it's necessary. I prefer…I need you to wait for me.

Your voice was hoarse and tight. I realized then the droplets falling on my back were not sweat from your brow. Your pride would keep me pinned on my belly so that I could not see your tears, so I tried to brush them away, dry them with my words.

I'll welcome your punishment if I unknowingly commit any other transgressions, but I promise that in the future I will always wait for you. I want to wait for you. Only for you.

So, I wait for you now in the dark.

The chain on my cuffs is unnecessarily shorter. I might conjure memories to torture, but would never touch myself while I wait. I belong to you. Your pleasure is mine. And so I wait.

You speak to the television, admonishing the referees, celebrating with your team, and take a phone call from a friend. I smile at the domestic feel, as though I'm sitting on the sofa next to you.

I'm not. I'm naked, face down on my bed, ass in the air, hands between my knees and shackled to my ankles. On the bed next to me are my favorite of your toys. The tight, latex harness is designed like a jockstrap and has an O-ring large enough to accommodate Big Jane, your fattest eight-inch purple dildo that stretches me tight and fills me beyond complete. Beside it is the matching purple vibrating butt plug—the medium-sized one. You know I can't handle the large one and Big Jane. And, of course, Big Jane and a bottle of lube.

Your shout from the other room makes me smile. You're enjoying yourself, and that makes me happy. You make me happy.

I was surprised to discover that, though quirky, you're shockingly vanilla in your sexual needs. You're not interested in more exotic fetishes like fisting, nipple clamps, gags, or bondage other than the cuffs or silk scarves. Punishment is rare and never administered with anything other than your bare hand. You simply need me to wait for you to fuck me.

So, I wait for you in the dark.

Soon now. My sex swells and throbs and lubricates in anticipation. The night is cooling, and a breeze whispers in the open window to cool my thighs where my arousal has wetted them still again.

The noise of the television abruptly ends, and the leather of the sofa creaks as you rise. I strain to hear your footsteps, but you've removed your boots and your socked feet make no sound on the wood floors. I hold my breath and follow the sound of the light switches clicking off as you darken the house. We need only the moonlight.

You gently turn my head to face you rather than the window and lie next to me so that our noses are inches apart. You lightly trail your fingers along the arch of my back and the curve of my hip, raising chill bumps on my skin.

"You are so beautiful."

You kiss me, gently, then with purpose. Your hands cup my face as your tongue takes possession of my mouth. You taste of cinnamon breath mints. When you leave my mouth, you trail kisses along my shoulder and back, fondle my breast, and tweak my nipple.

"I've been waiting for you."

"Yes, you have." You pause. "It was hard to concentrate on the game, knowing you were in here like this."

My chest swells and sings with the sweet epiphany. The waiting has become hard for you, too.

You stand and hold my gaze as you slowly strip. This is a new treat. I lick my lips when you drop your shirt to the floor. My hands itch to feel those broad shoulders. Your high small breasts are released from their almost unnecessary binding, and I take a deep breath with them. You peel your faded jeans and boxer briefs from your slim hips. You aren't packing today, and the neatly trimmed thatch of curls between your legs makes my mouth water. Perhaps tonight you'll permit me a rare taste of you.

You inspect what I've laid out for you and raise an eyebrow when you hold up Big Jane. I nod vigorously, and you shrug before stepping into the harness and settling the dildo into position. You climb onto the bed, and my heart beats double-time. Your hand rubs across my bottom, and I squirm when your fingers slide through my wet folds.

"We'll have to get you ready first."

You probe inside with your fingers, and I reflexively clench in an effort to grip them tighter. Then you trail my juices up to finger my anus and I go still. I don't want to miss any of the sensation. I jerk when you bite into my butt cheek and a second later discover that your finger has penetrated my ass while I was distracted by your teeth.

"That was easy enough. Maybe you don't need as much preparation as I thought."

Your finger, despite my pussy juices, is rather dry in my ass, so I'm happy to hear you pop the cap on the lube. I barely flinch at the cold dribbling down my crack as you spread it around and inside. It feels so good, so good. I clench my pussy over and over, wishing you would hurry. Your finger is sliding in and out easily and you add a second finger. I grunt at the added invasion, but I'm practiced at this now and push against you to open wider. Finally, you are satisfied and quickly substitute the butt plug for your fingers. It isn't as long, but is shaped to stay put. I shudder when you activate the vibrator inside it.

"Hurry, please."

I'm struggling to wait. The vibrations reaching my clit are too strong. I need Big Jane to intervene. You understand that my control has limits and smack my bottom sharply with your hand to distract me.

"You will not come until I tell you to come."

You slap my bottom a few more times, then caress my heated cheeks. I wonder if you are doing this because you know I enjoy a little pain or because you like to see your red handprints on my bottom.

At last, Big Jane's bulbous head nudges at my quim. You shove into me in one swift, clean stroke that makes my eyes bulge. My memory of her girth never equals the reality. Your first strokes are tantalizingly, agonizingly slow. In and out, in and out, in and out. I am filled before and aft, my clit stretched tight outside by Big Jane's bulk inside. I beg you to pump faster, but you glide in and out at an excruciatingly measured pace. In and out, in and out, in and out.

Still, the pressure builds.

"Please, oh, please."

"Yes, come for me."

I nearly sob in relief as you give permission and I relax into the pleasure that is riding me low in my belly. Another stroke, two strokes and my wave is cresting. My climax is more of a roll over than an explosion, and I tumble along in the myriad of sensations as you thrust smoothly into me.

The tendrils of my orgasm still tease me as you quicken the pace of your thrusts. Your fingers dig into my hips where you grip them to jerk me backward as you drive into me. I glance over my shoulder to find your gaze, but your eyes are on your cock where it slides relentlessly into my tight pussy. The erotic image—the fat dildo pushing in and pulling out of my red and straining sex—is a bolt of electricity to my cunt as you pound into it.

"I'm going to…again."

"Yes."

Your growls are as fierce as your battering ram, and your shout of victory throws me over the chasm, grenades of sensation bursting in my belly and bombarding my sex, my ass, my lungs, my heart, my brain, my legs, my toes—every part of my body. Slowly the brilliant colors, the exploding synapses fade. Soft moonlight and the familiar walls of my bedroom return.

You are panting, braced over me and still lodged inside me. You pull out carefully, then extract the anal plug with a sucking pop. I'm a mess of lube and cum, so you use the hand towel I'd discreetly laid out with the toys and dry me before you release my restraints.

You divest yourself of the harness and lie down next to me to let me cuddle into your side. After a moment, you kiss me and take my hand in yours to direct it to your breast. I massage gently, marveling at its soft contrast to your hard muscle, and then tug at your turgid nipple. You take my hand again and move it down your lean belly to your stiff curls. You're very wet. You press my fingers against your swollen clit.

"I'm still hard."

"I've been waiting, hoping you'd let me taste you."

"I think you've earned that."

You've only let me do this once before—you standing and me kneeling. This time, you simply push against my shoulders to direct me downward. I pepper your belly with kisses to show my gratitude. You casually bend one leg to give me better access. I'll take what I can get and wedge myself sideways between your legs.

I wait for your permission.

"Lick me, but don't suck. I don't want to pop off too soon."

You taste of musk and salt and faintly of latex. I clean the cum of your first orgasm from your folds and then narrow my strokes to the hard knot of nerves growing under my tongue. It's more prominent on the left side of your clit, and I know this will be the spot that will drive you to orgasm. I scrape my teeth over it and you groan.

"Inside. Two fingers."

I am so startled that I almost stop. You've never allowed this, never requested it. I press my fingers to your entrance. You're tight, so I work in and out gently as I wield my tongue. My fingertips find that rough spot inside and I press hard as I thrust. Your thighs tense and you bend your other leg up so that you are fully open to me.

I stroke you inside with my fingers and outside with my tongue. Stroke, stroke, stroke. I move my other hand to your belly and scrape my fingernails across your tense abs. You gasp and your hips buck.

"Now. Suck me now."

I obey, but scrape my teeth across your hard knot with each suck and you growl out your climax. I don't stop until you push my face away. I kiss your thighs and crawl up to cuddle again. You are limp, and I lick the salty sweat from your neck.

"I should make use of your mouth more often."

That pleases me. You please me.

"I'd like that, very much."

You roll me over, spoon against my back, and pull the sheet up to cover us. You sigh deeply and, in only a few moments, your breathing slows and evens out in sleep.

WAITING

I stare out the window at the moon in wonder. You're going to stay the night? My heart soars. I'm both tired and elated. The one time you'd stayed before, I'd awaken on my stomach with your weight pinning me, your thumb in my pussy, and your fingers sliding along my clit. I could only hope for it to happen again. I close my eyes, reveling in the warmth of your skin against mine, knowing I'll dream of you, ecstatic that you have given me something I hadn't realized was my deepest desire.

I should wait in the dark for you.

THE SYMMETRY OF TALKING IN CIRCLES

BY NICOLE BIRDSTONE

"THERE'S A STARBUCKS ACROSS THE street." Zoe rose on her tiptoes and peered through the dusty glass window of a china cabinet. "You're buying me a mocha if we ever manage to emerge from these catacombs." Her face scrunched in disgust when her breath disturbed the dust into a faint cloud.

Rebecca rolled her eyes. She could set her watch by Zoe's boredom threshold; it was never longer than fifteen minutes. She ran her fingertip over the surface of an oak roll-top writing desk, leaving a clean trail in the wake of her touch. "Antiques can be very valuable with a little love, and you know it wouldn't kill us to have some furniture that wasn't 'rescued,'" she air-quoted the word, "from some West Village garbage pickup."

"Hey! The sofa was—"

"Bought new, I know, but leather?" Rebecca glanced back over her shoulder at her girlfriend of the last four years, her lips twisted to suppress a smile. "I'm not letting you furnish our home like some metropolitan gigolo with a hard-on for postmodern decor." She waved her hand dismissively, continuing down the crowded aisle of furniture.

Zoe huffed a quick *tch* and crossed her arms over her chest.

Pretending not to see Zoe's pout, Rebecca crouched down to inspect a cherry wood hope chest. "And yet I'm expected to embrace this Pollyanna on the prairie shit you think is homey." Zoe wrinkled her nose at the word, gesturing toward the hope chest.

Rebecca just oohed quietly to herself over the price tag and ignored her entirely.

"You're still buying me Starbucks when we leave." Zoe groused.

Rebecca smiled at her affectionately. She took Zoe's hand and, in an attempt to placate, started toward the entrance of the shop. When she stopped a few steps later to peer at a tacky stained-glass lamp, Zoe kept walking past her. "If you want to get coffee, we should go to that Jo on the Go place," Rebecca said to her retreating back. "It's good to support local businesses, and Starbucks is the epitome of corporate greed in a branded cup."

"Oh my God, Rebecca, you have seriously got to stop listening to Sheila do her charity-of-the-month routines." She narrowly missed walking into a grandfather clock when she turned to fix Rebecca with an accusatory look. "Don't you remember that thing with the horses?"

"You certainly approved the switch to organic milk."

Rebecca was smug as she followed her up the aisle, and Zoe waited until Rebecca was closer to reply. "That's for health reasons. They pump some freaky shit into dairy cows for the...." She trailed off at the knowing smirk spreading Rebecca's lips. "Look, I just don't want Bessie the cow's menopause in my Peanut Butter Crunch, okay?"

Rebecca nodded with a condescending smile on her face. "Of course, sweetie."

Twenty minutes later, Zoe followed Rebecca out the door of the Starbucks across from the antique store, sipping her iced mocha with all the contentment the spoils of a battle won could offer.

She made a production of slurping her drink through the straw, the noise obnoxiously loud in the relative silence of the car. "Mmmm, corporate greed tastes so good, Bec." Her smile was broad and teasing.

Rebecca tried not to return it, but the corners of her mouth twitched. "Jerk. You're lucky you're hot or you'd be single."

"Obviously it's my sexual prowess that keeps you hooked." Zoe waited just a beat.

After four years together—and having known each other for all of high school before that—Rebecca knew what was coming before Zoe even started.

"And you know, of course, that *the hoook briiings youuu baaaacckkk.*" Zoe rolled her fingers to the tune while she sang the lyrics, her grin wide and dorky and impossibly cute.

Rebecca couldn't suppress the giggle that escaped with her eye-roll. "I don't think I'll ever break the brainwashing that Sheila and Blake did to you in that loft."

Zoe had spent her first year after high school—while Rebecca slaved away in college trying to keep her GPA acceptable—in a very RENT-esque loft in New York City with some very theatre-oriented friends. Rebecca never missed an opportunity to razz her about it, despite the fact that those same theatre friends were now their closest.

She started the engine and ignored the follow-up slurp Zoe threw in for good measure, wondering for the countless time how she managed to fall so hopelessly in love with such a brat. Between Rebecca's super-sensitivity and shutdown response and Zoe's tendency to lash out, they should have dissolved within the first two months. But four years later, they shared an insufferable cat, two car loans, and a tiny, overpriced apartment.

Rebecca watched Zoe's slender fingers flit across the touchscreen in the dash, looking for music, plump lower lip pulled into her mouth absently and dark brows drawn together in concentration. She was just so breathtakingly beautiful, such a perfect study of how softness and edges—both physically and emotionally—could blend into this stunning creature, and no matter how many times Becca looked at her, the thought still didn't fade. She realized she was staring a moment later, feeling silly for how easily she was distracted by the warmth that bloomed in her chest when she looked at her partner. They'd been together for years, yet she still felt like a besotted schoolgirl. Becca reasoned she must just be really lucky. Feeling a burst of simple happiness, she leaned over the console to suck Zoe's lip between her own.

"I love you." Becca sighed into the sweet kiss.

Zoe's smile looked confused when she sat back from the contact. Her expression didn't change as Becca settled back in her seat with a little bounce.

"I love you, too, pod person," Zoe stated evenly. "Do you put an alien in my brain now, or is that for after lunch?"

"Oh, hey, yeah—what do you feel like for lunch?" Rebecca asked.

"Um..." Zoe stalled, distracted by the stereo. She hummed a little *ah-hah*, and music started playing through the speakers. "I don't care. Pick something."

"You're still stuck on this song?" Rebecca's nose wrinkled. "Panera? They have that tomato basil soup you like."

"It's not eighty-seven degrees outside, sure." Zoe turned a high-wattage fake smile toward the driver's seat. "Should I also wear a parka?"

"Okay. Then... how about Chipotle? I could go for some carnitas."

"Hmm." Zoe looked thoughtful for a second before shaking her head. "I would say yes, but I'm already bloaty today." She circled her hand over her midsection. "Can't have Chipotle-belly goin' on in these shorts."

Rebecca inhaled slow and deep through her nose, a sigh more weary than irritated. "Well, what do you feel like eating?"

Zoe arched an eyebrow. One corner of her mouth lifted in a flash of a smirk before she parted her lips to reply.

"For lunch, Zoe. What do you feel like eating for lunch?"

"Really, I don't care. Just pick something that isn't gross."

They ended up going to a sushi place for Zoe, while Rebecca visited the Chipotle two doors down. They would never be mistaken for a fairytale match, but they'd figured out their own balance and it was working so far.

"You're gonna start doing your own laundry." Zoe accentuated the word by forcefully throwing the armload of clothing she'd collected from Rebecca's side of the bed into their laundry hamper. "If you can't put it in the hamper, three fucking feet away from this Goodwill discard pile you wanna hoard over here."

"I appreciate you!" Rebecca's voice floated in through the open door to the bathroom, and though the volume of it was muffled by the running shower water, the teasing lilt still carried through.

"There is almost an entire load of just scarves! How did you even accomplish that? I do laundry every weekend!" Zoe rolled her eyes and started separating their clothes by color into piles. She did their laundry, and in exchange Rebecca handled all cat-related maintenance and most dish duties— provided Zoe had actually put her dishes *in* the dishwasher and not in the sink. "Less than three fucking feet away."

Zoe had learned a thing or two about cars over summers as a kid spent at her uncle's garage, so she decided the first time Becca freaked out about a flat tire that she would deal with anything involving their vehicles. In turn, Rebecca was resident CFO of their operation since she was much more methodical and precise with financials. They tended to leave errands like grocery shopping for weekends when they could go together, and Zoe threatened physical violence any time one of the idiots they spent their free time with—usually those same theatre kids from Zoe's first apartment—brought up how adorably domesticated it was.

After the initial settling-in period when they moved in together, they fell into balance pretty easily. Zoe still marveled sometimes at how well they worked, considering they bitched at each other about what sometimes felt like everything. She was just grateful they did, because trying to imagine making life work without Rebecca, well... that was messy, and probably best left at she didn't get very far.

The water shut off, and Zoe finished separating the clothes just in time for Rebecca to appear wrapped in a towel. A wave of oatmeal and almond fragrance rose from Becca's warm skin and followed her into the bedroom.

"What?" Becca asked, the corners of her mouth turning up. She bent at the waist to tousle her fingers through her slick blonde strands.

Zoe just continued to stare at her. She unconsciously licked her lips and stepped in close to bump her hips into Rebecca's backside, the laundry forgotten. "What?" She murmured back, the pitch of her voice low and throaty. Her hands settled lightly on Rebecca's hips, and she nudged forward again, just enough to make Becca stumble a little and catch herself on the bed with her hands.

"What are you doing?" Rebecca giggled, but she was bumping back into Zoe.

Zoe pressed her body along Rebecca's back and inhaled deeply at the nape of her neck.

"Thinking." She smoothed her hands up under Rebecca's towel, palming over hips, belly, and ribs to brush teasing strokes along the bottom curve of each breast.

"About?" Rebecca's question was huskier this time.

Zoe cupped the warm flesh she'd been playing with under the towel, unsettling the loose knot that held it in place. She leaned back enough to let the fabric drop to the floor and hummed kisses into Becca's neck. "About how crazy hot it would be," her pelvis shifted against Rebecca's backside, undulating in a soft rocking motion while her fingers captured a nipple, "to fuck you like this." Zoe grinned into Rebecca's shoulder at the unsteady intake of breath she felt swell against her chest. "I could grab Charlie, and just..." She rolled her hips a few times, letting her breath ghost over the sensitive spot behind Rebecca's ear.

Pale fingers tightened in the comforter that covered their bed, but Rebecca shook her head. "You know I don't do that..." Her reply was even and still had a warm note to it; she was rejecting the suggestion but not rejecting Zoe.

It certainly wasn't the first time Zoe had brought up that particular subject, but there was a reason their strap-on was named Charlie—a play on Rebecca's middle name—she was the only one that had worn it. She'd given Zoe a mixed bag of reasons for the resistance, citing a fear that it would hurt as paramount. Zoe was sure there was more than that, though, because Becca herself had called it an irrational fear given the rough sex they'd had in the past. Honestly, she wouldn't be surprised to learn that it was the power trip of it all. Zoe knew Rebecca, and Becca loved to be in control of things.

Still though, sometimes...

Rebecca's eyes closed as Zoe moved against her. Her body responded to the press of soft breasts against her back and the damp breath at her ear instinctively, shifting back into Zoe's groin.

Sometimes, Zoe was positive she thought about it.

"Mmm, but just think," Zoe sucked Becca's earlobe into her mouth and slid one hand down to tease her nails through trimmed curls, "of all the other things..." She glided one fingertip between Rebecca's lips to brush over her clit. "...I could be doing with my hands." She dipped two fingers just barely inside and then removed them again, smiling to herself when Becca gasped.

"God."

"I could be doing all those other things, Becca, and I could still be inside you." Zoe's voice was a smooth purr directly in Rebecca's ear.

There was just something primal about the idea of having her like that. Zoe would never push at something Rebecca was truly uncomfortable about, but she also knew how Rebecca liked to demand more with three of Zoe's fingers pumping inside her. How she liked to share deep panting kisses while she came. That sexy rounded ass pushed back into her again, and Zoe's eyes rolled up with a shaky breath. She felt Becca's hand cover her own, and a moan escaped without her intention.

"And here I thought you could do that, anyway." Rebecca's taunt was a little breathless as she moved Zoe's fingers against her core with a gentle pressure.

"I've never heard you complaining."

Rebecca met Zoe's gaze over her shoulder and removed her guiding touch from Zoe's hand. Then Zoe was swallowing a groan as Becca bent over the bed, her bare backside still pressed tightly to Zoe's lap and her knees pushed into the side of the mattress.

"I think you need to refresh me." Widening her stance just slightly, Rebecca braced her feet along the sides of Zoe's and bounced her hips in invitation. "My recollection seems to be a little fuzzy."

Moments like these reminded Zoe that Becca knew her buttons and knew how to coax the exact reactions she was seeking out of Zoe. The pressure that was already building at Zoe's center started throbbing for attention. Their give and take was balanced, and Zoe's desire swelled with her affection at the thought. She gritted her teeth at the wave of pleasure when she slid two of her fingers smoothly into Rebecca from behind.

"You need reminding that you're mine?" Zoe immediately started a passionate rhythm, her other arm still wrapped around Rebecca's hips and trapped against the bed so her fingers could circle around the swelling knot of Becca's clit. "That can definitely be arranged."

Long minutes later Rebecca was coming with a groan muffled into the bedspread, one hand twisting at her own nipple while the other grasped desperately at Zoe behind her.

When Zoe came home the next afternoon, Becca was sitting in the chair by the bed, apparently waiting for her.

"Hey!" Zoe said in surprise while kicking her shoes into the closet. "Didn't expect to see you home." She unfastened her jeans and started pushing them down her legs, looking up to see Becca watching her closely with a small smile and her eyes dark. "Everything okay?" She stepped out of the denim and lifted her sweater over her head, raising a brow in question when Rebecca just nodded slowly with that same smile. Zoe was starting to feel like prey.

"Okay." Zoe took off her bra and walked over to the dresser in the nude, digging for her favorite sweatpants in their pajama drawer.

"You don't need any clothes."

Zoe stopped pilfering through their pajamas. She thought how funny it was that a sentence could sound so much like a direct order without actually being one. Rebecca's voice had that *thing* in it, that thing that meant she had something particular in mind.

"All right." Zoe drawled the word and slowly turned around to face Rebecca, resting her hands on her hips. She was confident in her body and its effect on her girlfriend. "What do I need, then?"

Rebecca's smile spread wider in approval, and she pointed to the end-table on her side of the bed, a few feet away from where she was sitting.

Zoe squinted in confusion but followed the direction, walking over to the table and opening the drawer. She stared for a couple beats—Charlie staring back at her—then looked at Rebecca for an explanation.

Rebecca's hands twisted together in her lap, and she nodded, her cheeks tinting pink. She cleared her throat and stiffened her spine to regain her composure.

Zoe certainly hadn't thought her evening would be playing out like this when she left work. She tried not to feel self-conscious about being watched while she fiddled with the buckles that secured the harness to her hips. After successfully affixing her new temporary appendage, she looked up at Rebecca with a goofy smile and swung her hips so the toy swayed side to side.

Rebecca giggled and shook her head. "How did I know that would be the first thing you'd do with a hard-on?" She stood up and closed the few steps between them, stopping centimeters from Zoe and licking her lips as she looked her up and down. She didn't move for several seconds, her expression growing more uncertain the longer the moment stretched on without any action.

"Hey." Zoe's voice was soft, a tender tone she didn't use very often, and her hands came up to cup Rebecca's cheeks. "You know you don't have to do this, Bec." She dipped her chin to meet hazel eyes, trying to convey all of her sincerity with the look.

Her patient reassurance seemed to flip some switch in Rebecca. Zoe watched as she stood taller, squared her shoulders, and tightened her jaw. She might've been appalled at herself for how her stomach twisted as she watched Rebecca's demeanor change, but instead Zoe was too preoccupied with not just throwing Rebecca on the bed and fucking her stupid to even care.

"I don't *have* to do anything, no." Rebecca stroked delicately over Zoe's collarbone with the comment.

Zoe inhaled sharply at the first touch, a sheepish chuckle following her gasp. Becca's presence weighed heavier than her fleeting touch, and Zoe was hypnotized.

"But this is definitely happening," Rebecca continued. She outlined the arch of Zoe's lips, her gaze following the motion.

There was a mark of leisurely possession in the caress that left Zoe breathless. The contradiction of the storm rolling in those eyes and the softness of Becca's contact set her nerves tingling. She didn't want to mess up Rebecca's plan—she knew better than that by now—but, hot damn, now that they were here and this was really about to happen, she was already impatient with the slow pace. She settled her hands lightly on Becca's hips as a test.

Becca's gaze snapped to hers.

"Down." The snap Zoe had been waiting for crackled in Rebecca's voice. Rebecca pushed at her shoulders, and Zoe sat back on the bed behind her. The phallus made her feel awkward in a way she was unfamiliar with, but her smile was wide, regardless.

"All the way." Becca flicked her finger to indicate Zoe should lie back against the pillows.

She tried to ignore how eagerly she shuffled to follow the instruction.

Rebecca didn't take her eyes off Zoe's while she unbuttoned her blouse, pushing off her heels and kicking them under the bed.

"I've been thinking about this all day." She unzipped her skirt and smiled a little at the hitch in Zoe's breathing when it dropped to the floor. Stepping out carefully, Becca pushed her blouse off her shoulders to join the skirt. "About how I wanted you to fuck me." She crawled onto the bed in her camisole and panties, moving to all fours over Zoe's prone form. The strap-on almost brushed against her. "About letting you do it with this."

Zoe dragged her tongue over dry lips and took a slow, shaky breath. When Becca clicked it on, she clicked it *on*, and Zoe was just trying to catch up with her body's immediate reactions.

"About how bad you want it." Rebecca dipped her hips to catch the toy against the fabric of her underwear. She sat on Zoe's upper thighs and deliberately tilted her pelvis down until Zoe gasped at the pressure. "Tell me how bad you want me, Zoe."

God, her voice had turned all low and guttural in seconds, and Zoe just knew she was so screwed at the sound of it. She lost the battle with her own will and reached for Rebecca, her hands each grasping a rounded cheek. Pulling forward with her grip at the same time as she rolled her hips up, Zoe groaned at the friction from the inside of the harness and the sound of Rebecca's responding moan.

"Fuck, Becca. I—" She stopped in the middle of answering when Becca braced her hands on Zoe's shoulders and rubbed back. All Zoe could do was stare as Rebecca's eyes closed and her jaw dropped open. It was overwhelmingly sexy, and Zoe pressed her fingers harder into the soft curves of Rebecca's ass with a growling sort of noise. Becca's pale complexion would have Zoe's fingerprints branding her for at least a few days, and Zoe couldn't be happier. She ran her hands up Rebecca's back under the cami and started to sit up.

Rebecca pushed Zoe's shoulders down into the bed again, her hips still grinding against the shaft of the toy. "Nope." She was a little breathless, and she smiled lazily. "This is mine."

She leaned down for a kiss, and Zoe met her in the middle, straining to press her mouth to Rebecca's while her hands tangled in blonde hair. The kiss started hungry and turned deep and searching within moments.

Rebecca eased her back down to the pillow by deliberately slowing the pace, then pulled back.

Zoe stifled a whimper at the loss of contact, instead dropping her hands to palm indulgently over Rebecca's thighs just to keep touching her.

"And... I think you'll like what happens if you give me what I want." Rebecca pushed up onto her knees over Zoe and shoved her own panties down her thighs. When her progress was blocked by Zoe's hands, she paused to lift an eyebrow.

Zoe looked down to help Rebecca angle out of the underwear and was entranced by the gleaming wetness on the inside of the material. She was suddenly breathing much heavier, and her hands seemed to have lost basic motor function. The physical evidence of how much Rebecca wanted this had her insides twisting pleasurably and her brain lust-fried.

Rebecca leaned back down to all fours once she had successfully kicked the scrap of fabric off her ankle, and Zoe couldn't breathe at the sight. Rebecca's blonde hair was wild and eyes were dark, the look in them burning like a touch.

"That depends." Zoe's voice sounded scratchy to her own ears, and she wasn't sure where the response even came from. She looked down between them to where Rebecca had widened her knees a tiny bit, dropping her hips the barest inch until the head of the toy was almost touching her again. They were so close, and even though Zoe knew she couldn't actually feel it, her clit still twitched and throbbed with every teasing hint of pressure.

"Oh, does it?" Rebecca's smile could be heard in her words as she circled her hips in one direction and then the other, nudging against the toy with every twist. "What does it depend on, Zoe?" She scooted down a little more, and her lips just barely spread over the tip, her eyes falling closed with a slow inhale.

Zoe ground her teeth and decided she deserved a fucking medal or something for not just thrusting upwards, when everything in her was screaming to do just that. Instead she ran her hands up the outsides of

Rebecca's thighs, following the lines of her body to draw designs along the curves of each breast.

"It depends," she rasped with her palms full of Rebecca's breasts, squeezing softly before catching both nipples with her thumbs. "On what you want."

When Rebecca bowed her chest down into the touch, Zoe leaned up again to steal a kiss. She nibbled at Rebecca's lip while she rolled hard peaks between her fingers and twitched her hips. The head of the toy was still nestled just below Rebecca's clit, and Zoe's little move rubbed it back and forth over the swollen nub.

Rebecca gasped. Her hips jerked, the kiss abandoned as the silicone rubbed over her a second time. She panted into Zoe's neck, rocking against the minute friction.

"I want *you*." Rebecca moaned into Zoe's skin. She turned her chin and took Zoe's mouth again, then reached down between them. Gripping the toy in her fist, Rebecca positioned it against herself and growled, "I want you to let me ride your cock," as she started to slide down the shaft. When it was halfway inside, Rebecca dropped her forehead to the bed over Zoe's shoulder, gasping out, "Oh my God."

Zoe held her breath. Becca had stilled above her while she adjusted to the new feeling. She wasn't acting as if she was in pain, but Zoe knew she wasn't used to that particular kind of stretching sensation. Zoe stroked aimlessly over Rebecca's sides and back with soothing murmurs, dropping kisses to any skin she could reach.

It wasn't long before Rebecca's apprehension seemed to fade, and she pressed down to take the rest of the shaft with one long exhale. "Let me ride it until I come all over it."

Zoe's hips jerked at the words, and her hands gripped Rebecca tighter. She bit down on her lower lip until she thought she tasted blood to stop herself from moving; waiting against the pressure at her core took everything she had.

"Fuck."

Rebecca's gasp hissed directly into Zoe's ear. She dragged her nails down Becca's back at the sound of it, scoring half-moons into the curve of Rebecca's ass at the end. She pulled until Rebecca whimpered as her hips tilted and the toy shifted inside her, sucking at the spot behind Rebecca's ear that made her breath catch.

Rebecca lifted her head enough to kiss Zoe, using her thighs to raise herself oh-so-slowly, then sinking down again a little bit quicker than the retreat.

"God, Rebecca." Zoe couldn't help the lift of her hips. Every painstaking motion of Becca's body made the harness push and pull over her until she'd slicked the inside of it, the understraps slipping between her lips and causing the most perfect friction. She'd never quite understood how Rebecca was able to come sometimes from using this, but the experience was so overwhelming, she was starting to understand.

Zoe tried to pull herself together as Rebecca pumped up and down again, the rhythm starting to smooth out now that she'd gotten accustomed to the penetration. She felt so incredibly good, but she wanted Rebecca to feel that way, too. Zoe knew she couldn't lose herself if she wanted to make Rebecca scream.

"Can you give me what I want, Zoe?" Rebecca's cockiness had reappeared with her confidence, and she looked down at Zoe through her lashes with the rasp.

The wet sound of their bodies sliding together was distracting, and Zoe nodded before she managed to speak. "I'll give you so much more than that…" The words had sounded more forceful in Zoe's head, but what actually escaped her mouth was a breathless and airy promise. She used her hold on Rebecca's backside to guide the rocking of their bodies, rolling her hips with each thrust to meet Rebecca before sinking back down to the bed. They moved together in sync, their panting breaths and the dull thud of wet flesh connecting the only sounds other than the occasional protest from the bedsprings.

Rebecca pushed upright again, bracing her hands against Zoe's ribs with a drawn-out whine of her name as she continued to ride the toy.

"Tell me what you need." Zoe's voice was low even to her own ears, and Rebecca winced at the sound. Zoe roamed her hands over the delicious body over hers, groping her ribs and sides and breasts before dragging her fingers down Rebecca's stomach to stop just above where they were joined. Her thumb slipped through the wetness until she found the knot of Rebecca's clit, brushing over it a few times before circling tight and fast.

"Baby, your hand—fuck." Rebecca threw her head back with the exclamation, leaning against Zoe's raised knees at her back.

Zoe could feel Becca trembling, and she wanted so badly to roll them over and bury herself inside Rebecca over and over. She resisted the urge because she knew her girlfriend had to do this her own way. Instead she concentrated on tilting her hips to hit the spot she knew was along the forward surface of Rebecca's walls, pressing a little harder with her thumb when she felt a throb under her touch.

"That what you needed, Becca?" Zoe half-sat up and wrapped her arm around Rebecca's back, pulling them closer together so she could suck a nipple between her teeth. "You gonna come for me?"

Rebecca nodded with her eyes closed, little whimpers huffing out of her every time their bodies met, and her nails biting into the back of Zoe's neck where she was holding on.

"I'm so deep, Bec. Do you feel that?" Zoe hissed around the flesh between her teeth.

Rebecca moaned a long, low note, not even fully rising off the toy anymore as she sped up her movement.

"C'mon, baby. Come on my cock."

Rebecca froze as soon as Zoe's words filtered through the fog of sex, her brows furrowing as her mouth dropped open. "Zo-Zoe!" Her hips spasmed wildly, and Zoe could barely keep contact. She twisted her wrist to keep stroking over Rebecca's clit, trying to prolong the orgasm wracking her girlfriend's body. Reaching up to grab the back of Rebecca's neck, Zoe pulled their mouths together and slid her tongue between Rebecca's lips while she quaked and shivered. The kiss eventually slowed as Zoe pulled them down to the bed, her hips still rocking gently and receiving random spasms for her efforts.

Rebecca finally separated their mouths long moments later. She grinned lazily down at Zoe, her eyes soft with a teasing sparkle in them. "You talk about this thing like it's actually part of you." She twitched her hips against the toy still inside her, her grin widening when Zoe inhaled sharply through her nose.

"Yeah, well. You ride it like I can feel it." She bumped back to Rebecca's twitch, and their faces were close enough together that she actually watched Rebecca's pupils dilate at the sensation.

The smile dropped, and Becca lifted herself off the toy in one smooth motion. Zoe's protest was halted when Rebecca immediately scooted down her body until her face was level with the hard-on standing up proudly. She wrapped her fingers around the base and pressed down, watching Zoe watch her with darkened eyes and her lips parted. "Let's see how much you feel this."

Rebecca sucked the head into her mouth, sliding her lips down the shaft until it bumped the back of her throat. She used her hand to push the harness harder into Zoe's body beneath it, keeping the eye contact.

"Oh my God, Rebecca." Zoe couldn't wrap her brain around what she was seeing down her body, but she definitely couldn't look away, either. She stared enraptured, watching the toy slide between Rebecca's lips. The urge to thrust into her mouth was hard to deny, and Zoe settled for tangling her fingers in Rebecca's hair.

At the tug, Rebecca smiled around the toy.

Zoe felt two fingers dig around the side of the strap until they were slipping inside her easily, the feeling exactly what she hadn't realized she was craving.

Zoe was surprised at how quickly the combined sensations overtook her, robbing her breath and tightening her belly. She could've almost been embarrassed by her lack of staying power, if Rebecca weren't so distracting.

Rebecca slid the toy out of her mouth with a wet pop while Zoe's scream was still echoing around the room. She scooted back up to lay across Zoe's body, nuzzling into her neck while her fingers continued to curl rhythmically inside her until the clenching stopped.

They lay there panting for a few moments while the sweat cooled overheated skin and the scent of sex was thick around them.

"Holy shit, that was incredible." Zoe didn't even try to keep the wonder out of her voice. If she ever wanted this to happen again—it was so freaking happening again—she knew letting Rebecca know how amazing she felt was the first step.

"I told you you'd like it if you gave me what I want." Rebecca replied with the haughty and smug quip, and Zoe decided with certainty that yeah, this was so freaking happening again. And next time she was going to be on top.

FEAR OF FALLING

BY SASHA SAPPHIRE

I LEAN MY HEAD AGAINST THE plastic window, enjoying the vibrato as the plane's engines start up and we begin taxiing away from the terminal. *Time to go home*, I think, then realize I no longer have any idea what home means. I'd thought it was San Francisco and Inès.

How different Paris will seem to me after seven years in San Francisco. I catch a glimpse of the burnt orange bridge, through threads of wispy, playful fog, before the plane makes a sharp turn inland, and before long thick November clouds cover California. Was it that easy, saying good-bye?

I place myself mentally on the street outside the building on Vallejo and Webster, where I've lived in for the past five years with Inès. What is she doing in this exact moment? Is she crying, walking aimlessly around the apartment, lost without me? Is she peering into another empty wine glass, the way she so often was, hunched over her computer, typing slowly, drunkenly, when I returned home from working late? I force myself to hold onto these memories, rather than the other ones, the happy ones, the irresistible ones, but even after everything, I can't think of Inès without seeing those long, slim legs, the tanned, shimmery skin, her coils of bronze hair. I feel myself becoming wet just thinking about last night.

We should have known better, both of us. Our relationship has been over for several weeks and I was due to fly out this morning, but yet again we were overcome by the fire that defined our entire relationship, and before I knew it, we were tearing each other's clothes off, scratching at skin, licking and sucking each other forcefully, pushing our lower bodies together, grinding against each other feverishly, Inès' hands tugging at my hair, my urgent, dirty words trembling between us, until we almost simultaneously came, laughing and heaving.

"Excuse-moi, Madame?" A woman who can be described as nothing less than an absolute vision brings me out of my reverie. I've got the whole row to myself, and she's leaning across the aisle seat, smiling sweetly, having clearly asked me a question while I was entertaining my smutty Sapphic fantasies of last night. I blush.

"Umm, yes?" I ask.

"What would you like to drink?" she asks again, still smiling, exposing her incisors, which are very sharp, making my thoughts dart wildly to vampires. She sounds British, and her voice is low and smooth. On her chest there's a BA nametag that reads HELENA. I imagine kneeling in front of her, holding up the skirt of her flight attendant uniform, slitting her open with my tongue, sucking at her wetness.

"White wine would be great," I say, in English, and smile at her, giving her a slight wink. She doesn't blush, or look confused the way you'd imagine a straight woman might; rather, she holds my eye a long while, leaving her lips slightly parted, letting her tongue pass quickly over those strange, irresistible teeth while passing me my drink. The energy between us is palpable, and I have to fight myself to not reach out and undo the tight bun her hair is gathered in. I want to watch it tumble out across her shoulders.

"Are you very afraid?" she suddenly asks too loudly, and I look in confusion from her to her male colleague, who is waiting for her with the trolley. "If you like, I can come and sit with you in a while, once we've prepared the cabin for the night."

"I... Uh, yes that would be great," I say. "Very kind. I am terribly afraid of flying."

She winks at me and disappears towards the front of the aircraft, leaving me all but completely breathless.

———— ✦ ————

Helena slips soundlessly into the middle seat next to me, smiling that dreamy smile which conjures up afterthoughts of danger, thanks to those teeth.

"Would you like to hold my hand, and I'll try to explain to you some of the techniques I believe can help in conquering a fear of flying?"

I nod, and she takes my hand from where it was resting on my thigh, brushing against me. The cabin is almost entirely dark, and outside, a swollen moon hovers above the North Atlantic. I can only see one other passenger from where I'm sitting, an old man, and he appears to be sleeping. Thin rivulets of spit crawl down his face, weaving in and out of his scraggly white beard.

"What are you most afraid of?" Helena asks, her face close to mine and glinting in the moonlight. She looks slightly younger than me, and she is exquisite. I want to photograph her, framing her face in the Leica. I want her naked in front of me, running a moist finger up her inner thigh. I want to take pictures as she throws her head back and opens her mouth in a moan.

"I... I'm afraid of falling."

She smiles and says, "Many people are. It doesn't feel entirely natural, does it, flying? Are you good at breathing properly?"

"Umm, yes, I think so," I whisper.

"Here, let me feel." She puts one hand against my abdomen and one against my lower back, where my sweater has ridden up, exposing bare skin.

I take a breath and she laughs softly, tutting.

"You're practically holding your breath," she says. "No wonder you are so tense. What's your name?"

"Aurélie."

"That's such a beautiful name. And you are French?"

"Mmm," I say, "yes," attempting another deep breath, Helena's hands still on me.

"Do you know what I think you need?" she whispers, so close now that her breath is dancing, sweet, in my hair.

"No..."

"I want to tie you up."

"Tie me up?"

"Uh huh." Helena removes her hand from my abdomen and takes hold of my hand. She places it underneath her skirt, high up on her thigh, which is very warm and firm. I glance briefly around, then let my hand slide further up, then further still, and where her legs meet, there is no slit of fabric like I'd expected, just a hot, wet gash. I can't suppress a moan as I slide two fingers into her.

"Shhh," she whispers and giggles. I finger her hard but slow, feeling her grab my fingers with impressive muscle control. She spreads her legs more, and I want to unbuckle my seatbelt and slide to the floor and bury my face in her wetness, but instead, I bring my fingers out of her and into my mouth, sucking at the amazingly sweet taste of her pussy.

"Don't stop," she says, peering quickly around the darkened cabin.

"But I must."

"Why?"

"More when you tie me up…"

"But why?"

"I'm afraid of falling," I say, and she smiles again, a sweet smile this time.

"Deal," she says and leans forward so she's less than an inch from my face. I want to press my lips against hers so badly, I almost whimper.

"Take a cab to the Hotel Westin Vendôme after we land, and ask for Helena Aubrie at the front desk. I'll be expecting you."

She leans forward, and quick as a snake, slips her tongue into my mouth, flicking its tip against mine. Then she's standing, and after smoothing her skirt down, she walks quietly towards the front galley without turning back.

———◆◇◆———

I debate back and forth, all the way here. How wise is it, to be standing in a plush beige hallway at the Westin, holding a bottle of Perrier-Jouët, waiting for the door to be opened by a ravishing flight attendant I'm unlikely ever to see again after this encounter, when my heart is already practically pulverized? I'm tired, I'm overwhelmed and I'm lost, feeling the stress and heartache of the last few years crash over me again, but Helena opens the door to me with a wide smile, her hair flowing around her shoulders in gentle dark-brown curls. She is wearing a lacy black tank top and tight ripped jeans, and it is clear to me that I want her, and this, more than I have ever wanted anything in this life. Her lips are on mine before the door is even shut, and I throw my duffel bag to the floor and put my arms around her, drawing her in close, breathing her scent, which is at once both feminine and darkly spicy.

"I had to touch myself in the plane toilet before landing," she says and we both laugh, hungrily, looking into each other's eyes between deep, demanding kisses. "The way you touched me… Oh my God," she whispers into my ear, while putting those warm, thin hands inside my shirt, running them up and down my back before easily unbuckling my bra. She's equally smooth with the zip on my jeans, and within moments I am on the bed, pinned down beneath her, wearing only a tiny, see-through white lace G-string. She inches slowly down my body, letting her hair caress my skin as she goes, licking and biting my stomach, the insides of my thigh, my wrist, my ankles… She rubs her nose against my clitoris through the soaked slit of my underwear, and slips one finger into me, tugging the fabric aside. I'm aware of moaning, of saying her name over and over, and have the sensation of standing on the edge of a cliff, gazing into a dark abyss below. She pulls the underwear off me and begins licking me unbearably slowly, nibbling on the hood of my clitoris with those full, soft lips. I feel my orgasm gather and build but before I can come, she suddenly stops and comes back up and kisses me deeply, a salty taste of me on her tongue. I peel her clothes off quickly and begin touching her all over, and like she did with me, I avoid her most sensitive zones for as long as I can, focusing on caressing and kissing the backs of her knees, between her shoulder blades, behind her ear. Every now and then, I quickly slide two fingers into her, withdrawing them just as quickly, teasing her. She squirms beneath me, and begins to beg.

"Please…" she whispers, pushing her pelvis up, rubbing herself against me as I trail my tongue slowly down her chest. "Please… Aurélie… down, down," she moans, but I resist, pushing three fingers into her tight, wet pussy instead. She bites my shoulder, hard, and then kisses me until I can taste blood in my mouth. I want to stir the beast in her, to see her abandon her polished, honed façade and crawl across the debris of everything she thought was important to get to me, I want to make her scream, I want to slip inside her mind and heart and to fuck her brains out, over and over. She's practically whimpering and I can feel that she's getting very close to coming, so I stop and kiss the exact spot where her shoulder molds into her neck, very softly. Then I lift her on top of me, spreading her legs out on either side of mine so we're scissoring, and collectively, we are so wet, she has to push very hard against me, moving fast to create enough friction. I come, hard, holding onto a fistful of her hair with one hand, and a perfect, firm breast with the other, and I can feel her contracting too, and before she's totally finished, I slither back down and run my tongue slowly along her labia until I get to her clit, which I lick very slowly and very lightly. Helena begins whimpering, trembling beneath me, pulling hard at my hair, and I slip two fingers into her pussy which is still contracting with her last orgasm, and feel her surge towards another one.

— ✦ —

I don't know what I expected for this morning; when we finally drifted off to sleep, holding onto each other's sweaty, spent bodies. Any thoughts were beyond me. But I didn't expect to see Helena sitting on a chair across from the bed, watching me, her eyes spilling over with tears. She's wearing nothing except a thick, white robe with "Westin Paris" embossed in swirly, gold writing over her right breast. I sit up fast and open my mouth to speak, but she swiftly brings her index finger to her lips and shakes her head quickly, closing her eyes hard, making more tears scatter down her face.

I walk over to her, feeling slightly self-conscious in the daylight, and kneel down on the floor next to her chair. I reach for her, and she collapses into my arms, sobs shaking her entire body. I feel terrible and try to think whether I've said or done something she wasn't comfortable with.

"I'm married," she whispers, finally.

I feel like something cold and ugly has been poured all over me and I push her away from me. Not hard, but enough. I don't want to sit here, holding someone else's wife.

Then she whispers, "To a man."

This, of course, is even worse. I feel so used, like something she just picked up and is now throwing away so that she can go back to her cozy, little heterosexual life.

"Are you angry?" She asks, in a low, weak voice as I get dressed as quickly as I got undressed last night.

"You could have told me."

"I didn't know how. You wouldn't have come here."

"Damn right I wouldn't."

"I don't think you understand," she says, wiping at more tears. "I really don't think you understand."

"Don't you think that I, too, have had to go through the process of coming to terms with who I am and what my orientation is?"

"I know we don't know each other very well, but within a second of laying eyes on you, I just…knew."

"Knew what, exactly?" I could hear the bitterness in my own voice… taste it.

"That it would be you. That we would…know each other."

I look at her, so vulnerable and small, drowning in the swathes of that big robe, and see sudden flashbacks of last night; of running my tongue in and around every crevice of her body, of laughing and drinking wine in bed after all the sex, of that first slow, sexy smile on the airplane, and I realize she's right. I felt it too, that we would know each other.

Silently, at first, I lead her by the hand over to the bed and fling the robe into a corner, closing my lips around one of her nipples.

"Come with me," I say, locking my gaze on hers, and she nods, swaying before me as I plant kisses down her tummy.

"Where?" she whispers.

"I'm going to Costa Rica next week, to stay in a cabin in the rain forest, taking pictures. Come." I kiss the top of her pubic bone and she lays back, spreading her legs for me. I lightly kiss and lick the pink folds, feeling her become wetter at my touch, and suddenly, maybe because of what she's told me, I want to fuck her with a strap-on, like a man. I want to hurt her, though only slightly. I want to watch her squirm and tremble as I slam into her, harder and harder, until she begs me to stop, and then I'd go down on her again, gently, gently...

"Yes," she whispers, then says it, then shouts it as I feel her approach orgasm. I'm massaging her clitoris with my index finger while sticking my tongue as far as I can up into her. "Yes!" I presume she's exclaiming out of passion and excitement, but after, when I've come too, when we are snuggling, tightly wound in each other, she says, "Of course I'll come with you."

In Costa Rica, Helena and I spend long mornings in bed, exploring each other; old faded scars, soft folds, warm skin shivering at an unexpected touch, searching mouths, sweaty lashes of hair under eager fingertips, and we emerge onto the teak deck that overlooks the jungle only when we can resist food and bathroom no longer. We then inevitably retreat back to the bedroom, sleeping close together for several hours beneath wispy muslin curtains when the sun is at its hottest. In the afternoons we wander around, never far from the eco camp we're staying at, while I photograph minute forest details, like a globule of rainwater suspended from a gnarled branch, or an iridescent insect wing discarded on squelchy red earth. I photograph her, too, my newfound muse. Helena swaying to the beat of rain under a canopy of waxy leaves. Helena leaning in to kiss me, the Leica catching a blurry edge of her face. Helena in bed, legs spread, shadows falling onto her, obscuring her lower half slightly, but scattering moonlight on her breasts.

At night we make love until our touch becomes slow and inconsistent and we drift off to sleep, until one of us wakes in the middle of the night, continuing where we left off, rousing the other from dreams with the touch of a soft, wet tongue.

"Don't leave me," she whispers to me on our second to last night.

"It isn't me who is doing the leaving," I whisper back, but turned away from her, so she has to mold herself around me in spoons. After a while, I can tell from her slightly jerking movements that she is crying, and I turn back round to face her, kissing away big tears falling from her eyes like beads from a broken necklace.

"What if I didn't leave you?" she says, eventually, burying her thin fingers in the hair at the nape of my neck.

"Then you have to leave *him*," I say.

The tears keep coming.

And then, this morning, she is propped up on her elbows in bed, watching me, when I wake.

"Tell me about your apartment in Paris," she says, with a gentle, radiant smile.

"It's on the fifth floor," I reply. "No elevator."

Helena nods and closes her eyes, as though imagining herself there.

"It has a big bedroom painted mauve, and a smaller room that I've turned into a darkroom," I continue, "and an open plan kitchen/dining room with two huge antique chandeliers. It's my favorite room in the world, and I can't wait to move back there."

"What do you mean?" asks Helena, and I wish I hadn't blurted out that I'd be returning to the apartment from somewhere else. "Have you not been living there for a long time?"

"I lived with my ex in San Francisco until fairly recently," I say, fixing my gaze on a spot high up on the ceiling, and as if on cue, a tiny gecko darts across it.

"A woman?" asks Helena.

"Yes."

"What was her name?"

"Inès."

"How long were you with her?"

"Six years."

"Wow. Have you ever been with a man?" she asks.

"Sexually, yes, on a couple of occasions. In a relationship, no."

"I suppose I'm the other way round. I've never been in a relationship with another woman, though I've had a couple of short-lived sexual relationships with women. I guess I never met a woman I wanted to pursue a relationship with, you know, like a full-on, fully-out, love relationship."

Her voice is so soft and pleasant in the still, near-darkness of the early dawn that I find myself zoning out slightly to the sound of it, but I snap back to attention when she says, "Until now."

I prop myself up on my elbows, too, so we lie facing each other, and Helena leans in and kisses me hard on the lips.

"I'm afraid," she says, smiling, but her eyes are wide and anxious.

"What are you afraid of?" I say, taking her hand and putting it on my left breast, so she can hear the skittish beat of my heart.

"Falling," she whispers.

I put my lips to a spot just above her left breast, feeling her heart thud against my lips, before coming back up to kiss her again deeply. We break away and look at each other, the trail of her tears still visible on her face. I ran a hand slowly up the inside of her thigh, my eyes never leaving hers for a moment, until I reach the spot where they met and ease a finger into her, withdrawing it very slowly, then pushing two back inside her. She trembles with my touch, but pushes herself hard against my fingers, becoming tighter and tighter as her orgasm builds, and when I feel she is nearing climax, I slip down and tease her clit with a firm, wet tongue. She has me in a headlock with her thin brown legs and her hands are in my hair, pulling it as hard as she came.

And after, when she's caught her breath and her legs have stopped shaking, she lies on top of me and scissors her legs with mine, so that we meet in a burst of wetness. She builds a delicious rhythm, and soon I come too, crying out as I do, and Helena silences me with her hard, searching kisses.

———◆━◇━◆———

"We could just live here, you and I, among the trees and the giant, rustling beetles, taking pictures and being together," says Helena, and we both laugh a little, letting our gazes sweep across this strange little hut that has been our room, our home, our very universe, this past week. Night is falling and mosquitoes are buzzing noisily around us. We are drinking a fine Argentine oaky chardonnay from lumpy, eco-center clay cups, and the Leica is on the table between us, Helena's face is vivid and beautiful in the light of the moon, which is just peeking above the trees. It is the last night, and tomorrow this will all be over. I'll return to Paris, alone, and Helena will return to her husband in London. What else is there to do? Dismantle long-established lives to pursue an impossible fantasy?

"We could," I say, "but we're not going to. You'd tire of me." I tease, but it isn't funny because we are both acutely aware of the seriousness in the undertones.

"Nothing could ever be this good in the long-run," said Helena, earlier, when we lay tightly wound in each other's arms, but I could tell from the way she spoke that it was a question rather than a statement. I ignored her, because on so many levels I am furious with myself for getting involved with someone new who is unavailable. But she is different, and a part of me actually believes that Helena and I would be this good in the long-run, whether we lived in a tree hut at a Costa Rican jungle eco camp, or in my bourgeois apartment, or even on a boat, a rolling little thing, bobbing around on Azure waters somewhere far away, where we could be together.

"I'd never tire of you," she says, now, fixing me with eyes so intense and full of feeling that I feel myself come undone just at the sight of her.

"You would," I say feebly, and take my eyes away from her, gazing back around this little hut high up in a tree, partially hidden in foliage, where two women sit on a wicker porch, loving each other, drinking chardonnay in the moonlight.

"I would not," she says, firmly, and reaches for my hand. On her ring finger is a pale band of flesh, the ghost of her wedding ring, which she'd taken off before coming here. And then she is sitting astride me again, pulling at my hair and my clothes, pushing her tongue into my mouth where it flickers deliciously against mine, freeing my breasts and taking them into small, warm hands.

"Come to Paris, then," I say, into the web of her hair, in spite of myself, in spite of everything. We break apart, disheveled and laughing, and stare at each other a long while, marveling at this night, this love.

"Yes."

After we've finished making love a second time, we stand closely together at the end of the wicker porch, looking down at the eerily illuminated eco camp far below, smoking a shared Vogue menthol slim cigarette.

"Are you still afraid of falling?" asks Helena.

"Nope," I answer. "Too late for that."

We both laugh softly, then I crush the cigarette into the empty wine bottle and we return to bed.

DINNER AND A SHOW

BY CATHERINE LANE

"What're you doing?"

I looked down to the plate of perfectly roasted chicken on the counter and then to the drumstick in my hand. "Eating."

I would've thought it was obvious.

My wife raised her hand in that defensive motion that she had picked up in the last year or two. "Trista's cooking dinner, you know."

I almost snorted the chicken out of my mouth. "Brown rice noodles because she doesn't eat gluten. Soy meatballs because she's a vegan. Tomato sauce without sugar or salt because she's a crazy health nut. She may be cooking, but believe me, it's not dinner."

Carin's hand, which was raised in objection only a minute before, shot out toward the chicken. "You're right. Can I have a piece, please?"

I handed over the drumstick, because it was her favorite, and tore off a piece of the breast for myself. We munched for a while in comfortable silence while I rolled the coming evening around in my head. Dinners with Trista came in only one flavor—barely edible food and predictable conversation. After two bites of a meal that resembled spaghetti and meatballs in name only, Trista would pick up her wine glass, throw her shoulders back, and regal us with crazy stories of her days as editor-and-chief of *Trim and True* magazine. I have to say, her adventures were funny and entertaining the first time, and even maybe the second, but on the third and fourth go-around... Well, let's just say I had to bite my tongue not to recite the stories right along with her.

Carin said she enjoyed the evenings, and that's why we went. She and Trista had a lot in common: obsessions with physical fitness, hiking, trekking in Nepal—which Trista had actually done and my wife had just dreamed about. But I'm not sure how closely Carin was listening, anyway. Her eyes would glitter with excitement as she watched Trista bounce about the kitchen in athletic clothes so tight they could've been painted on. The way she pivoted at the stove and whirled around the kitchen gave us an up close and personal view of firm breasts, a tight ass, and everything in between. I didn't blame Carin. If I'm being honest, I didn't mind the show, either. In fact, Trista's taut, little body made up a lot for the *I had a really crazy day at my super cool job* stories.

"What do you think she's going to be like?" Carin brought me back to the present as she dropped the chicken bone into the sink.

"Who?"

"PJ. The new girlfriend."

"She's going to be there? Really?"

"Yeah. She's staying with Trista all this week. I told you."

"And Addie? Is she going to be there, too?"

"I guess so. I mean, isn't she always?" Our gazes met and we both broke into wide, happy grins. Suddenly, this evening had taken a very exciting turn.

Trista's love life, to say the least, was complicated. Trista was out and proud. I had caught her looking at my chest enough times to be one-hundred-percent sure on that point, and if that weren't enough, she flew a rainbow flag on her front porch. But Addie, her best friend, claimed to be as straight as they came. Even so, she sniffed around Trista like a dog in heat. They didn't live together, but they might as well have. Addie had a key and was always, always there. Once, when Addie had the flu, we had heard pitiful, little moans coming from the guest room right off the kitchen as we twirled the brown rice pasta on our forks. Together, the *best friends* acted more like a couple than Carin and I, and we had been together for twelve years and shared two children, one dog and several revolving goldfish and hamsters.

"Let's go." I pulled the plate away from Carin, curled the plastic wrap back over the leftovers and shoved them back into the fridge.

"Now you're all gung-ho?"

"Yeah. I didn't realize that there was going to be dinner and a show."

Carin punched me squarely on the shoulder. "You're terrible."

"Ouch," I said in a playful whine. "You want to stay home, order a gluten-filled pizza with both fat and meat? We could mess around." Actually, with the kids at my parents' for the night, that alternative didn't sound at all bad.

"No way." She grabbed two bottles of the organic, nitrate-free wine from the counter. "I want to see what kind of girl Trista attracts. I bet she's gonna be just like her, with long hair, lipstick and little diamond earrings."

"I don't know. There's always a chance she's a jock. Opposites attract."

"Want to bet?" Carin raised her eyebrows in a challenge.

"Ten minute foot rub when we get home for the winner?" I thrust out my hand for a shake.

"Deal." She met my hand with a clap, and we grinned at each other once again.

When we got to her house, Trista welcomed us at the door with fierce but quick hugs. She always grabbed us as if she were marking her territory in some way.

Tonight, the hug lasted a little longer than usual, and it came with a heat that had never been there before. "So glad you came." Trista met my gaze and then dropped her eyes, paying her usual and flattering attention to my chest. "Oh, thank you. You brought wine."

How she actually saw the wine, I couldn't guess. I wasn't carrying it in my cleavage.

Our host was dressed in her usual pink and black Athletica workout clothes. Skin-tight and smelling of fresh lavender, they said it all. Trista was an incredibly fit woman who had walked out of the pages of her own magazine. She stepped back and invited us into her house.

As soon as I crossed over the threshold, something shifted in the air—a force, an energy so strong that it almost sucked the air from my lungs.

A woman, almost as tall as I was, stood smack in the middle of the entryway. Somehow she took up way more space than she should've, and I had to fight an urge to step closer just to feel that force more completely.

Black, wavy hair framed an oval face. She was looking down at Trista's cat, who was twisting himself around her legs, and then she raised her head. Her eyes were a deep, deep brown, almost black, and her gaze immediately, almost hungrily lit on me.

"Hi, I'm PJ." She approached with an outstretched hand. Her T-shirt, a basketball design with GIRLS RULE in big, curling letters, read as more of an announcement than a fashion statement, and the way her stride ate up the space told me she was an athlete. From the looks of it, probably a pretty good one.

"Oh, that's right," Trista said with a slight blush darting across her cheeks. "You guys don't know each other."

I reached my hand out, eager to meet the woman who could make Trista, the control freak, flustered. We shook, and then I knew how. My pulse leapt when our hands met. Her touch was almost electric and drove a jolt right up my arm.

"So where'd you play?" PJ asked.

"Play what?" I was dazed. "You mean basketball?"

PJ's gaze locked with mine—unsettling to say the least since our eyes were almost level, not an experience I had very often.

"Oregon St. But that was years..."

"Good program. So you're a Beaver?" I waited for the inevitable, crass joke, but, thankfully, it didn't come. She shifted to Carin's hand and pumped it once.

"How did you know?" I asked.

PJ grabbed my hand again and spread my fingers with her own. Another shiver ran through me. Trista stiffened. Annoyance and jealously rolled off her in a waves.

"The handshake," PJ said. "People who've handled a ball their entire lives have a certain touch."

"Really?" I pulled my hand out of PJ's and looked at my own fingers.

"You still play, too."

"Not really. I just coach. High school."

"PJ coaches, too. In college." Trista gave me an *eat that* kind of look, then linked her arm through PJ's possessively, dragging her away from us into the kitchen.

"I win. She's a jock," I said to Carin as she passed me.

"I think we both win." She wore a bemused expression as her gaze followed Trista and PJ. "This evening is going to be very interesting."

We moved from the closed-in entry hall into the great room. Trista's house spread all around us in a modern, open-concept plan where the living room ran into the dining room and kitchen without doors or walls. All of the bedrooms were just a step off the great room in every direction. It was perfect for a single person without kids, dogs, fish or hamsters. Instead of pictures, great big mirrors adorned the walls. They were works of art in themselves with ornate metallic frames. It wasn't until I had seen Trista glance at herself in first one, then another during our introductory dinner did I understand that Trista always needed an audience, even when she was alone.

"Hello, Carin, Eliza." Addie's voice was cold enough to freeze water. Dressed in a crisp blouse and straight skirt, she had apparently come straight from work and now stood in the kitchen stirring the red sauce. Despite the task, she couldn't take her eyes off Trista's arm laced though PJ's. "You're just in time. Dinner's almost ready."

"Sit down." PJ took command and pulled out a chair for me at the round table between the kitchen and the living room. Everyone's gaze hit me as we all jockeyed around the table: PJ looked as if she could eat me up with dinner; Trista seemed as if she would blow a gasket at any second; Addie was so green with jealously that she looked as if she would be ill. Only Carin, who still wore that bemused expression, was unfazed. She broke the silence by raking her chair across the floor and plopping down.

"I'm starving," she said. "What's for dinner?" She threw me a secret smile at our inside joke as I slid into my seat. PJ immediately took possession of the chair next to me as Trista pursed her lips beside us.

"Trista, can you give me a hand?" Addie asked.

Trista stood for a long moment glaring at the space between me and her girlfriend, and then finally moved into the kitchen area. She worked like a whirling dervish to get the pasta off the stove and into the colander in the sink. She ladled it up into the ceramic bowls on the counter as the globs of rice spaghetti dropped into the bowls with unappetizing plopping noises. She then slid them to Addie, who spooned on the sauce. Trista grabbed one bowl with each hand and walked them over to the table, placing them in front of PJ and the empty chair on the other side. She sat down and scooted the chair closer to her girlfriend.

"You forgot the meatballs." Addie brought the whole pan of them to the table and scooped three into each of the bowls.

Carin jumped up to help, which earned her a grateful look. I would've too, but suddenly PJ's arm was on mine with a force so possessive it pinned me in place.

"So what kind of offence do you run?"

"Uh….." I looked to Carin for help, but she was at the stove doing something with the sauce. Trista was ready to shoot daggers out of her eyes, but what was I supposed to do? Not answer the woman? "High-low."

"How do you penetrate the ball if you're running a high-low?"

"Let's not talk sports at the table," Trista said, filling her wine glass up almost to the brim with one of the bottles we brought, which had somehow found its way to the table.

"Come on, babe. It's not often I get to talk to a high school coach. It's interesting to me to see what the girls know before they get to us."

326

"No," Carin said as she filled up her own glass. "Eliza coaches a high school boys' team."

"Really? Athletic directors almost never give a boys' team to a woman coach. You must be really good." Respect darted into PJ's eyes. Sudden awareness of just how close she was prickled across my skin, and goose bumps ran up my arm where her hand still rested.

"It's a progressive private school." I pulled my arm into my lap and away from PJ's radiating energy.

"They're 5-0 this season." Carin's bemused expression had turned into full-on amusement. Her eyes sparkled with delight. I threw her a look asking her to tone it down. She was enjoying everyone's discomfort, especially mine, a little too much. "And they're playing without a true center."

"Now that's really impressive," PJ said and shifted her chair just a smidge in my direction.

And that's all it took. Trista slammed her glass down so hard, the bright red wine sloshed over the brim and spread out on the tablecloth like blood from a wound. She scraped her chair back and stormed out of the room through the first threshold on the right, that same room where Addie had suffered from the flu. Trista closed the door with a loud slam, so hard that a mirror on the opposite wall rattled in response.

"Oops." PJ blotted the wine that was edging toward her with a napkin. "My bad."

Then she too slid out of her seat and moved toward the guest room. On her way, she ran her hand across my back; her fingers lingered suggestively at the nape of my neck before making their way to my other shoulder. She disappeared inside the room, closing the door with a gentle click.

Trista started speaking. Not loud enough to make out exactly what she was saying through the closed door, but the heated tone of her words spoke volumes about how mad she was.

I looked at Carin, who met my questioning gaze with one of her own. "What do we do?" I mouthed silently.

She shrugged; the smile had died on her face. A deep sigh came from kitchen, and we shifted our attention to Addie. She looked as if her heart were breaking. She stood by the stove cradling three bowls of pasta and meatballs in her hands. Without a word she deposited a bowl in front of each of us, then dropped to her own chair and began to spoon the noodles into her mouth without looking up.

Another unintelligible string of words from the other room, this time from PJ. She was mad, too.

"How was your day, Addie?" I asked.

She looked up at me, her eyes narrowed to almost two slivers in her agony. "I've had better." Her gaze drifted to the closed door to the bedroom right off the great room.

Why had Trista chosen the guest room to throw her tantrum? Her bedroom would've been far more private, but then the realization hit me. Trista didn't want her hissy fit to be in some remote room; she wanted to throw it right in all of our faces.

"Fuck you!" She raised her voice just enough for us all to hear.

"Fine!" PJ's response was also loud and clear.

And then there was silence.

At the table, we three froze, waiting for what came next. But there was nothing. The quiet stretched out for so long that Addie began to squirm in her chair. I glanced again at Carin as if to ask "what do we do?", but her eyes were down on the pile of pasta in her bowl.

Suddenly there was a soft thump, as if one had pushed the other onto the bed. Then someone, I couldn't tell who, groaned with passion—a deep, guttural sound. My body reacted before it even registered in my mind. Heat flared up in me, and my center tightened with a jolt that ran straight to my groin.

It was so weird to hear the noise without seeing the action. Carin and I always turned off the sound when we slipped in one of the two girl-on-girl DVDs that we owned. The video seemed so fake, but this was the sound of real lovemaking.

I liked it!

Soft moaning, just barely audible, started up. I felt my nipples harden inside my shirt. I enjoyed the noises coming out of the room way too much.

"Maybe we should go," I said, starting to get up from the chair.

"No," Addie said. "I'll take care of this." Her green eyes had turned steely with purpose. She took the four steps to the door and opened it without knocking.

"Trista, you need to..." Her words died instantly on her tongue as she flinched at whatever was going on inside.

What was it? I craned my neck to try to look around her, but her body blocked the view. And then a motion out of the corner of my eye caught my attention. There on the wall opposite the guest room, the whole scene was playing out in one of Trista's big ornate mirrors, which was angled in just the right way to give me an up-close and personal view into the room.

Hot damn!

Trista, naked from the waist down, knelt with one knee on the bed, her back to PJ and now to Addie and me. The other leg was stretched out on the rail of the footboard at the end of the bed, and the position spread her legs open in the most delectable way. Trista's pink, soft sex was thrust out and back and unfurled for everyone who was looking.

And believe me, I was looking.

PJ's head was right there and left no question, at all, about what she was doing when Addie barged in.

PJ sat back on her heels. I couldn't see her face, but her body language was calm and controlled.

Trista turned her head just enough so she could meet Addie's gaze. "Join us," she said, her voice raspy and still a little breathless.

Addie took a step back, but PJ slid a hand to her calf and pulled her very gently into the room. "You can just watch."

"You want to, don't you?" Trista stared hungrily at Addie.

"Yes," Addie finally choked out.

Trista reached out her hand as an invitation, and when Addie slipped her hand into Trista's, she pulled her onto the bed. They formed a perfect twosome. I felt it rather than saw. The door, left ajar when Addie had stormed in, cut off their heads in the reflection in the mirror, and while I could see most of Trista's torso, Addie's face and reactions were lost to me. I yearned to reach into the mirror and reposition them all so I could see every delicious detail.

No such luck. Addie did something. What, I didn't know. Trista responded by yanking her shirt up and over her head. For the first time in over dozen dinners at Trista's house I saw the true benefits of her diet of denial.

Her body was magnificent—smooth and taut, not an ounce of fat, with curves and muscles in all the right places. But I could only see her back.

Turn around. Turn around.

And then she did. She twisted her torso to PJ and gave me the view I wanted. Trista's breasts were pert and made for nuzzling. Her nipples were already hard. I sucked in a breath.

"That felt great," she said to PJ, the anger long gone. "Start again?"

PJ rocked up on her knees and then to her feet, turning quickly toward the door. Were they going to shut us out? Panic raced through my body, especially when PJ's hand circled the door handle.

Please, don't close it. Please, don't close it.

As if she had heard me, PJ met my gaze in the mirror. As our eyes locked, a sexy, hot-to-trot smile jumped to her lips before she threw me an air kiss. Then she opened the door wider, so the reflection in the mirror caught the entire room. More importantly, it caught another mirror over a chest of drawers in the back corner. It was like a movie. I had the back view of Trista on the bed in the mirror in the great room and, shifting my gaze to the mirror in the bedroom, I had the front view of Trista. In short, I could see everything. Addie knelt on the bed only inches away from Trista.

Forget the dinner. The show came first. Oh boy!

I looked to Carin. Her eyes burned with anticipation and excitement. I didn't have to ask if she had as good a view as I did.

"Do you want to go?" My voice came out low and breathy. I prayed she didn't, but I wasn't going to stay if this was going to come between us in any way.

She shook her head. Relief whipped through me followed quickly by a slow heat that was just starting to radiate in my chest.

"Then come here." I tilted my head, inviting her closer.

She grinned, scooted closer, and I pulled her onto my lap. Carin was smaller than I was in almost every way, and her weight felt comfortable on my legs. I drew her body against mine, and she went lax with both desire and trust. I slid my hand up and under her shirt. Her skin felt hot to the touch. I nuzzled the back of her neck with my lips. She was warm there too, and already I could smell her arousal rising off her body. The scent was heady and intoxicating.

My gaze drifted over Carin's shoulder and back to the room. Things were in full swing. PJ had returned to her place between Trista's legs and her head bobbed up and down in a rhythm that made Trista moan with pleasure.

Trista grabbed Addie's hand and placed it on her breast. Addie pulled her hand back so quickly as if it had touched a fire.

"She's not ready." Carin said so softly her words were little more than a breath.

"Are you?" I asked. My fingers pushed up under her bra to tug at her nipple. It hardened immediately as a soft moan escaped her lips. I had my answer.

I rolled and squeezed her whole breasts—the nipples hot little nubs of heat at the center of my palms. Her back arched at my touch, and she thrust her body into my hands as if we would meld together.

"That's it. Right there," Trista cried. PJ had both hands clamped on Trista's behind to keep her in place while she dove into her with enthusiasm. But the real show was on the bed. Somehow Trista had fought through Addie's embarrassment, and Addie's hands traced wide circles around Trista's breasts. In the mirror in the bedroom they were pert, erect, and a huge turn on.

"Touch me. Please" Trista locked eyes with Addie and guided hand to her nipples. Addie slid her hand over one. Trista moaned with pleasure. "Squeeze it," she said hoarsely.

Out in the great room, I clasped both of Carin's breasts.

Addie gave Trista's breast a tentative squeeze.

"Harder," Trista commanded. Both Addie and I obeyed.

"My nipples," Trista said.

I tugged at Carin's nipples as Addie rolled her fingers over Trista's.

"PJ. Inside. Now," Trista said in her best editor-in-chief tone. There was no doubt in her voice that everyone would now jump to her demands.

PJ slid a hand from her behind and plunged it into Trista. Her hips bucked back, inviting the touch. There was nothing tender about PJ's movements, as she greedily possessed all that Trista offered her.

I, too, dropped my hand and found my way under Carin's skirt and into her underwear. She opened her legs for me so my entry was easy. She was so wet and snug. A moan escaped my lips as she ground into my hand. Immediately she tightened around me and I began to drive into her, moving my fingers to hit every part of her.

Fast and furious and full of passion, I matched PJ stroke for stroke. All five of us moved in unison, even Addie, who had dropped her head to nuzzle Trista's neck. Trista writhed in pleasure at the touch, and she gently guided Addie's head and mouth to her breasts. When Addie's mouth covered her nipple, Trista's groan of lust even made me shiver.

PJ's mouth dropped back to the apex between her thighs as she sucked and stroked every part of her. I too responded by forcing my other hand into Carin's underwear and inside her slick, soft folds to find that swollen place at the top. It was burning hot. She arched against my hand as I circled that one spot that I knew would send Carin into convulsions.

She was close. So was Trista. The moans coming from the bedroom rose an octave. Trista never did know how to do anything in halves, luckily for us. I was drawn in completely. And so was Carin. Her soft warmth clamped against my fingers. My other hand rolled, squeezed and pulled her clit until I could feel the heat and tension build almost to the breaking point.

"Make me come," Trista cried out from the other room.

I drove into Carin as she burst and rollicked around me, lost in the joy of my touch and naughtiness of the moment. At the same time, Trista cried out long and loud. She writhed as if she would break in two. Then her whole body stiffened as she rode out the intensity that racked her body. The performance ended with a deep sob and a collapse against Addie, who wrapped her arms around Trista and pulled her into her chest.

Trista clamped her legs shut, pushing PJ away from her as if now that the deed was done, Trista had no use for her supposed girlfriend anymore. PJ stood for a moment watching the pair on the bed. No mirror caught her face, but I could see as she shuffled back and forth on her balls of her feet, unsure what to do next.

Finally she turned toward us. Carin still quivered in my arms, and when PJ gathered what we had been up to, excitement leapt into her gaze. We both bounced up, Carin yanking down her skirt.

"There's another room down the hall," she said, her voice low with arousal.

I was worked up; there was no doubt about that. Everything in me pulsed with a need so strong I could barely speak. What I had just seen and what I had just done to Carin had put me so close to the edge, I could almost tip over it myself.

To my utter surprise, however, the last place I wanted to go was into that other room down the hall with PJ.

I shook my head and backed away from her.

"Sorry, PJ, she's mine." Carin took a step in front of me, her small body big with intent. "I'm not sharing."

PJ must have heard the determination in her answer, because she didn't argue.

Carin took my hand and led me to the front door.

"I'm serious, Eliza," she said as soon as we stepped over the threshold. "I want you all to myself, and I want you now." She dug the keys to the mini-van out of her pocket. A double beep and the passenger door slid open electronically. "Get in."

I climbed in to the main cab, where she pushed me into the bank of grey seats. The soft but aggressive shove turned me on even more. Then she reached around me for the seat rest and yanked the lever so the seat fell back and put me in a prone position.

"Top off." The door slid closed on its track. I strained at my shirt, and she helped to ease it over my head, then yanked my bra off with a practiced snap.

Her mouth was on my breasts before I even knew it. Her teeth teased my nipple, rolling it around in her mouth and savoring it. She released me and for a moment panted into my skin.

"God, Liza. I want you so much."

"I'm yours."

She returned to my breasts, teasing me into a near frenzy, before fumbling with my jeans button and zipper. She yanked my pants down and chafed my skin ripping my underwear down my legs. The elastic caught on my hip and dug into my sensitive flesh. I was so aroused that even the slight pain darting through me made me quicken. One of her hands dropped between my legs almost before my underwear was clear of my thighs. I spread shamelessly for her, my body arching in the anticipation of her touch. She didn't make me wait, thank God. Her finger slid inside me easily.

"You're so wet," she said, her words hoarse with lust.

I strained against the seat as I clenched eagerly around her hand, pulling her closer to my aching need. What had gone on inside had been hot, really hot, but this was better than hot. My eyes closed with the excruciating touch that was grounded in both lust and love.

I moaned. She pulled out and immediately pushed back in with two fingers. A shudder ran completely through me.

"Oh God." I braced myself on the armrests of the seat. My hips began to thrust against her hand as it drove deeper and deeper inside me.

Carin was breathing hard now, too. She curved over me and crushed my lips to hers. The first kiss of the entire night, aggressive and gentle all at the same time. Her lips were soft and yielding, but her tongue plunged inside my mouth with a pressure that made me writhe in pleasure.

I pressed my entire body against her and kissed her back. Hard. Our tongues met and stroked back and forth, quickly finding the same rhythm of her fingers below. She was driving into me on both ends, and her fingers seemed to be everywhere, stroking and probing, until she found that one sweet spot. She hit it once and then again as her fingers took full possession of me. My hips churned and my thighs clenched in response. I cried out as she drove me closer and closer to release.

"That's it, baby. You're so tight. I can feel how close you are."

She was right. I felt my orgasm building in monumental leaps with every stroke of her fingers. All feeling rushed to the center of my body. She plunged deep in me one final time, and I lost it. Every part of me tightened and tensed. I was so taut I thought I would explode. And then I did. My release rolled through me with an intense surge of pleasure and passion. A burst of fiery heat pulsed through my body as I quivered around her fingers, which were spread wide inside me, filling me completely.

"Oh God," I cried. The last waves of the orgasm made me buck up against her, my hands still gripping the armrest until my tremors subsided.

I sank back into the seat, breathing heavily with the aftermath of desire. As Carin's hand fell out of me, I sighed deeply.

"Oh, no you don't," Carin said. "We're not done yet."

I opened my eyes to look into hers. They were so close I could see the honey flakes in the deeper brown. They shone with love and, frankly much to my surprise, still with lust. She sank to her knees on the car floor and lifted my legs over her shoulders until they straddled either side of her head. My sex was still throbbing from our first go-around, and as the cool air from inside the car hit it, I shuddered. I couldn't remember a time, even in the beginning of our relationship, when I had felt so raw, so sensitive.

"Oh, sweetie." She leaned in and blew a hot breath over me. Her warmth mingled with mine, and desire ignited once again in me. My legs flexed against her back and my hips bucked slightly, bringing me closer to her mouth. She lowered her lips onto my throbbing clit until she just barely touched it. She didn't move, waiting until I relaxed into her. Then slowly she slid her soft tongue between my folds. First she used a darting motion, and then she held still without any real intent. She knew me so well. I was still so swollen and responsive that even the barest touch was something between agony and pleasure.

We stayed like that for a long moment until my hips moved slightly of their own accord, pushing me into her mouth. My wetness met hers, and she groaned in response. Her tongue flickered over my swollen clit.

My turn to moan. It felt so damn good. My hands rose to her head, and I tangled my fingers in her hair. If I could, I would've climbed inside her. As it was, she pushed her tongue inside me, sweeping along one side and then the other. My head pushed into the seat rest as I began to tighten again.

She became greedy with her tongue and her need for me, surprising and wonderful after everything that had already happened. Her desire sent another wave of heat rolling through me. Her hands cupped my bottom, pinning me in place while she worked with joy. She drew circles around my clit, darting over it every so often until she took me into her mouth. She sucked lightly at first, and then with more passion. I felt a second orgasm start to build as she sucked and licked and stroked.

An overload of sensations knocked me back into the seat. Surge after surge of pulsating heat and emotion rolled through me as my body tightened and convulsed until I cried out with release.

Carin wrapped her tongue and lips around me as I quivered under her, and she stayed there until the last shiver ran from my body.

Opening my eyes, I looked down at her.

Her eyes shone with the intense excitement of the moment we had just shared. But beneath that was something much more familiar and much more thrilling. Love.

My heart melted and delight mingled with the excitement until it was almost a new emotion, all together.

"I love you," I said.

"I bet you do." She laughed. It was low and throaty and full of tenderness. "It's been a long time since we had that much fun."

I chuckled. She was right. We had always been good together, but kids and a dog had a way of driving a happy, active sex life into limbo. "It's nice to know that it still can be."

"Yeah." She took my hand in hers and traced a finger along the palm. "You know, I love you, too. More than I can say."

"I know." I intertwined my hand with hers and raised her knuckles for a kiss.

We stayed like that for a long moment, enveloped in a space where there was only room for just us two.

I finally broke the silence. "What do you want to do now?"

"Didn't we just do it all? What's left?"

"We could get that pizza?"

"Oh, and I believe I owe you a foot rub."

The best sex I had in ages *and* a pizza and a foot rub. Honestly, it didn't get much better than that.

THE SOUVENIR
BY FLETCHER DELANCEY

"LADIES! TEN PERCENT OFF TONIGHT'S show! Gorgeous men, come on in!"

A flyer was thrust into Laura's face and she stopped short, bringing Veronica to a halt as well. The tourists streamed around them on the crowded sidewalk. "Seriously?" she asked. "Do we look like we want to see male strippers?"

The hawker seemed surprised, then smiled as he saw their clasped hands. "Nope. Never mind. Ladies!" he shouted to someone behind them, waving the flyer. "Ten percent off tonight's show! Gorgeous men, come on in!"

"Good lord," Veronica said, tugging on Laura's hand. "I have never been verbally assaulted so many times in a ten-minute period."

"You're the one who wanted to see Las Vegas." Laura allowed herself to be pulled along. "I was all for going straight to the North Rim."

"I still want to see Las Vegas. I just don't want to see this particular part of it." Veronica turned at the corner and headed down a slightly quieter street. "Let's get off the main strip."

"And 'strip' is the operative word, isn't it?"

They'd planned this vacation a year in advance, and Laura still couldn't believe they were actually here. A hike from the North Rim of the Grand Canyon all the way to the bottom—fourteen miles of steep downhill—two nights at Phantom Ranch next to the Colorado River, and then a long climb out, back the way they'd come.

But Veronica couldn't stand the idea of just driving straight out of the airport to the park, so they'd agreed to spend one night here and see the sights. Which, as far as Laura could see, consisted of sleaze, exploitation, litter, and more electricity usage than any desert city had a right to. Well, and a few really awesome fountains and some great shows, but still. She couldn't wait to get out of here and into the pristine beauty of the Grand Canyon.

"Hey, check this out! A toy store!"

For a brief moment Laura thought it seemed wildly incongruous to have a children's toy store in this location. Then she saw the window display.

"Huh. This is…surprisingly tasteful," she said.

Veronica turned, her hazel eyes alight with anticipation. "Let's go see."

"I don't know. Are we dressed for it?" Laura asked teasingly. They were both in shorts and tank tops, a look that she considered "sporty" on her big-boned, athletic frame, and "classically beautiful" on Veronica's smaller, slim body. With her dark auburn hair in its ponytail and her clothes outlining perfect curves, Veronica turned heads wherever she went.

"You're right. Maybe we're supposed to take everything off before we go in."

"That would be quite a barrier to sales," said a new voice. A woman with short-cropped dark hair walked up to them, holding a Starbucks cup in her hand. "Please, come on in. We don't require nudity, and I promise to stay behind the counter unless you have questions." She strolled past them into the store and called out, "Marlene! Your turn!"

"Thank god," said another voice. "I'm dying for my latte—oh! You sweetheart, you brought me one!"

Laura and Veronica trailed into the store, which felt like a refuge after the hot, noisy street outside. It was well lit but not glaringly so, cool and comfortable, and filled with classy display cases holding sex toys of every size and shape.

"Wow." Veronica stopped in front of a case featuring glass dildos with twisting streaks of color inside. "These are works of art."

"They really are. Especially this one with the blue starbursts."

"Those are flowers."

"Uh-uh. Starbursts."

"You have no sense of artistry. They are clearly stylized flowers."

"Do you want me to put flowers inside you or starbursts?"

Veronica's mouth fell open slightly. "Well, when you put it that way…"

Laura turned back to the display case, a little thrill shooting through her as she let her imagination loose. "I think we should buy it."

"Uh, honey, have you noticed the price tag?" Veronica whispered.

"How much could it—oh, holy shit."

Regretfully, they left the glass dildos behind. The rest of the store was full of equally well-made and tasteful toys, all of which had equally tasteful prices. Laura was starting to think their toy drawer at home was woefully low rent, especially when they found the silicone dildos and read the informational card on the benefits of pure silicone materials.

"If we can't get the glass dildo, we should at least get one of these," she said.

There was no answer.

She looked up to find her wife in the corner of the store by the checkout counter, in front of a black leather contraption the likes of which Laura had never seen. It hung from the ceiling on a thick strap, which led to a ring that then supported several other straps holding various parts of…what *was* that?

"It's a sex swing," Veronica said when Laura arrived.

"A what?"

"A sex swing."

"What the hell is that? And how do you know?"

Veronica pointed at the sign off to the side, which listed the name of the apparatus and a stratospheric price tag. "That's how I know. But I don't know how it works."

"Would you like me to show you?" the clerk asked from behind her counter.

"Um…" Laura said.

"Yes!" Veronica said brightly.

The clerk came over, a smile on her face. "I'm Jen, by the way."

"Veronica. And this is Laura."

"Where are you folks from?" Jen asked.

"Washington," Veronica answered.

"DC or the state?"

"The state. The quiet part of the state, which is why Las Vegas feels a little overwhelming."

"Oh, I can imagine. I'm from New Mexico. Much quieter there, too."

"You're not from around here?" Laura asked in surprise.

Jen snorted. "Please. Nobody is actually *from* Las Vegas. Anyway, let me show you how this works. It's designed to make sex more comfortable for both parties. The person in the swing can just relax while she's being cradled in the perfect position, and her partner can move the swing any way she wants to. If one of you would like to get in, I'll set it up and you can see."

Laura took a large step backward.

Jen laughed and turned to Veronica. "Looks like you're the brave one in this relationship."

"You got *that* right."

"Okay. I'll need you to take off your shoes first…thank you. Now you just sit in this sling part right here…good…and then your feet go in these stirrups."

Laura winced. "Stirrups" meant "pelvic exam" to her, and she couldn't find an iota of sexual appeal there.

"Oh," Veronica said in a surprised tone. "This is comfy."

It was? Laura looked more closely.

"It's nice, isn't it? But it looks like the stirrups are a little far for you. Let's adjust that." Jen flipped a buckle and tightened a strap, drawing Veronica's foot closer in. She did the same with the other and stepped back. "How's that?"

"Even more comfortable." Veronica wiggled happily. She was cradled in the sling with her torso leaned back, her pelvis thrust forward, her legs bent, and her feet raised in the air. She looked…

Laura's eyes widened. She looked like she was *perfectly* positioned for sex.

"I can see the potential," Veronica said. "Come here, honey."

Laura didn't remember moving, but suddenly she was standing between Veronica's legs. "Oh, wow," she breathed.

"Yeah. Wow." Veronica smiled up at her. "This is *really* comfortable. I could hang out in this for hours."

"She's a little low for you." Jen pointed to a small hand loop and then a large buckle on the main strap. "Grab that—it's to keep her from dropping when you undo the buckle—right, and now undo that, pull on the strap, and close the buckle when she's high enough."

Laura followed directions and watched in wonder as Veronica smoothly rose a few more inches into the air. She fastened the buckle again, then reached for the other two hand loops. "And these are for pulling her in?"

"Exactly."

Laura gave the hand loops an experimental pull. Veronica swung in, and with her legs spread by the stirrups, her crotch came in contact with Laura's zipper.

"Oh…my…god." Laura relaxed her grip and Veronica swung out again. Another tug and she swung in. "Can we spread her legs more?"

"Of course." Jen stepped up and showed her how to adjust the stirrups. Within seconds, Veronica's legs were spread wide. "Now if you dropped a pillow on the floor for your knees, she's in the perfect position for cunnilingus. Or if you *really* want to be comfortable, you just drag a chair over, sit down, and raise her high enough so she's at face level."

Laura began to get light-headed.

"That's the joy of this swing," Jen continued, apparently unaware of Laura's sudden loss of blood pressure. "It has a nice, broad sling and a headrest for the comfort of the person in it, hand grips for the person directing it, and adjustments for everything. As I said, it's designed to make sex more comfortable."

Veronica looked up, a lascivious grin spreading across her face. "I *like* it," she said.

"I want it," Laura announced.

Veronica's expression morphed into shock. "Really? Um, did you see—"

"I did, and I don't care. We need this."

Jen looked back and forth between them, waiting.

"Okay," Veronica said. "Then I guess we're taking it."

The Grand Canyon hike was so glorious that both women forgot about their Las Vegas purchase until they arrived home from the airport and found the FedEx box on their doorstep. Veronica let out a squeal and scooped it up. "It's here already! I'm so excited!"

"You know we can't actually use it until we install a hook in the ceiling, right?"

"Yeah, yeah. That'll take you ten minutes."

Laura recognized the tone of voice, which meant she was expected to move this task to her Veronica Needs This Now list. "I'd kind of like to unpack first..."

Veronica waved that off. "I didn't mean right now. We've been traveling half the day. Let's relax tonight and install it tomorrow. I want to try it out before we have to go back to work."

Sunday morning found Laura in the living room with her toolbox. They'd agreed that this was the only room large enough for the swing, and had a lively conversation about what they could hang from the hook when the chair wasn't in use. There weren't many things that required a hook with a holding capacity of three hundred pounds. Laura had joked that she'd need to take up boxing and hang a punching bag from it.

Of course, as with any home project, this one didn't take the ten minutes Veronica had so blithely estimated. First Laura had to locate a ceiling stud through the drywall, which only proved what she'd feared: there was no stud where she wanted to hang the swing. She'd have to install a crossbeam, which meant taking careful room measurements, cutting a two-by-four to fit, crawling into the attic and finding the right place for it under the insulation, and putting in metal brackets to reinforce the joints between the crossbeam and the studs. She hated working in the attic. Their insulation was fiberglass, and that stuff made nasty cuts. She'd have to wear coveralls.

It took half the day and three trips to the hardware store. The first was because she had to buy the brackets. No sooner had she gotten home with those than she opened her fishing tackle box with its collection of screws and realized she'd run out of wood screws in the right size.

"Didn't you check those before you went to the store?" Veronica asked, which was really not helpful.

Then she cut the cross brace a hair too long and needed to hammer the damn thing in place. She'd almost gotten it perfectly aligned when a hammer stroke hit wrong, bounced off, and knocked a hole through the ceiling drywall.

"Shit! Shit shit shit shit!" she yelled.

Now she'd have to plaster over the hole and repaint it, and she wouldn't be able to paint until tomorrow, when the plaster had dried.

Furiously she hammered the crossbar into its final position. Then she positioned one of the brackets, took out a brand new wood screw, and promptly stripped it with the drill.

"Fucking hell, of *course* I can't just screw the fuckers in," she said in exasperation. The wood was too hard; she'd have to pre-drill the holes.

Eight screws later, she climbed down from the attic, stripped off her dusty coveralls, pulled her bucket of plaster out of the cupboard, pried off the lid, and swore a blue streak when she saw the tiny smear left in the bottom. She'd meant to get a new bucket after her last project, but had forgotten.

"That kind of day, eh?" the hardware clerk asked when she slammed the plaster down on the counter.

By the time she'd gotten the hole plastered over and *finally* screwed the goddamned hook in place, she wasn't in the mood for anything except a shower and a cold beer. Maybe not in that order. She threw her tools back in the toolbox with more clatter than necessary, grumbling about stupid ideas and wives who thought every project would take ten minutes. The floor still needed to be vacuumed, but she was damn well going to leave that to Veronica. All she wanted was—

"Can we hang it now?" Veronica asked from the doorway.

Laura closed her eyes, her bent head hiding her expression. "I really can't deal with this anymore."

"I just want to see how it looks. Please?"

"The ladder's right there. Knock yourself out. I'm going to put my stuff away." She picked up her toolbox and strode out without looking at her wife. She didn't want to get into an argument, but she wasn't in the mood to even *see* that damn swing right now.

She took her time in the garage, needing a little space to turn herself back into a reasonable human being. The sound of the vacuum cleaner drifted out while she tidied up her workbench, which made her feel better. At least she'd walk back into a clean house.

By the time she went back inside, she was a little less stressed and actually curious to see how the swing looked. Striding down the hall, she called out, "Did you have any—?"

Her voice died when the living room came into view.

The swing was on its hook. And Veronica was in it.

Naked.

"No, I didn't have any problems," Veronica said in a low voice. "And it's just as comfortable here as it was in the store." She crooked a finger. "Come here."

"Honey, I need a shower…" But Laura's feet carried her to the swing anyway, where Veronica smiled up at her.

"I'm sorry this turned into such a long project. But it was worth it, wasn't it? Look at it." She spread her legs wider, opening up her center to Laura's gaze.

"Um…" Laura said stupidly.

"It's okay if you don't feel like using it right now. I know you're tired and dirty. But I hope you don't mind if I use it."

"What?" Laura's brain must have been addled by all the dust in the attic, because she didn't see how Veronica could use that swing alone.

"You didn't get all your tools, you know. You forgot your hammer." Veronica held it up.

Laura stared, not understanding. What did that have to do with…

All of her thought processes dried up as Veronica set the hammer on her stomach and ripped the top off a condom packet.

"You're very sexy when you do projects, did you know that? You're so… competent." Veronica rolled the condom over the hammer's handle, set it on her stomach, and ripped the top off a second packet. Rolling that one over the first, she said, "So I was looking at this hammer and I suddenly wondered what it would feel like inside me. Something you use so often…and it's long, and hard…"

"Veronica," Laura croaked in alarm. "Tell me you washed that. The insulation—"

"Of course I did." Veronica's smile was expectant. "Are you ready?"

Not ever. "That is—I can't—I'm not putting that inside you."

"No, you're not." Veronica dropped the empty packets onto the floor, wrapped her hand around the base of the condoms to hold them in place, and positioned the handle at her entrance. "I am."

With that, she slowly slid the handle inside herself.

Laura's knees nearly buckled. "Oh, my god," she whispered. It was a claw hammer, and seeing that curved, sharp-edged metal right outside her wife's most tender parts was disturbing. It was also extremely arousing, which made it even more disturbing. Her brain felt torn in half.

Veronica's head went back and she moaned. "Oh…yes. God, it's so hard inside me…I can't move around it. I feel every bit of it."

She pulled it partway out and then pushed it back in, setting up a slow, lazy thrusting. Her other hand drifted up and began squeezing a nipple, then twisted it.

Laura took another step forward, her eyes locked on the hammer. The hammer she'd used not very long ago to bang a crossbar into place. The hammer she'd used so many times for so many years that the handle was worn to a smooth polish. It had to be twenty years old at least, and in all that time, she'd never once considered using it for this.

Her hand moved of its own volition, touching Veronica's where it was wrapped around the handle, riding it as it moved in and out.

Veronica stopped her thrusting and gently moved Laura's hand away. "Your hands are filthy. Go wash them and then come back." Her eyes snapped to Laura's. "With the harness and our new dildo."

"It's not just my hands that are dirty," Laura protested, waving a hand down her body. "Let me take a shower."

Veronica shook her head. "I want you like this. Just like this, the way I've been watching you all morning and half the afternoon. I've been wet all this time, thinking about those hands on me. Those strong, capable hands..." Her voice drifted off as she pushed the hammer handle back in again. "Oh! Yes, I want you like this. Fully clothed. Dirty. Because you know what? It doesn't matter." The hammer moved out and in again. "Because this swing means you don't even have to touch me except with your hands, your lips, and the dildo." One more thrust for emphasis, this one harder than the others, and her head went back again. "Oh!"

She opened her eyes and stared at Laura. "Go wash your hands, now. I'll take care of myself while you're gone."

"Just...don't come until I get back," Laura said desperately. With one last look at that hammer sliding into glistening flesh, she fled down the hall.

She washed her hands twice, just to be sure. Then her face, and then her hands again. Feeling two hundred percent cleaner, she dashed into the bedroom and pulled on the harness over her jeans.

"You'd better hurry," Veronica called.

Laura grabbed the dildo from its drawer and ran back into the living room.

"Oh, good," Veronica purred. "Come on, love." She didn't stop what she was doing.

It was hard to focus on pushing the dildo through its O-ring and snapping it into place when she was constantly aware of Veronica and that damn hammer. At last, Laura raised her head and stepped forward. "Okay. I'm ready."

Without further ado, Veronica pulled out the hammer and tossed it onto the rug with a thud. "Good. Get over here and fuck me."

Laura stepped into place, but the swing was too low. She held it steady, loosened the main buckle, and lifted it higher.

Veronica let out a small squeal. "I think this might be a little too high."

"Not for what I want." Laura adjusted the stirrups to pull Veronica's legs further apart, then grabbed a pillow off the couch, threw it on the floor, and went down to her knees. "Because this is what I wanted to do in that store."

344

She took a moment to stare at the treasure in front of her, suspended in the air at exactly the right height, and felt herself grow wetter. Then she put her hands around Veronica's shapely ass and pulled her forward, right onto her tongue.

"Oh, yes," Veronica moaned.

Laura pulled her tongue out and swallowed. "You are so wet," she murmured. "I don't know why they call it eating out. I'm drinking you." She thrust her tongue in again, pulled it out, then ran it up the inside of one swollen, puffy lip and down the other.

Veronica jerked in the swing. "Jesus!"

Smiling to herself, Laura settled in, teasing her wife with the gentle touches that always drove her crazy, avoiding the clitoris until Veronica was driven to beg for it. Even then, she didn't satisfy, licking it only until she felt Veronica's hips jerking in that special way they did just before she came. When she sat back on her heels, Veronica let out a curse that rivaled the one Laura had shouted when she'd found her empty plaster bucket.

"Don't get mad at me," Laura said. "I'm just doing what you wanted."

She rose to her feet, kicked the pillow aside, lowered Veronica to the right height, and stood with her hands on the grip loops. "Didn't you say you wanted to be fucked?"

"I did." Veronica was panting and impatient. "But you're just standing there."

Laura tugged her in, and yes, it was right *there*. The dildo slid in without effort, and Veronica groaned.

A simple relaxing of her arms and the swing drifted back, pulling Veronica all the way off the dildo.

"Hm." Laura grinned at her. "Guess I can't let you go that far."

She pulled Veronica onto the dildo, let her slide back to the tip of it, then pulled her in again.

"This is effortless," she marveled. "I could do this all day."

"God, me too."

That was all Laura needed to know. She lost all track of time as she fucked Veronica slow and gentle, fast and hard, and every way in between. She found the buckles that changed the swing's angle and shifted Veronica into a more upright position, so that she could fuck her and suck her breasts at the same time. Then she leaned her back again and pounded her hard, her hips thrusting forcefully with every stroke. Next she tilted her slightly forward, went around to the other side, and took her from behind.

Veronica seemed to have lost the capacity for speech, reduced to moans and pleas as Laura fucked her endlessly and in every position she could think to try. This swing was *fantastic*, adjustable in so many ways, and worth every penny they'd paid for it. She planned to use it every chance they got. It was amazing how long she could go when she could just stand there at ease, without having to kneel or to hold her weight up on her hands or forearms.

She was back in front, sucking Veronica's reddened nipples while pacing her with slow, deep strokes, when the idea struck. Letting go of the nipple in her mouth, she kissed Veronica and whispered, "Don't go anywhere."

"What…"

"It's okay. I'll be right back. Just…relax."

Laura ran for the bedroom, yanked the bottle of lube from the drawer, and ran back.

Veronica swung gently, her head back and her eyes closed. She looked the picture of relaxation except for the fact that she was still breathing hard, and her chest was flushed with arousal.

Laura paused for a moment, admiring the scene and reveling in Veronica's beauty. It was hard to believe that she'd been so pissed earlier she hadn't even wanted to look at this swing. Veronica had a way of getting around her moods, and though her methods weren't usually as extreme as this, they were nearly always effective. It was such a cliché about your spouse making you a better person, but in their case, it was true. Laura had been a harder person to live with before Veronica had changed her. Normally she bristled at the idea of being handled, but when it was Veronica doing the handling, it just worked.

God, she loved this woman.

She moved into place behind her, pulled dark auburn hair away from an ear, and dropped a soft kiss on it. "Good, you're still here," she whispered.

Veronica shivered. "Not sure I could go anywhere if I wanted to."

Laura moved her mouth across her ear, onto a downy cheek, and then to the softest lips in the world, taking several minutes to communicate her feelings through gentle kisses. At last she pulled back and drizzled the lube onto her fingertip.

"I saw the clock while I was in the bedroom." She ran her coated finger around Veronica's other opening. "Do you know how long I've been fucking you?"

"Oh, god…" Veronica trembled at the touch. "Are you—"

"An hour and a half. Nonstop. That's how easy this is. But you need to come, and I know you. You're so far past it now that you won't come any of the usual ways." She drizzled more lube and spread it. "So I'm going to take you in the ass, honey, and you're going to make yourself come."

A sharp intake of breath was all Veronica seemed capable of. Laura drizzled lube onto the dildo, set the bottle down, positioned herself, and carefully slid the tip inside.

"Ah!" Veronica cried as it popped past the initial resistance. "Oh god, oh god…"

"Okay?" Laura waited.

"It's…it's okay. Go ahead."

Laura pushed it further in, pulled slightly out, then in again.

"Yes," Veronica said breathlessly. "I'm okay, just…oh…yes, like that…"

Laura watched raptly as the entire length of the dildo slid into Veronica's tight opening. "Oh, honey…you took it all. You have this whole thing inside you."

Veronica moaned.

"You look so amazing," Laura whispered, pushing the swing away from her and listening to the groan. "You're taking it all and you need to come, so do it. Take care of yourself there while I take care of you here." She pulled the swing back gently.

Veronica moaned again, then moved her hand down and began rubbing herself.

Laura kept the same slow speed for several more strokes, until she was sure the lube was thoroughly distributed. Then she moved more abruptly, smiling at the sound that elicited, and before long she was pounding Veronica in the ass just as hard as she'd pounded her pussy earlier. It never failed to amaze her how this small, slim woman could take such rough handling, but Veronica had made it clear a long time ago that when she was in a certain mood, gentle sex was not enough.

And this swing made it so easy. She could be gentle, she could be rough, she could be everything in between. Now she watched the dildo slide in and out, marveling at the sheer size of what Veronica was able to handle there and feeling her own arousal soaking her underwear.

"My nipples," Veronica gasped.

"What?"

"I need…god, I need you to…to twist them."

347

Laura looked down at her sweaty, filthy clothes. "I'll have to hold you against me."

"I don't care! Just…please…"

Laura stepped up against her, held her in place with one hand, and tightly pinched a nipple with the other. Then she twisted it and pulled outward.

Veronica threw her head back. "Yes!" Her hand moved frantically, rubbing harder than Laura would ever have dared. "Oh god, oh god, oh god," she chanted.

She was close. Laura kept her tight hold on the nipple and pulled her hips back, then pushed in again. She continued this light stroking with the dildo as she watched Veronica tremble and shake, her mouth opening silently.

Finally, when she judged that the time was right, Laura snapped her hips back in, shoving the dildo as far as it would go, and jerked on the nipple at the same time.

Veronica came with a roar, shaking so hard that Laura had to hold the swing steady. At last she flopped back, her hands dropping to the sides and hanging in the air, and looked as if she'd passed out.

Laura let go and began softly caressing her skin, bringing her down and whispering to her. "You are so beautiful. So beautiful, god, I could have watched you do that all day. You were mesmerizing."

At last Veronica stirred. "I don't think I can move."

Laura laughed and kissed her cheek. "The nice thing is, you don't have to."

"Yes, I do. I need to lie down."

"Okay. Then I'm going to pull out. Are you ready?"

Veronica nodded, clenching her jaw. She made a noise of discomfort as the dildo slowly came out, then let out a gusty sigh of relief.

"Stay there just a minute. I'll be right back." Laura hustled into the bathroom, took off the harness and dildo, and dropped everything in the sink. Back in the living room, she found Veronica trying to pull her foot out of the stirrup without much success.

"God, I'm dead," Veronica said as Laura helped her out. "You killed me." She took one step and wrapped her arms around Laura, slumping against her body.

"I'm going to take the 'you made me do it' defense." Laura glanced at the hammer lying on the floor. "And I hope you realize I'm never going to be able to use my hammer again."

Veronica gave a tired chuckle.

"You were amazing," Laura whispered.

"So were you," Veronica said in a slightly stronger voice. "So is that swing."

"It really is."

"Did I hear you say an hour and a half?"

"Yeah, but that was before I changed to your other side."

Veronica pushed herself away and stumbled down the hall to their bedroom. Laura followed and watched her collapse face first onto the bed.

"That swing might be the death of me," Veronica mumbled, her eyes closed.

Laura kissed her on the temple. "But what a way to go," she whispered.

Veronica didn't answer. She was already asleep.

It was a month before one of their friends noticed the hook in the ceiling. "That's new," she said during dinner one evening. "What are you planning to hang there?"

Laura waited for Veronica to give their agreed-upon explanation about a large hanging plant.

"We saw one of those swinging chairs in Las Vegas," Veronica said calmly, making Laura choke on her salad. "It looked so comfortable for reading. I was all excited about ordering it, and I even asked Laura to put up the hook. But then I thought more seriously about the layout of the living room and decided that it would have made things too crowded."

"So I put up that hook for nothing," Laura said, having recovered her breathing.

"Oh. Too bad," their friend said. "A chair from Las Vegas—that would have been a different sort of souvenir. So what *did* you bring home?"

"Nothing," Veronica said.

"Nothing? You don't have any souvenirs from your Grand Canyon trip?"

Laura pointed at the hook. "Just that. Think of that as our souvenir."

"And memories," Veronica added. "Lots of great memories. I get breathless just thinking about them."

Laura choked again. "Me, too."

"Well, I've heard it's a real workout," said their friend.

Laura and Veronica burst into laughter. "It really is," Laura said.

"Yes, it's best if you train for it before you try it," Veronica added.

Laura picked up her wine glass. "Here's to memories."

"And souvenirs." Veronica winked at her.

"And souvenirs," Laura echoed.

The three of them tapped their wine glasses together, and Laura glanced over at the hook. Below it and off to the side, her hammer lay on top of the bookcase. Maybe someday she'd be able to put it back in her toolbox and actually use it again.

But not yet.

ABOUT THE AUTHORS

VALERIE ALEXANDER

Valerie Alexander lives in L.A. and Phoenix. Her work has been published in The Best of Best Women's Erotica, Best Bondage Erotica, Under Her Thumb, Come Again, and other anthologies.

Connect with this author:
Website: http://www.valeriealexander.org
E-mail: Vaxder@gmail.com
Tumblr: http://valeriealexander.tumblr.com
Twitter: http://twitter.com/vaxder

ANNIE ANTHONY

Annie Anthony is a Chicago native who moved to Los Angeles in 2013. A professional holder of day jobs, she has handled complex insurance claims, worked for a dating service, edited more than fifty books in almost every genre, and managed the day-to-day operations of an indie e-book publisher until early 2015.

Annie holds an MFA in creative writing and has taught writing at the community college level and in writing workshops. She loves to crochet and donates much of what she makes to various hospitals. An avid volunteer, Annie has worked with medically fragile children and with nonprofits supporting GLBTQ issues since 2006.

Connect with this author:
Facebook: www.facebook.com/writer.annie.anthony
Blog: https://annieanthonydotcom.wordpress.com
E-mail: annie.anthony.author@gmail.com
Twitter: @anthony_annie

T.M. BALLION

T.M. Ballion lives in Newfoundland, Canada, with her wife and village of pets. She holds a graduate degree in the Social Sciences and enjoys writing lesbian fiction with her weekly writing group.

Connect with this author:
E-mail: tmballion@gmail.com
Twitter: @tmballion

JOVE BELLE

Jove Belle lives in Vancouver, Washington with her family. Her books include *The Job*, *Uncommon Romance*, *Love and Devotion*, *Indelible*, *Chaps*, *Split the Aces*, and *Edge of Darkness*.

Connect with this author:
Website: http://www.jovebelle.com

NICOLE BIRDSTONE

Nicole Birdstone has been writing short stories since she was a teenager, with roots in fan composition helping her develop the skill over the years. Ylva is her first foray into printed publication, though likely (hopefully!) not her last. Her day job in information technology keeps her busy in Houston, Texas, where she lives with two dogs, two cats, and two committed partners that make life worthwhile for her.

Connect with this author:
E-mail: nicole.birdstone@gmail.com

HARPER BLISS

Harper Bliss is the author of the novel *At the Water's Edge*, the *French Kissing* serial, the *High Rise* series, and several other lesbian erotica and romance titles. She is the co-founder of Ladylit Publishing, an independent press focusing on lesbian fiction. Harper lives on an outlying island in Hong Kong with her wife and, regrettably, zero pets.

Connect with this author:
Website: http://www.harperbliss.com/
Facebook: https://www.facebook.com/pages/Harper-Bliss/
E-mail: harperbliss@gmail.com
Twitter: https://twitter.com/HarperBliss

LILA BRUCE

Lila Bruce makes her home in the mountains of North Georgia, where the air is sweet and the summers are hot. Growing up in a military family, she traveled extensively as a child, living everywhere from Maine to Mississippi, Germany to Georgia, and a few parts in between. Lila loves to read and write contemporary lesbian romances and is a sucker for a happy ending.

When not writing, she spends her days adding to her ever-growing pack of basset hounds, consuming unhealthy amounts of coffee, and dreaming of the day she's able to leave her evil day job behind.

Connect with this author:
Facebook: https://www.facebook.com/profile.LilaBruce
E-mail: authorlilabruce@gmail.com

T.M. CROKE

T.M. Croke lives in Newfoundland, Canada, and hold degrees in English and Classics. She's always had a love of writing, but it was only a secret passion. Her voracious writing habit led to the creation of a weekly writing group, which inspired her to step out of her comfort zone and share her expansive portfolio of original lesbian fiction.

When not writing, she spends her time playing hockey, hiking with her dog, Karma, and reading. She is currently working on a full-length novel.

Connect with this author:
E-mail: tmcroke@gmail.com

CHERI CRYSTAL

Cheri Crystal is a healthcare professional by day and writes erotic romances by night. She is a native New Yorker who was born in Brooklyn and raised on Long Island. Recently, Cheri has crossed the pond to live in the United Kingdom with her loving wife. A day doesn't go by that she doesn't miss her three kids, technically adults, but thanks to Skype and lots of visits with her family, she enjoys living in England's southwest coast. Cheri began writing fiction in 2003 after reviewing for Lambda Book Report, *Just About Write*, *Independent Gay Writer*, and other e-zines. She is the author of *Attractions of the Heart*, a 2010 Golden Crown Literary Winner for lesbian erotica. In her spare time, she enjoys swimming, hiking, viewing wildlife, cooking, jigsaw puzzles, and spending quality time with family and friends.

Connect with this author:
Website: http://www.chericrystal.com
Facebook: http://www.facebook.com/chericrystal

MAY DAWNEY

May is a twenty-nine year old fiction and fan-fiction writer. As a lesbian, almost all her work focusses on portraying lesbian relationships, either within an existing franchise or in a world of her own design. She has been writing for as long as she can remember, making comic books with her mom as a child, finding her voice through on-line roleplay, and honing her skills through fanfiction. She is relatively new to original fiction, but is quickly growing addicted to the freedom it offers.

May lives with her long-term partner, and their eighteen year old cat, in The Netherlands where she balances far too many projects for her own good—and she loves every single one of them.

Connect with this author:
Website: http://maydawney.blogspot.com
Pinterest: http://www.pinterest.com/maydawney
Tumblr: http://bythedawn.tumblr.com
Twitter: https://twitter.com/ByTheDawnTW

FLETCHER DELANCEY

Fletcher DeLancey spent her early career as a science educator, which was the perfect combination of her two great loves: language and science. These days she combines them while writing science fiction.

She is an Oregon expatriate who left her beloved state when she met a Portuguese woman and had to choose between home and heart. She chose heart. Now she lives with her wife and son in the beautiful sunny Algarve, where she writes full-time, teaches Pilates, tries to learn the local birds and plants, and samples every regional Portuguese dish she can get her hands on. (There are many. It's going to take a while.)

She is best-known for *Mac vs. PC*, a geeky romance, and *The Caphenon*, an epic science fiction story with rich world-building and strong female characters. Currently, she is working on the sequels to *The Caphenon* and as an editor for Ylva Publishing.

Connect with this author:
Website: http://www.chroniclesofalsea.com
Facebook: https://www.facebook.com/fletcher.delancey
Blog: http://www.chroniclesofalsea.com/blog/
E-mail: fletcher@mailhaven.com
Twitter: https://twitter.com/alseaauthor

N.R. DUNHAM

N.R. Dunham lives in Wisconsin but doesn't like beer, so it's surprising that she hasn't been kicked out of the state yet. She took business classes in college, then realized what a terrible idea that was and switched fields. She earned an English degree, which she now uses to write reviews and articles on anything pertaining to pop culture.

When she's not doing that, she writes fan fiction. Her earliest attempts are perfect examples of why one has to keep writing in order to improve. If she's not reading or writing, she's probably playing with her dog or debating the merits of fictional characters with her girlfriend.

Connect with this author:
Facebook: https://www.facebook.com/NRDunham
E-mail: nr_dunham@yahoo.com
Tumblr: http://cblgblog.tumblr.com/

R.G. EMANUELLE

R.G. Emanuelle is a writer and editor living in New York City.

Her university degree in English and literature propelled her into publishing, where she spent 20 years as an editor, typesetter, and graphic designer. She is co-editor of *Skulls and Crossbones: Tales of Women Pirates*, and her short stories can be found in *Best Lesbian Erotica 2010; Lesbian Lust: Red Hot Erotica; Women in Uniform: Medics and Soldiers and Cops, Oh My!; Lesbian Cops: Erotic Investigations; Khimairal Ink; Read These Lips*, Volumes 4 and 5; and the online collection Oysters & Chocolate. When she was child, a neighbor called her a vampire because she only came out after dark, so it's fitting that her first novel, *Twice Bitten*, is about creatures of the night.

When she's not writing or editing, she can usually be found cooking or developing recipes, as she is also a culinary school graduate.

Connect with this author:
Facebook: https://www.facebook.com/RGEmanuelle
Blog: http://www.rgemanuelle.com
E-mail: rgemanuelle@gmail.com
Twitter: https://twitter.com/RGEmanuelle

EVE FRANCIS

Eve Francis's short stories have appeared in Wilde Magazine, The Fieldstone Review, Iris New Fiction, MicroHorror, and The Human Echoes Podcast. Romance and horror are her favourite genres to write in because everyone has felt love or fear in some form or another. She lives in Canada, where she often sleeps late, spends too much time online, and repeatedly watches old horror movies and *Orange Is The New Black*.

Connect with this author:
Website: http://evefrancis.wordpress.com
Tumblr: http://paintitback.tumblr.com

SACCHI GREEN

Sacchi Green is an award-winning writer and editor of erotica and other stimulating genres. Her stories have appeared in scores of publications, including eight volumes of *Best Lesbian Erotica*, four of *Best Women's Erotica*, and four of *Best Lesbian Romance*. In recent years she's taken to wielding the editorial whip, editing eight lesbian erotica anthologies, most recently 2010 Lambda Award Winner *Lesbian Cowboys*, *Girl Crazy*, *Lesbian Lust*, *Lesbian Cops*, *Girl Fever: 69 Stories of Sudden Sex for Lesbians*, and 2014 Lambda Award Winner *Wild Girls, Wild Nights*, all from Cleis Press.

Sacchi lives in the Five College area of western Massachusetts, with frequent stays in the White Mountains of New Hampshire, and can be found online at sacchi-green.blogspot.com, FaceBook (as Sacchi Green,) and Live Journal (as sacchig.)

Connect with this author:
Facebook: https://www.facebook.com/sacchi.green
Blog: http://sacchi-green.blogspot.com

CATHERINE LANE

Catherine Lane started to write fiction on a dare from her wife. She's thrilled to be a published author, even though she had to admit her wife was right. They live happily in Southern California with their son and a very mischievous pound puppy.

Catherine spends most of her time these days working, mothering, or writing. But when she finds herself at loose ends, she enjoys experimenting with recipes in the kitchen, paddling on long stretches of flat water, and browsing the stacks at libraries and bookstores. Oh, and trying unsuccessfully to outwit her dog.

She has published several short stories and is currently working on a second novel.

Connect with this author:
Website: https://catherinelanefiction.wordpress.com/
Facebook: https://www.facebook.com/catherinelane
E-mail: claneauthor01@gmail.com

JESS LEA

Jess lives in Melbourne, Australia, where she started out as an academic before working in the community sector. Historical fiction is her favourite obsession, especially for the way it lets us imagine the lives of women and people of unconventional genders and sexualities, so often left out of the official record. Jess spends her free time haunting the cafes of St Kilda, watching bad 60s horror films, and writing stories.

Connect with this author:
E-mail: Jessleacontact@gmail.com

D. JACKSON LEIGH

D. Jackson Leigh grew up barefoot and happy, swimming in farm ponds and riding rude ponies in rural south Georgia. Her passion for writing led her to a career in journalism and to North Carolina, where she edits breaking news at night and writes lesbian romance stories with equestrian settings by day.

She was awarded a 2010 Alice B. Lavender Certificate for Noteworthy Accomplishment, and was a finalist in the 2013 LGBT Rainbow Awards for erotic romance and in the 2014 Lambda Literary Awards romance category. She is the winner of a 2013 Golden Crown Literary Society Award in the paranormal romance category for "*Touch Me Gently*," and a 2014 GCLS Award in the romance category for "*Every Second Counts*."

Connect with this author:
Facebook: https://www.facebook.com/d.jackson.leigh
Twitter: @djacksonleigh

SAMANTHA LUCE

Samantha Luce was born and raised in the Mosquito state a.k.a. Florida. She is a total dork who became hooked on kick-ass women growing up in the eighties, seeing Sarah Connor of *Terminator* and Ellen Ripley of *Aliens*.

For the past ten years, Samantha has been working in law enforcement. She met the love of her life online through the wacky world of fan fic. The two have met in person just once, but their long-distance love separated by five states and a ton of snow has only grown stronger during the past few years.

In her spare time (Hmmm, what's that?) she writes fan fiction, reads whatever she can get her hands on, watches way too much TV, and is currently at work on a lesbian thriller featuring a kick-ass FDLE agent and a sexy deputy sheriff. Oh, and she has plans to hopefully contribute another short story to Ylva's Halloween anthology.

Connect with this author:
Facebook: https://www.facebook.com/people/Samantha-Luce/
E-mail: samanthaluce87@yahoo.com

ANDI MARQUETTE

Andi Marquette is a native of New Mexico and Colorado and an award-winning mystery, science fiction, and romance writer. She also has the dubious good fortune to be an editor who spent 15 years working in publishing, a career track that sucked her in while she was completing a doctorate in history. She is co-editor of Skulls and Crossbones: Tales of Women Pirates and All You Can Eat. A Buffet of Lesbian Erotica and Romance. Her most recent novels are Day of the Dead, the Goldie-nominated finalist The Edge of Rebellion, and the romance From the Hat Down, a follow-up to the novella From the Boots Up, a Rainbow Award runner-up.

When she's not writing novels, novellas, and stories or co-editing anthologies, she serves as both an editor for Luna Station Quarterly, an ezine that features speculative fiction written by women and as co-admin of the popular blogsite Women and Words. When she's not doing that, well, hopefully she's managing to get a bit of sleep.

Connect with this author:
Website: http://andimarquette.com
Twitter: @andimarquette

ANA MATICS

Ana Matics is in her mid-twenties, a long-time writer, and sometimes bank employee. When not writing, Ana enjoys running with her dog and exploring the vast countryside that her current state of North Carolina offers.

Connect with this author:
Tumblr: http://anamatics.tumblr.com/
Twitter: @anamatics

CASSANDRA MCMURPHY

Cassandra lives in Portland, Oregon, and works a day job in the financial sector. She spends her free time writing novels, drinking too many lattes, and cooking up inedible vegan food with her husband and daughter. She also started training for her first trail race. Her recent foray into short fiction has resulted in her first published work, set to appear in fall 2015.

Connect with this author:
Tumblr: http://CassandraMcMurphy.tumblr.com
E-mail: Cassandra.McMurphy@gmail.com

MEGHAN O'BRIEN

Meghan O'Brien lives in Northern California, with her wife, their son, and a motley collection of pets. She is the author of seven novels and various short stories from Bold Strokes Books, mostly of the romantic/erotic variety, and a two-time recipient of the GCLS Award for Lesbian Erotica. Meghan is a native of Royal Oak, Michigan, but can't say she misses the snow. You can connect with her on Facebook or Twitter.

Connect with this author:
Twitter: @meghanobrien78

L. M. PERRIN

L. M. Perrin is an English major who started writing fiction to break up the monotony of analytical essays. She lives in western Michigan with one exhaustingly energetic black Lab. Her first short story, "Viral Valentine," was published in Supposed Crimes's Love is a Mess anthology.

Connect with this author:
E-mail: perrintly@gmail.com
Twitter: @Perrintly

SASHA SAPPHIRE

Sasha Sapphire is an American author who divides her time between the UK and Norway. She holds an MA in Creative Writing from Bath University and an MSc in Business Management. Her first novel, a lesbian love story set in Paris and Central Africa, was published in 2013, and she is currently finalizing her second book.

RONNIE WILLOWS

Ronnie Willows is a full-time fiction editor and erotica writer. She loves travelling and is most at home in ancient surroundings by the sea.

Connect with this author:
Facebook: https://www.facebook.com/ronnie.willows
E-mail: ronniewillows@gmail.com

OTHER BOOKS FROM YLVA PUBLISHING

www.ylva-publishing.com

DON'T BE SHY

Volume One
ISBN: 978-3-95533-377-5 (mobi), 978-3-95533-378-2 (epub)
Length: 60,200 words

Volume Two
ISBN: 978-3-95533-380-5 (mobi), 978-3-95533-381-2 (epub)
Length: 79,000 words

In these two short story collections, available only in e-book format, twenty-six authors spin tales that focus on the sensual, red-hot delights of sex between women and the celebration of the female form in all its diverse hedonism.

You'll find intimate encounters between strangers, couples playing out their most titillating fantasies, one-night stands, and stories featuring slow, sultry weekends. Are you up for toys, hot sex, and fun?

Are you in the mood for something spicy?

HEART'S SURRENDER
Emma Weimann

ISBN: 978-3-95533-183-2
Length: 305 pages (63,000 words)

Neither Samantha Freedman nor Gillian Jennings are looking for a relationship when they begin a no-strings-attached affair. But soon simple attraction turns into something more.

What happens when the worlds of a handywoman and a pampered housewife collide? Can nights of hot, erotic fun lead to love, or will these two very different women go their separate ways?

BITTER FRUIT
Lois Cloarec Hart

ISBN: 978-3-95533-216-7
Length: 244 pages (50,000 words)

Jac accepts an unusual wager from her best friend. Jac has one month to seduce a young woman she's never met. Though Lauren is straight and engaged, Jac begins her campaign confident that she'll win the bet. But Jac's forgotten that if you sow an onion seed, you won't harvest a peach. When her plan goes awry, will she reap the bitter fruit of her deception? Or will Lauren turn the tables on her?

HOT LINE
Alison Grey

ISBN: 978-3-95533-048-4
Length: 114 pages (27,000 words)

Two women from different worlds.

Linda, a successful psychologist, uses her work to distance herself from her own loneliness.

Christina works for a sex hotline to make ends meet.

Their worlds collide when Linda calls Christina's sex line. Christina quickly realizes Linda is not her usual customer. Instead of wanting phone sex, Linda makes an unexpected proposition. Does Christina dare accept the offer that will change both their lives?

ALL YOU CAN EAT
Ed. by R.G. Emanuelle & Andi Marquette

ISBN: 978-3-95533-224-2
Length: 260 pages (58,000 words)

Chef R.G. Emanuelle and sous chef Andi Marquette locked themselves in the kitchen to create a menu that would explore the sensuous qualities of food and illustrate how the act of preparing and eating it can engage many more senses than simply taste and smell. They gathered a great group of cooks who put together an array of dishes that we hope will whet your appetite and send you back for seconds.

COMING FROM YLVA PUBLISHING

www.ylva-publishing.com

SERVE IT UP - A MENU OF LESBIAN ROMANCE AND EROTICA

Edited by R.G. Emanuelle and Andi Marquette

Fast food or gourmet meal—what's your pleasure? We bring you collection of short stories that combine the love for food, sex, and romance and will crank up the heat beneath you.

ACROSS THE POND

Cheri Crystal

After having been betrayed by her partner of thirteen years, Janalyn isn't looking for another relationship, especially not one separated by miles of ocean.

But when she travels to Devon, England, for a conference and meets a sporty Brit named Robyn, desires Janalyn thought were permanently lost are suddenly back and stronger than ever.

Despite cultural differences, poking fun at each other's use of the English language, and Robyn coming off as a player, Janalyn can't help the attraction she feels, no matter how hard she tries.

Can she and Robyn find a common ground upon which to make a life together? Will Janalyn throw caution to the wind and risk her heart again? If Janalyn does indeed venture across the pond, will love be her life preserver?

Don't Be Shy
Edited by Astrid Ohletz and Jae

ISBN: 978-3-95533-383-6

Published by Ylva Publishing, legal entity of Ylva Verlag, e.Kfr.

Ylva Verlag, e.Kfr.
Owner: Astrid Ohletz
Am Kirschgarten 2
65830 Kriftel
Germany

www.ylva-publishing.com

First edition: August 2015

The short stories in this book appeared in *Don't Be Shy* Volume 1 (June 2015) and Volume 2 (July 2015).

Credits
Edited by Michelle Aguilar Therese Arkenberg, Jeanne De Vita, Deni Dietz, R.G. Emanuelle, Sandra Gerth, CK King, Julie Klein, Sheri Milburn, Astrid Ohletz, Day Petersen, Deborah Schwartz
Cover Design and Formatting by Streetlight Graphics

CPSIA information can be obtained at www.ICGtesting.com
Printed in the USA
LVOW08s0113140716

496237LV00001B/73/P